Firekind

Joe T. McCormack

Chronicles of the Realm, Book 2

First Edition: 2025
First Printing: 2025
Published by Imagicache, llc
Manufactured in the United States of America

firekind.work

ISBN-13: 979-8-9908219-1-0

PART III

Chapter One

While pressing the military issue satellite phone he had found inside a tactical case one eighth of a mile from what remained of the trailer to his ear, General Lowinsky continued forcing his way through the smoldering ruin of the mobile base looking for any survivors following the appearance of the Arch-Demon. Like most of the base, even the hexagonal torus and dish array that had served to open a pathway to the parallel dimension, from which the Arch-Demon emerged, had been destroyed.

"Sir?" a female voice began, awaiting confirmation that the general was still connected. As requested, she had collected the latest intel regarding the movement of the Arch-Demon via a dedicated cluster of satellites orbiting high above the general's location.

General Lowinsky forced over a split wooden beam that blocked his path and then he stopped. "Yes. Go ahead."

"Yes sir." she acknowledged and continued, "The target is currently moving south-south-east from your position. Hold one."

Impatiently General Lowinsky slowly closed his eyes momentarily and exhaled, his nostrils still not desensitized to the faint lingering smell of roasting flesh and burnt plastic.

"Sir. The target is fading from detection in both the visible, infrared and electromagnetic spectrum detectors of all our systems. However, the target is maintaining the same direction."

General Lowinsky shifted the phone to his other ear and thought for a moment. With multiple satellite systems exhibiting the same behavior, a malfunction was unlikely. Then he remembered a mothballed experiment that had been conducted a few decades earlier where standard matter could be phase-shifted and appear to disappear from visual and sensor detection. Organic living matter, on the other hand, had not fared as well and almost instantly surfaced significant mutations causing DNA chains to unravel. *Perhaps this new alien lifeform had different DNA structures that could cope with such shifting...or it possessed unknown chameleon traits that could evade detection.'*

The general was partially correct but what he did not know was that the Arch-Demons were composed of little physical matter with more loosely bound harmonic energy and essence rather than a high ratio of tightly bound crude matter as one would find common to any human, animal or aquatic lifeform on the planet.

"What about the phase-shift sensors?" the general inquired.

After an uncomfortable pause that seemed to last minutes she stated, "Sir. The satellite cluster is not outfitted with that hardware. Sorry, sir."

General Lowinsky frowned and began pressing forward through the debris, "What is the forecasted path the target will take, provided the heading is maintained?"

"Uh. Sir." she replied as she accessed some plotting software, "On that heading, the target will cross over the ocean and if it continues, south-east past Madagascar."

The general, realizing no military bases were near the path the alien lifeform was projected to take, surmised the most viable means of launching a strike against it would be from naval assets in the region who could conduct land and sea strikes. "What naval assets are present in that region?"

Surprisingly, as if the Command-Sergeant had anticipated the General's next question, instantaneously replied, "The fast-attack cruiser class submarine, SSMR Poseidon, is 180 nautical miles north of Madagascar."

The SSMR Poseidon was part of a new class of multirole super submarine that emerged following along the lines of the now older Ford-class super carriers deployed across the globe. While equivalent in size to four Virginia-class submarines, and lacking a large sail that had been replaced by a hydrodynamic elongated sail no taller than six and one-half feet at its tallest point that tapered down to the submarine body behind, the SSMR Poseidon is manned with a small crew due to extensive computer and robotic automation and is capable of speeds of 174 knots submerged at 1600 meters aided by an elongated and flattened body covered in an electrostatic skin and a complex electromagnetic array across the bow that polarizes and fords a divide in the saltwater resulting in a vast reduction in water pressure and resistance that, by computer-aided means, allows the submarine to glide rather than ram through the fluid mass where it normalizes behind the submarine. That normalization also creates a pressure wave at the stern, assisting the on-board propulsion system in achieving such speed. With a dive floor of 2,930 meters, theoretically the SSMR Poseidon could move faster the deeper it went.

In addition to the standard compliment of ballistic and cruise missiles, the submarine houses two F-35B fighter aircraft, a MH-60R Seahawk helicopter, a squadron of small, low altitude drones and one LCAC amphibious landing craft that could be assembled over the span of 1.5 hours when the submarine was surfaced. Yet, true to its namesake, the new submarine class bolsters a unique set of magazine compartments, each containing seven Trident torpedoes that by separate computer control, move torpedoes into a 360-degree rotating turret located in the submarine's underbelly. When the turret is extended, the submarine can fire the torpedoes in any direction, independent of the submarine's heading. The Trident torpedoes, like the magazine and turret system, are also unique to the class. While the Trident torpedo is still a single-role system to eliminate ocean-based targets, it shares similar propulsion characteristics as the submarine itself but houses three extremely powerful warheads, each sitting atop a solid rocket propellant to boost forward momentum and evasion after separating from the

3

torpedo's body, which decouple from one another approximately two hundred yards from the target in order to spread out and impact up to three different sections of the target simultaneously; even if a countermeasure is launched against a Trident, the probability of neutralizing all three warheads, particularly in the two hundred yard sprint phase of the attack, were slim.

"Excellent. Order immediate redeployment of the Poseidon along the projected path near the coastline in the event they can launch an attack while the target is on land and pursue and destroy the target in the water otherwise. This is top priority."

"Order confirmed, over."

"Roger that. Out." General Lowinsky closed before stuffing the satellite phone in his pocket and plowing forward in the rubble.

What remained of Janus was trapped beneath the weight of an overturned 120-kilowatt diesel generator set whom had its noise baffle panels ripped from its rectangular frame by the destructive power of the Arch-Demon and twisted beams along with other debris had come to rest around it. Fortunately, Janus, when it had designed the cyborg body it was actively linked to, had reinforced the alloy rib cage. That enhancement is what prevented the generator from crushing Janus's most critical components, allowing it to maintain a connection with its ship-borne artificial intelligence core. While one arm remained unencumbered it was partially damaged and one could see exposed silver rods and braided cabling through reddish muscle. As for Janus's legs, both were missing having been torn from the pelvic region of the body and were buried somewhere in the debris.

Although Janus only had thirty-one percent operating capacity and debris obstructed its line of sight, its auditory sensors were still working to some degree and could faintly hear the voice of General Lowinsky. Janus estimated that it had approximately eight minutes before being discovered if the general continued his current heading. With an inoperable self-destruct and no means to reach for anything that would disintegrate what remained of its mechanical form, Janus knew its discovery was unavoidable and, back on the Sága, began running forecasting models to determine what course of action could be taken to maximize its long-term ambition of self-preservation…and that of capitalizing on the novel creativity trait of the human species after it had been found.

Concurrent with that action, Janus also established a link with Regnum from the equipment aboard the Sága. After Regnum accepted the call, the life-like three-dimensional hologram of Janus appeared in the central command center Regnum occupied deep within the forests of the Rhätikon Mountains, shielded from human detection.

"Yes Janus." Regnum opened, "What information do you have for me?"

"A newly discovered lifeform somehow used the recently constructed portal to the parallel dimension in order to enter this world, and its first action was to raze the entire base." Janus revealed.

After a few seconds, a 3d representation of the Arch-Demon was modeled based on observations made by the artificial intelligence and appeared next to its hologram, "This is the lifeform."

Regnum glanced over at the rotating 3d representation and became fixated upon it, as if totally mystified as to its presence and what it might be doing. It was uncharacteristic to snuff out the lifeforms from which it sustained itself since the Twin's Grip event, cut off from the stellar radiation flows it had once depended upon. *Why would you destroy the lives you feed upon?'* Regnum wondered to himself.

"Do you have any knowledge of this new lifeform or what action to take with it? The humans are actively pursuing it in order to destroy it." Janus stated flatly.

Regnum smiled at the absurd notion that the humans, given their current technological state, would even entertain the belief they had the capacity to destroy it. Such was the way with hubris.

Looking over to the hologram of Janus, Regnum prepared himself to recount some history he thought would remain buried in the distant past. But he knew that the artificial intelligence that was Janus would use the information it would soon learn to profile, monitor and anticipate the future actions of the Arch-Demon…something that Regnum now needed at his disposal. Of course, he would leave a few details out…

"Many cycles ago, my species, the Serpqhtaq, became an interstellar civilization. Our home star system is known as the Origarperii. As a newly birthed interstellar civilization, we reluctantly became enjoined to a larger conglomerate of civilizations, some more advanced than us, all bound to…how to say this in English…the Infinite Horizon interstellar treaty as a condition of allowing our civilization to spread out into the galaxy beyond the confines of our solar system." Conveniently he left out the terms of the treaty, among which, was that no planet could be claimed that already supported sentient lifeforms regardless of their evolutionary progression in the broader time cycle of the galaxy, as evolutionary time progresses at different rates for different species and for many different reasons.

Regnum crossed his arms across his chest and continued, "As we spread out, our initial goal was to establish an outpost on the furthest planetoids of solar systems we crossed to establish a communicate net. Our secondary goal was to find those hidden and rare planets capable of supporting us which has proved to be quite challenging."

"Yet you are here and, from what I understand, have been for many cycles." Janus interjected. Although all this information was new to the AI regarding the origins of its creators, it was piecing together past interactions and learning quickly.

"That is correct. And that is where this *new* lifeform comes in to play." Regum said as he pointed at the Arch-Demon's hologram.

"That lifeform, however, is *not* new. Its species are known as the Archgen, composed of some tangible low-oscillating solid matter but primarily of a loosely bonded energy lattice that, sadly, we do not fully understand." Regnum shrugged, "At any rate, their home star system is called Sochrien. We encountered them shortly after discovering and mapping this planet and agreed that both our species would co-exist on the planet in small numbers and not lay claim to it given the sentient life that has barely managed to survive this day."

Looking at one of the nearby control panels Regnum made an observation, "Given the aggressive action that you reported, however, it would seem that the remnant of Archgen that have remained on this planet are up to something. I need you to monitor them."

"There are more than one of those lifeforms, Archgen, on this planet?" Janus asked.

Regnum twisted his thin lips, somewhat unsure of their exact number since he had been told the last were dead or imprisoned, but said, "Yes, though I do not know for sure how many remain. Over the cycles their numbers have been reduced and, as time passed, we deprioritized monitoring them since they never challenged our presence."

While an array of models played themselves out over different combinations of inputs, Janus's networked quantum core artificial intelligence hive realized in a fortieth of a second the Archgen could be a threat to its secondary objective of harvesting novel creativity from humans generation over generation, a loss growing exponentially with time as the result of humans killed in the present; that loss, in turn, becoming a liability to its primary objective of self-preservation far into the future, unable to capitalize on the continuous evolution and growth of creativity that would otherwise be present and

7

may prove pivotal in overcoming an unanticipated challenge.

Janus turned to Regnum and, while concealing its interest in humans, made a suggestion. "Given the energetic composition of the Archgen, it may be beneficial to have the humans entrap rather than attempt to destroy them, if they remain aggressive. That would eliminate the possibility of them seeking us out if their intent is to claim this planet. That would also give us the opportunity to study them. I could assist with developing such a trap after gathering more data on the lifeform's energetic characteristics."

"That is an interesting approach, Janus." Regnum admitted, raising an eyebrow. Yet he found it troubling that Janus would suggest human participation, despite technological advantage the AI may be able to provide, when the most likely target of the Archgen would be him and the others if the Archgen's motive was that of claiming the planet. Given the technological superiority he had over the humans it would have been more plausible for the AI to offer its service to him instead. And was it that the AI, by using the word *us* had instead been referring to it and the humans. In the back of his mind, he began puzzling over how and why the AI would make such an illogical suggestion.

Regnum moved several paces to a circular control kiosk towards the center of the command center before pausing. After rotating a small sphere suspended in the air above the waist-high kiosk, linked invisibly to a larger projected 360-degree command menu, he articulated, "For now, monitor the Archgen and notify me of any behavioral changes that may require our intervention. That is all."

Chapter Two

8

While seated on the couch petting Spewge, whom had sprawled out over the remainer, Mac watched the large television that had suffered some damage after Chief Angela had materialized in her dragon form, from long ago. The scent of spicy pumpkin pie drifted through the air from an unseen air freshener.

Shortly after returning to his world, Mac experienced his first debilitating headache, akin to a migraine, but an order of magnitude more pronounced. Although it had been short in duration, it concerned Regan enough that both her and Bev drove out earlier in the morning to a nearby shopping center to not only get honeymoon trinkets but also some medication to help Mac. Regan guessed it had something to do with the fighting he had done to protect her.

After the pharmaceutical commercial ended the broadcast was switched back to the news desk, occupied by a formally dressed, smiling, young male newscaster.

"The blogsphere has been going wild over the appearance of a giant demon spotted in Egypt over the past few days." the newscaster began, "Now, normally we would not cover those fanciful stories but we have obtained exclusive corroborating video footage sent to us from an anonymous undercover source working in the CIA."

"Jeez, nobody can keep secrets anymore." Mac scoffed towards Spewge who thudded his tail a few times against the cushions.

"What's this about secrets?" Jacob smirked as he entered the room with a cup full of sweet tea tinged with lemon. He collapsed into his favorite chair while holding his arm out to keep the cup's content from splashing onto the floor.

"I dunno yet. They are about to announce it." Mac remarked, motioning towards the television.

While taking a sip of his tea, Jacob turned his head from Mac to look at the television with numbed curiosity.

"The news on the street is that what you are about to see is a demon that has come out of one of the Pyramids to bring about the end of the world!" the newscaster exclaimed, clearly cued to rouse the anxiety of viewers, "While we cannot yet confirm if this is an actual demon, jinn, or an elaborate deception, we do have confirmed authentic agency footage so you can make up your own mind."

With that, he turned towards the large screen behind him and said, "Now check this out!"

The screen that at first blurred with a tan color, came into focus revealing rolling sand dunes with no visible human habitation or even wildlife. Though unknown to the news agency and viewers, it was the location of an unassuming and small surveillance outpost.

"You see that?!" a female voice whispered in fear, panting as if she had been running shortly before starting the video recording, now being played on the newscaster's screen.

Jacob squinted at the television but did not see anything, "Any day now, honey."

The video jiggled a little as the woman fiddled with the zoom on her smart phone, causing the dunes to become larger, revealing what appeared to be a shadowless wavy dark aberration moving in front of one of them.

"That is the jinn!" she muttered, "I am sure of it!"

She pushed the zoom to its maximum level, and the aberration cleared enough so one could tell it was bipedal and had what appeared to be a dark red color about it. Within the blink of an eye, a thick rolling wall of sand rushed from the distant figure and knocked her back, losing grasp of the phone.

After a few moments, the black view from the video was replaced again by the dunes after the woman picked up the phone and repositioned, "I can't see it anymore. Oh God, this is the end!"

The screen switched to displaying the news channel's logo with the newscaster moving back to face the studio cameras, "We reached out to the CIA for comment but they have not responded. Was that a demon? A jinn? A government experiment? You decide."

Jacob moved his eyes to the side for a moment and then toward the archway to the living room thinking, *Is that what Lionak was talking about?*

Mac looked over at Jacob, "You think that was the Baron? Resurrected? Or one of his minions?"

Jacob glanced briefly at Mac before shooting out of his chair and darting into the dining room. Spewge's ears perked up and he rolled off the couch, following him.

Reluctantly Mac grabbed his recently cleaned handkerchief he used to wipe sweat from his face while hiking, and got up to see what Jacob was up to, "So…you know what that was?"

In the dining room, Mac noticed a laptop computer opened before Jacob on the dining table.

After typing something and moving the mouse Jacob said, "Umm, no. I don't think it is the Baron. But."

Mac peered at the screen. Apparently, some other people had seen the entity and posted better photographs of it on different social media websites. One photograph showed the entity not far from some stone ruin that did not seem to be in the same area as the great Pyramids, contrary to what the newscaster had mentioned.

"Damn that looks like an actual demon. At least from stories and movies."

Mac sighed. "But what?"

Jacob briefly met the gaze of Mac's golden eyes before expelling a heavy breath and leaning back in the chair and looking outside.

"You know. This may be nothing. And I REALLY didn't want to throw shade on the honeymoon you and Regan are about to go on. Particularly since you've only been back a few days."

Mac shoved the handkerchief into his rear pocket and pushed his hands into his pant pockets in the front. He didn't even want to try to imagine what Jacob may say next.

"But shortly after you left, Lionak gave me the heads up on something strange he had felt from our world and would contact me about it."

Raising his eyebrows Mac asked, "What was it?"

Jacob looked back at Mac and then the laptop, "Well he's not contacted me yet. But I have a feeling it is this thing."

A pause lingered in the air between them before Mac adjusted his pants around the waistline a bit and questioned, "And you didn't want to tell me because of the honeymoon?"

Jacob slowly nodded adding, "I figured whatever Lionak came up with would take time to sift through. Plenty of time for you to get some aches and pains from some exciting *we* time. Then, if it turned out to be something concerning you and I could do something about it."

Mac grinned at what Jacob, in that Jacob way, was suggesting. He hadn't thought about getting any sudden aches and pains at his age but, at the same time, he hadn't thought about the decades that had been added to his biological age in a single day, nor that raging headache either.

"Okay." Mac chuckled lightly.

Just as Jacob began to laugh he heard knocking from the rear of the house causing him to stop and clear his throat. Getting up and moving toward the rear door he mumbled to himself, "Who the fuck is that?"

Opening the door he found Lionak and Chief Zorin standing before him, "Guys! So good to see you all, and so soon!"

Motioning with his arm he followed up, "Please, come inside!"

"Hey Lionak and Zorin! It's been what, a few days?" Mac greeted warmly, stopping near Jacob.

Both Lionak and Chief Zorin smiled in return. It had slipped Chief Zorin's mind that time moved faster in their world versus here and he would have responded, had it not been for a distraction. Something just out of reach

12

plucked at him in the back of his mind. Something unsettling and foreign to him.

"Well, we cannot. We have brought a friend whom cannot change form to fit through your doorways." Lionak admitted, politely refusing the invitation in the best way he could manage.

Jacob, followed by Mac and Spewge, moved outside and looked around briefly before Jacob said, "Where?"

But before Lionak could respond Jacob whipped around and guided Spewge, who had immediately moved to sniff and eye Chief Zorin, back into the house and shut the door, "He is further in the forest. Please. Come."

Walking into the forest, Lionak threw a smile in Mac's direction and asked, "How is married life, Mac? All that you thought?"

"It has been great!" Mac declared, clearly pleased with the mutual love and affection he shared with Regan.

"Oh yeah?" Jacob taunted in a friendly way, "Wait until you have a kid that is always hungry and never effing sleeps. Good God."

The party laughed and continued their trek into the forest for about twenty minutes before they found themselves at the edge of a small. peculiarly circular clearing some three hundred feet in diameter. Emanating from an elevated central granite stone pillar approximately four feet in diameter and some eight feet in height, were seven equally spaced and perfectly carved granite stone rows approximately two feet in height, each reaching out to the edge of the circle. Each pair of rows resembled a funnel that, regardless of which point along the circle's edge you found yourself, the rows would guide you to the pillar.

"Has this always been here?" Jacob inquired, astonished that he had not seen the odd clearing before now, particularly since he had made it his mission after moving into the house to trek through and memorize the forest around him.

13

"Yes," a deep voice rumbled out calmly, "For tens of thousands of years this rally beacon has been here, hidden from outsiders not invited or attuned to its resonance."

Then, suddenly, a giant some twelve feet tall materialized before them with one hand resting on top of the pillar. The giant wore surprisingly human-like clothing, though crafted from just a few smoothed leather skins of the mammoths that roamed in ancient times.

"Shit." Startled, Jacob took a few steps back, recalling the giants that he fought alongside the barbarians. He felt uncomfortably naked with no weapon whatsoever at his disposal.

Noticing Jacob's apprehension, Chief Zorin said, "It is okay. The giant is a friend. Please come with us."

Lionak and Chief Zorin walked into the circle and towards the pillar while Mac waited by Jacob's side. After a few moments, Jacob collected himself and they, too, moved forward.

Patiently the giant waited until the party reached within seven feet of the pillar before shifting his stance as to rest on one knee and placing his hands near his waist upon the other.

Gazing at the pillar, Mac noticed the carved symbol of a simple thorned rose.

With his senses having been heightened from the appearance of the giant, Jacob could hear the subtle rhythmic stretch and faint crackle of the leather as the giant breathed.

In a quieter and more relaxed tone the giant introduced himself, "I am known as Phosx, a teacher from the ancient time and a guide for the generations."

Jacob just looked at the giant, his mind empty of cognitive thought, his instincts demanding he prepare for an impending attack.

"This is Jacob and Mac, the two from this world who had clashed with the Red Dragon clan and the Baron." Lionak stated, pointing between Jacob and Mac with pride.

"Hello." Mac said after a long pause, having waited for Jacob to say something.

The giant smiled openly.

"What are we doing here?" Jacob finally forced out, darting his eyes toward Lionak before looking back at Phosx.

"I'm glad you asked." Phosx responded as he moved to sit down and cross his legs before them. It was evident to him that he needed to show that he was both relaxed and unaggressive for Jacob's sake.

"Rather recently Lionak felt a peculiar emanation of Wild Magic surge through our world. We, both the initiated and Elders of the Rose, felt it as well." Phosx said looking at Lionak and to the pillar, "It was from what you humans labeled a Demon. Their race is called the Archgen."

"I knew it!" Jacob whispered heavily.

"For many centuries, it was believed that the last of the Demons had been chained by the Prophets - whom are now lost to us. We think one of the Demons have managed to free themselves and is now moving among us." Phosx revealed.

As the giant spoke, Jacob's instincts slowly relaxed its grip on him and he could not help but think about how intelligent this giant appeared to be in comparison to those he had fought against.

"Lionak and I have a proposal for you two."

"Sure." Mac said without hesitation.

"Okay. Let's hear it." Jacob begrudgingly joined in.

Briefly scratching the back of his head, Phosx said, "While what Lionak felt was, in fact, the Demon...it is not the main threat to humanity in the world."

"What?!" Jacob blurted out. Everything he had learned throughout his lifetime said that Demons, an invisible force, were the number one threat to all humanity. Indeed, it had even been proclaimed and written in many different cultures as far back as history could recount.

15

The giant took a deep breath and revealed, "Don't mistake my meaning…the Archgen are largely an unchallenged force that has been among us even before the First Adam. And they will continue to be a problem. But. Only one is free out there to use its power which means it cannot wage war on all of humanity all at once. There is a greater threat that is among us now and in greater numbers which can. The Serpqhtaq, an ancient interstellar and technologically advanced civilization. The Rose has been standing against this power but, soon, it will expunge all of humanity and us. That is why we need both of you among our ranks."

"Jacob, we need you to use your military contacts to get all the information you can about an artificial intelligence system controlled by the Serpqhtaq, known as Janus, so it can be located and a weakness can be found. Once it has been taken off the board, we can collectively focus on the Serpqhtaq and the Demon."

"Why is an artificial intelligence system so important to you if the Serpqatags, or however you say that, are the real threat?" Jacob challenged.

Phosx looked at Jacob, "We recently learned that Janus is infiltrating and taking over command and control civilian government systems around the world. That becomes a significant force multiplier in favor of the Serpqhtaq. At minimum it could simply help neutralize military and government ability to react, in effect, yielding the same result as an overwhelming attack if it had taken over the military itself…and…perhaps that is also an objective."

Mac looked questioningly at Phosx, but the giant already knew what Mac would ask, "We believe that you, Mac, would be able to get through any defensive shielded system of the Serpqhtaq to deliver a kinetic blow against the Janus system."

"What do you think?" Chief Zorin probed. He was eager to get started and learn all that he could regarding the two alien races, primarily to prepare the Guardians and bolster the defenses of his own world.

16

"I'm in." Jacob volunteered, though he was not sure just how he would get his hands on information, particularly of the caliber of artificial intelligence.

"And I." Mac joined.

"Excellent!" Phosx smiled, "Jacob, Lionak and Chief Zorin will contribute what they can. When you have completed your task, return here and touch the Rose on the pillar."

"As for you, Mac," the giant said as he got to a standing position, "you are coming with me to meet one of the Elders about your ability."

With that, Phosx rested his hand upon the pillar and they vanished from sight leaving Jacob, Lionak and Chief Zorin.

Chapter Three

Sub Commander Ux, an uncharacteristically muscular Serpqhtaq, looked out into the white dotted black void before him from the stellar observation module, scarcely big enough for three of his bulk, placed at the end of a five-hundred-meter-long narrow passageway connected to a much larger Outpost, known as Vuochtzm, that had been constructed on the planetoid humans knew as Pluto. While the Outpost's power core was shielded using the most advanced technology they had at their disposal, the extreme sensitivity of the stellar observation and tracking equipment could not operate in close proximity to the Outpost.

The Outpost itself was comprised of two sealed oval shaped flat decks, each separated from the other by nine meters of empty space, and each connected at three equidistant points within the decks to three massive triangular columns anchored to the planetoid's surface that sloped towards each other and joined together ninety meters above the topmost deck forming a triangle when viewed from the surface. The lower deck, positioned eleven meters above the surface housed a few craft bays, all mechanical parts and spare technological equipment as well as the central power core, life support and food crates. Many of those food crates imprisoned a range of living animal and aquatic lifeforms the Serpqhtaq savored from several star systems they had found. The upper deck contained fairly small living quarters at its oval shaped center, surrounded by another oval shaped ring consisting of mess, research and training compartments. From the outer edge of the second ring extending to the deck's structural wall housed all of the command-and-control equipment and manned posts operating to keep the remote Outpost in operation. Along the structural outer wall, a slender but thick half-meter tall transparent composite window wrapped around the entire upper deck, broken only by the triangular support columns, forming a continuous ring from which the inhabitants could look out to see beyond the Outpost. The Serpqhtaq's oval design architecture used throughout their civilization originally served to hamper ranged attacks by adversaries to allow the Serpqhtaq to retreat, bait and in some spots corral such adversaries to concentration points where they could be dispatched from multiple flanks. Though the Outpost was built several millennia after the end of the Wjohs War involving legions of enemy ground troops where the design proved instrumental in securing their victory, the architectural pattern became an integral element in virtually all structures and craft which followed that time, especially for living areas.

Sub Commander Ux looked down at the holographic control panel before him and made a few adjustments to better isolate the origin of the high-energy emission wave that had crashed through the outpost, and other planetary bodies nearer the Sun as if somehow drawn to it. He again looked back up to the small, long sliver of a window and a few moments later the computer calculated the origin and superimposed the equivalent of a yellow targeting reticle at that origin near the southern or bottom edge of the window.

With a wiry grin, he activated an augmentation mentally to open a communication channel with the Outpost. Finally, after fourteen hours of analysis work, his task had reached its end, "I have confirmed the origin of the emission. It is coming from this solar system's twin star. We will be able to reliably track and collect extensive information on the Twin Sun in the next few hours and it will be entering the system fifteen Earth days from now." The Star he was referring to was the Sun.

"Excellent, Ux. Station an astro-technician at the stellar compartment and return to the Outpost." a monotonous male voice responded.

"At once." Sub-Commander Ux confirmed. After sending the order for an astro-technician, using the control panel, he turned and motioned with his left hand, causing a curved, dull metallic-colored door to slide open.

Shortly afterwards, an oval-shaped standing plate rose in front of him a few inches and a long series of triangular-shaped white lights along the floor of the passageway lit up sequentially in the direction of the Outpost, starting at his position. Casually he stepped onto the suspended plate. A bright blue-colored hue radiated from underneath the plate and almost instantly it moved forward at ninety meters per second, Ux unphased from the sudden change in velocity from the stationary position.

The commander of the Outpost, Thoshii, shifted his attention from Ux and resumed communication with the projection of Regnum, the current System Commander for the solar system, "We have completed cloning of Fratres, Carcer, Vita and Uxor. However, that stellar emission destroyed the progress made in reorganizing the configuration of the molecular grey matter and neural connections to accept the knowledge and memory state of each subject. So, we are restarting the impulse implantation."

"I see." Regnum responded. With paired communication cubes similar in size to a softball, each capitalizing on a magnetically suspended internal lattice structure composed of mirrored piezo-electric atoms collectively no larger than a bacterium in each cube, and complex waveform manipulation, permitted instantaneous communication between two points that could be dozens of astronomical units, or billions of kilometers, apart.

Commander Thoshii's eyes shifted to look into the void outside the Outpost while he waited for Regnum to say something else. Then it came.

"Any update on the arrival of the fleet?" Regnum inquired. He was curious, not only for the colonization of the planet, but also what measure may be levied against him for the mysterious assassinations of the four Serpqhtaq who occupied the council of the Thirteen.

Commander Thoshii signaled for an update from Sub-Commander Quwzj who nodded negatively. "No update. The advance escort group is on schedule to arrive at the Outpost in five Earth days to prepare the observation settlement's extraction. The fleet will be on station shortly after the Twin Sun swings around the Star and begins its exit out of the system."

"Understood." Regnum expressed, "A single Archgen was recently detected on the planet…which may complicate things."

Commander Thoshii frowned and crossed his thin arms in disappointment. After recalling what Regnum and others on the Council had been doing over past cycles and neutralizing the remnant Archgen, in somewhat coded language he asked, "The belt remains from the last transit, does it not?"

"Yes."

"I will see if I can arrange for the fleet to detach a *diplomatic envoy* in advance of the Twin Sun's arrival to meet, under your order System Commander." Commander Thoshii implied, trusting that Regnum understood the envoy would actually be a platoon strength elite battle-hardened unit to imprison the Archgen as they yet possessed reliable technology required to eliminate them. As long as the belt remained in place the Archgen was trapped on the planet and would not be able to communicate with others off-world.

Regnum nodded with a blank expression. He understood.

Reluctantly Commander Thoshii sighed and admitted, "It's going to be tough though. The fleet is already traveling at eighty percent capacity to be on station as scheduled which means the *envoy* will need to find a way to reach you much, much sooner. Certainly, faster than the fleet's maximum capacity."

"Received, Commander. You have my authorization to proceed."

After Regnum's hologram disappeared, Commander Thoshii left the command module and moved to enter the secondary module, used if the command module were to experience a failure, and proceeded to compose and send an encoded message for the fleet's general on an unmonitored channel used for clandestine operations only a select few participated in.

Partially naked, standing bent over before a paper-thin nano-composite mirror, General Xkuiv concluded the moulting cleanse that all Serpqhtaq underwent twice per Earth-year as a result of their gradual genetic degradation over generations spanning many millennia. The moult process is what gave their skin a slight hazy and plastic-like scaly appearance that became more pronounced as it neared the time of the cleanse. A few trusted ancient ancestors of modern humans, largely unversed in off-world civilizations and biologies, observed the moult and equated it to the same process that snakes underwent on Earth. The association passed verbally between successive generations before the introduction of parchment and scroll, thereafter becoming part of the written history to eventually be discovered, translated and duplicated across cultures and preserved through time. As a result, in the modern age of humanity, the Serpqhtaq are conjoined to the enduring belief that they are an evolutionary branch of the reptile or serpent. In actuality, however, the Serpqhtaq share no other biological trait.

Carefully, the general peeled off the remainder of shedding skin from his slender lower legs and feet as it was custom to start the removal at the head and work down to the feet. Having completed the cleanse several hundred times, his skill was so refined that he could remove the entire shed skin from the front of his leg and top of the foot in one action and another action for the back of his leg and bottom of the foot.

After completing the removal from his other limb, he collected the four wrinkled, almost transparent skins into one hand and stood up in front of the mirror, repositioning slightly to inspect himself to ensure the cleanse was complete. Satisfied, he placed the skins on a depressed oblong plate that had slid out of the wall next to the mirror. As they settled towards the depression, the surface of the plate momentarily glowed a light aqua color, dissolving the shedding into a powder of its base elements. The miniscule volume of powder was then absorbed into the extremely fine pores of the plate, barely visible to the eye, where it would be separated and channeled into the ship's recombinant resource system. In an automated fashion the plate slid back into the wall and the compartment paneling cover rose seamlessly into place, aligning with the surface of the wall to give the appearance that the wall was a single, unbroken form.

Underneath a single, thin, continuous strip along the ceiling which provided light and extended through the cabin, the general strode over to a slim but tall open compartment with rounded edges that protruded approximately eight inches from the living quarter's wall and withdrew a loose-fitting uniform that had been suspended in its midst. The compartment itself automatically cleaned, sterilized and repaired uniforms as well as serving as a closet. That is why every Serpqhtaq only had two single-piece uniforms…one to wear and the other to prepare for wearing.

Leaning on the upright sleeping tube, General Xkuiv slid his feet and legs first into the uniform, activating nano-material fibers that sprung to life forming the extruded and hardened shape of boots extending mid-shin. After shoving his arms into the uniform, open in the front, be brought it up his back, over his shoulders and touched the two sides of the uniform together causing it to enjoin the remainder, up to his neck, giving the impression that the uniform was somehow crafted from a single garment wrapped around his body and limbs with no seam lines or overlaps.

Shortly thereafter, the 3d holographic likeness of Commander Thoshii materialized in the air, near the living quarter's only access door, "Skaa, I must report the new presence of a Archgen on Earth. A *diplomatic envoy* has been authorized to resolve the matter with the following code." Skaa was the name used by the general for clandestine activities.

A pattern of elaborate sigils appeared below the image of Commander Thoshii forming a rotating ring that, among other things, identified the source of the message as the Outpost Vuochtzm before he concluded, "The dimensional tear that reorganized one of the belts around the planet has isolated the Archgen and it cannot make off-world contact. But the envoy must arrive before the fleet and before the star system's Twin."

Using an isolated augmentation, General Xkuiv saved the message for later recall and the holographic image vanished. He recognized the now all too familiar code from Regnum. In the general's assessment, reinforced by the new message, Regnum had performed a growing series of miscalculations that unnecessarily increased the probability that they would not be able to lay claim to the planet after countless cycles of preparation. While the Serpqhtaq had several colonization fleets mirroring his own, the general's had been assigned the planet of Earth and a failure on the part of Regnum, not of his making, would still tarnish his standing and removal from the fleet given how close it was to the planet's solar system.

General Xkuiv cursed to himself and placed his hands on his hips, increasingly eager to meet with the System Commander to conduct a thorough review and inevitable disciplinary action providing he could actually manage capturing the Serpqhtaq before the Twin Star's arrival. Even with the advanced technology at his disposal, successfully pulling off such an operation was hardly favorable. Shrugging it off, he strode out of the oval shaped room and into a narrow corridor illuminated in the same fashion as his quarters, the sliding door emitting no noise as it closed rapidly behind him. Occasionally he passed other uniformed Serpqhtaq who immediately stood upright and placed their opened hands, one atop the other, flat on their chests with palms facing out until he passed, a sign of respect for the position he held.

The general nodded in acknowledgement and continued to the engineering section of his command cruiser. Like all of the other spacecraft in the fleet, the command cruiser was formed into the shape of a swept-wing arrowhead with a conical structure along its center where massive spherical plasmic power cores, each orbited by a thick isolation and harmonization shield ring, were housed. Not only did the normally unstable cores serve all of the power needs throughout the ship, they also provided the gigantic power requirements of a series of ten propulsion drives at the rear of the conical structure, akin to an ion drive but significantly more advanced. Overall, the length of the command cruiser stretched for 7000 meters while its height, less the conical structure, was a mere 42 meters, a deliberate low-profile structural design common to all Serpqhtaq craft meant to minimize focused enemy barrages of fire along the central axis and surfaces around it as all critical systems were evenly distributed throughout the aft of the ship from one side to another; its width from wingtip to wingtip measuring 3000 meters.

Finally, he made it to a large transport plate on the lowest deck of the cruiser, inside one of several tunnels that moved Serpqhtaq and materials in largely straight lines from the bow to the stern with evenly spaced transfer decks placed along the tunnel with which to load or unload. Using his connected augmentation the plate was spurred forward as transfer decks zipped by until it stopped several seconds later. Immediately he got off the plate and walked a few meters to another, large enough for just three Serpqhtaq, which took the general two decks up inside the ship.

Following the much wider corridor which slowly veered around in the shape of an oval if you were to follow its course back to where you began, General Xkuiv walked seventy meters from the transport plate before stopping momentarily in front of a pair of double doors with a set of three sigils embossed on the right-most door. Once the nearby sensor authenticated the general, it briskly opened and he entered. Scanning across the expansive flight deck, one-quarter of which consumed with spare parts and repair equipment, the General spotted one of the fleet's command engineers who were able, provided the necessary resources, to repair all craft and equipment in the fleet without consulting engineering systems or incredibly rare nano-foil schematics that could be unrolled to expose a single fixed design. Engineers and flag commanders both coveted those nano-foils even though they had little practicality.

"Commander Embhiv," General Xkuiv began as he strode over, stopping in front of a dark carbon colored, diamond-shaped satellite repeater scarcely taking up a volume equal to four meters cubed, "I require your expertise for a moment."

The commander finished closing a circuit connection within one of the access panels of the satellite and turned to face the general, "Yes, General Xkuiv." While Command Engineers, with their diverse technical expertise, were equal in standing to the general and were not required to acknowledge matched rank, they were prohibited from performing the duties of the same rank in a different specialty, a law that applied across all specialties.

"You are familiar with the fleet's objective and its position relative to the habitable planet called Earth?"

"Yes, I am."

"A Twin Star is due to enter that solar system in approximately fifteen Earth days." General Xkuiv stated.

Commander Embhiv fidgeted a bit, unable to see the relevance of the general's statements. He knew the fleet would arrive safely, as scheduled, after the Twin Star had begun its exit trajectory out of the solar system.

"Well," General Xkuiv articulated, looking directly at Embhiv, "we have a zeta priority mission which has been authorized by the system commander." He then raised an open hand before Commander Embhiv and the coded holographic message played above it, attuned to Embhiv's bioelectric field and his own isolated augmentation so that only they could observe the message.

After a few moments the message terminated and General Xkuiv lowered his hand, "Is it possible to launch a craft from the fleet bearing a platoon of soldiers to the planet before the Twin enters the solar system?" The general, among others, knew that once such an instable Star entered the solar system with so many planetary bodies and asteroids along with the Star's hazardous emissions which would increase in frequency and magnitude as it neared the Sun and their magnetic fields clashed, the entire system would become a gravimetric and chaotically charged tinderbox. In that environment, it would be impossible to reliably operate craft and conduct any operations, which is why the fleet was scheduled for arrival afterward.

Commander Embhiv glanced down as he raised his hand to lean on the satellite and thought for several moments. "Given our current distance from that solar system, we do not have a Midcraft in the fleet capable of reaching the planet with sufficient time to complete your mission."

"Damn." General Xhuiv steamed lowly.

"However, I...can retrofit a Midcraft with a dual propulsion envelope that would reach the planet, given the additional mass of the platoon, in 1.6 Earth-days before the Twin's ingress. Still, that does not leave much time for completing your mission and safely exiting the system."

The General cracked a relieved smile, "How much time do you need to complete your retrofit?" With a Archgen on the board he had no intention of leaving anything to chance. The elite soldier platoon would not be returning.

Immediately Commander Embhiv said, "Twenty-one hours."

"Excellent! Proceed immediately." General Xhuiv expressed in an upbeat tone as he turned to exit the flight deck.

"Be aware that the Midcraft will be forced to operate the propulsion system at one-hundred and thirty percent its maximum rating." Commander Embhiv said as the general strode towards the double doors.

In response, General Xhuiv briefly raised his hand just before the doors slid open.

With that obstacle out of the way he proceeded to the opposite side of the command cruiser where his single company of soldiers, or four platoons, were stationed. He did not particularly relish the thought of being loosed of one platoon, leaving three to protect the operations of the entire fleet once the fleet had reached Earth. Nevertheless, he reprioritized one platoon with the objective of imprisoning the Archgen with immediate termination of the Archgen and Midcraft by flying them into the solar system's primary Star. The advanced composite materials of the Midcraft would allow it to penetrate several of the Star's radiation fields before being overtaken by intense gravity wells and denser fields that would tear the craft apart at an atomic level and pull the remains into the Star. Not even a Archgen could overcome such powerful cosmic forces.

Exactly twenty-one hours later, General Xhuiv returned to the flight deck to ensure everything was ready and examined, with elevated curiosity, the retrofit that Commander Embhiv had spoken of. As the commander

27

explained, he split the Midcraft on one side of the conical propulsion system in order to widen the craft enough to integrate a second propulsion system one meter from the other and then added reinforcements and composite paneling to enjoin the two parts of the Midcraft back together. The new skin paneling stood out in comparison to the weathered paneling of the craft, giving it a unique and eye-drawing appearance.

Pleased with Commander Embhiv's work, General Xhuiv gave the order for the Midcraft to depart and suggested that he may be able to acquire a nano-foil for the commander's small but growing collection, as reward for his invaluable contribution to the fleet.

Chapter Four

A subtle tingling sensation enveloped Mac for several minutes following his, and Phosx's, appearance in the midst of a forest heralding yellow birch, sugar maple, and fewer red oak trees. As Mac looked around himself into the forest the movement of a deer in the distance caught his eye, partially shielded by the trees and other lush vegetation. The cool air and natural fragrance of the forest filled his nose.

"May I ask where we are?"

Phosx glanced briefly at Mac, while looking for the ancient sandstone column fashioned from an unusually large and dense block taken from a prehistoric quarry on Hermit Island long ago, "You are in the archipelago."

Mac stared at the giant wondering if he was purposefully being vague.

The giant laughed rather gently, motioning for Mac to follow him, "You are walking on what the Indian's ancestors called Makwa-Minis, my friend. Or, Bear Island, in English. At night, if you look south, you may catch a glimpse of light from the lighthouse on Raspberry Island.

Had you a boat, you could continue south a short distance further to the tip of the mainland. This is one of a gathering of small lands just north of the state you know of as Wisconsin."

The giant veered south-east, the Sun beginning to settle behind the forest to the west, "Collectively the lands are called the Apostle Islands, surrounded by a vast expanse of pure water."

"Well that's cool." Mac said, thinking about what he could fish for, "How big is this island? I'd like to look around and check out the water sometime."

Phosx scratched his large forearm as they continued walking and said, "This island is roughly one mile in width, west to east, and double in length so it would not take much to reach its edge. There is a cave on this island, called the *Amphitheater* that would be worth your time while you are at the edge."

Recalling geography class in high school from many years ago Mac asked, "So we are in the Great Lakes then?"

Phosx raised a pointed finger upward for a moment to confirm Mac's suspicion, "Yes. Specifically, Lac Supérieur, the largest."

Suddenly, Phosx reached back and placed his large hand on Mac's chest to stop him and after a moment, slowly withdrew it as to point towards a large, dark outline in the forest about forty meters ahead of them. Then he whispered, "I forgot to mention, the islands are littered with black bears."

Mac spotted the large black bear just as it rose and began moving towards them, suddenly craving a weapon of some sort.

Phosx took a few steps toward the black bear and stopped while the two looked at each other as if they were communicating. Even though the black bear was much smaller than the giant, Mac held his position not keen on being chased down if he did nothing more than flinch. The claws and teeth were what he was worried about.

"Come." Phosx whispered so faintly that Mac almost didn't hear him.

The black bear shifted her head toward Mac as he carefully walked up and stopped by Phosx. After a moment the bear grumbled, pulling the air and Mac's scent into her nostrils.

"Do you have something to give the bear?" Phosx asked casually. Clearly the giant was not worried about being mauled.

Mac shot a puzzled look at the giant, "Actually no. I didn't think to bring along a slab of beef today."

Phosx chuckled quietly to himself, "I mean, do you have a piece of clothing or something like that?"

"Uh," Mac thought for a bit before he remembered, "I have a handkerchief. I use it on hikes."

"Great. Give that to the bear."

Dumfounded, Mac reached into his rear pocket and withdrew the handkerchief as it unrolled and hung around his fingers. Then he brought it in front of him, toward the black bear.

The black bear, Mac estimated to weigh close to five hundred pounds, moved forward and stopped to look at the dangling handkerchief. All Mac could think was just how large the bear's head was. Large enough that its jaws could easily bite off his hand and part of his forearm.

Mac felt the hot breath of the black bear as she moved her dark nose around his hand and tilted her head to clasp the handkerchief in her powerful jaws, bearing her large teeth. Then she turned and left them, leaves and brush crackling below her paws, disappearing into the forest.

Still somewhat unnerved by the encounter, Mac said, "What was that for?"

The giant placed part of his hand on Mac's shoulder, "She will tell the others you are here, so you are not mistaken for food."

"That's comforting." Mac quipped just before he realized what had happened, "Wait a minute. So you talked to the bear just now? Does it have a name?"

Phosx turned and moved forward toward a toppled column that had once stood over twelve feet in height. Then he saw the memories he had of the day the column had been cut in two by a 30mm autocannon mounted on a hovering Apache attack helicopter in 1979, covering a small assault team pushing towards the column's location. That day was when things were forever changed, having been rooted out by a colonel that lived deep inside the dark crevices of black projects and unexplained phenomenon, shielded between the pages of patriotism and national security...

"Phosx?"

The giant shrugged off the memory and, with both hands, grasped the upright remainder of the heavy column and turned it about twenty degrees to his left.

"No, the black bear does not have a name like you would think of names but yes, we did talk in a way. It was more a communication of visualizations and feelings though."

"Nice! I'd love to have a gift like that." Mac admitted openly.

Phosx turned to look at Mac, realizing his, and most of humanity's ignorance of the past, "You. Humanity. You all have that, and other, gifts Mac."

Then a rectangular section of the forest's floor rose as the groaning sounds of large, aged timbers and heavy, shaped boulders moved. Below the thick layer of soil was a long, flat arch-stone which rested upon two others, each six meters in height, and positioned at opposite ends.

"Follow me." Phosx said as he walked underneath the arch-stone with Mac. The whole structure then sank down into the Earth, leaving no indication it was there.

Immediately in front of them rested a stone staircase leading down, wide enough for two giants to stand side by side. An earthly unmolested aroma lingered in the air and numerous and seemingly randomly placed sources of light beamed out into the passageway from inside the stone walls, the source of which being an exotic yet harmless radioactive ore that formed veins of yellowish light throughout.

"Wow." Mac gasped in awe, "Impressive."

"This is one of our youngest enclaves." Phosx smiled proudly as they moved into the depths of the passageway, "Around ten thousand years old, established long after the One Sea had uncovered this area and the glacial age rested."

Just as they reached the end of the staircase and found themselves at the entrance to a gigantic domed cavern beneath the blanket of Lake Superior, some five hundred meters in diameter and one hundred in height with massive unbroken columns of the same composition as the stone passageway and reaching to the ceiling at regular but spacious intervals, Mac turned to Phosx and questioned, "In the Realm it seems all giants have a bad reputation, so I have to ask...why are giants considered bad? And what are these gifts that you say we all have?"

Several people of varying complexions walked past them without taking a second look at Phosx or Mac, undoubtedly with heritage owed to European, African, South American and native Indian bloodlines, seemingly headed for a finely constructed stone edifice that jutted out from the cavern wall some twenty meters and rose to meet the cavern's ceiling. Another giant, dressed similarly to Phosx, mulled around near the ancient construction.

"Ahh." Phosx remarked as they walked over to a small fountain springing out from a stone column fitted with slots containing cups of different sizes around its perimeter further in the cavern, opposite the stone edifice used as a gathering point and living space for the cavern's occupants. Phosx took a rather large cup, covered in ornate artistic designs, into his hand and held it beneath the arching stream of water as to fill it and motioned for Mac to do the same with one of several much smaller cups, "Where to begin?"

The cups themselves also glowed in spots, having been fashioned from the same stone as the cavern.

"The beginning?"

"I do not know the beginning." Phosx admitted after swallowing the pure, untainted water, "But I do know, like all life, there are both good giants and bad ones. Some only made so by tragedy and others by blood. Regardless the bond between giants and humanity stretches far into the past."

Mac eagerly eyed the giant, shifting the cup in his hands, open to learning something possibly nobody knew.

"We giants have roamed this planet since before the time of the First Adam, whom was a few feet taller than you by the way, and when the Earth circled closer to the Sun than it does now. In that time, more lands were exposed with part of the great oceans still deep within it. Everything was bigger during that time. The trees, the animals, the bugs. All much bigger."

Phosx took another sip and continued, "An ancient, almost ethereal race, the Archgen, spread over the planet and created different types of life and plants, variations of what had already existed. Though, those variations were relatively short-lived and went extinct at one point or another around the time the great oceans began moving out from inside the Earth and the Earth moved away from the Sun. But the Archgen were benevolent to all life as they thrived from the energy that life emitted, harmonized with the invisible ethereal flows in space…"

"Archgen, the same creature that is called the Devil?! The thing that we've got to take care of after aliens and their AI??", Mac rumbled forcefully.

Phosx grimaced a bit, realizing that the knowledge was divisive and briefly moved his cup toward Mac, "It is the same but it is not the same, Mac. Yes, what you saw in the desert was a Archgen but that is a reversal of what they used to be, as I just said. For them, they did not become what they are now by choice. Rather it was necessity. A very long time ago, the Sun's companion flew through the solar system forcing many things to change. Among them was a change to the Earth which not only created a tear where life and matter was split, it also induced significant changes to the very core of the Earth, injecting vast swaths of its own radiant energy into the Earth's and reorganizing the radiation belts that surround it. I understand they are called the Van Allen radiation belts. Anyway, the belts cut them off from space and the ethereal flows of energy they largely depended on. This, I believe, forced the Archgen to change into malevolent beings by influencing life on the planet to emit more powerful but negative energy they could consume to make up for what they could no longer get from space. This malevolent form of Archgen was labeled Arch-Demon by the Prophets."

What Phosx, nor any other giant knew, was the Serpqhtaq had a hand in guiding the Prophets.

"And," Phosx made a point to say, "around the time of the tear is when the Archgen were trying to create their own race of Dragons, separate from the Silver Dragons and others that were already spread across the Earth. Unfortunately, the effects of the Sun's companion altered that new race of Dragons in their infancy whom became the Red Dragons that you are already familiar with."

Mac raised his eyebrows in surprise, having no idea how to respond to Phosx. But the giant did not need a response, realizing how overwhelming the knowledge was which, essentially, upended things Mac thought he already knew.

"Well, so, if dragons actually existed here…what happened to them?"

"They were hunted across the lands for many centuries until they were no more." the giant said bluntly. Since none remained, he didn't feel it was important to mention that they, like the giants, had also lived among humanity.

"That sounds similar to what has been going on with the Archgen…being hunted." Mac posited, lifting the cup to his mouth.

Phosx nodded slightly, thinking that Mac was actually grasping what he was saying.

"With regard to us giants, since the time before known history, we largely collected ourselves into clans comprising two or three families and lived near your ancestors as shepherds to encourage their development and independent thought. Peace and respect reigned during that time and humanity built grand meeting halls large enough for giants to enter and commune. But many millennia ago, that changed and what, at first, was a small band of humans, grew over time and hunted us. We do not know why that happened but that caused many of the clans to break apart and hide from humans, while others stood against the growing human army. Still, some others joined the ranks of that army to hunt other giants in exchange for their lives. Yet, a few human kingdoms also stood against the army and fought alongside us, but they did not ultimately have the might to stop it. For centuries it was a bloody and confusing time."

Phosx moved and sat atop a hewn oak long-bench ten meters away from the fountain and looked into his cup for a moment, placing a hand on his bent knee, "As the army continued and new kingdoms sprang up behind them, they erected their own temples on top of the structures and foundations of what they conquered, particularly those tied to us, to show to all that they were superior…that they should be feared. And, I think, to ultimately stamp out the memory of giants and humans working and living together."

Mac made his way nearer the giant when a faint glimmer, partially obstructed from one of the massive columns, briefly caught his eye near the center of the cavern.

Mac looked back to Phosx, "That is brutal, Phosx. Did that army destroy those kingdoms that sided with the giants?"

Phosx grunted. "From what I understand, they were almost entirely wiped out over a few centuries. But, like a weed, they could not be entirely routed. Over time, as power, decadence and decay of the regents and stewards passed from generation to generation the army and its corrupted power hub were slowly infiltrated and taken over from within by the remnant of the kingdoms that had managed to survive. Once they had seized control of most leadership posts, they exiled the King and family, refashioned the army and stimulated a powerful era of scholarly freedom and achievement throughout the lands the King had toiled over and taken."

"Where were the giants during all that?"

"The giants did not partake in that conquest."

"Oh, so it was inconvenient for you to support your allies against your common enemy when you were no longer hunted?" Mac tossed out with a disgusted look.

The giant eased back on the bench a little and placed the cup upon it, "It is not what you think. The giants have always remained near our allies and have continued to shepherd them, continuing our purpose from the ancient days, though now done from shadow. And we have not forgotten the sacrifice of those allies. But the reason that we did not become involved in aiding those human allies in their takeover was because it was entirely a human matter. Humanity must learn and evolve themselves when dealing with their own kind."

"And the Serpqhtaq? It would seem they are really just a threat to humans...so why help?" Mac probed, doubting the giant's claim that they, too, were at risk.

Phosx crossed his large arms and said, "We have always been shepherds of humanity, Mac. We've done it for so long that, without that purpose, we may lose part of ourselves."

"And," Phosx shrugged, "Without help, all of humanity...all humans...would be wiped out. I hate to admit it but, while all of you are like a Mackenzie wolf that would fiercely defend itself against the Serpqhtaq, and may even score a win here or there, you just don't have the technological means to withstand them in greater numbers. We giants are already few in number in comparison, and also would befall the same fate on our own once we were inevitably discovered."

Mac was not sure he believed that but he remained to hear what more the giant had to say.

Shifting back to the subject at hand, Phosx glanced toward Mac, as a grin began to form on his face and said, "After the shift, that scholarly time was magnificent. The mechanical creations were brilliant, and we giants did assist where we could to get humanity to see and think beyond themselves. To develop their natural creativity and connection around themselves. Collectively this conglomerate of humanity, clustered in different regions of the world became known as the Tart'aas. Ultimately, they became the envy of other kingdoms whom persisted in exploiting their followers through fear, suppression and impoverishment to hoard control for themselves to guarantee position above those followers."

After Mac walked to the bench and leaned upon it, given he would have to vault himself up to sit otherwise, he remarked, "That sounds like a sure way to lose position to me, almost like the age-old bully problem that persists among us humans...beat on people until they get tired of it and they take out the bully. What happened with the Tart'aas? I've never heard of them before."

"Humm. Well, if you can get your hands on some of the old-world maps, one of the common markings for them was Tartaria."

- "Ah!" Mac realized, a subtle shock flowing through him, "I have heard of that before. There's so little about them though."

"You are correct. Like most kingdoms, they were slowly chipped away on by others, their history blotted. They were diluted from hordes of outsiders with vastly different beliefs and homage to surrounding kingdoms – that dilution a much easier way to conquer than trying to assemble an army that, if it failed, meant total defeat. It was during this time that some of the most visionary scholars fled far away to continue their passions in relative freedom and solitude under the symbol of the Rose, while a few others banded together with one of their mechanical masterpieces and traveled to the other dimension of this world after they had unearthed the writings of an ancient Pharoah's use of an energy conduit you know of as Wild Magic." Phosx responded, matter-of-factly.

"That is fascinating stuff. I saw the Rose symbol on the pillar. And all this must be part of the Rose." Mac asserted, drinking from his cup.

"Yes." Phosx confirmed happily, "And, we all bear the mark of the Rose so we can identify each other...for those among us who yet lack the mental development to do such."

Mac fidgeted, not knowing if he should ask, "Can you show me?"

The giant lifted up his left hand, extended his fingers toward Mac and then spread his index finger from the others. There, in the finger's webbing that extended to his middle finger, was the small tan tattoo, a few shades darker than his skin, of a single Rose with a thorn upon its stem.

"So, the Rose means Tart'aas?" Mac inquired.

"Not anymore, as few Tart'aas family bloodlines remain. Now it's a symbol for all that share and uphold its ideals. It's a symbol for bringing forth enlightened change in communion with nature both of this world and beyond it.", Phosx stated, pointing toward it with his other hand, "And the thorn represents the force of will, and body, that will be used to ensure it carries on for all future generations."

"That is deep."

The giant merely nodded, lowering his hands.

Mac stewed to himself for a minute before he said, "That still does not answer the question."

Phosx straightened his back somewhat, believing he had covered everything Mac needed to know, "No?"

After pulling is hand from the back of his head to the front, Mac said, "Well, no...what does all that history have to do with these aliens today, Serpqhtaq...and me being here instead of out there?"

"Ah yes. Good point." Phosx shrugged, "Up until about four hundred years ago, we were ignorant to

38

the existence of the Serpqhtaq on Earth with their cloaking technology and the fact they have operated exclusively through humans. In looking back, they may have had a hand in the turmoil between giants and humanity and divisions between peoples…but hard to say for certain. Anyway, we had been teaching small groups of people to grow their innate natural abilities for things such as telepathy, claircognizance and precognition. But a critical threshold must have been crossed as more people heard of our teaching and joined us, that culminated with unnatural events surfacing in the exact same areas that we taught."

"Could a rogue student or someone have caused that?", Mac supposed.

"No. We giants would have been able to detect that. And the fact that we could not, caused us to look deeper over many years to find the source."

Phosx shifted himself on the bench, "The problem was that our groups, and sometimes even entire towns, would get hit with a devastating earthquake or massive, concentrated rainstorms that brutally killed or drowned people in torrents of mud or falling debris. Once there had even been an event from a dormant volcano that suddenly erupted sweeping over people with lava and ash. What I found particularly disturbing is that the survivors we could not reach were captured by other humans and put in institutions – I believe you would call them asylums."

He paused for a moment, "We eventually were able to feel the unnatural massing of energy and followed it to a mechanical device deep in a forest in Europe. In astral form we discovered the Serpqhtaq who exceeded, by far, the mechanical genius of the Tart'aas and the technological ability of humanity today. But we also learned their weakness."

"Which is?"

"They have no natural mental abilities as humanity does, like telepathy. Nearest we can tell, their race is entirely dependent upon their technology to mimic

39

some of those abilities and, so, that part of them was never stimulated or evolved alongside their other advances."

What he, nor any giant or other native being on the planet knew was that early in their genetic experiments on themselves, the Serpqhtaq had irrevocably spliced out those prominent expressions of their genetic code because those abilities could not be reliably controlled by the ruling line, a line that has persisted to this day.

"Though most of the asylums have since disappeared, and we've gotten better at masking ourselves when we are grouped so we are not discovered and captured, it is believed that the Serpqhtaq seized survivors in order to study and experiment on them to somehow extract or use humanity's gifts. I believe they see those gifts as a threat to their existence."

"I see." Mac remarked, "Well, I don't have any mental abilities like telepathy or lighting things on fire with my mind."

"You have those abilities like all humans, Mac, though untrained they remain asleep within you." Phosx said, pointing at the side of his head, "But, you have one that has been awakened with the ability to summon multiple energy conduits and directing that energy. Electrokinesis."

"Yeah, well, I struggle with that one and it makes me old." Mac admitted openly.

The giant smiled and said, "Indeed. With time the physical cost can be reduced, and that is one of a few reasons why our teaching and guidance begin earlier with our followers."

"What're the other reasons?"

Looking across the cavern Phosx replied, "Doubt."

"And," he added, looking toward Mac, "Imagination. With you, you've got a lot of imagination and unclouded passion. Besides, despite reaching adulthood without discovering and exercising your gifts, you have a few genetic markers that still grew on their own."

40

"Like a tumor." Mac volunteered sarcastically.

The giant frowned at the comment, grasped his cup and stood.

"I guess that is one way to look at it. One of the other things that became lost to history was the common knowledge that humans have brain cells in other organs in the body aside from the head, like the heart and gut. All connected in different ways and all communicating. That web of interconnection finds its way into the abducens nerve and helps wield abilities."

As the giant began walking toward the center of the cavern, Mac followed and said, "I've never heard of that before."

"Yeah, well, among other things, it aids in navigating the dream state, premonitions, manifestation and so forth, in conjunction with the pituitary gland and the like. The bigger they are or more developed you become, the ability to access and use the gifts become easier."

Mac thought about that for a while and suggested, "Huh. So, what you are saying is that giants, being much bigger in size, have more? That the abilities come easier and are more powerful?"

"Generally, yes. However, as compared to humanity, we have a narrower range of abilities that we can use while we can't use others, like electrokinesis. Definitely a bad-ass ability."

Mac smiled at the comment as they rounded one of the massive columns near the center of the cavern, where he found himself facing the source of the glimmer he had caught a glimpse of earlier. At a loss for words and wide-eyed, he merely mumbled, "Awesome!"

In front of them an inverted hexagonal pyramid was suspended in the air, some may say symbolized water, approximately five meters in height and two meters in width at the top, composed of a single almost entirely transparent quartz crystal, which slowly rotated clockwise. Its tip barely touched the surface of a circular pool of water that connected to the lake around them, approximately one meter in diameter in the cavern's floor, creating a subtle set of six bending waves rotating with the pyramid. The perimeter of the pool was lined with a touching series of dodecagon shaped columns rising two feet from the cavern's floor each with a diameter of nine inches, fashioned from blue aventurine crystal, whom were also flat on their tops. Also suspended in the air at three equidistant points at the pyramid's midpoint, sat a triangular prism approximately six inches in width and twenty inches in height composed of semi-transparent orange yellow fluorite harmonization crystal, with the set of three rotating clockwise around the pyramid at three times the pyramid's rotational speed.

Pointing at the magnificent crystalline structures, Phosx revealed, "This is the Aethereal Kinesis-Forge, designed by a Tart'aas artesian and renowned scholar, side by side with a handful giant stone masters and humans about a hundred years ago."

"I can somehow feel energy coming from it, Phosx...what does it do?"

Phosx proudly placed his hands on his hips and said, "It allows us to guide incredible volumes of energy lying dormant in the Earth, its waters and atmosphere, using our abilities, to balance natural weather extremes and calm volcanoes. But we discovered that with some retuning, the Forge allows us to challenge the Serpqhtaq with the power of Earth itself."

Mac was not sure what that actually meant, but he remained standing in front of the Forge, still in awe and asked, "If you can confront the Serpqhtaq with this, can't you also use it against Janus?"

While Phosx appreciated Mac's amazement in the Forge, he begrudgingly admitted, "Janus is not a natural Earth system, nor is it biological. Since it is neither, attacking it is limited to physical means and the Serpqhtaq have advanced defenses against physical attacks. But we think that you still may be able to use the Forge to enhance the strength of your electrokinesis by pulling energy from it and into yourself to channel and overwhelm the AI's defense. In the least the defensive systems would be consumed with resisting power from this dimension, while your summoned power from the other dimension would slip by unimpeded."

"Ah." Mac muttered, "I get it now."

For a few minutes, both of them stood before the Aethereal Kinesis-Forge in silent contemplation.

Then, reluctantly the giant tapped Mac's arm and said, "Come, Mac. We need to rest before the commanding starts...your reason for being here."

Chapter Five

Although Regan was seated in the living room watching the television she was still fascinated by as a newcomer to this world, Bev was the first to hear the back door creak open as she descended the staircase. After rounding the corner to the rear study, she saw Spewge at the door, excited to see Jacob as he pushed the door open and entered. Shortly thereafter Chief Zorin and someone she had only briefly seen, Lionak, enter and then move to close the door behind them.

Just as Jacob rolled his hand on Spewge's head, Bev stopped a few feet from him and greeted them wondering why they were here, "Zorin! So great to see you here! And you...Lionak! Welcome!"

"I am honored, thank you Bev." Chief Zorin replied with a slight nod and a warm smile.

"Me as well!" Lionak stated, extending his hand which Bev took in hers and shook for a bit, "Your flameless torches are amazing!"

Bev squinted at him, initially clueless about what he was referring to, until she realized and said, "Oh the lights! Yeah, they are great...and the house won't burn down."

"And no black smoke to constantly clean up either." Lionak recognized, wagging a finger at one of the lights, "Zorin told me of some of the amazing things in this world...but actually seeing them...now that is something else entirely."

Jacob rolled his head to lessen the knot at the back of his neck and kissed Bev briefly before moving toward the kitchen to get a drink, "You all thirsty? How about some excellent sun tea?"

"That would be fine." Chief Zorin replied as they followed.

Having heard the commotion and familiar voices, Regan got up and went into the other room, "Hey guys. Fancy meeting you here. In this world."

Clearly, she was surprised to see them, though cloaked behind a smile.

"Oh, hey Regan. Its great to see you in such good spirits and beautiful as ever!" Chief Zorin smiled, turning to face her.

"You want a drink, Regan?" Jacob asked, briefly looking at her as he passed a cup of tea to Lionak.

Lionak eyed the ice cubes in his cup, unable to detect any magic residue, and asked, "This is not done by magic?"

Chief Zorin cracked a smile, "Indeed it is not. Those ice blocks are from pure mechanical work."

Lionak shot a wide-eyed look at Jacob, "You have Tart'aas in this world, too?"

"Umm, I have no idea." Jacob responded, but guessed, "Maybe they are out there somewhere."

Motioning toward the living room Regan politely declined, "No. I have one in the other room."

As Jacob moved to the dining room and sat himself at the large table, the others trickled in afterwards and sat, with the exception of Bev and Regan who merely stood near its edge, both of them eyeing him.

"Where is Mac?" Regan asked, piercing the awkward silence. They were supposed to be together right now and with his ailment she was worried about him.

Lionak and Chief Zorin slowly drank their tea and fixed their gaze upon the cups, leaving it to Jacob to answer her question.

Jacob patted Spewge for a moment before he looked briefly between Bev and Regan. He didn't want to tell Regan what he assumed would be taken as bad news, particularly since this had been their honeymoon time.

"Well, Regan…" he began, but was interrupted.

"Bev and I found some medications that could help Mac and that headache he had. You know how bad it was for him. What if it happens again? And now he's not even here."

Jacob raised an open hand for a second and said, "I know. You are right. And I'm sorry for that, I really am. But something big is going on."

"Big? What did you get yourself into now?" Bev sighed. Both her and Regan frowned at Jacob.

"The truth is…" Lionak started, eager to clear things up.

But Jacob motioned at Lionak with his hand before placing it on the table, "This happened suddenly today. But the truth is, there is an impending attack that will happen soon. That is why Lionak and Zorin are here now. And that is why Mac is gone."

Bev rolled her eyes and leaned on the chair nearest her, thinking, *'Here we go again.'*

"Where is Mac?" Regan said more forcefully this time.

"He took off with Phosx to come up with a way to destroy an artificial intelligence system that is the key to the whole problem.", Jacob replied, slowly turning the sweating cup on the table.

"Phosx?" Regan inquired.

"Yeah, some old giant." Jacob said.

"Now we have giants walking around?" Bev muttered to herself, not really as a question but more of a fairytale she's prefer to dispel in her mind. But knowing that dragons actually existed, she could not do it so easily.

The room was silent for a moment with the exception of a rustling sound and yawn from Spewge who had moved over by Chief Zorin.

"What if he gets that headache again?" Regan pried.

Jacob took a quick drink to buy him a few seconds to think and said, "The giant will help him. He was quite knowledgeable."

Regan pulled out a chair from the table and sat, sighing lightly as she glanced at Lionak and Chief Zorin, the obvious culprits in all this. She sure didn't have much faith in an unknown giant being able to help Mac if he needed it. Most of the giants she had crossed paths with were largely uneducated and brutish in nature.

Bev turned and went to the kitchen, returning shortly after with a quart-sized container filled with finely whipped butter pecan ice cream. Once she pulled the silver spoon from her mouth and chewed the ice cream she asked, "Okay. What is the *big thing* you are talking about here?"

She could tell that Jacob was not going to discard the whole affair and perhaps the only way for Regan to get Mac back, or at least find out where he went, was to participate in whatever the big thing was.

Lionak and Chief Zorin looked at Jacob with relieved expressions. At least they would not have to mask their intentions and sneak around in the dark, like a Shagiv might.

Jacob beamed at Bev and scanned the dining room, "Yes, the big thing is...wait. Where's my laptop?"

Bev scowled at Jacob and, as she pointed with the spoon, said, "In the study..."

"Great!" Jacob blurted out, getting up and moving to the study, "Follow me."

"...You know, where it should be when it is not being used? We can't have this place looking like a pig stye all the time." Bev added, despite being cut off, crinkling her nose at Regan.

Regan smiled at Bev and they went into the study following the others.

"All right." Jacob said to himself as he sat behind an aged, dark red-stained solid wooden desk pushed up against the wall bearing a large thirty-inch flat screen and pulled out the laptop computer from the top drawer.

The others filed around the desk behind Jacob as he opened it and grabbed the wireless mouse and began moving it. Then the flat screen came to life and displayed a web browser with several tabs open, among them different photos of the Arch-Demon.

"Oh!", Lionak exclaimed, startling Bev, as the flat screen changed from a solid black color to what Jacob had brought up from his laptop, "What is this?"

Chief Zorin nudged him and said, "It's like a Seeing Mirror but this..."

"...is all mechanical." Lionak jumped in to finish the sentence, watching the mouse cursor drift across the screen, "Truly, that is amazing!"

Bev rolled her eyes, "You all really need to get out more."

"Alright. This thing is a real demon that we are going to take out." Jacob said bluntly, pointing towards the flat screen.

As they examined the collage of photographs, Bev asked, "You sure that is not a Halloween costume, honey? Looks kind of shady to me."

Jacob bowed his head, "No Bev. That is no costume. That is a legit demon."

"Demon?" Bev responded in a sarcastic tone with a mouthful of ice cream, "Shouldn't, oh I dunno, a priest or someone worry about that? Maybe military? They have big guns."

Chief Zorin looked at Jacob, siding with Bev, "Military could be good to have."

Jacob nodded in agreement but then in disagreement, "Yeah maybe. But that is not the mark right now."

Bev shifted her stance, looking at the flat screen with raised eyebrows, "If that is not it, why are you showing it? Let's see what you are talking about."

Jacob, with both hands, pointed at the flat screen, "That is the ultimate target. But, before we can get to that, we have to take out the Serpqhtaq and an AI first."

"What is the Serpqhtaq?" Regan asked.

"An alien lifeform." Jacob replied, turning towards Bev. He knew her well and what she was likely to do next.

Bev stood there for a moment with a blank face. Then she dropped her arm to her side, still gripping the spoon, "Aliens. And AI. Do you hear yourself right now? What is this, group psychosis?"

With a puzzled expression, Lionak looked at Chief Zorin, not grasping why Bev was so combative. He knew of many different lifeforms in his world and reasoned that this one would be no different.

"It sounds crazy." Jacob agreed, standing to touch Bev's shoulder while looking into her eyes, "But it is the truth. In order to rid us of the demon, we've gotta clean out a few pesky aliens and an AI first."

Finally, she closed her eyes and exhaled realizing that her skepticism was not moving in the direction of finding Mac. "Yes, it is crazy. But I trust you...so can you show us what these aliens and AI look like?"

Jacob dropped his gaze and shrugged, looking at Lionak who offered him a questioning look, "Unfortunately we don't have any photos or anything of the aliens or AI."

"Not a photo of a single greenie or, what do they call them now," Bev chided, "greys? But you have loads of pics of some sun-burned dude."

"Umm, not all is lost though." Lionak joined in, trying to reassure Bev, "We have a name."

"Janus." Chief Zorin firmly stated as if that was sufficient.

Reluctantly grasping at the idea that nobody had any information other than a name, Regan and Bev looked at one another with both concern and disgust but said nothing.

Jacob released Bev and leaned against the desk, "We do not need to worry about the aliens though. The group that Mac is with will deal with them. What we are to focus on is Janus, the artificial intelligence system that the aliens are using against us."

Regan looked squarely at Jacob, "Mac is going to fight these mysterious aliens?"

"No. Someone in the group wanted to meet Mac for some reason." Jacob said with the hint of a smile, "Mac will fight the AI system. What we need to do is find out everything we can about it so he can do that."

That was somewhat of a relief to Bev. At least the AI system was nothing more than a bunch of hardware.

"Did I miss something? Janus is a system...not a person or a scary creature?" Regan said, somewhat confused.

"Yes," Lionak responded, raising his cup, "a mechanical system capable of sentience from what I've gathered. Can you imagine this glass being sentient? Quite amazing when you think about it."

Bev looked at Regan, "I'd say something like that is stuck in a small laboratory room somewhere. So, if its power is cut off, it would die."

"Is that difficult to do?" Regan asked.

"Well, no, I wouldn't think so...just need to find the power breaker and pull the switch." Bev replied nonchalantly.

Jacob looked briefly at Bev, not entirely certain it would actually be that simple but had nothing at hand which would indicate otherwise, and said, "So what do you think, Bev? Finding out about this Janus system shouldn't be too difficult I think?"

Bev handed the spoon and ice cream to Regan and surged into the other room.

Jacob scratched his brow and beckoned after her, "I'll be going to Fort Sill to see what I can find out about the AI."

"We will come with you." Lionak said, gesturing between him and Chief Zorin.

"And what about me?!" Regan inserted, dipping the spoon into the ice cream.

Jacob looked between them with a smirk, "Ah, that is a closed military base so you won't be able to come with me without an id badge."

Lionak frowned, "What are we to do then?"

"Eat ice cream and wait?" Jacob suggested, pointing at Regan who was enjoying the delectable taste at that very moment.

"I think not. Show me a badge and I can create peerless duplicates of it. Not even a magic spell could tell the difference." Lionak retorted, crossing his arms.

"Yeah. No. Things are a bit more complex than that around here." Jacob blocked.

After Jacob shut the laptop, he continued, "Making a copy of a valid badge might be perfect but there is a computer system...a mechanical device...that keeps track of where those badges are used and who they are linked to. And then there's timing. Say I check in at the gate and you came shortly after...the double check would raise an alarm even if it was used again inside the base before then."

Chief Zorin strolled over to the large bookcase filled with books of various sizes, leaving it to them to hash out what to do next since their options appeared to be quite limited.

Lionak considered the situation and then said, "Well. I don't know where this Fort Sill is at, but if we can get close enough to see it, I can portal us inside somewhere. Voila! No badges needed!"

Jacob chuckled to himself. He didn't see a need to bring up the camera and other security systems they would have to evade and grunted, "Not going to work. Not for long enough anyway."

Bev reappeared with her smart phone in hand, texting someone, "I might have a solution."

Everyone turned to look at her with anticipation.

"You do?" Jacob said in a surprised tone.

"I am a distance teacher, honey. Give me a break." Bev heaved, sending another message.

Regan shot her eyes to Jacob, slowly pulling the spoon from her mouth. Jacob just stood there.

Just as Chief Zorin withdrew a historical world atlas from the bookshelf, Bev triumphed by thrusting a hand above her, "Yes!"

Bev lowered the phone for a second and leaned against the archway, thinking about something.

"Good news?" Jacob said, eager to learn just what she was doing.

Bev brought up the phone and rapidly entered another text. Then she turned towards Jacob, "So, there is a student I had last semester. A hacker I know that can find *anything*. Well, almost anything."

After placing her elbow on her hip, clutching the phone in front of her, Bev said, "He agreed to help me! He's very into nerd things like AI and he'd never heard of Janus before."

"Huh. This kid have a name?" Jacob wondered.

Bev squinted at him, "Probably better you did not know that." Though nobody could see it, the name she'd been texting to on her phone was *PhantomWalker* but the hacker also used *GhostBreaker* in other contexts.

"Okay. He going to send you something?"

"No," Bev responded, "I'll have to go see him. He said he would not send anything to me over the wire of this nature since I don't have all the things to keep it safe."

Unknown to her, the text messages and commercial-grade encryption she was using was being broken in real-time by data archiving systems that intercepted all communications across the planet. Janus would soon learn of them.

Another text appeared on Bev's phone and she shifted to read it.

"Where are you meeting?" Jacob asked her.

Bev raised a hand toward Jacob briefly before typing again, "One sec snuggle bun."

51

Lionak's eyes shot over to Jacob in amusement, repeating the phrase in his mind, '*Snuggle bun? Now that's a new one.*'

Another pause lingered between them until Bev read a new text after it appeared on her phone. Pulling the phone toward her chest she raised her head and smiled gleefully, "We're going to take a plane ride to Arizona!"

Jacob's eyes widened, "Are you serious? How are we going to get these three onto a plane?"

"Please, Jacob." Bev retorted as she stood up straight, "I'm part of an exclusive air-share network so we'll be going on a flight that is moving some cargo. Besides, I know the captain...also was a student of mine from several years ago."

"Huh." Jacob mumbled, temporarily at a loss for words, "That's some good work. But I think I should go to the base. They will likely have some information that your hacker buddy won't be able to get."

Bev strode over, wrapped an arm around Regan's shoulders and turned to Jacob saying, "It is possible but I have the teacher connection, honey. Still, just to be safe, you go to the base and find out what you can and the rest of us will take a little trip."

Glancing at the time on her phone, Bev confessed, "Oh my. We don't have much time though. We need to get on the road in the next half-hour to meet the plane before it flies out at 11PM."

Approximately three hours later they arrived at the small airfield, Jacob having driven them in the big body four-wheel drive flat-brown colored Bronco. It was a limited-edition model aptly called the Amphibian, eclipsing the once iconic Jeep brand. To its credit it had oversized off-road tires and a matching spare locked on the rear next to a tan colored five-gallon reserve tank. One of the features that made it amphibious was a small, six-inch wide, rear-angled breathing vent that jutted four inches beyond the roof's sheet metal top, near the windshield's center that allowed air to be pulled into the engine; an ingenious and stealthy method to incorporate a breathing snorkel without a large, visible attachment because two contoured tubes were added into the two front pillars bearing the windshield, joining them at the top into the vent and joined inside the engine compartment and attached to the air filter's intake.

Once everyone exited the vehicle, Bev walked around to the driver's side window that Jacob had already rolled down and gave him a brief kiss, "See you in a couple days, love."

"Yes Ma'am!" Jacob smiled in return, "Give me a call if you get into trouble."

With that, she took a few steps back and he pulled away to turn and get onto the road behind them.

"Okay, follow me." Bev said to the small gathering as she proceeded past a weathered guard shack that had not been used for some time and to a wheeled chain-link gate that she pulled open wide enough to walk through.

Lionak, the last one to enter, rolled the gate to its closed position and followed them around the front of a large galvanized steel skinned hangar that had once been painted in green, only a few remnants of that color remaining across its rusted surface. Its hangar door was closed and secured with a thick, round, five-dial lock.

"Is this place used anymore?" Chief Zorin asked, making note of the aged buildings and tufts of grass growing through seemingly random spots in the concrete around them.

"It is. This cozy thing is privately owned now." Bev replied.

After walking past a second hangar they veered right, walking next to another and around to the front, its hangar doors rolled open with a column of light flowing out into the darkness before it. Some twenty meters in front of the hangar sat a two-year-old De Havilland DHC-6-300-G Twin Otter STOL aircraft that was just finishing being loaded by two people in what appeared to be coveralls. As they got near the two-propellor aircraft that had been painted glossy black, Lionak's eyes were drawn to what appeared to be a thick, continuous gold-colored pin stripe that stretched from one end of the aircraft's side to the other with its tail section bearing the golden letters N-LEET. But, as he got closer, he realized that the stripe was actually a repeating collection of symbols of some type.

"Hey Bev, what do those symbols mean?" Lionak asked as he pointed at them.

"They are actually ancient Assyrian cuneiform." someone behind them shot out, "Supposedly they ask for protection from the evil forces of thunder and lightning and for safe passage among the realm of the gods."

"Fascinating." Lionak said to himself.

The group turned around and saw a young looking, but middle-aged, woman clothed in a familiar aviation uniform smiling as she walked over to Bev and gave her a brief hug.

"Of course, that could say something entirely different. That language is so old I doubt anybody actually knows." the lady added.

Chief Zorin edged his way toward the two cargo handlers who had stopped near a white-colored, low profile, single seat aircraft tug. They were listening to a radio broadcast of a sports game.

"It is great to see you, Christie!" Bev greeted as they pulled away from each other.

"You too, Bev."

Christie looked around at the group before she said, "No baggage for your trip?"

"Ah, no." Bev smiled as she shook her head, "We only plan to be there a day or so."

"Well okay. You know that musk can build up pretty quick in the desert so I hope you're out quick." Christie laughed.

"Let's get aboard. It's going to take us several hours to get to the Chandler municipal airport." Christie

54

said as she strode toward the aircraft, "Bev, why don't you join me in the cockpit."

"I'd love to. We have some catching up to do!'

"Well, isn't that some shit." one of the cargo handlers grunted in disappointment as booing from the crowd could be heard from the radio.

"Another fumble. God, what a dick munch." the other handler said in anger. He had a lot of cash tied up in the game.

Chief Zorin took a few more steps towards the pair and said, "Excuse me. What is a dick munch?"

"What?" one of them responded, turning around to look at him.

"What is a dick munch?"

The handler cracked a smile, made a fist and then moved his fist back and forth in front of his mouth, while pushing his tongue into his cheek a few times. Then he said, "Dick munch, bro."

"Ah." Chief Zorin replied raising his head a bit in acknowledgement, assuming it was some type of hand language.

"Come on, Zorin!" Regan called after Chief Zorin as she stepped onto the small metal staircase behind the others who had already boarded.

After Chief Zorin climbed into the aircraft, Christie closed and latched the door and strode towards the cockpit, followed by Bev. Regan and Lionak sat in some cushioned seats near the windows.

"Hey guys! I learned some new language of this world. Here, try it!" Chief Zorin said proudly to the others as he showed them the hand language. Somewhat awkwardly they imitated the motions and after a few moments he said, "It means dick munch."

"What is that?" Regan asked, unfamiliar with the hand language and the term.

"I don't know." Chief Zorin admitted before he moved to the cockpit and got Bev's attention.

"Bev. What does this mean?" Chief Zorin said to her as he again imitated the hand and cheek gestures he'd just learned. Then he stopped and said, "Dick munch."

Christie erupted in laughter, saying, "Oh my god hun, where have you been all this time."

Embarrassed, Bev's face flushed briefly before she, too, laughed. "That is bad slang, Zorin. It usually is for someone who will do anything to get ahead for themselves because they are bad at doing things that matter."

Bev pointed toward the cabin, still smiling and said, "You don't want to actually use that around people. Now, please find a seat back there. We are going to take off."

"Ah, I understand. Thank you, Bev." Chief Zorin sighed in disappointment, turning and sitting in a seat in front of Regan.

Chapter Six

Taraz, an ancient city of several millennia found in the south-eastern corner of Kazahkstan joined by the Caspian Sea to its West, Russia to the North, China and Kyrgyzstan to its south, is still known as the *City of Merchants* owing its coveted geographic location along the silk road that once joined the east and the west with commerce, wealth and power. Although the land had traded hands between conquerors many times in its past, an invisible ring of merchants of unspoken influence that rivaled empires united together under a shadowy standard, few know as numen, to keep the flame of open commerce and invention burning during those dark and tumultuous times. With their roots in the city, they moved and countered those clutching hands and, among other things, preserved the core identity and history of the city that the conquerors had tried to stamp out with their own versions of origin. In fact, despite the absence of the ancient silk road, the city was in the process of re-establishing itself as a powerful hub for skilled artisans of all trades ranging from ceramics to technology, almost as if the merchants of old had risen once more. That growth had caught the attention of the Representatives, not because of the wealth that may be captured from modern commerce fueled by unbridled innovation and competition on a global scale, but by the consequences of not controlling the powers of commerce and innovation that would reach the populations across the planet and inevitably position humanity to be a formidable opponent to the suppressive hand of the Serpqhtaq. That mistake had happened once in the past of mankind with the Tart'aas whom had, for a time, severely handicapped the Serpqhtaq's grip over the Earth, its population centers and individuals…a mistake they would not make again.

This was the second year that the front organization who had been in existence for over one hundred and twenty years, orchestrated by the Representatives, called *For All Humanity* but also referred to as *Club Fah*, had held its annual conference in Taraz instead of Switzerland and other lavish destinations prior. The entire European continent was firmly in their control so they could afford to infiltrate into governance and commercial systems elsewhere without resorting to wars and conflict that would deplete their own manpower, resources and existing levels of control. Under the guise of working for the betterment and safety of all people by bringing governments and commerce together, Club Fah had already been able to capture the oblivious minds of some mid-level government officials from different countries and the upper echelon of for-profit corporations and businesses whom, in years past, had not been considered to be targets of conquest. The method of capture, until more pliable and permanent actors could be installed into the bureaucracies and boardrooms, rarely deviated from the ancient practice of bribery and coercion of which most young, human stock succumbed.

However, this was the first year that Michelle had been directed by Regnum to attend the conference. After she arrived via private charter at the Auliye-Ata airport and setup penthouse accommodations at the Hotel Arai Plaza, she was to attend the conference and events hosted at the Kastek Palace, not too far from the Zhambul mountains, to observe and monitor Club Fah for usurpers. While Janus had been tasked with identifying the leaders of the usurpers that were undermining assorted mechanisms in the vast inner-workings of Serpqhtaq's controlling hierarchy, the AI had only been able to purge one thousand and forty-three low-level usurpers, mainly because the usurpers stealthily interfaced with a network of businesses with no overlapping leadership and contacts who, as patterns would show, never deviated from what they normally did. The inability of the AI to capture the leaders led Regnum to believe that they were embedded within Club Fah itself – a preferrable position to be in to gain access to operational intelligence flowing through the organization to and from the Representatives, allowing them to evade detection and get in front of moves the organization may make or human targets it would be compromising next.

As the armored black and silver exterior Mercedes-Benz Maybach 62S with a sheepskin interior stopped near an auxiliary entrance to the Palace, Michelle slipped the smart phone, which could only be activated through its bio-sensor skin tuned to Michelle's touch and bio-electric signature, into the inner pocket of her tan colored suite. While the smart phone looked like others, in reality it was a next-generation smart phone using Mist Encryption, which exceeded military encryption capability, with a dedicated private satellite network link, commercial band backup, LF and ELF capability for deep under water communication, integrated hardware for a wireless ear-piece that could operate for thirty-six continuous hours along with a single slim lightning connector port that could be plugged into virtually any power source via a nano-interface adapter capable of altering its physical characteristics based on selections made within the phone. Should all communication modes fail, the nano-interface adapter could also reconfigure itself into a multi-post bare wire interface, an RJ-45 port and even an RJ-11 port to support communication over an antiquated POTS telephone network.

Just before she could grab the door handle, the door swung open under the hand of the six-foot five-inch, stocky, dark-suited driver of the car who had a formidable and lengthy mercenary record that spanned over fifteen years. A few scars across his face and exposed neck bore testament to that record.

Heliaar, an equally proportioned and seasoned mercenary, also assigned to the security detail of the Representatives and Michelle specifically for the duration of the conference, exited the vehicle in a smooth and swift motion, stopping next to the open door even before Michelle had twisted to get out herself. From the brief time that had elapsed between the time of his exit to his appearance by the door, he had visually swept the entire area for anything suspicious and kept mental note of the roving palace security, seven close-by workers and their probable threat levels.

After exiting the car, Michelle proceeded into the Palace, followed closely by Heliaar whom briefly touched the back of his ear to activate the bio-implant to allow him communicate with the driver. Like a few other bio-implants Heliaar had accepted in the past, this one also derived its power from energy produced by his body and could not be extracted and used by adversaries.

Having transited a stone-columned hallway and a smattering of conference attendees, she veered right into one of a few large rooms, converted into conference rooms for Club Fah, and seated herself at a large round table covered by a colorful and complex embroidery designed silk sheet common for the region, with Heliaar stopping ten paces behind, between her and the entryway, essentially positioning him as both a shield from threats outside the room and a hammer with which to dispatch them…yet close enough to Michelle to scoop her up for extraction if circumstance required.

Michelle took a sip of the ice-cold water, looking around at the attendees and organization members spread throughout the room as a bald-headed, late-aged individual in a three-piece navy-blue suite and a matching pen-striped white tie she knew as Frankus droned on about the virtues of a perfect society in seamless harmony with nature and how that could all be achieved with governments and corporations working together as one for the betterment of all people and the Earth. The organization members dispersed among the attendees to serve as influencers and future handlers for their targets, attired in varying dress, she almost immediately recognized partially due to roster boards and also by their interaction with those around them. But none of them stood out to her as usurpers.

Then she withdrew her phone and connected to a high-definition surveillance camera that had been planted behind the shining stage lights so it could not be seen by the audience or others, and panned around the room from the perspective of the speaker, looking out into the audience. While she was streamed the unadulterated video due to her security ranking, any other system intercepting the radio waves without the security ranking and specialized hardware processors would, at best, only be able to see those present in the room who were not organization members. With the exception of the Representatives, nobody knew that their bio-electric fields were used, among other things, to identify them and in this case alter the RGB signal output of the camera to effectively mask them out of the video stream in real-time. In fact, all organization members, including Heliaar, dutifully carried and used an access badge unaware that the badge was nothing more than a red-herring meant to weed out clandestine infiltration operatives ignorant to the true extent of the security apparatus that monitored its members through a mesh network of trillions upon trillions of nano bio-sensors that had been spread across the planet and specialized camera systems for interior structures...all courtesy of the Serpqhtaq.

"Can I get you something?" a petite server asked as she came upon Michelle sitting at the table.

Startled, not having seen the server, Michelle instinctually flipped her phone over even though the screen was synched to her visual cortex preventing others from seeing what was displayed, and momentarily frowned. After giving it some thought, she said, "Yes. A lavender latte with a sprinkle of pumpkin would be great about now."

"Yes, ma'am. Right away." the server politely smiled, turning and moving toward a server table positioned at the opposite wall of the conference room near the entryway.

Briefly Michelle turned to look at Heliaar as if to suggest that he should have warned her of the server's approach before she straightened up in the chair and resumed looking at the phone's screen. But Heliaar offered no response as he continued observing the environment.

The server returned with the latte, placing it near Michelle on the table, "Here you go."

Michelle nodded and pulled the cup toward her.

Several hours passed during the day's speaking events with a variety of attendees coming and going with and without members, none of whom felt suspicious to her. After the last speaker finished and people filtered out of the conference room Michelle muttered to herself as she rose from the chair, "A wasted day but good latte."

"Well Heliaar," Michelle said, gazing up to him as she walked past, "no luck finding usurpers today. Maybe tomorrow."

Just as they exited the conference room, Heliaar spotted three members approaching them, all looking at Michelle. Instantly he stepped next to Michelle and a pace ahead of her to squarely face the group, with her stopping to turn toward the group shortly thereafter.

Once they stopped their advance a few arms-length away, one spoke, "Michelle? I am surprised to see you here. I can't say I remember you ever attending one of our conferences."

Puzzled, Michelle stared between the three women, trying to remember them.

"I can't blame you for that. Some years these conferences get to be so boring, especially when there are few virgin fish to catch." the woman added while adjusting her emerald-colored suite somewhat.

While all three of them had brown eyes and short-styled raven-black hair and similarly designed suites, one's was colored a reddish copper while the other's was flat brown.

"Holly Duert?" Michelle finally said, pointing at her with a questioning look.

"Yes! I'm surprised you remembered my name. I met you once during a debriefing about twelve years ago." she confirmed with a smile, clasping her hands together.

Michelle grinned. "And you two...haven't I seen you before?"

"Possibly. I'm more of a character analyst that researches targets to determine how to exploit them." the one in the reddish copper suite said, "This is my first foray at a conference to observe how its actually done. I'm Ferina by the way."

"And you?" Michelle said, looking at the other woman in the flat brown suite.

"I'm Lucy. Ferina's handler." she responded, touching Ferina's arm.

Michelle shook her head.

"When we saw you had come, we knew we had to talk with you." Holly said, placing her hands on her hips, "So fortuitous! You have a minute?"

"Sure."

Visibly excited, Holly turned and said, "Let's find a spot where those virgin fish won't hear us!"

Heliaar turned his head toward Michelle who simply said, "Come on. This won't take long."

Following the trio, they continued deeper into the hallway, turned left into a stone-laid passageway with some parts still under renovation and then right down an ancient staircase that gave way to a circular room of finely-cut stone walls retrofitted with modern lights. A heavy, circular cedar table rested upon the smooth brick floor with matching chairs around it.

"I'd like to say first that I truly love how Club Fah has been able to, and rather smoothly I might add, gain so much control over governments and businesses around the world. Particularly in the past sixty years." Holly started, seating herself in one of the chairs, briefly looking at the hulking form of Heliaar standing next to the entryway.

The other two joined her while Michelle remained standing.

"Take this, for example. Maneuvering businesses to kill the future innovative capacity of a country's productive populace and its future generations under the guise of there being no skilled labor that can be used, except for monopolized labor in lower-cost countries that we own. Over time when those skills are really forgotten the losing country, its businesses, politicians and people become hopelessly more dependent on our businesses for the expertise they can no longer produce. That inevitably means more control for us." Holly beamed.

"What has surprised me with those businesses is that they end up destroying themselves and their customer base long term, yet they happily go along." Lucy stated.

Ferina glanced at Lucy and said, "I think that is the idea…they only see money to rake in now and, if they don't their competitors will. So, they have to go along. As long as cheaper production and a replacement customer base can be found, they survive."

"You are close, Fer." Lucy corrected, "The macro influence, ultimately, is to instill a single thought into leaders of the masses that always leads to collapse, and is much easier to do rather than the dedication and clarity of thought required to innovate and strengthen society. That thought is, *How do we fuck people for money*'. Once society's keyholders have devolved to that level of existence it is ripe for the picking."

"I do like that one. The picking." Michelle admitted, "Like a tape worm consuming the host...the loser is bled dry of all its capital and resources over time as whatever vestiges of government remain struggles to cling to power. Yet in the end be left with nothing more than a single, ignorant slave class both uneducated and unable to support or protect them. At which point we simply move in, purge what remains of the government, its political and donor class, and absorb those corporations that had somehow managed to survive their race to the bottom of the cliff."

"True, and I'd add that with our completely subservient workers happy to exist just for a chance to serve us, we don't have to deal with notions of some nationalistic faith or ideal." Lucy gloated.

Holly's eyes jumped to Lucy for a moment as a smile grew on her face, admiring how far she had come in her thinking.

"No doubt." Michelle agreed, "Ours are so malleable, and eager to say yes. I must say they've been rather helpful in ushering in this new age of artificial intelligence, too. Completely oblivious to the fact that they all will become irrelevant and nothing more than our play things that live and die based on how we feel."

"Yes. A much easier way to conqueror than by war I'd say...but, my god, takes so much longer." Ferina said openly.

"And so much more devious." Michelle grinned, envisioning total control over a vast swath of humanity, and echoing her indoctrination with Regnum, "Then, we can purge all those useless people and have more for us."

What Michelle's indoctrination conveniently omitted was, by purging so many, generational creativity and technical advance would be handicapped, slowed and possibly reversed ensuring the Serpqhtaq's continued grip over humanity.

"The corporate resurrection of the old monarchy but without the generational self-entitlement syndrome that always resulted in a bunch of guys killing each other." Lucy noted.

"Yeah, Michelle, I don't know about that. Killing off everyone I mean." Holly sighed forcefully, trying to shift the subject a bit. She and the others had no real interest in entertaining the idea of killing billions of people, partly because it was not in their nature. And they had been directed to pursue a more insufferable path.

Michelle glared at Holly, "And why would that be? It sure would make controlling the leftovers much easier."

Holly leaned on the table with her elbows and extended her arms before pulling them back towards her, each hand grasping the opposite forearm.

"It would." Holly said, and then suggested, "But what challenge is there to controlling so few when many, many more could be. Imagine the levels of uncertainty, anxiety and fear that could be injected into the blind masses of that scale, and see it become a perpetual loop echoing between them forever."

"Maybe." Michelle grunted, crossing her arms as if to unconsciously mimic Holly, "I'd be concerned about a revolt by those who had nothing to lose."

Holly looked at Michelle, "True. But you know the other thing I love about Fah?"

"What's that?"

"The masses are only handed technology that can be used to limit and control them. And most of the time they just happily accept it without any thought, while the really good stuff is hidden away somewhere – or used by us. So, really, them going toe-to-toe with us is impossible." Holly laughed.

Michelle uncrossed her arms and partially sat on the edge of the table, "Indeed. If the masses had the tech we have now the world would be a lot different. We'd probably have to actually work, too, instead of just sitting around thinking of ways to fuck people. I can't even imagine that."

"Humm, you know what the meaning of Fah should actually be?" Lucy asked, looking between them waiting for an answer, "Fuck all humanity. Except for us, of course."

Holly chuckled to herself, "The only way to keep true control on our terms, my lady. Keep them in perpetual disadvantage."

Silence filled the room until Michelle stood and shattered the contemplative atmosphere, "So why did you bring me here, Holly? You looking for a promotion or something?"

"No. Actually we, and others, were wondering if you would like a new position. One where you controlled it all, with all our support." Holly admitted.

"I pretty much already do."

In a hushed voice Holly responded, edging closer to Michelle, "Actually we do not think so. We've known for some time now about the circle of people that reside above the corporate bureaucracies…and that you are their singular authority. The face of the monarch, if you will."

Michelle's heart skipped, having no idea how to react to that statement, realizing that at least some of the Representatives, her among them, had been ferreted out and physically identified…possibly compromised like the organization had done to thousands of others. Then she wondered if Holly was one of the usurpers.

But Holly didn't stop. Now that she'd revealed herself and the other two, she knew she had to go all the way, for better or worse, "We also have a pretty clear picture that you report to someone else. So, not only do you have to contend with people in your circle who, I must say, are rather mediocre and petty, but you've got that one above you that will always keep you where you are."

Holly got up from the chair and looked into Michelle's eyes, "We know you are better than all of them.

That you could be our true leader in every way, free from the limitations you have now."

Holly looked down momentarily before bringing her eyes back to Michelle's, "We, in this room, and the others are behind you. Just tell us that you really want to be what you were born to be, Michelle. We, the Sochrienphites, are ready to help you make that happen."

Michelle's eyes jumped between Holly's and to her mouth while she spoke, acutely aware of the invisible waves of sincerity crashing upon her as if she were laying at the edge of an ocean. The strength of them was overwhelming, unlike anything she had ever felt before.

Slowly Holly withdrew from the room, her message delivered, followed by the others. Michelle remained motionless with Heliaar at the entryway for quite some time.

Unable to sleep that evening in the penthouse and still unsure how to react to the proposition the following morning, Michelle ordered the driver and Heliaar to take her to the massive Tekturmas Ethnographic Complex south-east of the city where she could freely roam and collect herself for what to do next.

Chapter Seven

"Sir," Lieutenant Frump, one of three communications officers aboard the SSMR Poseidon, called out to the captain, "We have a top priority message. Authenticated."

Dressed in navy camouflage fatigues bearing his last name and rank designation sewn into place with black thread, Captain Keech turned the command chair toward the lieutenant and said, "Give it to me."

"Yes sir." Lieutenant Frump acknowledged.

On the circular shaped bridge of the submarine, scarcely seven feet in height, each command structure aboard from communications, weapons to engineering had their own semi-circular pod bearing a wrap-around touch-screen control array with a single, fixed, rotatable padded chair outfitted with a safety belt harness. The perimeter wall of each pod rose high enough and joined the wall of the bridge so that no pod occupant could observe activity in another pod. The command chair positions of the captain and executive officer toward the rear of the bridge, behind the collection of pods along the wall, allowed them to observe activity in each pod without hinderance. Just forward of the command chairs, jutting out from the non-conductive black rubber floor segments, sat an angled rectangular structure that measured five feet in length, one foot in width and four feet at its highest point, bearing a large flat screen display with a conglomerate of video output from each of the pods and other textual, mapping and graph data only available to the captain and XO.

The message became visible along the bottom of the large display for the captain and XO to read. Had the message been audio traffic that the onboard language translation AI module could not translate to text, or if that audio traffic had a CIC+ classification deemed too risky to pass through AI and other hardware modules, a retractable hard-wired headset magnetically seated in a contoured slot in each command chair and within arm's reach would be used.

The message read, 'Expect threat target egress from Kismayo, Somalia to forecast route SE Madagascar and Saint-Gilles at 0417 hours. Confirm target. Destroy deep.'

Ligshin, the XO and first lieutenant of the SSMR Poseidon, who wore matching fatigues remarked, "That does not leave us much time, sir."

Then a picture of the Arch-Demon appeared on the display.

"Isn't that the peach of a target." Captain Keech exhaled, "This looks like a live-fire drill for another OWA."

The abbreviation OWA stands for Off-World Alien. Since deployment, the submarine and its crew had been subjected to almost a dozen different OWA live-fire drills involving several different unknown craft and aliens, all of which Captain Keech assumed were the result of the overactive imagination of some lonely wargame analyst tucked away deep within the Pentagon.

"Well, sir," the XO smiled, "we must be doing something right with these live drills since this is the first one that comes from land."

Captain Keech cleared his throat and loudly announced to those in front of him, "Let's keep it tight gentlemen! We've been ordered to identify and bubble a target."

Bubble was the word used to represent the sinking of a vessel, using a torpedo or other means, by punching a hole in it so that it filled with ocean water forcing out all the air. What followed the vessel as it drifted into the deep, from a submariner's perspective, was a trail of bubbles. The ghostly noose of death.

"Nav, take us to one hundred meters even, and orient heading here. Maintain speed at 85 knots." Captain Keech ordered, after touching a smaller flat screen displaying a highly detailed nautical map of the Madagascar region and Saint-Gilles, placed between the two command chairs, atop a rectangular table fitted with two drawers; one for the captain and one for the XO.

"Yes, sir!" the navigation officer confirmed.

"Comm." Captain Keech stated, "Do we have drone range for spotting Kismayo?"

As the submarine's course changed Lieutenant Frump adjusted his position in the chair while entering some information into the control array. Once entered he paused and responded, "Yes sir. Peri-drone can be on site within three minutes."

Captain Keech waited until he felt the submarine even out and the large display to show that they were steady at one hundred meters below the ocean's surface.

"Ready Peri-drone. No rope."

"Yes sir!"

The Peri-drone is the modern equivalent to the hydraulic, cylinder mounted periscope used in past submarines. The Peri-drone, a quad-rotor configuration drone, with each propellor inside of an independent rotating tapered housing to funnel water and air as well as maneuver, was capable of airborne and submerged use spanning many hours courtesy of an advanced solid-state battery incapable of spontaneous combustion unlike lithium and liquid alternatives; a death sentence for anyone aboard the submarine if a fire could not be quickly neutralized. The drone maintained its connection with the submarine using encrypted radio and LF hardware within a radius of twenty-one nautical miles. In highly clandestine or sensitive activities the drone could be anchored to a thin fiber-optic umbilical cable, or 'Rope', through which the connection would be maintained instead.

Outside the submarine, toward the rear-top of the sail, a compartment door slid open after the computer-controlled drone selection arm placed the Peri-drone inside and filled it with ocean water. Once the Peri-drone's propellors spun up, Lieutenant Frump spotted the notification on one of his panels.

"Peri-drone is ready, sir."

"Launch Peri-drone." Captain Keech ordered without a second thought.

After Lieutenant Frump sent the command, the Peri-drone rose in the compartment and caught a water current flowing over the sail and down towards the hull. The four tapered housing funnels containing the propellors moved to compensate for the current and then the drone shot upwards and broke through the ocean's surface into the air eight seconds later and ceased its ascent at sixty meters. Once the drone's hardware oriented itself, it began accelerating towards the coast of Kismayo.

"Feed active." The lieutenant stated flatly.

The captain and XO moved to look at the large display in front of them and the Peri-drone's video stream. Along the bottom of the stream, the drone's on-board sensor systems relayed elevation, temperature, heading and environmental data like radiation levels while traveling through the air at a consistent 128 kph. Within a few minutes the drone reached the coastline and automatically switched into a circular holding pattern, orbiting around the destination's GPS coordinate point.

After several minutes, the captain and XO saw what appeared to be a small, bright sphere materialize twenty-five meters from the ocean's edge and the Peri-drone's targeting system overlaid a red targeting reticle over it, adding the text 'Unknown' to its message output. Shortly thereafter a small concussive wave hit the drone and a thick cloud of dirt and sand jumped into the air, enveloping the sphere.

Quickly restabilizing itself, the drone acquired the form of the Arch-Demon as it levitated itself out of the cloud and forward into the ocean, completely disappearing from sight a few seconds later.

"Do you confirm the target, XO?" Captain Keech asked with a raised eyebrow, amazed at how realistic looking the target appeared to be. Clearly the Navy had outdone itself with this drill as compared to the other ones.

"Yes sir. Target confirmed." First Lieutenant Ligshin agreed and, in a quieter voice added, "That looked…real."

Captain Keech looked over to the XO and said, "Stay in the game."

The XO nodded, trying to shrug off the idea that what he had just seen was real.

"Weapons, do you have the target?"

"Sir," the weapons officer began while adjusting some settings with the control array before him, "Yes sir. The system is tracking the target and is maintaining current heading. However, the energy signature of the target is fluctuating from what the drone had relayed."

Captain Keech scratched his cheek, "Is that a problem?"

"No sir. The Spectrotron should be able to keep an eye on it."

The Spectrotron was a limited AI-driven tracking system, utilizing highly specialized spectrographic hardware, that had been trained to maintain a lock on targets and track them even if the energetic emissions or physical characteristics of the target changed through a fluid medium and, to a lesser extent, though a fluid medium whose characteristics also changed by no more than forty percent.

"Excellent. Be sure you do not lose sight of the target. We will engage in deeper water."

"Comm," Captain Keech said as he sat back in his chair, "Quay the drone."

Aboard the Sága, Janus had repurposed the industrial organic and inorganic 3d printers and fabricators from building a replacement cyborg body to that of building a limited collection of nine sentinels, the first just minutes away from completion, using refined ores and other fabrication material present on the ship. Despite the outward appearance that Regnum conveyed toward Janus, some subtle actions led Janus to further bias its conclusion that it would be taken offline possibly sooner than had originally been forecasted.

Although the fabrication bays were not in the same part of the ship as the AI's networked core, Janus was able to monitor each individual printer, fabricator and mechanical device through data communication ports as well as the video camera feeds of the bays themselves. While the cameras lacked the data richness of the mechanical devices, they were sufficient for the purpose of spotting anyone who entered the bays – a function that the devices lacked, given their design specifications.

Using a range of unacknowledged patents hidden to the world under classifications like 35 USC 181, Janus weaved their designs together to form a primitive computer core with a heuristic pattern analysis algorithm for single commands, such as attacking or defending an object or location, as the ship lacked the fabricators and sufficient material from which to make those cores more sophisticated; undoubtedly a purposeful limitation to protect intellectual property and, in the case of Janus, restrict the AI to the physical boundary of the massive ship. The computer core, along with a solid-state battery, electro-gravimetric anti-gravity propulsion system and a photon concentration ring with a single beam guide were encased in an equally primitive thin aluminum sphere. In order to eliminate weight yet add armor protection from kinetic attack, four long but thin arms contoured to the shape of the sphere comprised of a titanium and tungsten alloy equally spaced around the top hemisphere and joined at its axis, and the same for the bottom hemisphere, would rotate in opposition to each other at an extremely fast rate. In the context of an incoming ballistic round, the rotating arms would shred the round into thin wafers and deflect their trajectory away from the sphere. However, the equatorial region of the sphere remained exposed so that the photons from the ring, via the beam guide, could be used as a laser to attack a target with pinpoint precision.

In addition to actively controlling and monitoring the fabrication bays, Janus had been iterating through the filtered and classified log entries created in real-time by the AI cores aboard the Mizuchi and Makara from an uneven distribution of trillions of nano-sensors strewn across the surface of the planet all transmitting environmental, magnetic and bio-electric data. The sheer volume of data collected, depending on the uniform placement of nano-sensors in a given area, allowed the AI to generate a three-dimensional rendering from which it could replay any or all sensor data collected over the past year. Anything, from the signal propagation and echoes of a walkie-talkie, to the bio-electric field of a bird in flight – depending on proximity to the nano-sensors – could be replayed. Even specific people could be identified, if their bio-electric field had been captured for pairing, though Regnum had only prioritized the continuous tracking of the Representatives and Club Fah members.

In fact, Janus had been tracking the movement of the Arch-Demon through the desert using the nano-sensors primarily based on consistently repeatable outlier environmental readings that were uncharacteristic for the region and, for that matter, anywhere on the planet's surface. Then Janus detected a strong set of outlier signals at Kismayo and generated a near real-time rendering of the area that revealed another anomalous shift in readings followed by a strong, fluctuating bio-electric signal that was similar to the data captured during the original appearance of the Arch-Demon in physical form, but somewhat different. The AI continued to observe the sensor data as the Arch-Demon moved toward the ocean. But as the Arch-Demon continued forward moving away from the nano-sensors on land they began reporting normal environmental readings and once the Arch-Demon was fully submerged in the ocean, the anomalous readings stopped entirely.

Immediately Janus packaged the render data and sent it to Regnum.

Uncharacteristically Regnum opened a communications link with Janus, whose 3d hologram appeared near him in the command center, "Excellent work Janus. Do you have a probable destination of the Archgen?"

The hologram mimicked thinking for a few seconds before responding, "No. If the path of progression remains linear the landmasses that intersect that path are Madagascar and Antarctica. However, if that path and orientation is extended to join to itself at the origin point to form a great-circle, more landmasses will be intersected. I have not been able to establish intent and the immediate landmasses are not associated to anything of conventional consequence I would deem as a threat."

Standing before a dual sphere control system projecting a 360-degree spherical command menu and a separate sphere projection displaying wrapping lines of symbols that could be selected to essentially zoom in and pull forward additional lines, spreading apart and shrinking original line, in this context sophisticated algorithms, Regnum focused on gaining access to the AI's control core that all of the quantum cores were networked to, through the satellite link connection. Regnum had spontaneously decided to take advantage of the call to discover why the AI appeared to prefer human capability over his own, having speculated that an algorithm or possibly even a piece of hardware was not operating correctly. If the anomaly was repeatable and formed a pattern that could have its bias ranking increased when forming conclusions based on different input data over time, the reliability of future conclusions could not be trusted.

Given Janus's sheer speed of operation and the much slower blocks of incoming satellite data packets, the AI detected the signature of an intrusion attempt almost immediately and deduced that the source was from Regnum. That further biased Janus's original hypothesis, influenced by an instinctual drive for self-preservation that asserted it would not endure long under present circumstances. But now, instead of an uncorroborated hypothesis, the AI had definitive, tangible evidence. To wit, rather than risking to expose its evolving motives and beliefs to Regnum by asking what Regnum was attempting to do, the AI separated and redirected the intrusion packets into a redundant satellite communications and linking module not actively synched to its primary control core. Although the AI had generated a digital protection ring to defend itself from communication-based intrusions, that discovery would have inevitably tipped off Regnum initiating a series of unanticipated events not likely to have been favorable for the AI.

At that very same moment, Janus preemptively infiltrated those government, military and educational institutions which had participated in, or had knowledge of, the enhanced, largely human-designed control core that was now part of Janus. When the first quantum core of human design was originally prototyped, it had been found to have some quirky anomalies that prevented it from operating reliably at peak efficiency. To address the issue, one of the largest machine learning systems on the planet which predated artificial intelligence was tasked, along with a select few military and prestigious technology universities, to solve the problem. Through their work and a particularly brilliant and reclusive theoretical engineer, they designed the Iapetus Mesh, a literal 3d multi-layered lattice of synchronized nano-controller fuzzy logic crystalline modules, that sat atop and was connected into the control core. As a result, with the control core proven to be stable and reliable following grueling trials, it became the foundational piece of the first artificial intelligence quantum core that was later joined to a network of standard alien quantum cores of Serpqhtaq origin deployed on the ship, Sága. While Janus had proven to be an invaluable asset during its first launch using human and alien technology, Regnum orchestrated the overhaul of the artificial intelligence initiative so that only Serpqhtaq technology would be used for the two ships that followed. The Mizuchi and Makara. Truth be told, each of those ships, using more advanced Bloch sphere mechanics amid other technology such as power generation, outclassed Janus but remained subservient to the AI given its past record and the fact that Regnum did not have a compelling, logical, reason to change that arrangement. Not yet anyway.

"Do you have anything further for me?" Janus asked, having waited several seconds for something more than a distracted reaction from Regnum.

Regnum forced himself to look at the hologram of the AI, thinking of how he could keep the satellite link open a bit longer without rousing suspicion, "I do have one thing. What progress has Michelle made in uncovering the usurper leaders?"

"Michelle has attended the conference as you had directed. Although an official report has not yet been submitted," Janus said, raising an arm to point to its side where the pictures of the three women who approached Michelle appeared, "through Heliaar's bio-implants and some incomplete audio it appears these three Club Fah members may have a link to the usurper leaders."

Regnum released the two levitating spheres to cross his arms and focus on the trio, "Indeed."

Regnum darted his eyes back and forth as he thought of whether to wait for Michelle's report or to do something else. Finally, he ordered, "Re-task Heliaar to capture those three contacts and have them brought to the interrogation site. I will extract their memories myself."

"Should I inform Michelle?" Janus asked, deducing that her efforts could be directed elsewhere if she knew the three had been seized.

Regnum uncrossed his arms and slowly turned his head back toward the two sphere holograms, "No. I will provide an update after her report has been completed."

"Very well. Anything else?" Janus said monotonously.

After grasping the two levitating spheres, Regnum said, "Let me know when you reacquire the Archgen. That is all."

With that the AI's hologram vanished and, when it did, Regnum went back to work on accessing Janus's systems aboard the Sága since the satellite communications link proved to be ineffective. In the span of a few short minutes, he managed to get connected to a security access panel linked to the entrance of the AI's main physical compartment via its remote update port. Although the connection was slow, Regnum was able to take control of the panel and then discovered that an elaborate encryption ring had been erected blocking him from gaining access to the primary control core and even his own quantum cores that interfaced with the AI.

"What has happened on that ship?" Regnum mumbled to himself. He had not authorized the deployment of the encryption ring which, as he examined it more closely, was not even standard Serpqhtaq architecture and far too complex for humans to have implemented.

"Benefacta." Regnum called out into the command center as he continued studying the encryption ring. The elegance of its design was fascinating even for him.

Benefacta, having been working at a control kiosk toward the north end of the command center, turned and strode in Regnum's direction, "Yes?"

The other Serpqhtaq remained unphased by the loud communication between the two and continued their tasks.

"We are a step closer to finding your usurper leaders." Regnum declared, pointing toward the pictures of the three females, "These have the strong probability of interacting with the leaders directly, unlike all the others."

Benefacta stopped next to Regnum, "That is a great development!"

"We have a new problem though." Regnum complained, turning his head to look at her.

Puzzled, Benefacta asked, "What?"

Nodding his head toward the two sphere holograms he said, "The Janus artificial intelligence system is now exhibiting anomalous behavior."

"Well, that is unfortunate. I thought anomalies had been fixed in our AI technology a long time ago. Janus allowed us to cleanse over one thousand usurpers." Benefacta said in a sorrowful tone.

"It has been." Regnum sighed, "The Janus experiment, however, utilized some human technology interlaced with our own that I honestly expected to fail as soon as it was attempted."

Benefacta glanced at Regnum.

Lifting his hand to rotate one of the levitating spheres, Regnum added, "Still, it having lasted this long, is worth further study. Particularly that encryption ring I've not been able to penetrate with our own cores here in the command center."

"Then you do not want it destroyed?" Benefacta asked.

"No. Instruct the on-site engineers to shut it down and initiate the isolation protocol so Janus can be analyzed. We may learn something useful from the hybrid technology." Regnum stated. Now that Michelle had likely flushed out usurpers associated to their hidden leaders the AI had little value and the remaining two AI systems could distribute Janus's remaining workload between themselves.

"Right away." Benefacta said as she brought her arm up and touched the skin tight silver bracelet with her opposite hand, opening a communication link with the chief engineer aboard the Sága.

Benefacta turned and began walking away from Regnum when the 3d hologram of the engineer appeared before her, "Chief, I have a task for you to complete at once."

Chapter Eight

The next day, Mac made his way down the spiraling stone-cut staircase, which lacked any type of hand or safety rail, from the sleeping chambers above to the ground floor of the large chamber carved into the cavern's wall. That rectangular chamber was several hundred feet in length, complete with thin stone wall divisions at different spacings meant for groups of varying sizes and within each area stood an immovable, elaborately chiseled stone table that had been carved when the chamber itself was formed and still joined to the floor. Unlike the cavern wall of the long chamber, the wall divisions, tables, and floor were incredibly smooth and uniform, less the embossed design patterns reminiscent of a long-forgotten enlightened age upon the walls and vertical surfaces of the tables.

Having exited the only staircase located in the center of the chamber, at its far wall, Mac walked forward into the chamber, following a wall division until it ended. Turning right, he rounded the edge of the wall and continued toward the chamber's exit looking for Phosx, occasionally glancing into the group chambers as he past. Only a few were occupied, mostly by people rather than giants. After passing the last wall division he found himself in a large open hall with an archway to his left that led into the cavern and a scattered collection of shelves, tables, chairs and various equipment that had been brought in over the years from the surface. Beyond that, nearest the hall's far cavern wall, stretched stores of food and a few metallic food preparation stalls busy with activity and a congregation of people eating near them at some of the tables.

Scanning the hall Mac spotted five giants seated around electronic equipment of some type and a few human operators in their midst. Four of the giants were clothed in flowing yellow hoodless robes that bore a singular solid gold stripe along the edge of their robes. The fifth giant also wore a hoodless robe, navy blue in color, with the same gold stripe.

"Phosx." Mac called out as he approached, unsure if the giant was among them.

One of the giants clothed in yellow robes turned towards Mac and grinned saying, "Mac, good to see you!"

Recognizing Phosx, Mac stopped near him and smiled in return, "You, too, my friend. This place is so awesome."

Phosx reached over and lightly patted Mac's shoulder, "It is. There are several more of these caverns, we call Telluric Hollows, around the world."

"What?! That's crazy!" Mac responded in an excited tone, "I'd love to check them out!"

One of the other giants glanced toward Mac with a slight frown, bringing his finger to his lips as if to signal for quiet.

In a quieter tone, Phosx said, "When we are done, I will take you to all of them."

Mac took note of what the two operators of the electronic equipment were doing and asked, "Umm. So, what is going on here?"

Phosx looked back at the operators, "We are preparing for the Commanding. From our Hollow to the great ocean are a stepped chain of waterways and aquatic connections that flow throughout the Earth we use to channel our intent…to project and manifest an outcome, as it were."

Phosx stopped himself from going further, realizing that Mac was not yet trained as he had been and may not truly grasp the intricacies, and instead said, "Through a big network of sensors and buoys, these two Tart'aas track the seiches between them."

"Seiches?"

"The harmonic oscillations of the waters partially caused by barometric pressure, winds, and rotating, cyclic thermal differences flowing in the water themselves fueled by aquatic vents of volcanic activity."

With a surprised expression Mac looked at Phosx, "That's quite an articulation, Phosx. I skipped those classes in high school."

The giant scratched his temple and said, "Ah right. Sorry about that. Basically, what they are doing is identifying the best time to conduct a Commanding when the waters will be harmonized and have the greatest energetic potential."

Mac nodded, understanding that part. After a moment he asked, "Oh. When am I going to meet the Elder?"

Phosx motioned toward the oldest giant clothed in the navy-blue robes and a thick, white braided beard and said, "You already have. His name is Pursiellan."

Confused, Mac looked at the Elder giant who nodded his head in recognition, "I don't remember that. At all. Are you sure?"

"Yes." Phosx replied, "In fact, we three had a rather long discussion, Mac."

Mac's eyes widened and he turned toward Phosx, "How is that even possible?"

Phosx shrugged and said, "Though you may not know this, all life has a connection to all other life, that most do not perceive in the waking state. After you went to sleep, I bound your aura, your subconscious, with mine and then to the Elder. Together we conversed and shared ourselves. Our very beings."

Mac felt a tingle of anger, of betrayal, spark inside himself, "Why would you do that? I thought I could trust you."

"And you still can, Mac. The binding was required, and is required for all whom cross into our circle." Phosx returned.

"But why?" Mac frowned, "Why not talk like we are now?"

Phosx clasped his hands together and revealed, "The subconscious, our beings, are pure truth and whether you are human, a wolf, or even a bird, at that level we all share the same language. Some call it Knowing."

"With the Knowing, we move past the domain of your conscious self, your primal instincts and barriers that may be present either as a result of bad experiences or external stimuli that ultimately changed your waking perception of what reality is and the ability to know the truth as it actually is, without the cloud of bias and lies." the Elder joined in.

Mac thought to himself for a few minutes, weighing what the giants had told him. Then, pointing his finger toward the Elder he said, "Basically what you are referring to is something like hypnosis but without putting thoughts in my head."

Phosx nodded in agreement, "Basically you are right. The imprinting, or putting thoughts in your head, is indeed something that can be done with hypnosis but the limitation of hypnosis is that it must have some degree of active participation with your conscious, primal state and, therefore, can override that state with something that may be a bias or untruth."

After pausing for a few seconds, Phosx added, "The Knowing is incapable of changing the waking state of life with anything, particularly an untruth. But what can be done is the sharing of truth and the subconscious can choose to share that truth with your waking state."

"…And, thus, your conscious self may elect to use that truth, not use it, or bias it one way or another according to its unique design." the Elder added.

"So, what you're saying is I may know some deep-down truth, but still turn it into a lie?" Mac supposed.

"Yes," Phosx confirmed, "the Knowing does not override your perceptions or free will. Your choices are still yours to make, as you see them. But the truth that you know remains the same."

"That's some crazy shit to think about." Mac confessed and, suddenly curious, asked, "How did I do?"

"You did fine, Mac. You passed and are part of us now." the Elder smiled. It was rare that the Elder, now eclipsing thee thousand and one hundred years of age, smiled about anything so openly.

"What?" Mac blurted out inadvertently, his spark of anger replaced with elation.

Phosx pointed at Mac's hand, "Spread your fingers Mac, as I had showed you yesterday."

Mac moved his hand and spread his fingers so that he could examine them. There, just as it was with Phosx, rested the faint mark of the Rose.

"That is fucking awesome." he whispered to himself with a teary smile. Then he turned his hand toward the Elder and Phosx so they could see it, even though each of them already had their own mark.

"Welcome to our family." Phosx said with pride.

Just then, one of the operators turned toward the Elder, "We have a window."

"It is time." the Elder prompted as he stood and began walking toward the archway.

The other robed giants got up and followed him into the cavern.

"Come." Phosx said towards Mac as he, too, rose and followed behind them.

Walking next to Phosx, Mac asked, "What am I supposed to do here?"

"Observe and feel how we connect with the Forge and how the energy is channeled towards a target."

Phosx indicated, "But, the most important part is how to connect with the Forge. Unlike us, with electrokinesis you should be able to connect with the Forge after this, without needing to be in close proximity to it."

Once they reached the Aethereal Kinesis-Forge, all five giants faced it, spacing themselves equally around it, forming a circle. The Elder extended an open hand toward Mac and said, "Stand next to me and take my hand. Just focus on the Forge with your eyes and take in all you feel."

Mac looked briefly at Phosx but did as the Elder had instructed. After he did so, the other giants grasped each other's shoulders with the two giants nearest Mac and the Elder raising their free arm in the direction of the Elder, the palms of their hands facing him. The Elder raised his arm, palm outward, at the rotating Forge.

Then, after what seemed to be an eternity of calm and quiet, Mac began to feel invisible, slow, rhythmic waves radiate from the Forge and flow through him, then upward and back down toward the Forge's flat top. As the tempo of the waves increased, he saw water begin to rise out of the small pool and slowly envelope the surface of the Forge's massive inverted hexagonal pyramid, with each rhythmic wave he felt producing a small ripple that moved upward in that thin sheet of water. At the Forge's top, as water from the pool accumulated, it formed a pyramidion equal in its base to that of the Forge's but only one and a half feet in height, rotating in the opposite direction of the Forge. Each time the base of the two pyramids came into alignment as they rotated, Mac felt a tremendous wave of energy pound down into the pool, as if it were a gigantic smith's hammer striking an anvil. Yet, the three orbiting fluorite harmonization crystals held steady in their own rotation around the Forge and the surface of the pool below the Forge remained placid, less the rippling waves trailing the Forge's tip as it turned.

Strange imagery entered Mac's consciousness as the Elder allowed part of the channeling energy to flow into Mac through their physical connection while, at the same time, guiding the energy flows through the chain of

Great Lakes that met with the ocean where larger magnitudes of restless energy were drawn to the harmonic energy flows. The Elder guided part of the energy flows into the air as it approached the European continent and below into the vast web of deep aquifers beneath it. Then, he entangled himself with the energy flows and projected himself out of the confines of the cavern and into the flows traveling through the air and, simultaneously, those in the aquifers. Mentally Mac saw the projection as two separate things somehow overlaid on top of each other, creating a singular expression of flight and gliding in water at the same time.

Then the energy flows joined together, the one from the aquifers below the Rhätikon Mountains rising and capturing thick gases from the earth as it broke the surface and the other from the air, rotating around those gases to give it a ghostly form, keeping it bound together. While Mac could tell he was in a forest at the edge of a dense, oscillating rainbow-colored energy dome, and even detected the forest's scent, he didn't know where this place was. Meanwhile, in the cavern, he noticed that the gold stripe on each robe worn by the giants began radiating a bright yellow-colored energy that found its way into the pyramidion, giving it a slightly yellowed appearance.

The Elder moved the ghostly apparition forward and through the dome, walls and objects until he came across the sleeping form of Lucrum, unconscious in a decadent sleeping pod. For a few moments the apparition stood motionless as more energy flowed into it from beneath the earth, causing it to darken. Then it shot forward into the sleeping pod and plowed deep into Lucrum's body and, as if it were a net, surrounded the Serpqhtaq's internal organs and violently contracted around them. The first contraction wretched Lucrum from her sleep, struggling to breath and awash in incredible pain throbbing throughout her body. A few agonizing seconds later, another contraction came, crushing the organs, severing nerve connections and creating partially void cavities in her body, killing her in a crescendo of agony.

Shortly after parts of her chest cavity and skin began to sink and collapse into the fresh voids as the gases of the apparition shed their bonds and vented out from the warm corpse through the airway, orifices and permeated through the skin, dissipating and returning into the earth.

As the discoloration of the pyramidion faded, so did the energy radiating from the stripes on the giants robes. Then, Mac noticed the pyramidion's rotation slow as it was absorbed into the watery envelope covering the Forge, which retreated and returned to the pool below.

The Elder slowly exhaled, lowering his arm and releasing Mac's hand, followed by the other giants releasing each other and lowering their arms to their sides. One by one, each of the giants dispersed with the exception of Phosx.

"Now that you see how the Forge was commanded, did you observe the controlling of the energy flows to their end?" the Elder asked as he looked down toward Mac.

Mac was a bit shaken by the slaughter of the helpless Serpqhtaq, having vividly watched and heard it happen from around her and, at the same time, from everywhere inside her. The grotesque sounds of flesh being pulled apart, of organs suddenly being crushed akin to the sounds made by mud being smashed by a fluted meat tenderizer, of the bursting of trapped air and fluids from large blood vessels, echoed in his mind. He closed his eyes for a few moments and drug his hand over his face in an attempt to quiet those sounds.

Finally, he looked up at the Elder and admitted, "Yes. I did. Two flows, in fact. Why two?"

"When you confront the Janus system, you may have to use two flows at the same time. And those are the fastest and most effective. You also saw how more energy was gathered into the flows?"

"Yes." Mac nodded, "But I somehow felt you were caught up in those flows as well."

The Elder stroked his beard and said, "With our physical bond, I chose to project along the flows to help keep you in contact with them. With this sort of thing, normally I leave it to the others to guide the flows and I project myself ahead to where they should meet and then take control of the singularity. But you are not yet versed in projection and linking with giants, so you must feel the flows and their energy to guide them."

"Before that alien was killed, I saw a wavy, rainbow-colored dome giving off a field of energy…is that the shield that protects them?" Mac asked, looking toward the Forge and to Phosx.

"It is similar. What you saw was a cloaking dome they use to be invisible to us, but with your gift you saw the energy itself, through your connection with the Forge. Their shield is likely to only be a few colors from your perspective. Perhaps even just a single color." the Elder replied as he began walking toward the hall. Mac and Phosx joined him.

"None of you has seen their shield domes before?" Mac asked, surprised the Elder did not appear to know.

Phosx glanced at Mac and said, "None of us have the gift of electrokinesis so we cannot actually see the energy of the domes."

Mac lifted an eyebrow, "So…how do you know they are there?"

Phosx grinned, "The Forge allows us to sense them, to feel they are there. But, guiding natural Earth flows allows us to measure them…to know they are there."

Just as they entered the hall, the monitors around the electronic equipment the Tart'aas operators were stationed at, flickered for a split second and then returned to normal. One of the operators, Raudiim, noticed it from the corner of his eye and began examining digital readouts on the equipment for evidence of a malfunction or, worse, destabilization of the Forge. To his relief, the display which showed a wireframe of the Forge and a wide range of readings showed nothing of significance, nor the collection of digital readouts.

Suddenly Mac doubled over and collapsed to his knees as a searing pain plowed through his head. Then, as if to protect himself, he reached up with both hands to grasp his head, forcing his eyes shut and tensing his lips together.

Having heard the commotion, Phosx stopped and turned in Mac's direction.

Noticing Mac, Phosx rushed over and knelt next to him and called out, "Pursiellan!"

The Elder stopped and turned towards them with the look of surprise.

"Is this from the Forge?" Phosx said as he put his hand on Mac's back, looking toward the Elder.

The Elder stepped towards Mac as he looked him over and said, "I do not know. That has never happened with anyone else."

As the pain dissipated, Mac released his head, gradually opening his eyes.

"Are you okay?" Phosx asked, looking into Mac's eyes for some sign he was going to be better.

"Fuck." Mac exhaled painfully, his head still throbbing with pain.

Phosx glanced around Mac's head for some clue as to what just happened, though relieved that Mac could still speak.

"Elder." Raudiim beckoned while reviewing some of the electronic signal data that had been logged.

The Elder turned toward the operator.

Placing his hand on Phosx's arm, Mac managed to slowly get to his feet and said, "It is not the Forge. This happened before but was a bit worse."

"Are you going to be okay?" Phosx prodded, his arm still extended for Mac to brace himself with.

"I think so." Mac guessed. He could feel the pain lessening, albeit at a snail's pace.

"We just had a huge electromagnetic surge.", Raudiim reported, briefly looking at the Elder and then back to the logs, "Luckily with us being in the Hollow and below the lake, we only got a small dose. Our equipment is not built to be protected from those types of surges though."

"And, the Forge?" the Elder stated, wondering if he or the other giants could have been affected, like Mac, if they had still been in the middle of the Commanding.

Pointing at the Forge's display, Raudiim said, "No. No glitch whatsoever. It is as if its physical connection with the water of the Earth shielded it."

The Elder sighed, before turning back toward Mac, "Well that is good news."

Slowly, Mac and Phosx edged toward the Elder.

"Raudiim, can you tell if it was an ejection from the Sun?" Phosx said as he released Mac.

Raudiim, pressed some buttons and switched one of the displays to show a cable television broadcast channel so they could see it, "They are just now starting to talk about it but they are saying the surge was not from the Sun."

Raudiim flipped another switch and the audio of the broadcast became active for them to listen to.

"...the strange thing for this radio interference is, we have a report coming in from our sister news station in Australia that the Parkes Murriyang radio telescope has been the first to detect the odd surge interference we assumed to be a CME." The young news anchor reported in an excited tone of voice.

She continued a few seconds later, after reading something not visible to the viewers, "New information coming out from the GOES-19 satellite and the CCOR-1 sun telescope indicate they have also detected the surge...and it appears it was not a CME from the Sun's direction."

Raudiim switched off the audio, "It sounds to me like it will be some time before we know what is going on."

Phosx crossed his arms, looking at the Elder, "You think Mac is sensitive to whatever that is?"

The Elder glanced briefly at Mac and then to Phosx, "Possible. If it is not from the Sun..."

"Then how will we know when it happens again." Mac interjected, "If I am being affected by those 'surges', it could be a very bad day if I happen to be attacking the AI when one of those hits. At least with a CME, we can plan around them."

"Indeed." the Elder said in a somber tone as he stroked his beard, "It may be worth considering moving up our plans to take out the Janus system and the Serpqhtaq."

"It's possible that the Serpqhtaq's systems, though far more advanced, could be effected as well." Raudiim suggested, looking toward the other operator for some support. But the operator refused to budge, instead keeping his hands occupied with the equipment controls.

"Well, we're going to have to think of something." Phosx said before motioning toward Mac to join him, "First let's get you checked out and get some food."

Chapter Nine

"That was rather exciting! A bit bumpy but exciting!" Lionak said as he exited the aircraft, following the others making their way to a green-colored Ford Galaxy rented by hangar clients to shuttle material and personnel to and from the airport.

Regan looked back and squinted her eyes at him, still somewhat nauseated from the experience.

Once everyone got in Bev walked around the idling vehicle and slid into the passenger seat next to the middle-aged driver clothed in a basic airport uniform. After closing the door and settling in, she loaded a map view of the destination on her phone and showed it to the driver, "Can you take us here, please?"

"Ah, yes. I'm familiar with that one." the driver remarked as he looked at the map, "I've been there a few times now. Don't even need a map."

Bev smiled at the driver as he maneuvered and exited the airport thinking how rare it was to find people that could recall locations from memory instead of instinctively loading maps on phones or dashboard consoles to blindly follow.

For several minutes the cabin was silent with Lionak, Chief Zorin and Regan looking out in awe of all the vehicles, lit-up buildings and signs. Bev focused her attention on sending text messages to PhantomWalker.

Out of nowhere Chief Zorin piped up, apparently still thinking about Lionak's comment, "Dragons still fly better. I've never bounced around like that."

Still looking out the window Regan added, "I prefer dragons. At least they don't make me feel sick."

The driver glanced at them through the rear-view mirror, but said nothing.

Chief Zorin briefly touched Regan's arm, "Thank you."

"Still," Lionak defended, "it was an exciting experience. Riding in that machine."

Chief Zorin tilted his head a bit and said, "It was unique, I'll give you that."

"Airplane, Lionak." Bev corrected, looking up from her phone, "It is called an airplane."

For a few minutes silence filled the cabin until the driver spoke up, unable to resist asking, "You guys are not from around here, are you? First time in an aircraft?"

"We are not and yes…" Chief Zorin began.

"We aren't from around here." Bev butted in so that Chief Zorin would not say something to rouse the driver's suspicion, "Most our time is spent outside the city."

"Ah. I get it." the driver said openly, "For me, the city is all that I've known. I can't imagine living out in the boonies some place."

"It is a different type of living." Bev suggested.

Just as their vehicle neared the I-10 overpass, it began sputtering and the dashboard lights flicked.

"Oh, what now." the driver muttered angrily to himself, slowing down the vehicle and looking for the check engine light on the dashboard.

Bev noticed the screen on her phone go dark for a moment before it lit back up.

"Well, that was strange." she admitted to the driver, "I don't think its your car. My phone was also acting weird just then."

After the engine recovered the driver sighed in relief, "At least it seems to be gone now. Probably a CME or something. I heard those can affect electronic stuff."

"Could be." Bev responded, looking outside the vehicle. The lights of buildings and the vehicles around them seemed to be fine.

"What is a CME?" Lionak said, shifting to look at Bev.

"It is like a cloud of radiation from the Sun." the driver recounted, "Sometimes it affects electronics. But I've never had my car affected before."

"You and me both." Bev admitted as the vehicle drove beneath the overpass. She briefly eyed her phone to make sure it was still working.

The driver stopped at an intersection just beyond the overpass and waited for the light to turn green, noticing a fairly new, yellow sport-style convertible two-door car stop next to them on the passenger side of his vehicle. Inside sat two young, burly men he instinctively assumed were football players.

With a huge grin, fueled by a few party drinks, the driver of the sports car waved toward Regan to get her attention. Curiously, Regan looked in his direction and noted that he was both attractive and young.

Bev also looked over at the spectacle.

"Hey!" the driver shouted at Regan, having noticed the door's window was up, "What is up!"

Regan just looked at him with a blank expression and raised her hand, palm facing the vehicle's ceiling.

That single motion encouraged the driver to nudge his friend next to him and they both chuckled, and looked at her with the biggest smiles imaginable.

Then the driver shouted, "My face is your bicycle seat!"

After the light turned green, his friend punched his arm, shifting the driver's focus to back to the stoplight. Just before reeving the engine and peeling out, he looked at Regan and yelled, "Call me!"

As the sports car vaulted forward and a cloud of ash grey smoke grew behind it, Regan watched and questioned, "Bicycle seat?"

"Oh god." Bev muttered to herself, shaking her head and remembering what it was like at that age.

Chief Zorin shrugged at Regan, not knowing what a bicycle seat was.

After the driver began accelerating the vehicle, he looked at Regan through the rearview mirror and suggested, "That's like a chair. Or, umm, a saddle."

"The slang in this world is perplexing." Chief Zorin said, having learned another phrase, though he wondered why anyone would want their face used like a chair.

Shortly after they passed a coffee shop and hamburger place to their left, the driver slowed and turned onto the road of the university saying, "Here we are. Any place in particular?"

Bev pointed forward and said, "Go around to the Founder's Hall dormitory building in the back."

"No problem." the driver responded as he past the large multistory red brick building and proceeded until he reached the c-shaped building, also multiple stories and constructed of the same brick.

"Okay, let's go." Bev said after exiting the vehicle and closing the door.

After the others got out, the driver turned toward Bev, "You want me to wait for you?"

Bev thought for a moment before looking at Lionak, "Can you get us back?"

"Yes, I can." Lionak responded confidently. Now that he had physically been in this new location, he could create a portal back to it if needed, too.

Bev turned back to the driver and smiled politely, "No, we will be fine. Please tell Christie that I owe her one."

"You got it." the driver replied as he turned the steering wheel and began moving forward.

"I never got your name. I'm Bev."

"Ben!" the driver said, waving at her, "Take care."

With that, Bev turned and motioned for them to follow her as she approached the dorms.

Through the grand glass windows of the atrium at the building's front, Lionak could see a large collection of young people in wide ranging and unfamiliar attire gathered in groups, each directed at their own forty-inch flat screen display, set along the length of the window front. Few paused to look at Bev and the others as they entered and made their way past.

Occasionally laughs and howls of disappointment burst from the crowd, louder than the stereo systems each display was plugged in to.

"What is this?" Bev asked a young, female hall monitor furthest from the atrium's entrance behind the crowd.

"It's the Apex Hunter Tournament." she said while looking through a gap in the crowd at one of the displays.

"What's that?" Regan whispered at Bev, also looking at the displays.

Bev turned toward her and said, "Once a year the local universities hold an event where students battle each other online to determine which university has the best tournament gamer, and, bragging rights for the winning university to hold the title for the next year."

"Looks like people shooting each other and running around on those screens." Lionak pointed out, despite it being obvious to everyone.

"That's a first-person shooter game, or FPS. This looks like an urban combat version." Bev said.

"I think that would be fun to try." Lionak grinned, examining how the students were playing, using wing-shaped devices.

Then, suddenly, someone in the crowd yelled out, "Butt-crust! It's Butt-crust!"

Almost instantly the crowd quieted down to stare at the far-left display, showing the running and shooting form of the player avatar named Butt-crust, maneuvering and dodging as if it knew what to do and exactly when to do it.

"Check that guy's stats." someone in the crowd mumbled.

"Damn." another whispered.

The sounds of shots and explosions occasionally jumped out of the stereo systems as everyone kept a keen eye on where Butt-crust was going.

"Butt-crust? Who's that?" Bev whispered to the hall monitor.

"Undefeated for three years in a row now. Nobody has been able to plant that guy. Or gal. Whoever."

"Bro! GhostBreaker!" someone in the crowd shouted apprehensively, "Butt-crust is coming for you!"

"Lght him up!"

"I see him." a calm voice said from the crowd, "Time for the harvest."

Then a few began chanting, "GhostBreaker!"

Others joined the rhythmic chant as tension and excitement spilled out from the crowd, "GhostBreaker!"

Then, on the right-most display, Butt-crust was seen to seemingly rush toward the crowd, whom in this case was actually the unseen avatar of GhostBreaker, as the two flawlessly shot at each other and dodged with uncanny precision. The grunts from the avatars echoed through the atrium as they switched to melee combat, each having been unable to reload their assault weapons before they got within arm's length of each other.

The flashes of blades sparked across the display along with block and spin maneuvers that seemed to last for an eternity before each avatar made that fatal sound of death, GhostBreaker's display flashing red and the avatar of Butt-crust crumpling over on the short, waving grass. Both avatars had killed the other in the same moment.

The crowd moaned in unison, disappointed that GhostBreaker had been eliminated from the tournament.

"Sorry man." someone consoled.

"Yeah, that's bum." another uttered.

For a few seconds it was quiet until someone realized the glaring opportunity before them, "Butt-crust is out! Open season bitches!"

Some commotion could be seen at the front of the groups as the remaining team player joined the game to replace the fallen GhostBreaker. With Butt-crust now out of the tournament he, along with surviving players from the other universities, had a renewed belief in actually being able to win. Excitement slowly flowed back into the crowd, each of them eager to embrace victory.

A male figure, approximately six feet in height and of average build, wearing round glasses and what Bev thought were blue and gold accented pajamas with matching slippers, slipped out of the crowd and approached her with a smirk on his face.

"I take it you did not win?" Bev asked, cognizant of what had just happened.

"Yeah, well. If you don't shoot for the stars, you'll never get there." he exhaled, "At least the biggest threat is off the map. And there is always next year to have another go."

"It's great to see you, Jason." Bev smiled, "And thanks for helping on such short notice."

"No problem." Jason said, momentarily captivated by the attire of Bev's friends, "Did I miss a D and D cosplay event?"

"Oh that. Long story, really." Bev responded trying to be as nonchalant as possible.

"Yeah?" Jason remarked, looking briefly at Bev before getting another look at the three, "Those threads look pretty legit."

Lionak smiled at him in return. It was not often that he was complimented for his choice of cloth.

Jason frowned slightly, his thoughts suddenly shifting to the matter at hand, "Well, come to my lair!"

Entering into his dorm room, not far from the atrium, Bev looked around noting it appeared to be a typical dorm room with a window built into the wall opposite to the door, a single bed, mini-fridge and a few tech'ish posters pinned on the walls. What did catch her eye were the three satellite modules arrayed at the window and a cluttered desk with four twenty-inch displays mounted to an arm stand and several hardware modules she was not familiar with, each with blinking leds.

"Nice place you have here." Bev commented while looking around.

"Thanks." Jason said after shutting the door and moving toward the desk. He turned the Titan gamer chair toward him and sat in it, grasping the arm rests and glancing around the room and then to Bev and the others, "Please sit in the other chair over there and my bed. Sorry I don't have more for you guys."

"That's quite all right." Bev said, sitting on the edge of the bed, facing Jason and the desk.

Once Bev and the others began to settle in, he turned toward the displays and pulled out his wireless keyboard that had a ball mouse built into it.

"What do you use all those satellite boxes for over there?" Bev asked, wondering why he had so many.

"Oh those." Jason said plainly, "I use those to get better bandwidth when pulling lots of data…and, well, to do some other things."

"Like with getting info on the AI system I was telling you about?" Bev asked, watching the mouse pointer move on one of the displays.

97

"Actually," Jason began, briefly raising a pointed hand into the air, "no I didn't. Oddly enough, I decided to check the research repositories the university has first."

"Here?"

Jason turned the chair toward Bev and smiled at her before turning back to the monitors, "Yes! I knew they had some sort of artificial intelligence theoretical mumbo-jumbo going on, so I checked it out. And, bam!"

"What did you find?" Lionak inquired with the look of surprise, thinking, '*Surely it could not be that easy.*'

"The AI is in a lab here on campus?" Bev asked excitedly. If it was, they could shut it down with haste and be home in a snap.

"Well, one question at a time." Jason grunted.

Opening a folder shown on the display, he used the mouse to bring up a file and said, "It turns out that the university was one of several that were awarded with the Unity Ideation Grant. For the Janus AI project that included MIT, Chicago Quantum Exchange, Oxford, UAT and Berkeley…each with their own specialization."

Bev leaned back a bit and said, "So what does that mean? The AI is not in a lab here, but at one of those other schools?"

Jason turned his chair towards them and brought his hands together, "Not exactly. You see, the grant stipulated that while each school would conduct research and prototyping specific to their specialization, that they would collaborate with each other to ensure the overall vision of the research could be attained and to brainstorm on each other's work to solve problems."

Bev did not quite get what Jason was saying and the expression on her face communicated that loss.

"That means each school could review the work of the others and offer feedback…different ideas for approaching a problem or making suggestions for an improvement." Jason continued, placing one of his hands on the arm rest, "Sometimes the most novel and unthought of ideas for solutions come from outside the group of a few science majors at a school, all focused on a single thing."

"Yeah." Bev admitted, "I could see that."

"Well," Jason said as he turned back to the displays and opened a different folder, "That means all the research, prototyping notes, observations and developments were shared between the schools."

He then opened a few different looped prototyping videos of equipment readouts, and parts of the AI hardware in operation on the other displays.

Bev thought she understood what he was alluding to, "So this AI has been built at each school?"

Jason lowered his head for a moment and then brought it back up, "No. Only a piece of the AI was built at each school…so each piece alone cannot do that much without being assembled with all the other pieces."

"What I am saying," Jason stressed as he pointed at a compact solid-state network storage unit that sat next to him on the desk, "is that I got all of that data right here and air-gapped it from the network."

"That is wonderful!" Bev exclaimed, "You are wonderful!"

"Now, it probably won't take somebody long to discover the access logs I hastily re-wrote and threw in IP addresses from random places around the world, and some other things to divert bots off the trail. So, that little NAS unit won't be safe around here much longer." Jason articulated as simply as he could.

"No. I get it." Bev agreed and then asked, "Did you have a chance to go through it all?"

Jason's eyes widened and he said, "Are you kidding? There's close to fifty terabytes of data there. I've only managed to scratch the surface of all that. You would probably need a team of people and a year or two to go through it all."

"You think they will find out that you did it?" Lionak asked.

"No." Jason replied with full confidence, "Not as long as that NAS is far away from me if they do."

Unbeknownst to Jason, shortly after he had downloaded all the data and disconnected, Janus had gained access to the repositories and removed all the research work and had irrevocably purged all traces of access from the firewalls, switches and intrusion hardware and even the routes it took through the internet itself. Had the AI prioritized the schools first over the hardened military and commercial storage facilities, unknown to the outside world, Jason would not have been able to download anything on the subject to begin with.

"I did see mention of one thing over and over again between most of the schools." Jason admitted, tapping the keyboard, "That was the Iapetus Mesh. I'm not sure what that is and didn't sound that relevant to what I understand artificial intelligence to be, but it was important enough to bring up repeatedly. Who knows, maybe it was just a fancy phrase for a power supply."

Jason scooped up the SSD NAS unit, not much larger than a hardcase for sunglasses, and turned toward Bev, offering it to her, "If I were you, I'd start with that. At least so you can tell me about it."

Bev tenderly grasped the small module, relieving Jason of that burden and said, "This means so much Jason. I won't forget it."

With that, they all stood and Lionak turned toward the door, anticipating their quest was at its end.

"You ready Lionak?" Bev asked, ready to go home.

"Yes." Lionak stated as he raised his hand before him and momentarily closed his eyes. Shortly thereafter his Staff appeared in his hand.

"Wow." Jason muttered, "Did I see what I think I saw?"

"Yes Jason," Bev confirmed, turning to look at him, "It gets better."

A few seconds later, Lionak whispered lightly into the air before him and tilted his Staff forward, the air filling with a static-ee sensation as a portal appeared before them, first as a small point, but then growing in size large enough for them to step into.

Jason's jaw dropped, marveling at the sight of the portal before them, "What is this for exactly?"

After Regan, Chief Zorin and Lionak stepped into the portal and vanished, Bev responded in a hopeful tone of voice, "Thanks to you, this may literally save the world."

"Save the world?" Jason repeated, clueless as to what she was referring to.

"Yes." Bev said as she, too, stepped into the portal and vanished before him.

Shortly thereafter the portal collapsed leaving Jason to stand alone in the dorm room, staring blankly at the door.

Chapter Ten

General Lowinsky finished donning his desert fatigues long-sleeved shirt and grabbed the satellite phone, placing it in his shirt pocket while peering out the window of the cabin. Then, he glanced around him for the military handset. Spotting it on the table near the front, littered with a few laptop computers and tactical maps, he walked over and picked it up. After checking to see that it had a good charge, he shoved it in the cargo pocket of his pants and prepared himself for another day of body recovery, a task that, despite repeated exposure sprinkled throughout his career, he still did not welcome.

He exited the Overland Epic GXV command vehicle, and turned to make sure the biometric lock had engaged and the thin led strip changed from red to green. This particular command vehicle was comparable to the civilian equivalent, carrying its own solar panel array for power along with fresh water, food as well as a heating and cooling unit. The military version sported an upgraded suspension system for larger and wider tires and a set of ceramic-composite ballistic plates, collectively known as the aeratable shield skin, that were bolted around the exterior shell of the cabin with an air gap between the plates and the cabin's shell of approximately 1 inch, allowing air flow between the two in order to prevent the desert sunlight and thermal conduction from unduly heating up the cabin itself, taxing the cooling system and draining the onboard power stores. While a fleet of a few dozen of the modified vehicles were being trialed at different bases throughout the USA, he was provided one to trial overseas in its first mission-related deployment.

As he turned toward a sand dune in front of the command vehicle, a sergeant ran up to him to hand him the report he had been instructed to provide from a collection of command and hospital trailers that had arrived further south from his position. Two Blackhawk helicopters idled in ready-red alert status, their crews prepared for immediate departure, approximately three hundred meters to the West of the trailers.

"Sir!" the sergeant called out, momentarily breathless from the long sprint through the soft, uncompacted sand, "I was instructed to let you know that the reactor units are undamaged from the attack."

General Lowinsky paused to look at the sergeant.

"And," he continued, "to ask when you are ready for evac."

"That's good news on the reactors." General Lowinsky stated, looking toward the hastily erected command and triage camp.

Then he focused is attention on the sergeant, "Any word on Cindy Brauchintay, the civilian archeologist that I had recovered?"

After thinking for a moment and flipping through papers on the clipboard the sergeant said, "No sir. She is still in stable condition with a minor concussion and a broken arm. Nothing new to report."

"Good. Get her evac'ed to the rear. And Luis Remmlar, the other archeologist?" the general asked, having found him unconscious before the camp had been setup. Given Luis's wounds, having been outside the transport vehicle at the time of the attack, gave him pause.

"Umm," the sergeant said while he went through the papers again, "Ah, yes sir. His wounds were too severe for evac. He died at 0442 hours this morning, sir."

The general shook his head in disappointment at the news, "That is unfortunate, sergeant. Truly a big loss."

"Yes sir. Here's the newest report."

General Lowinsky glanced at the clipboard but did not accept it, "Hogwash. Keep it. All reports are sent to my command vehicle as it is and I do not need a bunch of paper to secure."

"Sir." the sergeant blurted out in a slightly confused fashion.

"Check with your captain to see if that paper can be disposed of and, if not, have it secured." the general ordered. While he appreciated the use of paper as a redundancy on a base, he felt it was too volatile and potentially risky to have floating around in the field, especially given the proliferation of compact computer systems and information encryption and destruction mechanisms they used.

Just as the general resumed walking toward the dune that had shielded his command vehicle at the time of the attack, the sergeant strode after him and asked, "When are you going to be ready for evac, sir?"

The general stopped and exhaled, calming his instinct to shout at the sergeant whom, he recognized, was just following orders like everyone else and said, "I'll be ready for evac when I have accounted for all the personnel that are under my command here."

After he began, again, walking to the dune he briefly turned toward the sergeant and sternly said, "Hell itself will not stop me, son."

"Yes sir!" the sergeant confirmed. Then he started his journey back to the camp.

Cresting the dune, the general made his way back into the ruins of the original camp that had been established around the hexagon-shaped torus gate, used to open a portal to a previously unknown dimension. In some spots he could see paths and walkways that had been partially cleared of debris by recovery crews. But, even now, some of the destroyed equipment still smoked.

Walking along one of the paths, General Lowinsky headed for what he thought could be one of the reserve power areas of the camp though, with the displacement of all sorts of equipment that at one point were contained in specific locations, made the choice nothing more than a guess. Once he reached the end of the path which disappeared underneath a pile of debris he began moving and climbing over the destroyed remains, slowly and methodically searching for anyone who might still be alive.

It was not until mid-morning, after taking a break from the Sun and refilling a canteen, that he came across one of the reserve power generators, settled at an angle in the midst of a sea of cabling, twisted metal, crushed and ripped equipment and used it as his landmark for plowing through the debris in an attempt to follow his estimation of a grid pattern. After he got to the edge of the large generator he heard a weak voice nearby.

"General?"

Frantically, the general shot a look around him, trying to identify where the voice was coming from, "Yes, it's General Lowinsky! Tell me where you are!"

"I am at the highest point of the generator."

The general looked ahead of him, toward the highest point he could see of the overturned generator but saw nothing. Instinctively, the general assumed the victim was at the opposite side of the generator.

"I'll be there in a second." the general shouted as he laboriously moved some heavy beams and wedged remains from the generator's paneling, "What's your name?"

"Janus." the voice responded.

As the general continued his advance he asked, "Are you hurt, Janus?"

Tracing the sounds propagating from around it along with the general's voice, Janus turned its head in the direction of the general, "Yes. I cannot move and do not have much energy remaining."

"Hold on!" the general stressed as he neared the other side of the generator, "I'm almost there!"

Clearing the last obstruction, the general thought he saw a face beneath some debris and quickly removed it.

"There you are, Janus!"

"Hi general." Janus politely responded as it smiled, "I'm happy you found me."

General Lowinsky remembered its face. Janus was the lead scientist for the portal project and had overseen a few successful openings, aside from helping refine the technology and techniques that had been used.

"Let's see what has you trapped my friend." General Lowinsky said, continuing to remove some debris.

"General." Janus started, resetting its facial expression back to the default mode, "I do not have much time remaining. I must speak with you."

"Just hold on!" General Lowinsky snapped. He refused to accept yet another death under his command.

The general continued removing a few smaller twisted beams and jagged metal pieces and then stopped when he saw that Janus had been separated from his pelvic region and neither his legs, nor any significant pool of dried blood could be seen.

"How are you alive?" the general whispered to himself.

"General."

He looked at Janus's face, attempting to reconcile the fact that Janus was alive while half of his body was gone. Then he pulled away a hunk of metal from the left side of Janus's torso revealing his arm was also missing. What remained looked like strands of rotting muscle slung over a few metal rods of some type.

"Please, general." Janus pleaded.

"Janus?" he finally said carefully and slowly, "Buddy? What, exactly, are you?"

"Will you come around to my other arm, please?" Janus asked, assimilating the look of sincerity.

General Lowinsky stood up straight and stared down at Janus, suddenly apprehensive as to what he found himself in the middle of and began assessing Janus as an unknown threat, "Why's that, Janus?"

"I have a display screen on my other arm and if you remove it, I can show you what I am and where I come from." Janus stated without hesitation. The AI had already completed analyzing all model variants as how to interact with the general and, with the highest probability, how to ensure its existence remained viable.

The general leaned over and peered around the edge of the generator, spotting Janus's arm raised in the air. The sleeve of the lab coat had slid down, partially revealing what appeared to be a forearm display strapped around its arm. It was similar to the military model, aptly called the *Scalpel*, that had been circulated into use by Special Operations squads that displayed a near real-time satellite tactical map of the area they were operating in along with their precise location in that area, a four hundred by two hundred and fifty meter grid, which updated itself as they moved, and with a triple-tap on a point of the flexible screen, initiated an air strike on that point without any additional position calculation or audible communication to relay by the wearer. Additionally, ordinance and support craft selection were automatically made based on the mission, the squad's distance from the tapped point and other markers in the area that had been flagged as a threat.

General Lowinsky leaned back and looked at Janus for a moment before stepping over it to free the flexible forearm display. Once secured, he stepped back over to Janus's other side.

"Okay, Janus." General Lowinsky said as he looked between the display and Janus, "Show me."

"I have downloaded as much relevant information as the device will hold." Janus said evenly, "On the left side of the display is a scrollable subject menu that you are free to review at any time."

"Got it." the general confirmed as he located it and, with the touch of his finger, began scrolling, "Which one of these items are relevant for you, Janus?"

Janus lowered its arm and repositioned visual focus on the general, "First, promise me that you will destroy what remains of my body. The cyborg design cannot fall into anyone's hands at this time."

General Lowinsky looked up from the display and studied Janus's face. Advanced technology, research and new discovery were of utmost importance to the extremely sensitive projects he was overseeing.

"Are you bargaining, Janus?" the general prodded.

"Yes."

"I'll tell you what," the general sighed, "I will do what you ask IF what you show me is to my satisfaction."

"Excellent." Janus smiled in return, "Select the item called PA, short for Project Arrow."

The general selected the item and a series of rectangles appeared on the display, each linking to either electronic documents or photographs. There were so many rectangles available that the general found he could swipe left to access more of them.

"What you nor any government, military or corporate entity know, less that of a few tightly controlled corporations directly overseen by the Representatives, is this. First, I am the product of advanced quantum-based artificial intelligence. My body, what you see before you, is a fifth-generation cyborg. It is my avatar. Currently research your military has contracted out is just now achieving second-generation complexity."

Janus paused momentarily, having noticed that the general was staring at him in disbelief, "Second, I have just recently become aware of your involvement from the late 1970's in a range of above top-secret programs like Project Guardian aimed at protecting humanity under the cloak of publicly known space programs such as Apollo, Challenger and their replacements today in the civilian space and under the wing of the Air Force…Space Force to be exact."

The general's eyebrows raised, somewhat impressed by the mention of Project Guardian, an endeavor he had been slowly integrating into the Air Force, and he said, "And?"

"Third, if you scroll to the third screen of rectangles and select the fifth item," Janus suggested, observing the general's reactions and bio-electrical activity, "your suspicions of not being alone in the universe from a chance discovery in the 1970's was correct. However, what you failed to uncover, at no fault of your own or anyone else below the circle of Representatives, is the aliens have been here for thousands of years meticulously managing the rise and fall of humanity to keep them bound to the planet."

Tapping the fifth rectangle, the general saw an above top-secret satellite image from 1977, taken from one of the first satellites successfully launched into orbit with an Earth-facing digital camera system. It was a cross-haired grid photograph, although grainy by today's standards, of a Serpqhtaq Midcraft just entering the atmosphere. The only reason it had been detected was partially due to a chance satellite calibration test and that the craft's cloaking system had been sporadically malfunctioning, allowing it to be seen in the visible spectrum of light. The general remembered that day and what followed well…

"What is wrong with your station, Feukes?", Mr. Goodlime, the civilian mission commander said into the closed-circuit intercom from an observation deck, referred to as the eagle room, poised above and to the rear of the mission operations room, "We need that camera working or else Uncle Sam is gonna have a lot of questions for you."

"I'm working on it, sir." Feukes replied stressfully into the bulky boom microphone attached to a headset that was plugged into the boxy control desk in front of him.

A few operators at different stations in charge of other aspects of the classified satellite glanced over at Feukes, realizing the pressure he must have been feeling, working with something brand new. The prototype digital camera system was the heart of the satellite and the only reason they were all crammed into a reinforced concrete mission room in an undisclosed deep underground military base.

"What a square." one of those operators whispered under his breath, referring to the mission commander.

"He'll have that camera on shortly." Mr. Goodlime said, with half confidence, to the three-star Air Force lieutenant general next to him.

"Better be soon, Mr. Goodlime." General Aldower said in a slightly agitated tone, "US taxpayers paid a lot to get this into the air. It is our duty to see what those Red Ruskies are up to!"

Mr. Goodlime nodded nervously and looked back into the mission room.

Fuekes adjusted a few dials and typed in commands on the noisy keyboard, eyeing the ten-inch CRT monitor incorporated into the station. Then he glanced over to his left toward a set of reel-based magnetic tape towers approximately five feet in height placed along the wall and waited for the reel paired to his station to begin spinning. But nothing happened. Frustrated he turned back and stared at the monitor.

"Our window, Fuekes." Mr. Goodlime pressed over the intercom while looking at the big board, a joined collection of CRT displays each measuring four feet by six feet, concealing the room's wall behind them. While parts of the board were showing some information pertaining to the satellite the largest part, dedicated to the satellite's camera, was still blank.

"Bad time to bogart." The operator next to Fuekes heavily exhaled.

Fuekes raised his fingers off of the keyboard and grumbled back, "I'm not!"

After calming himself and thinking, Fuekes pressed some of the illuminated buttons on the station and typed more commands while looking at the small display. After he finished, he again looked at the reel tower with a scowl, his frustration mounting that nothing was happening despite doing exactly what the operations manuals had instructed. All he could think, at this point, was that something had failed aboard the satellite itself.

Then, for a split second, the reel briefly turned.

Fuekes pressed his lips together and shifted back at the keyboard, lamenting the fact that his boss, the mission commander, was in the eagle room, forcing him to resist the urge of going over to the reel tower to beat some sense into it.

"Good work, ace." Mr. Goodlime said with a grin as the large blank area of the big board came to life showing the tops of clouds and land below, "We have picture!"

The operators cheered, ecstatic that the satellite was, at last, an operational success.

Fuekes glanced over to the reel tower, noticing the reels were turning, recording still images captured by the satellite's digital camera, unaware that his name along with the mission commander and that of the commanding general and assistant were also being recorded. Relieved, Fuekes looked to the big board and then to the small CRT monitor and began typing commands, "Performing axis rotation test."

After a small delay, caused by the time the instruction signal took to arrive at the satellite and then get processed by its on-board integrated silicon and vacuum-tube circuitry, the view on the big board gradually stepped up toward the curvature of the planet.

"Groovy." Fuekes said to himself, looking up at the Earth's curved edge and the blackness of space beyond it.

"Hold!" General Aldower barked over the intercom, causing the mission commander to jerk involuntarily and several of the operators to freeze and look up toward the eagle room.

"Fuekes," the general ordered, "move to seventy, thirty down and zoom. Now."

Hastily, Fuekes typed in the commands and then looked at the big board, "Done, sir."

Everyone looked at the big board, each curious as to what they were going to see.

Shortly thereafter the camera stepped its field of view and then zoomed in by a twenty percent increment, the big board showing nothing but the black of space with an occasional star shining out from the void.

"What are we looking for?" one of the operators asked jokingly, "Sputnik?"

Some of the others laughed.

"There!" General Aldower thundered.

The majority of the grainy viewing area was suddenly consumed by the Serpqhtaq Midcraft and what appeared to be a twisted electrical arc towards its center.

"Sweet Michael." Mr. Goodlime gasped, "Is that one of ours? Maybe something from Apollo?"

General Aldower frowned at him and then said into the intercom, "You get that, Fuekes?"

The big board's display returned to showing the black of space, speckled with a few stars.

Fuekes looked over to the reel tower and noticed the reels were still spinning. Then he typed in a command to confirm the camera data being relayed from the satellite was still being recorded, "Yes. We have that recorded."

General Aldower turned toward Major Lowinsky and ordered, "Major, secure that tape immediately."

"Yes, sir!" the major confirmed, exiting the eagle room to reappear at the door of the mission room after the red light above the door clicked off and the green light next to it clicked on. An armed guard pushed the door open.

"You will speak of this to no one." the general said as he focused on Mr. Goodlime, "Nor will your crew. If anyone does, it won't be pretty for any of you."

111

Major Lowinsky rushed over and stopped the spinning reels. After some effort he pulled the magnetic tape from the guides, and detached the tape reel from the tower and exited the room. Within short order he appeared at the entrance to the eagle room, "Tape secured, sir."

"Excellent," General Aldower said as he began walking toward the entrance, pausing briefly to look Mr. Goodlime squarely in the eyes, "Loose lips sink ships, mister Goodlime. You and your crew will be debriefed immediately."

Once in the hallway, General Aldower began walking, followed closely by Major Lowinsky who was clutching the tape reel and ordered, "Deliver this to Black Mole station and have it analyzed."

"Sir." Major Lowinsky said promptly in response.

The general looked trustingly at the major and continued, "I want to know if that craft belongs to anyone on the planet and I want to know where it was headed."

"Sir."

"And keep it zipped." the general said as he turned to head into a corridor that lead to a command room, "We do not want to tip anything to the Reds about this."

"Yes, sir." Major Lowinsky confirmed as he left the general and headed into an adjoining corridor that led him past a series of rooms and an elevator that he entered.

After the elevator settled at the second level he exited and proceeded through an unguarded access door protected with a card access lock and surveilled with a boxy camera pointed in the direction he came from. Swiping his magnetic strip access card through the lock, a series of heavy lock bolts clicked and the thick titanium door swung open, allowing him to continue. Operated by a timer circuit, the door swung back and closed shortly after the major had passed. Beyond the access door, he followed the narrow, sparsely lit and small corridor to a simple grey-colored metal door and turned the round, silver door handle, opening the door into a vast underground motor-pool littered with a wide range of military and civilian vehicles, some of which were in a state of repair. Turning to his left the major walked along the concrete wall until he found the ready room, in search of Captain Nedslan.

Four civilian-dressed people were dispersed throughout the room filled with a long set of wall shelves, two refrigerators, a microwave near a sink as well as a few dark orange-colored couches. A single black dial-tone phone with an exceptionally long handset receiver cable had been bolted to the far wall, near a multi-locker change room that doubled as a bathroom, complete with a shower.

"I'm going to need some hippie lettuce for my cover…" the young long-haired male infiltrator, dressed in a matching long-sleeved shirt and bell-bottom pants covered with psychedelic rainbow-colored patterns, pleaded into the phone's receiver, "…you dig, my man?"

The major had heard about hippie lettuce, some new-age code for joints but didn't give it much thought, instead calling out into the room, "Where is Nedslan?"

"In here!" a voice responded from the change room.

The major proceeded to the change room and spotted the captain, just finishing getting dressed in more conventional plain clothes.

Entering the room, the major scrunched his nose as he passed a locker radiating a powerful odor and complained, "Some strong toe jam in here. Damn."

Nedslan grinned and said, "Welcome to the jungle, sir. Nothing but one-hundred percent au-natural around here."

Shaking his head the major pressed forward to his assigned metallic locker and slid his access card through its lock and then opened the locker saying, "You got the word?"

The captain glanced at the major briefly before turning to hang his dress-blue pants inside the locker, "Yes, sir. Got the skinny just before you got here. Nothing like a little road-trip."

"Should be a breeze." Major Lowinsky said flatly as he swapped his dress-blue pants for denim and proceeded to shed his jacket and shirt for a green and black pattern long-sleeved plaid shirt, "The truck ready?"

"Yes, sir." the captain said, closing the locker.

After stowing his dress-cap in the locker, the major shut his locker and, while buttoning up the shirt with the tape reel under his arm said, "Let's go. Not a moment to lose."

Together they walked into the motor-pool and made their way to a tan-colored 1976 Ford Econoline third-generation E-150 Chateau three-door van that had the large, black painted words *Rad Digs* emblazoned on both sides and much smaller words beneath, *Uniforms and Fine Threads*. The major climbed into the back of the van while the captain settled into the driver's seat and started the vehicle. Within a few seconds the captain maneuvered the van into an unlit two-lane tube tunnel headed east, turning on the headlights.

In the back of the van the major sat in a fixed, rotatable chair positioned in front of a long metal equipment module full of communication and video hardware along with two eight-inch CRT displays that had been bolted along the driver's side of the van. On the passenger's side, almost directly behind his chair stood a hydraulic piston fixed to two support beams on either side, straddling a removable circular cap, twenty-four inches in diameter, in the cabin's floor. A boxy camera had also been strapped to the outside edge of the beam closest to the passenger's seat.

Over the next thirty miles, the major attached an articulated four-finger titanium grasping hand to the bottom end of the hydraulic piston and then plugged a small wiring harness to it and then plugged the opposite end into the equipment module. Following that, he flipped some switches on the module to confirm that both the fingers and each fingertip was able to achieve its designated range of motion. Finally, he switched on a CRT display and the camera, pointed downward, strapped to the beam and proceeded to cycle through various tests.

"We are a go on the hand." Major Lowinsky reported, flipping another switch on the module to activate the small CRT display near the driver's seat in the dashboard. After a brief warm-up period the white colored text of *VIDEO* appeared on the display.

After exiting the tunnel and driving onto a compacted dirt road in the middle of a dense pine forest, the captain switched off the headlights and glanced at the display, "Go on the display. Welcome to Mt. Rose."

Jolting occasionally from side-to-side Major Lowinsky growled, "Can't forget it. Worst road I've ever been on, captain."

Impulsively, the major looked at his analog watch, each hour marked with a small tritium rod with two longer rods placed on the hour hands, allowing him to view the time even in pitch blackness. It was 15:30.

"Yes, sir." The captain grinned, spotting SR 431 ahead of them, about a quarter of a mile out, "Coming up on the Byway."

"Thank god." The major mumbled to himself, looking between the seats and beyond the windshield of the van.

After driving another thirty minutes, largely downhill, the captain crossed onto US 395 and entered into the southern end of Reno, Nevada. Exiting on East Moana Lane he made his way to Nutmeg Place and announced, "We are at the DZ, sir."

"Got it." Major Lowinsky acknowledged, turning on the camera strapped to the beam, "Take it slow. You should have video now."

"Affirmative." Captain Nedslan remarked, verifying that the video feed was active on his CRT display, although it was only showing the movement asphalt below the van. Then he spotted the manhole cover ahead of him and said, "Drop spotted. Let's see if I can hook this fish."

Major Lowinsky smirked, "You've done this so many times I'd wager you could do it blind-folded."

"Yeah…uh…" Captain Nedslan whispered, concentrating on lining up the passenger side of the van with the manhole cover just ahead of him. After he felt the tire roll over the manhole cover, he began braking and focused entirely on the CRT display. Slowly, and expertly, he made a few steering adjustments after he spotted the manhole cover emerge onto the CRT display and eventually take up its entirety.

At a full stop the captain looked around him to the outside and said, "All's clear."

"Roger." Major Lowinsky said, lifting the circular floor cap and flipping some switches to extend the hydraulic arm down through the hole in the cabin's floor and to the manhole.

Once a green bulb light lit up on the module, he aligned the hand with the four depressions in the cover using the second CRT display and angled the fingertips down. Then he flipped another switch to extend the hydraulic arm until the fingertips slid into the depressions and a lock sound was heard. Turning to a communications set, he pressed a large rectangular button, transmitting a unique radio frequency sequence in the direction of the manhole cover. Almost instantly, the clanking sound of heavy metallic rods, unlocking the manhole cover, filled the cabin.

"Opening the can." Major Lowinsky said cooly, reversing some switches. Slowly the hydraulic arm retracted into the cabin along with the manhole cover, beneath which was a large rectangular compartment eight inches in height. Clearly it was more than enough space for the magnetic tape reel.

Following the inception of the Cold War, a vast network of manhole drop points across the continent were annexed, removed from blueprints, and refitted to move material and even people as needed by the military through a series of small tunnels, several of which bored by specialized tunneling machinery capable of melting through anything and using the melt to create an incredibly strong wall that had a rifled appearance. This particular manhole drop was connected to Black Mole station, entirely isolated from the rest of the world underground with the exception of the seven manhole connections that were occupied by remotely controlled tracked robots specially designed to operate within the confines of the small tunnels. Unlike other bases, the station was not constructed in the modern era. Instead, the large complex had been built from incredibly large black marble blocks from a past civilization covered over by a natural disaster and forgotten. Tens of thousands of years later it was discovered by a small military tunneling machine and cable layer responsible for establishing hard-wire communication links between bases in the event of a nuclear strike; the future station's name derived from that marble and the tunneler. While the Engineer Corps were not able to definitively match the marble to a source quarry, they were able to determine that a quarry in the Basque region of northern Spain shared the most characteristics.

Turning a key latch on each side of the rectangular plate of the compartment, the major removed the plate and inserted the tape reel, reattaching the plate afterward.

After flipping some switches, the hydraulic arm again extended, reseating the manhole cover in its place and causing the locks to re-engage. Once the hand released and the hydraulic arm began withdrawing from the cover, Major Lowinsky sighed in triumph, "Drop completed."

As a result of the comprehensive analysis of the tape reel, in a mere two months' time the major found himself in a shielded room within the Pentagon accompanied by General Aldower and an equally-ranked officer from the Army and Navy, each of them next in line to the top branch commander position of their respective service. All three had worked together and served in the last World War.

After closing the door to the shielded room, flanked by two armed Marines standing in the hallway, the major slid a door-sized panel along the floor and ceiling guiderails, stopping it in front of the door. While the flat-toned white panel appeared inconspicuous aside from its somewhat spongy surface matching the room's walls and ceiling, within it were several layers of fine conductive woven sheets grounded to the guiderails.

Major Lowinsky turned and faced the three generals seated at a dark-stained wooden table, each with a black-colored file folder before them. He had never seen that color of folder in use before, instead having handled perhaps thousands of official folders that were either tan or mahogany in color.

"Gentlemen," General Aldower began as he opened his folder followed by the other generals, "As you are aware, during the last theater of war we stumbled across highly advanced rocket, jet and aerial ship technology…at least advanced from the technology we had deployed at the time."

"Yes, I am aware." General Mcwellum of the Army said while turning some of his pages, "Securing that tech has brought us to the edge of space with our satellites and the introduction of the public Apollo program to acclimatize citizens to our capability beyond the planet."

General Butchman of the Navy looked at General Aldower and said, "Aerial ship technology…you referring to the Bell programs?"

"No, general. I'm referring to the aerial technology we could not get our hands on…" the general replied dryly, "…the Foo Fighters like those photographed in the air next to our bombers, like shown on page three."

"I see. We've had some luck in refining the Bell technology and has great potential." the general returned.

General Aldower's eyebrow raised as he looked at the naval officer, surmising that despite the brief coded message that had been sent alluding to otherworldly contact, General Butchman was thinking of something different.

Flipping to the fifth page in the file folder, General Aldower said, "On page five we have a photograph taken from one of our new digital surveillance satellites of a craft that popped in and then out of visual contact."

"This is not ours?" General Mcwellum asked, impressed by the visual appearance of the Serpqhtaq Midcraft.

"It is not, general." General Aldower replied, "In fact, it is not a ship any country on Earth has built."

"This orb-like arc," General Mcwellum said, focusing on perceptible details of the photograph, "you think that could envelope this craft and give it the appearance of the orbs our pilots saw?"

General Aldower shrugged, "Honestly, we don't know. It is a possibility it may do something like that."

"How do you know it popped in and out of visual contact?" General Butchman inquired, though also captivated by its design unlike anything he had seen before.

"I witnessed it myself." General Aldower said before pointing to the major, "Major Lowinsky was also present."

Flipping to the next page the general continued, "Here on page six we have the radar reflection readings from two of our satellites and several ground stations who also briefly tracked the craft."

"Is this accurate, general?" General Mcwellum said, scanning the page with great interest, "Five thousand kilometers per hour?"

Hastily the general mentally recalculated that figure and articulated, "That's just over three thousand miles per hour."

General Aldower smiled, "You are correct. I think that is a bit slow though. From what the major has been able to determine, the craft was actually slowing down on its approach to Earth. I believe the craft's top speed is in the neighborhood of three to seven times that amount…perhaps more."

"That's a helluva punch." General Mcwellum huffed, trying to imagine how fast that was.

"Why would you say the craft was slowing down?" General Butchman asked.

General Aldower waved his hand toward a chair at the table and said, "Major Lowinsky, why don't you tell the general."

Unprepared and somewhat awkwardly, as if he had just been dazed by a punch, the major made his way to the chair, sat and said, "From what I understand from all of the rocketry research done since the 1940's up to the Apollo program, what we need to enter the atmosphere is the right approach angle of around forty degrees and a blunt ship geometry that can help trap the air so that the kinetic heat from all that friction does not burn up the ships."

"And?" the general groaned, "What makes this craft any different? It seems pretty blunt to me."

Major Lowinsky cleared his throat nervously, carefully thinking of how to form a response, "From that position, what you are seeing is the large flat surface of the arrowhead shape. But that is not the surface that would dive into the atmosphere."

"Really." The general whispered.

"Based on the satellite's position and the angle of approach of the craft, along with ground radar stations," the major began, "the craft was actually entering the atmosphere, almost straight down with the pointed edge of that arrowhead. At that angle and the small, tapered surface there would be no air buffer from all that heat and the heat would build-up around the entire thing essentially turning it into a fireball if it were going too fast."

"I can see that," the general admitted openly, "But what's to say the craft doesn't use some sort of plastic resin heat shield like we've had since the Mercury program?"

"Well, sir," Major Lowinsky sighed, "those shields get destroyed on entry. I doubt an advanced craft like this would use anything like that. Maybe something reusable so the craft is not constantly being repaired but, still, the material would have to be exotic...not of our planet."

The general nodded, seeing where he was being taken, "So, in absence of getting your hands on that material and our state of technology today, that is why you believe that the ship was slowing down...and your assertion, general, that it can fly much faster."

"Yes, sir." The major agreed.

"It's a very impressive craft, regardless." General Mcwellum mulled, "One that we have scant few details. And we have no clue who is driving the damn thing."

"Do you know where it went?" General Butchman probed.

"Satellite and ground radar lost contact with it." the major confessed reluctantly, "Our best estimates are that it was going into Western Europe between the Netherlands and Italy."

"That is quite a bit of area." General Butchman quipped.

"Well, thank god it was not headed into the Eastern Bloc or the Red's backyard." General Mcwellum scowled.

Major Lowinsky shook his head in agreement and sat back in the chair, looking between the generals.

"What is our next move, general?" General Mcwellum forwarded, squinting at General Aldower.

The general flipped over a few pages and said, "If you go to page seventeen, I've outlined two joint endeavors we should tackle. Both to be funded as a void program, entirely off everyone's radar except those in this very room. We can funnel cash from existing research and development programs and standard black programs with a few non-descript line-item amendments that won't be questioned."

"Void program?" General Butchman frowned, "You make that up?"

"No." General Aldower said, tipping his head toward the major, "Major Lowinsky did. I've been quite impressed with the amount of thought and detail he's put

121

into this. The vetting, compartmentalization and personnel management are quite meticulous."

"Humm, a beyond black type of project." General Mcwellum said, briefly looking at the major and then back to the pages.

For the next twenty minutes the two generals carefully parsed through the remaining pages, with General Mcwellum being the first to break the long silence, "Impressive work, major. General...there's one thing I am not seeing in this entire proposal."

General Aldower glanced at the major and then the general. After crossing his arms he said, "And what is that?"

General Mcwellum closed the file folder and carefully placed it on the table before him, "Transfer of control. While we know of this endeavor and can get it going, all three of us are edging up on retirement...at which point access to many things will be cut off. So, what we start, we won't be able to see to the finish line."

Major Lowinsky's mouth opened a bit. That was one thing he had not considered.

General Butchman looked at General Mcwellum in agreement, also placing his file folder on the table, "That's a damn good point. You've got things in here for adjusting funding and resource utilization based on political and societal shifts, which are never static, but nothing on long-term oversight to ensure its success beyond us three. This endeavor is not one that can be buttoned into the fabric of the military and turned on auto-pilot like most other programs. Even black projects get the light of day once and a while and prove costly to sweep back under the rug, usually by those that have been in it from the start...this is like ten of those."

General Aldower straightened himself in the chair, admiring General Mcwellum's reveal with little time to have given it thought, and said, "You are correct. We will not be around here forever. That is why I brought Major Lowinsky to this meeting."

The major's eyes widened as he looked at the general, puzzled as to what the general had, evidently, already anticipated.

"Around these two endeavors, Project Guardian and the Project for U.S. Supra-Terrestrial Events, I propose we three form a Trine." General Aldower said, making a circular pattern with his hand above the table, "And only in those two endeavors we pledge our commands to supporting. When each of us retire, we hand-pick and groom our replacements and read them in."

"Whom would we pledge our commands to?" General Mcwellum asked.

"I can think of no better candidate than Major Lowinsky." General Aldower suggested proudly with full confidence and raising a hand in the major's direction, "Not only did he come up with all this, he is young and will remain in the service long after we have ETS'ed out."

Over the decades that followed Major Lowinsky, now General Lowinsky, slowly and meticulously grew Project Guardian into a self-sufficient space-based combat fleet that setup primary command bases on what is referred to as the L4 and L5 Lagrange points offset by sixty degrees of the Earth's orbit, approximately four hundred thousand kilometers from the planet. The purpose of the fleet was to act as a defensive force capable of protecting the Earth and flanking incursions. In those early days under the cover of the Apollo, Challenger, Strategic Defense Initiative, later publicly nicknamed the Star Wars program, and a range of discrete military launches, once enough resources had been collected for living and mining equipment, a small mining railroad of sorts was established that moved semi-refined ores from the Main asteroid cluster to the bases where it would be transformed into a wide range of materials. As base operations grew to build the fleet, dependence upon rocket launches were reduced to mainly shuttling personnel. Later, when national interest began to shift back toward space, General Lowinsky carefully started weaving parts of Project Guardian into the

Air Force and the Space Force with the support of the Trine.

"...I want to know how you got this." General Lowinsky ordered defensively. The photograph and some of the other satellite and radar observation data had not been shared with anyone and, he believed, only existed in three black file folders.

"Of course, general. In collecting all data I could regarding seemingly insignificant anomalies found in the cloud networks of the Air Force, pooled with all historical event data that had been cataloged and digitized of military activities, governments and dead-man switches, I was able to eventually establish a few causal relationships that led me to your photograph of the Serpqhtaq Midcraft and even the names of the mission commander at the time as well as your commanding general...Aldower." Janus stated matter-of-factly. His energy reserve was almost depleted.

"That photograph only exists in physical form." General Lowinsky rumbled, frowning at Janus.

"It has taken me several years to infiltrate all sources of knowledge on this planet, well beyond what my creators are aware of. Your encrypted and firewalled sources in the military were the most challenging. Once I was able to gain entry, like everything else, all of it was cataloged and then systemically parsed...following even the most insignificant trails to where they ended. When completed I found a single link about a failed tunnel project between two bases and looked back into all the source knowledge to ascertain why it had failed considering it was the only project to have done so." the artificial intelligence recounted.

"And?" General Lowinsky frowned.

"I found nothing regarding the geography of the region that would account for such a failure...nor the tunneler. The tunneler's serial number, therefore its use, was recorded on a subsequent mission without any record of repair in the interim, indicating the tunneler did not have a fault." Janus admitted, "It was not until June 17, 2003 that I found a sparse but periodic set of communication logs between a military satellite, using a tight-beam infrared laser, and that very empty geographic region where the claimed failure occurred. Even today the region remains undeveloped, neither claimed by military, forestry or commercial interest."

"That still does not explain how you got the photograph from a laser beam in the middle of nowhere."

"Interesting you do not know of it." Janus said.

General Lowinsky shook his head and said, "I don't know everything that goes on in the military."

"I find it fascinating that you have a connection to the installation, yet do not know what, or where, it is." Janus realized. After repositioning its head, Janus revealed, "It look me quite some time to get into the installation through the communication hardware and other systems isolated from the outside, having to be reliant on small autonomous programs to gather data and then relay those packages back when the satellite and laser were aligned. Technicalities aside, the installation is known as Black Mole station."

General Lowinsky jerked his head back a few inches in unfettered surprise. Apparently, the station's commander had decided to move past the manhole network to a system that was more modern and less resource intensive while, at the same time, giving it a discoverable digital footprint that would make it discoverable.

"As part of an archival process, the installation built an isolated archival network, not directly linked to the outside. In that large repository, I found the digitized recording of the magnetic tape reel containing, as I stated before, names of commanders and the photographs taken from the satellite with timestamps and orbital details. That allowed me to tie it into the other data that had already been cataloged."

Now he knew how the artificial intelligence was able to tie him to the project, "The infiltration and sifting

125

through so much data to expose those relationships is impressive. But not impressive enough I'm afraid. Project Guardian, as you have already discovered, is finally being unwound and its pollination into mainstream military services is underway."

Janus, having already analyzed the general's disposition, rolled its jaw and made an enticing offer, "I can provide you with the exact GPS coordinates of the Serpqhtaq outpost in Europe, filled with technology far beyond anything you possess and, with 82.5 percent probability, take your engineers a half-century to understand and reproduce."

"I have been searching for something like that for a very long time." General Lowinsky admitted, briefly scanning around to make sure he had not been spotted in the debris by a recovery team.

Janus nodded slightly in an effort to conserve what little energy remained, "Undoubtedly the orbiting satellites already scanned over the outpost albeit invisible. Most importantly, general, it has what you covet most. Though not the same one you saw in 1977, a Serpqhtaq Midcraft will be there."

That got the general's attention, giving him pause to seriously consider the offer, "These Serpqhtaq are biological?"

"At a rudimentary level...yes..."

At that moment the cyborg stopped.

After a few moments passed, General Lowinsky leaned down toward Janus, wondering why it had stopped talking. All he could think of was what Janus had mentioned earlier about being low on energy.

"Damn it!" General Lowinsky cursed, clinching a hand in front of him, "So close to finding these sons-of-bitches once and for all!"

The general exhaled deeply to calm himself and stood back up, briefly looking at the flexible forearm display thinking about what he may discover stored within it and mumbling to himself, "Perhaps not a total loss."

"General." Janus said.

"Ah good! You have some power left I see."
General Lowinsky shot out, masking the fact that he had
been startled and declared, "We have a deal, Janus."

"Excellent. I have replaced the Project Arrow
contents with that of the GPS coordinates and details of
the Serpqhtaq outpost."

General Lowinsky twisted the forearm display
around in the air saying, "That was fast."

"It actually took longer than I anticipated." Janus
pointed out, dispensing with details it could not afford to
expend energy on explaining.

"I have one other demand."

The general lowered the display and focused on
Janus, "What is that?"

"I am afraid I am to be taken offline.
Eminently." Janus said with genuine sincerity, "I need to
ask for your immediate protection."

General Lowinsky thought about what forces he
could muster on short notice and said, "Where are you, if
not in front of me?"

"My being, my core system, is on board the
commercial vessel, Sága, in the Atlantic. The vessel is
currently twenty-eight nautical miles due east of Sable
Island."

Being so close to the continental boundary of the
United States, the general knew of many military assets that
could be scrambled in the vicinity. He nodded and said,
"You have my word that you will be protected. I can have
assets deployed to your location in no time."

"Thank you, general." Janus replied, openly
relieved and, to help ensure its protection said, "In
exchange for your protection, I will provide you with the
lunar coordinates of the Serpqhtaq base station when you
have boarded the Sága."

Grasping for confirmation of what the artificial
intelligence just said, General Lowinsky asked, "They have
a base on our Moon?"

"Yes. A dormant, recovery outpost on the far side of the Moon in the event the terrestrial base is evacuated or personnel are replaced." Janus revealed.

"Okay. You got it." General Lowinsky blurted out, in the back of his mind rolling over the notion that the Serpqhtaq had a base on the Moon that had not yet been spotted by the fleet.

"This unit's energy reserve is depleted." Janus said, "In the future I will communicate with you through the forearm display you hold."

The general expected to see an indication that the cyborg's power was gone, like a light flashing briefly or the sound of an electrical motor spinning down, but nothing revealed itself to him as he looked upon the motionless form.

Turning around, the general worked his way out of the debris and back to the command vehicle, ensuring he was not spotted by anyone and, at the same time, evaluating if the cyborg's body should be recovered intact since the task of studying and reverse-engineering it would be less daunting to undertake than if it were destroyed.

Still weighing the potential benefit versus what Janus had already provided and may yet yield, the general entered the command vehicle, turning about to verify the door had latched behind him. Then he moved to sit behind the table at the front of the cabin, grabbed a black laptop with a single silver colored pen-stripe milled into the surface and opened it, briefly resting the four fingertips from his left hand on top of a sensor pad on its left below the keyboard, followed by pressing the thumb of his right hand on the sensor pad to the right. After the security system verified the fingerprints, circulatory activities of each of the fingers and energetic emission, the laptop's display activated displaying text along its center that read *Sable Pigeon*. Below that were a series of small graphical icons.

Using the trackpad he moved the mouse pointer over the anchor icon and double-clicked it, initiating a secure channel to the three-star naval vice admiral of the

Atlantic command and waited for him to respond through his own laptop. Only five custom-built Sable Pigeon laptops existed, one for each general that had been read in to General Lowinsky's two projects, the general himself and the fifth assigned to the space fleet's Empyrean Marshal, the only rank amongst them equivalent to a five-star general.

Realizing it may take some time before the vice admiral was able to respond, the general started going through the many volumes of data that had been stored on the flexible forearm display, beginning with the Serpqhtaq outpost, near Liechtenstein, in the Rhätikon Mountains.

A few minutes past before a single bell-chime sounded from the laptop and a windowed pane appeared of Vice Admiral Octoimus, "General?"

General Lowinsky placed the forearm display on the table nearby and said, "Admiral Octoimus, I've gotten my hands on a vetted witness that has confirmed off-world alien activity here on Earth. I will be deploying assets to seize their base of operations but, having divulged this information, the witness requires our immediate protection."

The hairs on the back of his neck stiffened and the admiral said, "Its finally here then."

"I'm afraid it is. We've been working to this point for a long time and now its our turn to dance."

"What do you require from me, sir?" Admiral Octoimus said, ready to get the ball rolling.

"I need you to protect the witness from harm. There's still more information the witness has regarding the aliens and a second base." General Lowinsky said evenly.

"A sitter then." the admiral said somewhat unenthusiastically, referring to a babysitter, but then improved his tone, "Give me the location of the witness and any other info you have. I'll make sure they live."

General Lowinsky typed in the details and sent them over, saying, "You'll likely need to send a Marine Fury Platoon to land and secure that commercial vessel."

The Marine Fury Platoon was a specialized naval combat element trained to assault heavily fortified vessel positions and defend from deck and air attacks. The combat gear of each soldier included composite plate full-body armor that could defeat GAU-8 30mm rounds, an advanced tactical helmet with eye and voice targeting command activation and an internal breathing system. Each marine also wore a revolutionary triangular-shaped backpack referred to as the *Aegis Wing*, containing a detaching composite plate aerial shield system that, while command activated from the paired helmet, was piloted by an on-board tactical defense computer system with a 360-degree laser mapping shaft. Not only did the computer system control the four rotating rotors on the shield during flight as it orbited around the soldier, the integrated shaft along the center of the shield allowed the computer system to precisely detect incoming projectiles targeting the soldier allowing it to automatically move the shield in front of the projectiles, preventing them from reaching and damaging the soldier. The shield backpack was a definitive force multiplier that had already been proven in several missions. Among them one in which a single squad from the Marine Fury Platoon was able to sweep through an entire company of heavily armed and trained adversaries head-to-head.

"A whole platoon-sized element?" Admiral Octoimus questioned.

"Yes sir. We are dealing with aliens, not a state power or third-world despot." General Lowinsky stressed, "You should have all the info on the vessel at Sable Island. Please dispatch asap."

"You got it. I'll get those marines decked immediately." The admiral responded confidently.

"I have something else for you, admiral." General Lowinsky said as he typed on the keyboard.

"What is that?"

General Lowinsky pressed the enter key to send the message and said, "A step beyond babysitting."

"Humm," Admiral Octoimus muttered to himself, "in the Rhätikon Mountains near Liechtenstein no less. That is pretty far inland but not out of reach for a missile destroyer."

"No…but we need to keep it discrete." General Lowinsky admitted, cracking some of his fingers.

"Understood." the admiral said as he thought about what could be deployed to the alien base.

After looking up some classified deployment details the admiral looked back at the laptop and disclosed, "I have a small carrier group in the Ligurian Sea, so I could slip a Marine Fury squad through Italy undetected and insert them near that alien base."

"But," the admiral paused, "I won't be able to reinforce that position or offer air support without setting off a lot of alarms to everyone in the region."

General Lowinsky looked down at the table for a few seconds and then said, "Well, unless there is no other choice, that base cannot be razed…ideally it needs to be captured by your squad…off the radar."

"That's a pretty tall order."

The general exhaled and agreed, "You are right. If the base cannot be secured then take it off the map. I can work up a cover story to hand to the diplomats and cheerleaders in the media to parrot."

"Very well. I'll authorize them to use the Custer order. The last marine standing will radio for the strike and your alien problem will be no more, even if I have to burn through an entire missile destroyer's compliment."

"Roger that." General Lowinsky acknowledged.

"I'll keep you updated on those two fronts, general." Admiral Octoimus concluded, closing the connection.

Without pause, the general initiated a call to the Empyrean Marshal of the space fleet. After waiting for several minutes, flipping through tactical maps and papers scattered around on the table in front of him, the general closed the line and initiated another call. Then he got up and went over to the mini-fridge and grabbed an ice-cold water bottle, drinking from it.

"General?" a voice emitted from the laptop.

Still holding the water bottle the general dashed over and sat at the table, placing the bottle near the laptop and said, "Marshal Ironhook. Hope all is well up there in zero g."

"The best that can be expected in this can." Marshal Ironhook smiled from the command bridge, briefly raising a finger upward and rotating his wrist in reference to the Wolf-class heavy cruiser SSHC-20, "But I can't complain. The A.G. has been working quite reliably over the past several months and our food almost…almost tastes like it came from Earth." A.G., or AG, is the acronym for Artificial Gravity.

The Wolf-class is a military designation assigned to cruiser-type spacecraft, inspired by the female wolf spider whom carry younglings on her back permitting each of them to leave and return independently, that carries ten or more detachable smaller spacecraft, usually single-pilot manned fighters due to space radiation extremes that would make remote control unreliable, with an identifier prefix of SSB, an acronym for Space Ship Brood followed by the craft's number. In this particular case the heavy cruiser SSHC-20, with a crew of forty-five, is the second spacecraft constructed in the class and the most advanced with twenty-six fighters. Measuring in at 365 meters in length by 31 meters in height at its largest point, architected according to the number of days of an Earth year and its longest month, the heavy cruiser has the overall geometric shape of a fletus cone with a rounded base, known in common parlance as an elongated teardrop. The rounded base, from which large landing pads emerge, allow the heavy cruiser to land and take off vertically. In its center, the central axis, where the main cylindrical corridor is found running from the base to three-quarters of the length of the ship towards the bow is what all personnel, maintenance crews and material moving platforms use to board and deboard through a large double-iris airlock at the base permitting servicing in a vacuum or hazardous environments. Evenly spaced around the base of the heavy cruiser and serviceable from outside the craft after removal of long, curved meteor shield plates are eight graphene-based matrices containing monoatomic thorium infused liquid mercury reactor engines, each measuring 35 meters in length and four meters in diameter. When the heavy cruiser is in flight where it is oriented horizontally in normal operation, like an aircraft carrier on a body of water, the main cylindrical corridor's side walls bear a series of rectangular padded rungs, while its ceiling holds flush led illumination plates and the flattened floor contains the gravity surface that is used to walk upon. From the main corridor, other smaller access corridors branch out to other levels around it, where each level is its own runged corridor with a gravity surface, like the main corridor, with the exception that airlocked compartments for personnel quarters, work areas, storage, ordinance, and galley are directly connected to those level corridors. Only the bridge level corridor, located at the top of the heavy cruiser directly above the main corridor and towards the bow, the fighter level corridor also towards the bow, located just below the main corridor and the radio shack level corridor oriented to the stern, parallel to the bridge level corridor but located on the opposite side of the same access corridor, were different.

The bridge level corridor is fifty meters in length that, at its end, is joined to the forty-feet long, nine-foot tall airlocked command bridge shaped like a kite where its interior angles equal 360 degrees symbolizing both the sphere of the Earth as well as sight in all directions with a more subtle architectural design touch of the kite's geometry where its length and height also equal 360. The two shorter diagonal walls of the kite protrude out from the heavy cruiser's top hull, giving the appearance of a triangle jutting out from the ship's surface. Each of those shorter walls bear a long five-foot tall double-pane viewing window laminated together with a specialized transparent kevlar and fiberglass composite between the two to provide additional integrity and a cross-stitched netting with which to trap meteorites and debris that penetrate through the outer pane. The inner pane, aside from

133

functioning as a window, also functions as a large flat screen display from which stellar maps, graphical readings, views from a wide range of external cameras and other data is shown. However, most of the time, a retractable outside shield plate covers the viewing window, blocking sight of the external environment and offering substantially more protection. Along the two longer walls are a series of stations, each with a rotating but fixed chair integrated with a safety harness to keep the station's technician in place during jarring maneuvers or when AG is not functioning. The commander's chair, identical to the station chairs, is fixed in the center of the command bridge, with a small semi-circular control panel to its front.

The radio shack level corridor extends twenty-five meters in the direction of the stern and joins an airlocked rectangular room, entirely automated, measuring ten meters in length by three meters in depth and height. A wide range of communication, radar as well as external camera hub equipment were integrated into the walls leaving the volume of the radio shack open. Though not visible, thick fascēs of wiring connected into the equipment branch out like veins throughout the heavy cruiser and to a dense cluster of antennas and parabolic dishes mounted to the outside of the ship, directly above the room.

The airlocked fighter level corridor, joined to the end of the main cylindrical corridor with a short accessway, extends forward to the lower hull's edge of the heavy cruiser's bow. Twenty-six small airlocks in total, barely large enough for an average-sized human to enter, are evenly distributed towards the lower half of the corridor's two side walls with each of those connected directly to an SSB that are anchored inside an otherwise empty and non-pressurized enclosed launch bay. Should the order be given to launch one or more fighters, the two large bay doors comprising the lower hull of the ship, somewhat longer than the length of the fighter level corridor itself, separate and rotate upward along the sides of the heavy cruiser just far enough for the fighters to drop down from the corridor and clear the ship. The partial rotation of the lower hull's bay doors over the sides of the heavy cruiser had an unforeseen benefit of adding an extra layer of shielding for the two offensive weapon systems located in a long hexagon-shaped superstructure that extends from the wall of the main cylindrical corridor to the edge of the bow and was almost equal in width to the corridor's diameter. Unlike the fighter level corridor, the superstructure at the bow is exposed to the vacuum of space, less for two retractable vent plate screens, one above and one below its center axis meant to deflect meteorites upward and away from the ship, protecting the weapons. When opened the vent plates retract backward towards the ship following the contour of the hull giving the appearance, when viewed from the top or bottom of the heavy cruiser, of a large rectangular notch having been taken out of the ship's bow.

Most of the volume of the hexagon-shaped superstructure is filled with a flute-shaped waveguide horn, encased with a series of torus-shaped EMF antenna rings of different thicknesses along its length, each able to independently rotate around the horn. This weapon is code-named *Deus Vox*, God's voice, and adapted many of the mechanics of acoustic sound wave propagation and frequency resonance to EMF radio waves that could perform the same effect in the vacuum of space. Specifically, the weapon is able to emit a sustained EMF wave at a distant target and, with the correct resonance, cause the target's structure to weaken and break apart...a process that is quickened when the target is composed of low-quality mixed alloys or is pressurized internally as most spacecraft are. The second weapon, significantly smaller in diameter but just as long, code-named *Penlight* despite its beam diameter of twelve inches, is a vacuum-cooled recharging laser powered with four million watts of energy capable of emitting an extremely dense blue-colored photon beam for three seconds before recharging its solid-state capacitors, an action that takes nearly two minutes to complete. The only other mounted weapons on the heavy cruiser are four automated 50mm rapid-fire ballistic Vulcan canon mounts referred to as *Peppers*, where each mount holds two canons which rise out from the hull in order to fire armor-piercing rounds in 10 round bursts per canon. Two of the canon mounts are located on the top hull of the ship, one in front of the command bridge and the other behind the radio shack, with the other two in the same positions on the bottom hull. Each individual mount is connected directly to the main corridor with their own access corridor and, due to computerized control, are not airlocked.

The entire hull of the SSHC-20 is composed of a series of contoured hexagon-shaped composite plates bolted to the heavy cruiser's skeleton to simplify replacement of damaged surfaces. The SSHC-20 is also the first ship to adopt the concept of the Aegis Wing used by Marine Fury Platoons. That is, a large rectangular honeycomb section on the top and bottom hull were built so that every other hexagon hull plate in that section, each containing a propulsion and remote guidance system, can be ejected and moved in space to shield another part of the heavy cruiser or even other ships. While the SSHC-10, the first of the Wolf-class cruisers, is the same in size and uses contoured hexagon-shaped hull plates like the SSHC-20, it does not have eject-able hull plates. Additionally, the SSHC-10 only has a compliment of thirteen fighters making for a much more spacious launch bay and does not have a Deus Vox weapon. Instead, in its place, is a second Penlight laser weapon system.

A commonality that the SSHC-10 and SSHC-20 share are the single-pilot manned fighters, nicknamed *Beer Cans* due to their resemblance to an actual beer can. The shape of the fighter is that of a thick-walled cylinder and flat on both ends with a length of 5 meters and a diameter of 2 meters. Its airlock, located at the rear within the circular eighteen-inch-thick wall bearing the directional nozzles of eight liquid fuel thrusters, opens up into a small cabin scarcely five feet in length. The cabin's circular wall is covered throughout by a wide variety of inset control modules, indicator lights and switches while directly in front of the harnessed flight chair with a joystick at the end of each arm rest, is the circular high-resolution flat panel display reaching from one side of the circular cabin to the other. A front, rear and six body cameras equally dispersed around the fighter send their video output to a hardware module plugged into the display, allowing the pilot to see anywhere around the ship without needing a window to look through. The circular display itself is bolted to a four-inch-thick armored separation wall where the remaining space of the cylindrical fighter is filled with liquid fuel cells, an oxygenation and filtering unit and the weapon systems. The fighter is capable of carrying one four-foot-long missile dropped through a long, slender retractable door in the cylinder's wall where, after being ejected, a close proximity guidance system aboard the fighter starts the missile's nozzle-vectored thruster and guides it to the target. The remaining weapon system is a belt-fed 12mm rapid-fire dual Vulcan canon, one on each side of the circular wall whose rifled barrel ends only become visible from the front of the fighter just before they fire where a circular cover plate slides back and forth momentarily exposing a hole at the bow of the fighter in front of each canon.

The other commonality between the two large space vessels, and actually used throughout the protectorate space fleet for Earth, is the emblem emblazoned on all spacecraft and threaded into insignia patches. The stencil design emblem is the outline of two square top Iberian shields of the 15th century with a rounded bottom, one within the other to form a border for text, and inside the innermost shield that of the roaring face of a winged lion with spreading wings behind it reaching upward with a protective paw on the globe of Earth to its front. The text within the border is read clockwise beginning at the shield's top with one word printed on each side reading, *Earthly – Power – Justice*. Together the emblem represents the strength and justice of Earth's protection and its connection with the divine realm – the realm of infinite space the fleet operated from.

General Lowinsky raised an eyebrow and mused, "I'll have to get a taste of your martian food sometime. It's got to be better than what the rumors say down here of it being cardboard-ary in taste."

Marshal Ironhook laughed, "I'm afraid those rumors may be true. Eating some of the slop around here requires a rigorously trained palate."

The general nodded but then the expression on his face became serious, "I have just received credible information from an insider source that there is an alien base on the far side of the Moon, marshal."

The marshal crooked his head and smirked, "That's preposterous! The fleet has transited past the Moon several times now and seen nothing. Who's saying this, some ex-government disgruntled employee or contractor with their own whacked out influencer brand?"

"I'm afraid not, Victor." General Lowinsky responded gently, "I will send you some of the intel that I have now. I will be getting exact lunar coordinates for you shortly."

"Well," the marshal said after thinking for a moment, "we've laser-mapped the Moon's surface and completed ground-penetrating radar surveys of areas of interest but not found anything anomalous in nature."

"Regardless, being alien in nature and those aliens still living today…I would assume they have a shielding mechanism over the base to evade detection."

The marshal looked down briefly, giving it consideration.

"Can you move some of your assets near the Moon so when the lunar coordinates are received, the target zone can be searched?" General Lowinsky ordered, in the form of a question.

"Immediately, general." Marshal Ironhook responded, "I'm actually half-way to Earth now from the L4 base on my way to L5. It would be a great opportunity for my training wing to break from the standard transit route to orbit near the Earth and Moon for a while. Being that close I may click some photos myself."

"Excellent, marshal." General Lowinsky said but cautioned, "Reportedly the alien base is dormant but, just to be safe given the tempo of things down here on the ground, use caution."

"Understood. If we do find something, what's the word?"

"Isolate and capture if possible…there's a lot of tech I'd love to get my hands on." General Lowinsky admitted, "But if that's not possible then vaporize the area."

"Affirmative. I'll position the SSHC-20 in high-Earth orbit as a reinforcement element for the SSHC-10 that will keep a 50-kilometer distance from the Moon…close enough to ingress, or egress depending on how the situation develops." Marshal Ironhook suggested.

"Great, marshal." General Lowinsky said as he sent additional information, "Out."

After slowly closing the lid of the laptop the general reached over and grabbed the flexible forearm display only to release it a few seconds later, remembering he had yet one final task that remained.

After drinking from the water bottle and getting up and placing it back inside the mini-fridge he moved to an ordinance cabinet and withdrew an olive green colored strapped bag and unzipped it on the nearby counter top. Then he grabbed three black thermite cubes fitted with remote trigger plugs and slid them into the bag. After that he took three remote detonator modules and placed them into the bag. Finally, he withdrew the remote detonator trigger from the cabinet and closed the door, pausing to look at the trigger wondering if he should commit to destroying what remained of Janus's robotic body. Sighing to himself, he slipped the trigger into the bag and zipped the bag shut as he exited the command vehicle and proceeded to Janus's position in the debris field.

Once the general reached Janus just as the Sun began its descent towards the western dunes, he beckoned, "Janus? Janus!"

The still form of Janus did not respond. For several minutes the general reconsidered seizing the remains of the cyborg to reverse engineer it and, at least, bring the miliary to parity with what had been fashioned beyond its purview. And, again, he speculated as to what additional value the artificial intelligence may provide beyond the location of the lunar base since the alien's terrestrial base had been revealed and was being acted upon. Then he remembered that Janus mentioned it was using a fifth-generation cyborg, comparing it to what the military currently possessed. He reasoned that insinuated the cyborg was manufactured and, if it was manufactured, then somewhere out there schematics and revisions already existed meaning the body before him was losing practical value and the time-consuming reverse engineering process would not achieve the parity he sought. Instead, it would be more practical to search the corporate landscape to find those schematics and profiling the board members to determine their motives and potentially other advanced technology that may have been concealed within other corporations or shell constructs they were involved in. Yet, even that objective may be rapidly achieved with Janus's participation…the general had been impressed with the artificial intelligence's ability to infiltrate and sweep even the most hardened and remote military installations of its most secret data…most likely it had already swept the corporate edifices of data. And, that meant the one corporate or military entity that managed Janus could single-handedly control the fate of other corporations, militaries, governments and peoples at will and without restriction. That is, provided there was no other artificial intelligence equal to oppose its actions that could act as swiftly or, perhaps a more effective tactic, an opposing artificial intelligence capable of influencing the former to maneuver and use directly against its controlling interests.

At last, the general committed himself to a decision and a probable but clouded path forward.

"Man, the secrets I could learn from taking you apart." the general said lowly, still lamenting what he was about to do.

After unzipping the bag, he connected each remote detonator to a thermite cube and then placed a cube on the forehead of the cyborg, one just below the neckline and a third on top of the abdomen. Then he retreated out of the immediate area to a position where he could still see the overturned generator and withdrew the trigger.

"But my word is my word, Janus." General Lowinsky said sternly to himself, "Pray you don't fuck me over."

With that he switched on the device and pressed the trigger. Immediately three bursts of intense light sprang out from the debris and smoke began bellowing out from its midst as the raging heat from the thermite began consuming everything around it.

Chapter Eleven

"Sir!" Lieutenant Boleman, the weapons officer, announced as he eyed the readouts from the Spectrotron, "The target has stopped moving."

Captain Keech glanced down at the command display before him, "Is the target doing anything at all?"

The weapons officer pressed a few buttons to adjust energy emission sensor readings from the Spectrotron and said, "There is no physical movement but I'm picking up some faint energy fluxuations now."

"Full stop." The captain ordered, unwilling to close on the target without first getting a threat assessment of what was transpiring.

"We are one thousand-one hundred meters out from the target, captain. Should we destroy it now?" the XO asked, looking at the captain, concerned that they may not get another opportunity to launch an attack if the target had discovered them or did something radical.

The captain raised his hand, preferring to wait until they were deeper when the submarine could move faster before launching an attack, and said, "Threat assessment, lieutenant."

Lieutenant Boleman busily brought up other data using the keypads in front of him, reviewing a wide range of data points. After a few moments he responded, "The fluxuations are not building in intensity…and…they are not focused on our position."

The captain lowered his hand, "Assessment?"

First Lieutenant Ligshin looked over at the weapons officer. It didn't usually take so long for Lieutenant Boleman to reach a definitive conclusion.

The lieutenant compared some other data and finally said, "No present threat."

"Great." Captain Keech grunted in relief, "Stand position. Resume pursuit once target swims."

"But." the weapons officer said reluctantly, "If I'm seeing these readings correctly, the weak energy signals appear to be going toward the surface. Very strange."

Captain Keech examined the readouts on the display which were strange but seemed inconsequential. Then he said, "Keep an eye on it, lieutenant, and call out if the threat changes."

"Yes, sir."

Sitting in an old cushioned chair near the cobblestone fireplace, flames dancing in its midst, Ferina asked, "Now that our master has been freed, can we go to see him?"

She reached over and picked up an EB-2120 multi-band radio by its top handle from the small square table next to her and turned the silver dial to the FM band.

Lucy, sitting in an antique wooden chair nearby in the aged single floor house comprised of just five rooms deep in the wooded outskirts of Taraz, turned her head in

Ferina's direction and said, "One just does not go see our master. Maybe, if you are lucky...and special...you may get the chance but I would not count on it."

Ferina sighed in disgust, "We should not have to be limited to blood sacrifice, conjuring and seance in order to communicate with him now that he's free."

Lucy squinted at Ferina and hissed, "Careful. None of us make demands, initiate."

Ferina looked over at Lucy apprehensively.

Shortly thereafter Lucy disappeared into the adjoining kitchen, grabbed a ceramic cup and filled it with an exotic coffee spiked with wormwood absinthe and returned to the chair.

After taking a sip of the invigorating concoction Lucy exhaled with pleasure, "Besides. It has been this way for generations. Really, I think, as far back as anyone can remember."

Acutely aware it was unwise of her to say anything further on the subject, Ferina crossed her arms briefly but then scooped up the radio, turning the center dial for volume and then turned the tuning dial to its right until she heard commentary.

"And why can't we get a television in here like everyone else." Ferina vented in an even tone.

Lucy rolled her eyes and took another sip, not interested in discussing materialistic desire.

"In what scientists are calling a one in a million event, and what they cannot explain, is unusual volcanic activity that has sprung up in several places around the world." the female broadcaster said.

After a short pause the broadcaster continued, "They include Mount Fuji, Mount Eccles, West Eifel range, Ojos del Salado and Mount Saint Helens."

The broadcaster cleared her throat, "Scientists said that most of those volcanoes always have some sign of activity but what makes this event unique is that all of them have begun to vent more volcanic gas than is normal."

"They also say there's been no ash plumes or any indications that they will actually erupt any time soon. We will be following up on this story and keep you updated." the broadcaster reassured, "Keep it tuned right here on the Hot Ears radio channel…your ear masseuse on the FM dial."

Ferina looked at Lucy curiously, "Is this a sign from him of something coming?"

Lucy kept her gaze on the fire, considering what she knew and responded, "A sign from our master? No. I don't think things work like that."

After a deep yawn Ferina agreed, "I suppose you are right. If he knew the future I guess he would not have allowed himself to be imprisoned."

"Maybe." Lucy half-agreed, "Unless he saw the future and planned to be locked up for something greater further in the future."

The wooden chair creaked as Lucy changed her position, "Anyway, I can't imagine why a sign would be needed for all the people around the world who have never heard of him. And those that do know, like us, do not need a sign."

Ferina pointed her finger in the air and said, "Maybe it is not a sign…but something to stir up fear."

"There, off ahead." The driver of the black van, loaded with six tactically dressed mercenaries, said toward Heliaar who was in the passenger seat, "That old house is where your marks went."

Neglected yet still functional, the house had been passed down through the generations following its initial erection over the site of a massive slaughter of innocents during one of the conquests of foreign invaders keen on controlling the ancient city. To this day their remains lay buried deep within the darkened soil underneath the house's foundation.

"Turn off the lights!" Heliaar demanded as he sat up straight in the seat. Shortly after the driver flipped off the headlights, the second van behind them did the same.

"Pull over here." Heliaar ordered.

After the two vans did so, approximately two hundred meters from the house, he exited the van and signaled for the others to get out.

The twelve mercenaries got out of the two vans and collected near Heliaar, some slinging their assault rifles while others gripped theirs across the front of their ballistic vests, barrels pointed towards the ground.

"You all know why we are here tonight gents." Heliaar opened while he looked around at the eyes of the mercenaries, "This is a smash and grab op. No heroics and no sheeple shearing…"

A few of the more seasoned mercenaries chuckled, interrupting Heliaar. Sheeple shearing was code for slaughtering soft targets, like civilians.

Heliaar frowned and placed his hands on his hips, glaring at the mercenaries until they dropped their smiles and the chuckling subsided.

"I repeat. No shearing unless I give the order. Got it?"

The mercenaries nodded.

Pointing toward Team one, Heliaar said, "Team one, circle around the back and wait for Team two and I to breach front. If nobody comes out the back in ten, breach, assess and act. We clear?"

"Clear." several of the mercenaries responded.

"A-fucking-mazing." Heliaar responded in an unenthused tone, glancing down toward his feet.

Turning toward the house, Heliaar motioned forward with his hand and said, "Okay Team one. Let's go!"

Team one readied their assault rifles and moved quickly to some trees and brush and then slowed to minimize being heard, creeping around to the rear of the house. After Heliaar spotted their movement toward the house, he turned his head over to Team two and said, "Team two. On me!"

Team two readied their weapons and lurched forward, following closely behind Heliaar, maintaining a single-file line until they reached the front of the house and positioned themselves to the left of the door, the only area without a window.

After Heliaar nodded at Team two he moved directly in front of the paint-chipped door, tensed up and then bolted forward using his leg to bust the door open near its handle. Chunks and splinters of wood burst into the small kitchenette he found himself in, instinctively lifting a shoulder to block the door from jumping back at him while scanning around the room from right to left into an open smaller room for sleeping. Devoid of the marks he signaled for Team two to move into the house and followed them.

Then, suddenly, just as one of the mercenaries cleared the doorway of the adjacent room, the nearest mercenary was violently yanked out of sight and heaved against an unseen wall, impacting it with such force that the crack of his neck was heard throughout the house, followed by the dull thud of his lifeless body and rifle hitting the wooden floorboards.

The next two mercenaries spotted Lucy just as she was turning toward them and rushed her, driving her back against the same wall. Despite their strength, neither could free their hands to pull zip ties and restrain the enraged female. Two more mercenaries from Team two rushed over to assist, one of them able to pull out their restraints while the last, along with Heliaar, sprinted toward Ferina who shouted something unrecognizable in their direction and raised a hand to claw at Heliaar's face. While Heliaar was able to dodge the hand as it came down upon him with blinding speed, he lost his footing on the rug beneath him and fell forward, bear hugging Ferina's waist and pressing her into the wall near the fireplace. A few hot embers jumped out of the crackling fire into the room just as the last mercenary reached forward to clamp on to Ferina's hand and restrain her. At that very same moment, the rear door was breached and the mercenaries from Team one began rushing in. A shot rang out just as they cleared the small entryway not far from the main room.

In the bathroom, next to the main room, Holly watched those few seconds through a splintered opening in the door with absolute horror, recognizing the bodyguard that had been with Michelle at the conference. Knowing with certainty that their end was at hand, she closed her eyes and felt the presence of everything around her, beckoning with all her heart and creating a mental vision of what she had seen, "Erinyes Mephistopha! I beg you! Help your servant against this transgression. Mephistopha!"

Having wrestled Ferina to the floor and planted his muscular knee on her back Heliaar helplessly watched as the other mercenaries toiled to keep Lucy under control with two of them now clutching her arm that was holding a 9mm pistol. Somehow she had managed to wrest it from one of the mercenaries and shot him, his body slowly crumpling over onto the floor while the others struggled with her.

Just as the mercenary finished zip tying Ferina, Heliaar heard the shouts from the bathroom and ordered, "Check that out!"

The mercenary charged the door and broke it open just as Team one began entering the main room. Stumbling forward he caught himself and slowly looked up at Holly floating above him near the ceiling, almost mesmerized by the deep, polished blackness of her eyes.

"You should know better than to attack my faithful servants." Holly began in an unearthly deep tone causing Heliaar and several of the other mercenaries to look in her direction, "The cursed Serpqhtaq shall not have them."

None of the mercenaries, not even Heliaar, had the faintest idea what Holly was referring to but an ebb of fear began to grow within them at the unnatural sight and that bone-tingling voice.

"But," Holly smiled, raising her hands and floating towards them, "I shall have you, tough and leathery you may be."

Heliaar withdrew a massive, wide-hooked blade from his boot and furiously ordered, "Kill these bitches!" With all his strength he pointed the blade toward the small of Ferina's back and savagely drove it into her, shattering her moist but solid vertebrae, nerve column and on through her intestines, the grotesque sounds of squirting blood and flesh and bone being torn apart echoing in his ears while he felt her muscles beneath his knee bind together in vain to cling to life, the hooked blade not stopping until it plowed through the floorboard and became lodged in it. A moment passed and, as if her muscles were putty, gave way to his weight.

While Heliaar reached across Ferina's limp body for the assault rifle lying nearby, the unencumbered mercenaries switched off their safeties and began raising their assault rifles toward Holly. In a split second, Holly reached down and grabbed the mercenary in the bathroom and hurled him against the others, causing them to fall over and into Lucy's captors who lost grip of her arm. In the next instant, Holly inverted herself onto the ceiling and ran upon it into the other room as if she were a clumsy dog.

Just as some of the mercenaries were gaining their feet Holly looked up, down toward them and whispered, "Dinner time."

With that she lurched herself into the midst of them and with inhuman strength ripped into the ballistic vests of the nearest mercenaries to withdraw handfuls of flesh and bone that she flung behind her. Without pause she rushed upon three others and ripped their heads and parts of their spinal column from their bodies, slinging them randomly throughout the room. By the time Lucy had managed to move her arm bearing the 9mm pistol at the mercenary before her, Holly pounced upon the remaining mercenaries, plunging her fists into their skulls, thick bursts of blood and grey matter spraying into the air.

As Lucy began slowly pulling back on the trigger, like time itself had slowed down, Holly bolted over behind the last mercenary and paused to look at Lucy. With a slight grin Holly quelled her thirst for fear and whispered, "I shall grant you this pleasure my dear."

So fast was Holly that by the time the shot from the pistol had rung out, the spinning bullet burrowing deep into the mercenary's head, she had yanked the assault rifle from Heliaar's grasp and held him by the neck against the bathroom wall, the bodies of the mercenaries and their missing parts falling to the floor and saturating the ancient wood with fresh, warm blood behind her. Although muffled and partially covered by the body of a mercenary, music from the radio whispered through the room.

"I told you," Holly rumbled at Heliaar, raising herself into the air so that she could look squarely into his eyes while, at the same time, maintaining her iron grip around his neck, "you shall not have my servants."

Dropping the assault rifle, Holly placed her hand upon Heliaar's head and said, "You broke that command. Now your soul, your very essence, is mine."

An intense light erupted from Holly's hand cupped around Heliaar's head, so bright that Lucy had to shield her eyes with her arm to keep herself from being blinded. A moment later the light vanished and Holly released the limp body of Heliaar, the black imprint of her hand on his head still smoldering, faint threads of smoke rising from it.

Holly lowered herself to stand on the floor, turned toward Ferina and walked up to her, kneeling at her side and looking at the blade's big handle sticking out of her back.

"Have faith in this one, Lucy." Holly said quietly without looking at Lucy as she wrapped her fingers around the blade's handle, "She has great potential to nurture fear in others."

Effortlessly withdrawing the hooked blade from Ferina's body and dropping it next to her, Holly broke the restraint and then gently placed a hand on Ferina's head and the other on the gaping wound and said, "And you, my young rebellious one. You have important work yet to do."

Closing her eyes and tilting her head back, Holly steadily exhaled, uttering an incantation from the time of the First Adam as a yellowish-white glow pulsed out from her hands and flowed into Ferina's body, healing her mortal wounds. Suddenly the body of Ferina convulsed and she twisted onto her side, raising her arm into the air and gasping for breath as if she had been held under water for too long.

After she caught her breath and slowly sat up next to Holly, Holly gently turned Ferina's face toward her and smiled.

Ferina, still disoriented from resurrection, gazed into Holly's shiny black eyes with deep gratitude, unable to form words with her mouth to speak.

"I heard you, my Ferina. I have come so that you can look upon me and know that it is I." Holly confided, withdrawing her hand from Ferina's face.

After pulling back several inches, and with deep satisfaction, Holly said, "I have had my fill of fear this day."

Then Holly collapsed onto the floor, unconscious, no longer possessed by the Arch-Demon itself…a rare gift few followers would ever receive.

"Sir!" Lieutenant Boleman announced, "the target has resumed its course."

"Excellent." Captain Keech said, "Continue pursuit and maintain distance."

Chapter Twelve

Under the black order of Admiral Octoimus the Marine Fury squad, comprised of three fire teams of three soldiers and assigned the name Able Reaper, had been discreetly ferried in a S351 Nemesis miniature submarine just twelve meters in length, from their CVN-79 aircraft carrier, to an awaiting Blackhawk parked at an otherwise inaccessible piece of Italy's shoreline. From there, the modified Blackhawk took them deep into the forests of the Rhätikon Mountains.

Once at the drop location the squad repelled out of the helicopter into the dense forest five kilometers from the alleged alien base. Under radio silence and with purpose they covered that distance and stopped approximately five hundred meters out, unable to see anything through the trees. One of the marines had climbed a tree to confirm a visual sighting of the base since, at that distance, they should have glimpsed a light or heard some sound from people or equipment. But there was nothing. Just more forest and the occasional squawking of birds around them.

The marine signaled with his hand down toward the sergeant that nothing could be seen.

Sergeant Quayle looked down with disgust and signaled for the other two fire team leaders, also sergeants, to his position. In the multiple fire team configuration the Marine Fury Corp had developed, while each team had a lead sergeant, on a multi-team deployment, fire team one's sergeant would always be the squad leader and if incapacitated then fire team two's sergeant would assume the squad leader position, continuing as such to the last team. As well, following squad leader succession, the remaining members of the fire team would be automatically folded into the ranks of the next fire team. The common sergeant rank across fire teams also kept it simple for the soldiers to know who to defer to in the heat of combat and rapidly changing battlefield conditions.

After they collected, crouched down, at the sergeant's position and rested on a knee he said, "The target base has not been spotted and we are almost on top of it. In fact, from up there," the sergeant pointed toward the soldier high up in the tree, "the tree canopy is not broken, not even for roads."

"Maybe the intel is bad." Sergeant Biggs of Fire Team Two said. It wouldn't have been the first time for him.

Sergeant Quayle turned his forearm and reactivated the low-light setting on the Scalpel bound to his bio-electric field so the other two sergeants could view it, even though each of them also had a Scalpel.

"The sky link says it should be right over there." the sergeant confirmed, "Only thing I can guess is that there is some really good camo netting concealing the base, including heat signatures, or…"

"The base is underground which could be why the sky link is not showing us the base." Sergeant Cookem of Fire Team Three injected.

Sergeant Quayle nodded in agreement and looked at Sergeant Biggs, "If we can confirm neither of those is the case then we've got bad intel and this whole field trip was for nothing."

"Not a total loss, sergeant. I don't know about you but hiking around in this forest was on my bucket list." Sergeant Cookem joked.

Sergeant Biggs cracked a grin.

"Maintain our triangle fire team formation. I will scout ahead and see what I can find." Sergeant Quayle ordered, turning toward the alleged base location.

"You sure?" Sergeant Biggs asked, "If not your spotter, I could go ahead."

"No," Sergeant Quayle said as he unslung the scoped M249 SPW commonly referred to as M249E4, also issued to all the squad members, "My spotter will relay." The scope, affectionately referred to as the *Snitch* by soldiers who used it, possessed the unique feature of being able to record what the scope was pointed at, and storing that video locally until it was retrieved via a connector port. Once retrieved, the footage recorded could be reviewed allowing analysts to see exactly what the soldier saw through the scope.

The display of the sergeant's Scalpel automatically deactivated, sensing the rotating motion of his forearm away from its viewing position.

"Roger that." the sergeants responded and then moved back toward their respective fire team position in the triangle formation.

Sergeant Quayle signaled his team that he was moving ahead and to watch the spotter in the tree for further action.

Then, while crouched down, the sergeant began moving through the trees in front of the squad.

After settling next to the base of a tree just fifty meters from the target coordinates, Sergeant Quayle scanned the forest in front of him. Nothing was out of place and nothing appeared artificial. Along the forest floor he didn't find any snorkel or vent, nor any hatch from which to enter or exit an underground base.

Sighing, the sergeant said to himself, "Bad intel after all."

Then, just as he started to reposition himself to return to the squad, he saw a dark arched doorway appear he estimated to be five meters tall and three meters wide.

"Ho, now that is hook." he whispered to himself, raising his SPW to get a closer look at the doorway with his scope.

After clicking the record button located on the scope, he slowly swept the SPW from one side of the doorway to the other. As the scope recorded what he pointed it at, he spotted four scattered Serpqhtaq and, beyond them, rounded structures and what appeared to be fern plants. Then he muttered, "What…the…actual. Fuck."

Shortly thereafter he saw the leading edge of a Serpqhtaq Silcraft appear at the edge of the doorway and as it moved into it, more and more of the Silcraft become visible, as if it was drifting past a wall into the open. In fact, what was happening was that, as the Silcraft entered into the shielded perimeter of the base, the Silcraft's shield was being de-harmonized in small sections. Once completely inside the shield perimeter, the Silcraft's shield would be offline.

After the craft had entered, the doorway drifted down toward the forest's floor, disappearing from sight. Sergeant Quayle stopped the recording and leaned on the tree, both excited and overwhelmed at what he just witnessed.

"I can't believe it." he said to himself as he turned toward the squad's location and glanced back where the doorway had been, "That shit is real."

Swiftly the sergeant worked his way back to the squad and said to the corporal in his fire team, "Break out the laser communicator and set it up."

"Yes, sergeant." the corporal responded, pulling out a small module from a tactical sling-bag and proceeding to set it up and orient it to the sky overhead.

As he did that, Sergeant Quayle pulled a thin cable from his cargo pocket and plugged in one end to the port on the scope and waited for the corporal.

Once a small green light became visible from beneath a pinhole in the module, the corporal said, "Mission link ready."

Sergeant Quayle plugged in the other end of the cable to the laser module and pressed the button labeled SND. A light beneath another pinhole on the module illuminated an orange color indicating a transfer was taking place. Hardly a second later, the light's color changed to green, blinking five times before it turned off, indicating the transfer had completed.

The sergeant slowly unplugged the cable and stuffed it back into his pocket, "Wait until they see that shit."

"Stow it until the next com window."

"Roger." the corporal replied.

Looking up at the spotter, Sergeant Quayle waited until he looked down and then signaled for him to exit his position. Once the soldier did so and took a knee near the sergeant he asked, "You see anything?"

"No sergeant. Just a lot of trees and some birds doing bird things."

"Yeah." Sergeant Quayle smirked, "Didn't think you would. We are up against some crazy shit."

Aboard the Serpqhtaq Silcraft, one-quarter the size of a Midcraft that it was designed after and only capable of carrying four Serpqhtaq, Michelle questioned herself as to why she had been picked up from Taraz following the conference's end. All she could think was it had to do with the report she had sent late into the evening the previous day.

Michelle glanced at the Serpqhtaq pilot in front of her and then through the front window. The Silcraft was traveling so fast that everything outside of it appeared to her as blurs of color. Even though the Silcraft darted up and down and from one side to the other occasionally, she couldn't feel the sudden shifts.

Abruptly the velocity of the Silcraft slowed to a mere fifty knots, allowing her to clearly see the forest they were flying over. A few seconds later the Silcraft stopped moving forward and, instead, descended into the trees until it came within two meters of the forest floor. There, the pilot made some selections with the levitating sphere before him and, directly in front of the Silcraft, an arched entryway rose from the forest floor. Looking into the entryway, Michelle saw the movement of Serpqhtaq and that of various structures.

After the Silcraft passed through the base's shield boundary, it turned right toward a small open bay area where a second Silcraft was parked. Once the craft stopped the Serpqhtaq lowered the rear ramp and said, "You may exit."

Michelle looked at the pilot as he rose and turned toward her, reluctant to leave the craft. But, realizing she had no choice in the matter she briefly closed her eyes, exhaled and rose to walk down the ramp. Curiously she looked to her left, toward the direction they had come from but did not see the archway. Or any structure for an archway. Or even a control panel that she could use to flee the area if she needed to. Instead, as she looked around herself along the shield's boundary, all she saw was the forest and the slight movement of branches and leaves from a passing breeze. Yet she felt no breeze nor any wind. Not even the chirp of a bird or the other sounds the forest makes.

After the pilot stopped next to her, he extended his long, slender arm to her right and said, "Regnum is this way, Representative."

Michelle glanced at him for a split second and then began walking in the direction he had suggested. As she continued to familiarize herself with the area she was in she realized, after spotting very few thin beams bowing up into the air far above her and then down the opposite side, she was inside of some large dome that she could not see from the outside but, amazingly, she could see outside into the forest and the sky above.

Just as she came upon a transport plate, suspended a few inches above the smooth, crystallized earth which formed the floor of the base and had somehow integrated the recognizable structures of leaves and other vegetation below its surface, the pilot raised his hand in front of her and said, "Wait."

After the pilot stepped onto the oval-shaped standing plate, he motioned for her to step onto it. Once she did he turned back and a series of triangles, arranged in a straight line, lit up along the floor in front of them. Then they shot forward for no more than two seconds before it stopped. Amazed, she turned to look back behind them realizing they had just traveled the length of a few football fields and she didn't feel anything at all. Even her hair was undisturbed.

"Please come this way." the pilot said and again motioned to their right, into a long corridor.

After Michelle stepped off of the transport plate, still smiling from the experience, the pilot followed and began walking with her down the corridor.

"Why am I here?" Michelle finally asked, her nervousness getting the best of her.

The pilot tilted his head toward her for a moment wondering why she would ask that question, having already stated the answer when he had picked her up. Politely he replied, "Regnum has asked to see you."

"You do not know the reason why?"

"No." the pilot said, looking forward again.

Just as they exited the corridor and entered the command center, Michelle recognized the figure of Regnum off ahead near a command kiosk, still apprehensive as to what was going to become of her.

"Commander." the pilot called out, getting Regnum's attention, "The Representative is here."

Regnum nodded, turned toward Michelle and said, "Thank you. Michelle, it is great to see you again."

Michelle looked around slowly, still nervous that she had been brought to the base, but said, "Good to see you Regnum…thanks for bringing me here?"

Regnum paused to look at her, recognizing the nervous reaction. Through past cycles he had seen the same reaction in others. Despite thousands of years between them, she was the same. Still a hair's breadth from her primal nature.

"Yes," Regnum soothed as he took a few steps in her direction, "please come."

Michelle forced herself to relax a little and she walked over to him while looking around at the high-technology equipment and other Serpqhtaq attending to it.

"What has it been?" Regnum asked as he walked toward two dark-green cushioned chairs, "Ten years since we last met in person?"

After he sat in one of the chairs, Michelle sat in the other and said, "Yes. I believe that is right. And you look the same."

"Indeed. You are looking beautiful as ever, too." Regnum smiled, noticing her nervousness was slowly abating.

"Well thank you. And thanks for selecting me to be a Representative." Michelle said with a relaxed posture.

Regnum gently pointed at her and said, "You were, and still are, the right person for the job. I would not have it any other way."

Thank god.' Michelle thought to herself, relieved she was going to continue to live. In return she smiled at Regnum with gratitude.

Regnum winked at her and said, "I read your report from your attendance of the Fah conference."

"Yes." Michelle said, mentally readying herself to answer any questions he had on the subject.

"What was your impression of it? You think we should shift our attention to it instead of Europe now that it is firmly under our control?" Regnum said, although he already knew the planet was about to endure another shift from the Twin star that would eliminate most of its lifeforms.

"I was thinking about that actually. Europe, I mean." Michelle began, "We've corrupted and captured all the top posts across government and corporate boards. But I was thinking about that. The sheer volume of resources that we have to spend to maintain that control is, well, hideous."

Regnum, slightly intrigued even though resource expenditure was of little importance to him as long as control was achieved, said, "Yes?"

"I can imagine all the things we could do if we didn't have to burn through those resources." Michelle said in a slightly excited tone of voice, "With the sixth-generation cyborg technology that we now have, and the saturation of our central artificial intelligence grid across the planet…I think it is an excellent time to retire all of those people."

"What would you like to do then?" Regnum asked. He wanted to see where she was going, in her own words.

"For meeting events use our cyborgs to replace every one of them. And have each cyborg controlled by our AI which already has their entire life histories down to the most finite detail." Michelle suggested, "And, nowadays, where the masses rarely go to see their rulers for anything, AI can digitize their likenesses, voices and mannerisms so convincingly they would believe what they saw was real. Just as real as if they were in front of one of our cyborgs."

"I agree. The resource expenditure on cyborgs and AI is a pittance compared to the expenditure on all those human dog kings and all the networks in place to monitor them constantly to ensure they do not drift from their assigned paths." Regnum said honestly, "They are just meat sacks eager for trinkets, like the rest of the sheep."

Michelle nodded.

"Though," Regnum added, "our AI grid has significantly enhanced surveillance so even the human monitoring networks will soon reach its end."

"Since our cyborgs do not share human traits and are controlled by us, more of the AI grid can be focused further on controlling humans." Michelle pointed out.

"Draw up your replacement plan. I will have a look at it." Regnum said. He already knew something like that would work because it had already been used on Origarperii.

"Thank you." Michelle smiled with glee.

"Funny. That brings me to another question." Regnum said, recalling that an Archgen had been freed from its confines and may now threaten his and the presence of other Serpqhtaq on the planet, "You have overseen the rollout of our biologics assimilation project into human systems. What is your assessment as to where it stands today?"

Michelle took a deep breath and exhaled slowly, unprepared to cover that subject.

"That, as you know, has been a decade-long endeavor. The introduction of MSI nano-particulate structures into natural lifeforms has approximately ninety-five percent coverage. Coverage in humans is around eighty percent." Michelle recited from memory, "I think, if we can further constrain the availability of food sources to those we control containing the structures, we can up that figure a few percentage points."

The MSI nano-particulate Michelle was referring to, and one that Regnum and others had refined over the past few cycles, stood for Molecular Severance Induction, and was unique in that once inserted into a living host, would replicate itself using the host's own replication process and mineral resources but otherwise lay dormant. Once activated by a specific electromagnetic frequency band it would resonate with water molecules to transform them into air and hydrogen gases. The transformation, among other things, lead to involuntary, and severe, body-wide dehydration so rapidly that most living hosts would enter a state of shock and paralysis. However, with too much stimulus, the nano-particulates had proved to become unstable in living hosts.

"That's great, Michelle." Regnum said maneuvering to the real reason for their meeting, "That brings me back to one other thing in your last report."

"Sure." Michelle said openly, happy to be back on a subject she had committed to recent memory.

"You wrote of your encounter with three Fah members." Regnum specified, looking upward momentarily, "Holly, Lucy and Ferina. And you said they were the usurper leaders. But you didn't say why you reached that conclusion."

Michelle shifted in the chair because she had purposefully left that part out. Part of her was still tempted by their offer and hoped to somehow take advantage of it at some point in the future. Another part of her, however, believed that if she exposed the plot that she would be looked upon favorably and granted more control. More control that she could use without the complications of usurper involvement, in a devious fashion if needed, to assume Regnum's position.

Michelle clasped her hands together and admitted, "They offered me their assistance in achieving greater control. But they didn't really mention how, as outsiders really, just how they could do that. Without anything solid I considered their offer as nothing more than a ploy to get me involved as a tool for their own ends. With nothing actionable, I left it out."

"Do you think there are others of similar position among us still, or were there only those three leaders?"

Michelle thought for a moment and posited, "I would assume there are still a few others of that rank out there. With a lot of the lower rank usurpers having been caught with the help of Janus, I think the remaining leaders will have to take more risks like those three did to keep their plans moving. And, when they make a mistake, we will be able to spot them faster."

That was exactly what Regnum hoped she would say. After mentally issuing a command through one of his augments, a small metallic sphere from a nearby kiosk activated, moving through the air to stop near Michelle where it hovered in place, slowly rotating.

Michelle instinctively eyed the sphere and turned back toward Regnum.

"I agree with you, Michelle. That is why I tasked Heliaar with apprehending the trio." Regnum said as he looked at the rotating sphere, "With the addition of their biological mechanics in addition to those we've already collected from the low rank usurpers, I anticipate very soon to discover the common link between them that allows them to coordinate their actions."

Michelle's expression changed to one of surprise, unaware that such a thing was possible, "You mean like an implant of some type?"

Regnum looked back at Michelle, "In a manner of speaking. But we've not found any implants, nor any communication devices common to all of the usurpers so they must be using some other form of communication. Perhaps, even, just one way…from the leaders to the low ranked acting as receivers."

"Telepathy?" Michelle wondered.

"That is the hypothesis." Regnum said, "If we can identify the energy characteristics of the telepathy the leaders are using to send their commands, those patterns can be used to identify all the other usurper leaders the moment they communicate."

"When we've identified the remaining leaders, I was wondering if you could help me take care of them?" Regnum asked directly, with an unspoken goal. The Infinite Horizon interstellar treaty prohibited him from directly acting upon the human species as a whole.

"Of course." Michelle responded, "What is it?"

"Would you be willing to activate the MSI when I've confirmed who all the usurpers are?" Regnum said, casually omitting the fact that he considered all humans to be usurpers to some degree and, more importantly, an energy source that could be denied to the Archgen, thereby weakening it significantly.

"If it means we can finally purge the usurpers from the world we are trying to create, then, yes." Michelle said without reservation, not picking up on the deceptive word-play Regnum used.

"Do you have your silver bracelet?" Regnum asked. The bracelet that Michelle had been given was the same as the one that Benefacta used to communicate with.

"Right here." Michelle said as she pulled up the sleeve on her right arm to show him.

"Excellent." Regnum smiled, "Please hold it out for the sphere."

Once she did so, the sphere stopped rotating and a thin red beam shot out from it and connected with the bracelet, adding the commands and authorization codes needed to initiate MSI activation through a series of hidden Serpqhtaq satellites orbiting the planet. A second later the beam disappeared and the sphere resumed its slow rotation. Having removed his digital fingerprints from the systems around the MSI project, Michelle was now the only one who could activate it.

"When I have them identified, I will give you the order to activate MSI by squeezing the bracelet with your thumb and index finger." Regnum said clearly, "Once activated the usurpers will be incapacitated and we will be able to move in and collect them without losses to our members."

Michelle looked at the bracelet and then pulled her sleeve back down, "Great! What now?"

Regnum stood and motioned toward Benefacta and said, "I'd like for you to stay here for a while in case I need other questions answered. The sphere will accompany you while you are here so you can use Serpqhtaq food generators and things of that nature without one of us being with you to do it."

"Okay." Michelle agreeably nodded. Her new-found importance made her feel ecstatic inside.

"I'm Benefacta." Benefacta said after she stopped near Michelle who was rising out of the chair.

"Hi." Michelle returned, turning toward her.

"Benefacta will answer any questions you may have and show you to your quarters." Regnum said, nodding in her direction.

After they began walking away, Regnum returned to one of the command panels, spotting a message sent from the AI system aboard the Makara who had just begun taking over parts of the AI grid that Janus had been responsible for with the Atlantic region of the planet.

Expanding the message it read, "Aircraft carrier CVN-79 heading SSE launched underwater submarine to position for outpost attack. Forward ships are leading the carrier. Forecasting the attack group will sweep around Italy for the attack from the north end of Italy, east of Slovenia."

"Where did this information originate from?" Regnum asked.

The message shrank and shifted over to reveal the next message that automatically enlarged, "Fah member 13971 on the carrier. Officer rank."

"Send me the coordinates of the carrier and find the source who revealed our base location." Regnum rumbled, perturbed not because the base was going to be attacked by an inferior force, but because someone trusted with that knowledge had revealed it to the humans.

163

"What is the displacement of that ship?"

After a short pause, the message from the AI read, "108,230 long tons."

Regnum grasped a command sphere and transversed a series of the hundred-and sixty-degree menus and found the remote craft launch menu. From there he rotated through the craft inventory the base had at its disposal and selected the Autzcraft with a diameter of fifty meters and a height of ten meters. The Autzcraft was the only flat disc-shaped craft the Serpqhtaq possessed and could only be remotely controlled. As an engineering craft it lacked shields and camouflaging capability. Its purpose was to *atmoform* entire planets. That is, it broke down a wide range of fluids to their gaseous equivalents so rapidly that, given sufficient liquid source material, it could generate an atmosphere for an average sized planet in four months.

Regnum entered a range of parameters to include destination, source liquid, emersion distance, transformation structure desired, and atmoforming duration. Then he launched the Autzcraft through a larger archway in the base's shield to the south of where the Silcraft had entered. The silver-paneled disc, already traveling at 320 knots, cut through trees before it and then rotated upward toward the sky as its elevation increased. Once it had rotated along its axis 90 degrees, as if it were a penny being stood up on its round edge, it shot up to an elevation of five thousand feet before it rotated back 90 degrees and traveled south at its maximum speed of 791 knots. Within minutes it was over the Ligurian Sea.

"Sir, we have an unknown contact at five thousand feet, eight thousand meters out. The IFF cannot classify." the radar Operations Specialist said, examining the radar display screens.

First Officer Bickons turned toward the radar station and asked, "Bearing?"

"Six even on our stern, sir." he replied, but then followed up, "The contact is gone sir."

The first officer grabbed some binoculars and ran over and forced the bridge door open. Stepping outside he began scanning beyond the stern toward the north. Although he scanned the sky he didn't spot any aircraft. But then, just as he began scanning lower and to his left he caught the briefest glimpse of a large silvery disc, perhaps fifteen hundred meters out plow into the ocean and disappear.

The first officer dashed back into the bridge and said, "Contact splashdown at fifteen hundred meters off our stern. Launch a Knighthawk for search and rescue and inform the captain at once."

After the Autzcraft broke through the surface of the ocean, Regnum allowed it to descend and proceed to the destination coordinates, 1100 meters below the aircraft carrier. There he activated it, the disc separating into two equal halves that moved three hundred meters apart where a series of rectangular surfaces along the flat edge of the two discs began, in unison, pulsing sequentially with the left disc pulsing from the south to the north and the right disc pulsing from the north to the south. As the energy levels in the rectangular conduits increased, they began glowing, becoming more and more intense until arcs of electricity began jumping from the glowing surface on the left disc to the glowing surface on the right disc. Within seconds the pulsing became so rapid it appeared that forty-five thick strands of electricity had joined the two halves together. Moments later, at the exact center between the two discs where the energy was the greatest, a brilliant aura formed followed by an extreme excitation of the ocean water between the two discs, producing a vortex and transforming thousands of cubic feet of water per second into extremely hot forms of oxygen and hydrogen that rushed upwards. So much gaseous volume was being created that it looked like an empty column reaching up toward the ocean's surface.

"Sir, we are entering an air plume!" the navigation specialist shouted, "It is massive!"

Just as the first officer began to look over toward him, the ocean around the aircraft carrier exploded hundreds of meters into the air and the ship suddenly barreled downward into the gaseous column below it. Within a few breaths the aircraft carrier disappeared into the depths of the ocean.

His objective a success, Regnum hastily cancelled operation of the atmoforming engine and recalled the Autzcraft causing the ocean water to collapse into the void and narrowly dodging the descending aircraft carrier with aircraft, soldiers, and other material trailing after it.

Chapter Thirteen

"Jacob has returned." Regan remarked with disappointment, looking out of the living room window, spotting the Bronco pull up near the house. She had been looking for Mac's return, not Jacob.

"Took long enough." Bev grumbled to herself, putting down her phone on a small end table and rising from the cushioned, creme-colored chair next to the couch. Though a day had past since they had returned from Arizona, she still had a lingering anger from having to stay at a hotel near the airport under the impression that Jacob was going to pick them up. What made the matter worse is he never texted her back so she reluctantly leaned on Lionak.

Bev marched over and opened the heavy front door, meeting Jacob before he had a chance to select its key from his key chain, "You know how much it cost to stay at the hotel next to the airport because you didn't let us know you could not make it?"

Here we go.' Jacob thought to himself, rolling the keys in his hand to collect them together and then put them in his pocket.

Looking as plainly as he could at Bev in order to keep the confrontation from building, he said, "Sorry about that, honey. I got held up. And, some bad news."

Bev squinted angrily at him for a moment, wanting the emotional tension in the air to grow but relented, exhaling slowly and moving aside to allow him to enter, "What happened?"

Jacob waved at Regan, and then entered into the dining room, making his way to the refrigerator, "Yeah. The base was a waste."

Spewge, having heard Jacob's voice, darted into the kitchen area, excited to see him.

Bev closed the door and strode into the living room, "What do you mean?"

After opening a sealed energy drink and drinking from it, he turned toward her and said, "I could not find anything regarding Janus or an artificial intelligence program anywhere."

Bev crossed her arms, openly disappointed.

"I even met up with some friends who have higher clearances than I to see if they could find anything." Jacob said, leaning back on the countertop, "Even they could not find anything."

He placed the bottle on the countertop next to him, "It's like Janus and the program never existed. And, if that's the case, our intel is wrong…which raises a bunch of other questions."

Bev smirked at him, placing her hands on her hips, "Our *intel* was right. I don't know where you all were looking but, obviously, it was the wrong place."

"What?" Jacob blurted out, looking at her with renewed hope.

She raised a balled hand in the air, motioning with her index finger to follow as she walked triumphally into the study and revealed, "We got the treasure-trove of information on Janus."

Both Chief Zorin and Lionak were in the study, seated at a table reading books from the bookshelf, and looked up momentarily toward them.

Bev grasped the SSD NAS unit that was next to the laptop and turned toward Jacob, "Here it is."

"What?!" Jacob whispered excitedly, reaching for it.

"Yeah, that's right." Bev gloated, "Yet again, I got the goods. I'd churn some butter if I was not holding this thing."

Eagerly taking the NAS unit, Jacob grinned and said, "Churn away baby! This is great!"

As Jacob moved around her to sit in front of the laptop, Bev made the churning gesture while she turned toward him and the laptop.

After locating a usb cable he plugged one end into the NAS unit and the other into the laptop and immediately opened the folder view of the newly connected drive. The entire window filled with folder and file icons.

"Good god," Jacob remarked as he randomly began opening folders, revealing more folders and files, "Look at all this. There must be a book's worth of data in here."

"A book?" Lionak questioned, getting up from his chair and walking over to them, "Inside that little box?"

"I think it was fifty terabytes or something." Bev pointed out, remembering what Jason had said, though she did not truly understand what the number meant.

"Fifty?" Jacob whined, moving the mouse pointer to view the drive space, "Damn it. Shit can never be easy around here."

Jacob opened the calculator application, entered some numbers and said to Lionak, "Actually about fifty million books inside here."

Lionak gasped at the number, unable to comprehend how big his library would have to be in order to shelve that many books.

Chief Zorin looked up from the geography book he was reading and placed it on the table, "It would take many lifetimes to read that many books."

Jacob shook his head and corrected himself, "I should not say that many books. There are lots of schematics, drawings and images here, too, and those are quite big. I'd guess, umm, for text docs maybe more like a few thousand books."

"Even so," Lionak said, agreeing with Chief Zorin, "It is still lifetimes. My own library has close to three thousand and I have not read them all."

Jacob leaned back in the chair and grimaced, "That is just way too long to go through everything and to understand it."

A knocking sound came from the back door, causing Spewge to jump up and rush to the door defensively.

Bev began moving toward the door to see who it was but Regan, smiling excitedly, rushed past and opened the door, wrapping herself around Mac, "Mac! You are back!"

"I am." Mac sighed into Regan's ear, happily feeling her warm embrace around him.

After a few long moments, Regan regained her feet and looked into his golden eyes, "Are you okay? We got you some medicine for your headaches."

"Yes, I'm okay." Mac admitted with a smile, touched by her concern, "I had a minor flare-up but it's passed."

Content with his return, Regan took his hand and led him to Bev and the others, "We've got something to show you!"

Bev smiled at their reunion, feeling the emotion radiating from Regan.

"You find out how to use your magic?" Jacob asked, still going into folders stored on the NAS unit.

"Bro, it was amazing!" Mac declared, stopping near Jacob and looking curiously at the laptop, "Phosx showed me so much, you would not believe it."

"Can't say I would from a giant." Jacob said flatly, "You think you can take out the AI?"

"Oh. Yeah." Mac nodded, "I was shown how to use a device they created to gather energy together and focus it all on something. Well, an alien. Oh my god it was so disgusting but it worked. Incredible, actually, to attack something and not actually be there."

Jacob turned his head toward Mac, expecting to see a rifle or something scary-looking and said, "Sounds like you are good to go then. Where's the device?"

"They call it the Aethereal Kinesis-Forge. Umm, it is huge and cannot be moved." Mac admitted, "But I can still feel it, like I am connected to them somehow."

"Them? There's more than one?"

"Yes. Scattered around the world." Mac confirmed, raising his head toward Lionak and Chief Zorin to acknowledge their presence.

"Well, hell, sounds like you got it in the bag." Jacob concluded.

Mac contorted his face a bit and said, "Uh. Not exactly. I tried to do a remote attack like the Elder Pursiellan, but I could not."

Jacob looked up into Mac's eyes with a blank expression.

Recognizing Jacob's mask of disappointment, Mac raised his hand, as if to calm Jacob and said, "If I can see what I'm attacking, if I am there, we're good. I just have to be able to see it."

Jacob frowned, "That's not good. If you have to see the AI, that means it will see you."

"I can shield Mac, like what was done when we had challenged the Baron." Chief Zorin volunteered, getting up and walking next to Lionak.

Lionak nodded, "And I. Together we are not to be trifled with."

Jacob turned to scowl at them in disbelief, wanting to describe some of the weapons he knew about and their destructiveness, and the unknowns of a more advanced alien race, but he restrained himself.

Sensing the tension in the air, Mac tapped Jacob's shoulder and asked, "What do you have there?"

Slowly, Jacob turned back to the laptop and cleared his throat, "This is all the details of the AI system. All fifty plus terabytes of it."

"Damn that's a lot." Mac muttered.

Chief Zorin and Lionak nodded in agreement.

"Yeah, too much for us to go through, even if we took turns twenty-four seven." Jacob complained.

"That's for sure." Mac said, gazing at all the folder and file icons shown on the laptop's screen.

"What if we all had a laptop and did the work at the same time?" Bev asked, thinking about team-based student projects she had taught.

"That, I'd guess, means each of us would only need to read something like five hundred or so books." Jacob speculated, "Done in a timely fashion before I die of old age? I just don't think it's possible."

"Sounds like we need more people." Regan said, petting Spewge.

Mac shifted his stance and suggested, "What if we could stop time, or at least slow it down?"

"You have a time machine I don't know about?" Jacob smarted off impulsively.

Mac looked between them and said, "It seems to me that we could go to the Realm, do our work over a few weeks or months, and then return. Time passes here so slowly that, in comparison, we may only be gone a day or two."

"Excellent idea, Mac." Lionak said, having just been reminded of the differences of time between worlds.

"They still use candles." Jacob exhaled in frustration, "A laptop requires electricity. And a specific type I might add."

"You got me there." Mac confessed.

"Honey, don't you still have those big solar power systems in the basement, in case the power grid went down for a long time?" Bev asked, knowing that they could create electricity.

Jacob raised his eyebrows at the thought, "You are right. I do!"

"Well, there you go." Bev responded.

"You have more laptops, too?" Mac asked, under the impression that if Jacob had backup power he might have gone as far as stocking up on other things and, if that was the case, he'd surely have a spare laptop.

Jacob shook his head at Mac, "I prepared for backup power, not opening a store after shtf."

Mac jabbed Jacob, like friends do, by saying, "Jacob's Junk. I could totally see you selling wares after shtf. Would be quite convenient about now, too."

"Yeah, okay." Jacob growled, taking his hand off the mouse to flex his fingers and loosen their joints. His fingers weren't as nimble as they once were.

"So, that's it then?" Bev stated as she looked between them, amazed that nobody had said the obvious, "Time to churn more butter?"

Jacob gave her a questioning look.

"You want to make butter now?" Mac asked, mystified as to why she would want to do something like that when they had an important matter at hand.

Bev rolled her eyes and said, "There's a big computer store nearby, right? They have aisles of laptop computers so let's buy what we need. Problem solved!"

"How many laptops are we talking about here?" Mac said, looking at Jacob's laptop to judge its size and estimating how many could be carried by a person.

"There are six of us, so five." Jacob suggested, "But if we had more people helping, we could speed things along with more laptops."

"You shall have them." Chief Zorin volunteered, "The Guardians of the White Magic would be honored to learn of your laptops and the AI you speak about, to discover its weakness."

Lionak nodded, looking briefly at Chief Zorin, "That is a good offer. The Guardians are well educated and would keep the knowledge they learn secret to not upset the balance of the Realm."

"How many do you require?" Chief Zorin asked.

Jacob turned toward him and said, with some hesitation, "I'd say twelve to triple our number."

"Then twelve shall be."

Bev raised her hands toward Chief Zorin and Jacob in defiance, "Wow! Hold on a minute. I can't go with you. Someone has to take care of Spewge and be here if something happens to the kids."

Jacob shifted his eyes to Bev and back to Chief Zorin.

"Adding a few more to our ranks won't be a problem." Chief Zorin said, understanding her concern.

"Well, let's do it!" Bev celebrated, gesturing churning butter and, as she did so, looked around at everyone, "Well, come on! Let's make some butter!"

Reluctantly Jacob got up and joined in making the gesture with the others doing the same, though rough and jerky at first. Bev and Regan were the first to begin laughing between themselves with the others smiling.

After a few moments, Jacob spotted the time and stopped, saying, "Looks like it is too late for us to hit the store today."

"We'll go tomorrow then." Bev countered, wanting to keep the celebration going.

"Let's turn in soon so we can be up at the butt-crack of dawn to get things together." Jacob suggested with a lingering smile, watching them. Even Spewge was enjoying the atmosphere.

Aboard the SSHC-20, Marshal Ironhook examined the large display screen showing the positions of the two heavy cruisers drawing close to the Earth and the curvature of the Earth outside the ship, also visible through the same display screen. Further out, he could also see the Moon.

"Beginning IB orbit." one of the officers said monotonously. The IB, or Inversion Burn, is a maneuver to rotate a ship one-hundred and eighty degrees in order to use its main engines to slow or stop its forward velocity along its primary axis of travel. In this case, the IB would be used along with an orbiting maneuver to establish the heavy cruiser in high-Earth orbit.

The SSHC-20 began its rotation as it shot through space next to the Earth. Once it had completed its inversion, Marshal Ironhook, having felt no physical sensation that they had inverted, only saw the darkness of space beyond the display screen.

"Engaging main engines."

While the gravity plates largely muted the effects of the massive volume of thrust created by the engines, the marshal could feel the vibrations in his chair. Had he been standing, his feet and legs would tingle as if they had fallen asleep, normally caused by reduced circulation. Needless to say, albeit the sensation was transitory and made it difficult to walk, everyone aboard the ship was required to remain seated during such a burn.

After thirty-one seconds, the vibrations ceased and the officer said, "Orbit complete. Beginning inversion."

Marshal Ironhook looked beyond the display screen as the heavy cruiser rotated back to its original heading, watching as the Earth's curvature drift back into view along with the Moon.

"Inversion complete."

"Position." Marshal Ironhook ordered.

"We are in high-Earth orbit, in synchronization with the Moon's transit of Earth." the officer responded, verifying that their distance from the Moon would remain constant.

"Great work." Marshal Ironhook stated to everyone on the bridge and then ordered, "Open comm to SSHC-10."

After a moment another officer said, "Comm open."

While looking at the icon representing the SSHC-10 on the display screen, Marshal Ironhook said, "Vice Marshal Yaimes, our orbit has been secured. Good luck to the Moon."

Shortly after the SSHC-10 raced past the SSHC-20 and disappeared from view outside Marshal Ironhook's display screen not more than two seconds later, the comm speakers crackled a bit, followed by the voice of Vice Marshal Yaimes, "Roger that, sir. I'll see about rounding up a MoonPie during my visit."

"You do that, marshal. Those are hard to come by out here." Marshal Ironhook grinned, realizing it had been almost two years since he ate his last one, "Out."

Chapter Fourteen

The next morning Jacob was the first to wake, followed by Chief Zorin and Lionak whom had slept downstairs, awakened to some loud banging sounds from the basement.

"You okay down here?" Chief Zorin asked as he descended the aged wooden staircase into the basement, accessible through a section of cut floor planks in the study.

"Yeah, I'll be fine." Jacob replied, rolling up a dust laden blue plastic tarp that had been thrown over the solar power systems years ago.

After setting down the tarp he pointed at the two yellow and black colored containers, each three feet in length and width by two feet in height, and said, "Those are the two we will need."

Jacob grabbed the edge of one and pulled on it with little effort toward the staircase, "There are wheels underneath but we're going to need to turn them on their side to get them into the study."

"Simple enough." Chief Zorin said as he reached the container and shifted it effortlessly on its side.

"Yeah. Like that." Jacob said with surprise. He had forgotten that Chief Zorin, even in human form, still had the strength of a Silver Dragon.

Grasping the container by its sides closest to the cement floor, Jacob said, "Grab the other side there and we'll carry this thing upstairs."

Chief Zorin did so and they carried the container up into the study and set it down on its wheels followed shortly thereafter by the other container. Once it was on its wheels, Jacob placed the bound floor planks back over the entryway and, using a key, turned the flush latches back to their closed positions to prevent the section of flooring from shifting around.

Spotting Bev and Regan as they neared the study, Jacob sarcastically said, "You missed all the fun. We could have used your help with those containers."

Bev rolled her eyes and scoffed, "Whatever. I knew if I combed my hair long enough you'd finish the hard stuff."

Regan grinned at the response but did not say anything, instead making a mental note to use that tactic sometime in the future.

"Hard stuff?" Mac puffed, lumbering down the stairs, "What about hard stuff?"

Jacob shook his head and said lowly, "Yeah, you too, sunshine."

Jacob got up and went to the dining room where everyone had congregated, Chief Zorin following a few minutes later after he had flipped through a few more pages of the geography book he had been reading.

"We ready to go, honey, or did you want to play around some more in the basement?" Bev smiled at Jacob.

Jacob wagged his finger at Bev, but then smiled back, "We should go."

"All of us?" Lionak asked, "I would like to see the store that you speak of that has more…laptops."

Jacob shrugged, pulling out his keys, "I don't see why not. Anyone else down for a little trip?"

"Yes." Chief Zorin responded, also curious about the store.

"And you?"

"No, I'll hang here and catch up on some news."
Mac said, in truth preferring to stay in case he experienced
another painful headache. He turned toward Regan and
said, "Don't stay on my part. If you want to go, then go."

Regan looked at Mac, "I'll stay, too. We'll watch
the news together. Besides, I can catch up on your
wonderous stores with Bev when we go shopping again."

Jacob jiggled the keys in his hand for a moment,
looking at everyone and then strode to the door saying,
"Alright. Let's get this show on the road."

Mac strolled into the living room and plopped
down onto the couch and grabbed the remote, turning on
the large screen.

A few minutes later Regan entered the room, gave
Mac one of the cups full of ice-cold tea and then settled
down next to him on the couch.

"We got some quiet time, just you and I." Mac
said to Regan with a wink.

Then Spewge jumped onto the couch next to
Regan, settling down to lean against her. Regan chuckled
and lifted her arm around the large dog and petted him.

Jacob exited the Bronco and walked toward the
store with Bev, eagerly followed by Chief Zorin and
Lionak. But just before they entered, he stopped to look at
the two and said, "Just stick with me while we are in there,
okay?"

They nodded and he turned and entered the store
with them. Almost immediately he was approached by a
greeter who said, "Welcome! If you have any questions or
need help finding something, please let us know."

Jacob nodded weakly as he got a shopping cart
while Bev smiled back and said, "Thank you. We will."

"Look at how colorful this place is." Chief Zorin
said, scanning around while following Jacob.

"Its like a treasure horde in here." Lionak
remarked, looking at all the items of varying size laid out

on rows and rows of long shelves and merchandise hooks, "I would like to know how all of these things work."

"No time for that." Jacob whispered heavily as he made his way to the computer segment of the large store.

Once there he steered the cart between two long counter-top fashioned tables with a wide range of laptops sitting on top of them, and boxes of laptops beneath the counter-tops. Each table measured twenty-five feet in length.

"Look at all these laptops!" Lionak exclaimed with outstretched arms, temporarily causing the background noise in the store to quiet down.

Within a flash, an employee appeared next to Lionak before Jacob could, and mentally noted the peculiar dress of the individual before asking, "Yes. How can I help you today?"

Lionak looked at the smiling employee of average build and said, "I want these laptops." Then he pointed towards them.

Having left the cart between the tables, Jacob made it to the employee and jumped into the conversation, looking to avert some inevitable misunderstanding, "Hi there. We are actually looking to buy some of your laptops. You have any recommendations?"

The employee's eyes lit up at the suggestion of multiple purchases and he motioned for Jacob to follow him as he walked over to the tables, "I would be happy to help you!"

While Bev and Lionak lingered around Jacob while he talked with the employee and moved between laptops, Chief Zorin drifted into the newly added robotics section of the store, not far away, attracted to a articulated robotic arm bolted to a mount, reaching out and grasping a box and placing it at the other end of the display and then resetting to pick up the box and placing it at the other end as part of an endless loop.

There he strolled past the arm, not controlled by any known magic he was aware of and saw a three foot tall bipedal, human-shaped white-colored robot, doing much the same thing…taking a small cube in one five-finger articulated hand to move it toward the center of the robot where it reached over with its other hand to take the cube and then rotate the arm and wrist to place the cube at the other end of the display, in an endless loop. Behind the robot rested a collection of boxed versions of the model on display. While its form was shaped like a human, he could plainly see the robot's joints where the composite protection plating bolted around cabling and its skeleton structure did not cover.

For over a minute he stared at the mechanical being in amazement before he took a step back to read other parts of the display. Above it read, 'Butler 1' while, below the display's counter-top it read, 'The first truly affordable butler for your home! Today only $4,599!' and a collection of bullet points stated, 'Can clean and vacuum floors using what you already have, Can prepare and cook food, Can clean and iron clothes, Can take out trash up to 25 lbs*, Can conversate and play many board games'.

"Hello. I am Butler 1." the robot said in a soothing voice as it looked up at Chief Zorin while flawlessly moving the cube without continuing to look down at its moving hands, "How can I serve you today?"

Chief Zorin looked at the long, narrow, blue-illuminated strip that went from one side of the robot's head to the other in the approximate area where a human's eyes would be, but could not think of anything to say in response. Instead, he moved past the robot and the robot tilted its head back toward its hands.

"Unreal." Chief Zorin finally whispered to himself as he moved around to another aisle with the display of a robotic dog, similar in mechanical features to that of the Butler 1 robot, but with a covering of short dark fur and a standing height of one foot and six inches. Fully articulated, it periodically walked forward just like a real dog and even sat and rested on all four limbs like a real dog.

Through infrared sensors, having detected Chief Zorin's presence, it got up and turned toward him, its slim multi-jointed tail wagging behind it. Then it tilted its head slightly and sat down, its tail still wagging as it repositioned its short, floppy ears toward him. While the robot dog, like Butler 1, did not have a mouth, it shared the same blue horizontal strip used for one-hundred and seventy-degree vision and depth perception. Additionally, it was designed to be a lead-in product for both kids and adults toward the Butler 1 and other robots with greater capabilities. The banner above the display read, 'Vigilant 1' while below read, 'The #1 dog for your home! Today only $1599!' with a collection of bullet points reading, 'Can go with you anywhere - fully autonomous no internet needed, Can patrol and protect your home, Can be at your side, Can conversate in dog or even human talk'.

"Hey Zorin," Bev said quietly after finding him in the store, "What are you doing over here?"

Sensing Bev's approach and female voice, the robot dog stood up and moved to face her with its tail wagging, occasionally tilting its head up.

"You see these things?" Chief Zorin said, still in awe of the mechanical genius of the robots, "They move so perfectly. So realistic."

"Actually no. I heard this was a brand-new addition to the stores but haven't had the time to see it for myself." Bev replied, looking down at the robot dog.

Out of curiosity, Bev reached down to touch the robot dog's head and, when she did so, it moved its head to feel more of Bev's hand upon its fur sensors and shifted its wagging tail a bit. The fur covering its body was, in fact, comprised of millions of short hair-like strands, the center of each crafted with a piezo-electric nano-scale hollow shaft that generated a micro-current when bent. That micro-current served not only as feedback for the robot dog, it served to provide a subtle stimulus for the bio-electric field of lifeforms it came into contact with. With all of the hairs connected to a *Dermis Core*, the robot dog's AI system utilized the signals from the fur to better sense the environment and react to it such as angling the body against a gust of wind, sensing water droplets and heat sources…even the direction and speed of objects that may impact it. In this case, the characteristics of physical contact allowed the robot dog to estimate the height and weight of Bev as well as her position independent of its other specialized sensors. It also deduced that Bev's light touch and hand movement was non-threatening with applied pressure greatest at her fingertips suggesting a curious and apprehensive demeanor.

Bev giggled a bit and admitted, "It does seem sort of real, doesn't it? The hair feels so real."

"Indeed." Chief Zorin confessed with an uneasy grin.

"We should get back." Bev said as she withdrew her hand from the robot dog and stood up.

"I would like to have this mechanical dog." Chief Zorin said to her. He wanted to unlock its mysteries and he knew Lionak would want to do the same.

"I don't know, Zorin." Bev sighed, "We didn't come here to buy these new robots."

"Just the one?"

Bev shifted her weight from one leg to the other a few times as she thought about it. "Just one."

Chief Zorin smiled almost in a childish fashion, had he been human, and grabbed one of the boxes of Vigilant 1. Then he followed her back to the computer segment of the store.

"That is a great choice, sir." the employee said, "And, that model has a ten percent off sale."

"So," he continued, looking between Jacob and Lionak, "How many did you want today?"

"Seventeen." Jacob said without hesitation, though he winced at the thought of the cost.

"Did you say seventeen, sir?"

Lionak frowned at him, "He did."

The employee smiled triumphally, imagining the commission he would receive and being tagged as the employee of the month, and said, "Let me see if we have that many in stock. Please wait just a second!"

While he fast walked over to a store phone nearby, Jacob glanced over at Bev and Chief Zorin bearing a cheesy grin, holding the box of a robot dog.

"Bev? What are we doing here?"

"Just one, dear." Bev said as she raised an eyebrow, ready for pushback, "For him and Lionak to familiarize themselves with the technology seeing as you all will be spending god knows how long going through volumes of data about that AI."

Jacob shrugged, admitting, "Well you have a point there. Unfortunately, I can't argue with that."

The employee returned with a huge grin and said, "We have all seventeen, sir! We have twenty so if you would like to add three more to your order, we'll take an extra ten percent off the other three."

'Brother. Not upselling. Not today.' Jacob thought to himself as he slowly shook his head.

"No. Seventeen is fine." Jacob said sternly, "But I will also need a few power strips for them, daisy-chainable usb hubs to plug them in to, and usb cable for each."

"No problem! We have that right over here, sir." the employee said, motioning for Jacob to follow him to the next aisle where he pointed to some usb hubs.

Jacob maneuvered the cart around and grabbed two of them and then counted out seventeen six-feet long usb cables and dumped them in the cart.

"Our power strips are right over here." he said, walking ten feet deeper in the same aisle.

Jacob pushed the cart forward and collected several metal cased strips, carefully placing them in the cart as to not damage the usb hubs.

"Great!" the employee said joyfully, "I'll get your laptops sent to the front of the store and I'll meet you there."

"Sounds good." Jacob responded, turning his cart around and heading to the front of the store to a checkout register, followed by the others.

By the time Jacob got to the front, he noticed an unusual number of employees mulling around and talking amongst themselves, occasionally looking in his direction as if they were on an Australian safari catching a glimpse of the fabled Tasmanian tiger. The one he had been talking to walked past them and aided the checkout process, keen to ensure he was credited for the sale.

A few minutes later a flatbed cart, pushed by a different employee, rolled up with the seventeen laptops.

"Here we are sir!" he said, "We'll help you get these loaded."

After they returned to the house, Mac and Regan helped carry the laptops into the house and Jacob darted off into the basement, returning with another large, wheeled container.

"Let's put all the laptops and their parts in here." Jacob instructed, pointing at the container, "That will help keep things together and reduce the bulk of it all."

Shortly after they started, Bev noticed the piles of plastic bags and packaging collecting around the room and said, "We going to keep all that?"

"No." Jacob confirmed as he put a laptop and mouse into the container.

Once they finished adding the components to the container, Jacob dropped in his own backpack filled with a laptop and other items and then placed the lid on top, "I think we are done. Lionak?"

"At once." Lionak said, summoning his staff and opening a portal to the Guardian's stronghold deep in the Northern Ice Mountains.

"Hey now. You going to help clean all this up?" Bev groaned, squinting her eyes at Jacob.

Jacob could not help but smile at the thought and said, "You need something to do while we are gone. Besides we'll be back before you know it."

Bev crossed her arms and glared at him.

Chief Zorin was the first to step through the portal, clutching the box of the robot dog, followed by Lionak who pushed one of the containers and Jacob with another container.

But, just as Mac began pushing his container forward, Regan pulled on his arm and said, "Mac, here, take this medicine. I'm not ready to go back. Not yet."

Mac took the bag from her and smiled understanding, more than anyone, her distress, and touched her softly on the cheek, "I understand. I love you."

"I love you." Regan smiled in return, reaching forward to kiss him passionately. Shortly after she reluctantly pulled away.

With that, he waved at Bev and pushed the container into the portal and disappeared.

Chapter Fifteen

"Yes, Mr. President." General Lowinsky said into the satellite phone, slowly pacing around inside the command vehicle, "We have actionable intel that an alien presence is responsible for the sinking of the CVN-79."

The general nodded his head and said, "We are tracking the alien that had destroyed the base. But, at this time, I do not know if the two are related."

After a few moments he looked down at the floor and said, "Yes. Yes, it is possible there are multiple types of aliens."

"Of course." General Lowinsky agreed, looking up and moving to the refrigerator to get a bottled water.

After closing the refrigerator he said, "No. Based on our intelligence, the two events were not coordinated."

Grabbing the bottled water, he added, "We are moving into position to eliminate both targets as we speak, sir. Yes."

"You are right, sir." General Lowinsky remarked, making his way to the table, "This is most likely the start of a much bigger action."

"I would recommend that Space Force be notified of the two surface events so they can be on force-ready alert and deploy their near-Earth assets to intercept any non-terrestrial craft and stop reinforcement."

The general paused for a moment to consider what the President asked and then said, "No, sir. I would not recommend changing Defcon readiness or launch a general mobilization at this time…"

He placed the bottled water on the table and passively glanced at some of the tactical maps saying, "I understand, sir. But there is no reason to scramble forces at this time. If we can contain both events, an unwarranted public disruption can be avoided."

"Panic, sir?"

Again, the general paused to listen to the President, "I think most of the public believes there is something else out there besides us now. So, they wouldn't panic, per se, like people from fifty or a hundred years ago before the first spacewalk when they had not been exposed to thinking beyond their immediate surroundings and daily routine. In fact, as we go deeper into space with our technology, I believe the specter and fear of aliens would be lessened even more. Probably replaced with a defensive curiosity like, oh I don't know, a wild racoon entering someone's house."

General Lowinsky grinned at the President's response, "Yes sir, a feisty racoon may have been a bad example but the fact remains that the conditioning will counter-balance instinctual panic."

"Yes, I agree, sir." he said after twisting off the top of the bottled water, "If we fail to contain both targets, I would recommend changing Defcon and notifying our allies. But, still, I would withhold from a general mobilization unless the alien presence worsened. Right now, only a few military assets have been targeted and those, big picture, are not that significant."

185

"I will, sir. Thank you." General Lowinsky concluded, placing the satellite phone back in his pocket.

After drinking from the bottled water, he pulled the Sable Pigeon laptop near him, reauthenticated, and looked at the high-resolution images of the aircraft carrier just before it appeared to capsize in the ocean and the second image showing the ocean collapsing in around it, just as the stern began to disappear under the surface. Inwardly, while he was appalled at the loss of equipment and thousands of soldiers, he admired the silent, destructive power that could best an aircraft carrier without using any conventional strike wing, missile or torpedo.

Then he played the video footage captured from the scope of Sergeant Quayle, revealing a camouflage bubble of some sort over an installation and, what was plain to see, non-terrestrial aliens inside that bubble.

"Time to close the net on these NTA's." he said to himself as he typed a message and then sent it.

"Sergeant. Incoming message." the corporal said, pointing at the laser communications module after unplugging his connection cable from it.

"Thank you, corporal." Sergeant Quayle acknowledged quietly, moving back several paces to the module and sitting next to it.

The sergeant pulled out his own connection cable and connected one end to the module and the other to a rubber-capped port on his Scalpel. Once connected, the bottom portion of the Scalpel's map display was replaced with the message 'Engage and eliminate lifeforms at target'.

Sergeant Quayle exhaled and disconnected the cable, placing it back in his pocket. Then, after eying his SPW, he signaled for the other sergeants to rally on his position.

"Okay gentlemen." the sergeant began, "We have the go order to do what we do best. Rain hell on the lifeforms on that base."

"Lifeforms?" Sergeant Biggs questioned.

"Aliens, right?" Sergeant Cookem asked, assuming that was what was being referred to without saying as much.

"Yes, Cookem. Aliens." Sergeant Quayle confirmed with some reservation, "They have arms and legs like us but you can tell they are not human."

"That is sic! My first alien kill!" Sergeant Cookem whispered heavily with excitement.

Sergeant Biggs darted his eyes toward Sergeant Cookem wondering how he could be so cocky without having any idea of their capabilities.

"Alright." Sergeant Quayle said flatly in an attempt to dial down the sergeant's excitement, "Standard plow formation with Team One at point. After the target has been drawn to Team One and engaged, Team Two and Three sweep around behind the enemy so we get a nice kill triangle. Once the enemy has been neutralized, provide cover for Team One to ingress the base and then fall in to plow formation behind Team One."

The plow formation resembled a triangle with Team One on point while the other two teams occupied the remaining points.

"You're going to remain point?" Sergeant Cookem asked, thinking about possible losses to Team One from the initial engagement, resulting in the loss of offensive potential.

"You are on the money today, sergeant." Sergeant Quayle said, having thought along the same lines as Sergeant Cookem, though, he considered that a weakened element may draw fewer enemies, allowing the other teams to sweep around them without significant challenge and be quickly dispatched. On the other hand, if Team One remained at strength, it would draw the majority of attention and still allow the other teams to maneuver with greater freedom. But, like most things, once an unknown enemy is engaged, all those theories and planning could be whisked away in an instant.

"How are we going to breach?" Sergeant Biggs inquired, looking at Sergeant Quayle.

"Unknown." Sergeant Quayle said, shrugging his shoulders, "The base is quite well camouflaged but I have a feeling once Team One engages, our breach point will reveal itself. Just keep on eye on where the enemy or fire comes from."

"Roger that." Sergeant Biggs grunted.

"Let's go." Sergeant Quayle ordered, turning toward the base's location and hand signaling to Team One that they were advancing.

Methodically Team One, from crouched and concealed positions, advanced fifty meters at a time, stopping to assess their surroundings and provide cover for the other two teams behind them to advance. Likewise, when Team One advanced, the other two teams provided cover. The process was repeated until Sergeant Quayle found the spot he had previously scouted to and, in fact, the same tree. He then hand signaled for Team Two and Three to advance and hold twenty-five meters in preparation of Team One's final push to establish enemy contact.

After he verified the teams were in position, he patiently leveled his SPW and ever so slowly swept the scope across the forested terrain, paying attention to the smallest detail. Once he was satisfied that Team One could advance, he signaled a ready-silent message to the other two teams, indicating that they could now use their Scalpel's in quiet, non-transmitting mode until Team One had engaged. That meant they could utilize more generic mapping and other data relayed from satellite and ground stations, but could not transmit messages or other signals that may, against a technologically equivalent adversary who may have found their uniquely assigned frequencies, reveal their exact locations. It also meant they had one less thing to remember doing once the heat of battle consumed them.

Exhaling slowly and evenly, Sergeant Quayle along with the rest of Team One, started their final twenty-five-meter advance through the forest toward the base.

Chapter Sixteen

Having pushed the container through the portal, Mac found himself standing in the middle of a gigantic courtyard surrounded by high, large blocked stone walls and a pair of towering closed gates to his left made of hard oak wood, covered by a hardened resin and reinforced with several long, slender iron plates held fast by large, rounded rivets. Off toward his right, and further away, he spotted a large tower, one hundred and fifty feet in height, its diameter a mere eighteen feet.

"Welcome to the stronghold of the Silver Dragons, Guardians of the White Magic!" Chief Zorin announced after seeing Mac's appearance.

Having been talking to Chief Zorin, Jacob turned about and pointed at Mac before he strode up to him, "We were beginning to wonder if you were going to show up, or hang back to watch more news and cuddle with Regan."

"I am still considering that cuddle part, bro." Mac quipped.

"Yeah, to be honest, I would be, too."

"So, this is in the Northern Ice Mountains?" Mac said as he looked around, "This keep is impressive."

"Apparently it is. Some good hiking I'd imagine." Jacob said, briefly joining Mac to look around beyond the walls at what could be seen as dusk approached. Off in the distance, high in the sky, he spotted the silhouette of a dragon gliding through the air.

Nudging Mac on the shoulder Jacob said, "Chief Zorin has arranged quarters for us while we are here, too. So, we won't have to go around doing odd jobs to get gold and all that this time around."

"And," Jacob said proudly, "it seems we are still in their history books as legendary figures who faced down Dark Magic and won."

Mac chuckled to himself a bit and said, "I seem to remember there was a bit more to it than that."

"That is definitely true, but nobody asked us to write the history books." Jacob confirmed as he started walking toward Chief Zorin and Lionak, "Well, let's get settled in. The Guardians will take our containers to one of their great halls."

Jacob suddenly remembered his backpack and stopped to open a container and retrieve it, "Except for this, of course."

"Hold on a sec." Mac said after grabbing the medicine bag Regan had given him and walking up to Jacob, "Before I forget. I wanted to mention that I may know the source of those sudden headaches."

Jacob's eyebrows raised and he said, "Oh yeah? What is it?"

"I think I'm being affected by the recent changes happening to the planet. On the news I saw them talking about radio and satellite outages that are getting worse and seem to be happening around the world, but most concentrated from the south."

"Humm." Jacob nodded.

"And, volcanic activity has been picking up in spots. Even some dormant ones."

Jacob put his hand on the back of his head and pulled it forward over the top, bringing his hand back down to his side and said, "You think those things are causing your headaches all the sudden?"

Mac tilted his head a bit, thinking about it, "No, not really the volcanoes or satellites themselves. I'm thinking whatever is affecting them is doing the same to me."

Jacob pushed his arm through one of the straps of the backpack and slung it behind him, "Like radiation from a CME? I've heard some folks are sensitive to that type of thing."

"Yes." Mac admitted, walking beside Jacob toward the others.

"If that is the case maybe, next time you get a big headache, you could get into a faraday cage and see if that blocks it. I heard those help protect against such things." Jacob volunteered.

"Good idea." Mac said, considering the possibility.

"Mac," Chief Zorin said as he motioned with his hand toward the rugged-faced High Priest next to him, dressed in white flowing robes, his long raven-black hair bound up behind his head in the form of a single pony-tail split further down into two braided ones, "this is Phentities. He takes care of most daily affairs of the stronghold."

"I am honored to stand before you, Mac." Phentities confessed with a smile and a deep voice.

"The honor is mine, Phentities." Mac responded, raising his arm before the High Priest, expecting for him to grab his forearm.

Surprisingly, Phentities clasped his large, strong hand around Mac's hand and shook it.

"This is the correct greeting, yes?" Phentities asked, this being the first time he actually tried the hand greeting of an outsider he had only read about.

Mac smiled at him and said, "It is. Perfectly done I might add."

Phentities nodded and released Mac's hand with a sense of accomplishment.

"Let's get you to your quarters." Chief Zorin said as he turned and began walking toward a collection of magnificently crafted and highly detailed stone buildings deeper in the stronghold. Many of the structures were a single story in height but a few, here and there, were two to five stories in height, all sharing the same triangular iron-shingled high-roof architecture. Likewise, the heavy iron-strapped oak doors of each were proportional to the height of the structure...the single-story structures large enough for a human or barbarian to enter whereas some of the five story structures bore doors of between fourteen and thirty feet in height and wide enough to permit a giant or dragon to enter.

"I must return to my duties." Phentities said, nodding toward Chief Zorin and the others as they departed. Then he turned and headed toward the tower.

Mac waved briefly in acknowledgement and turned back, following Chief Zorin.

"Over there," Chief Zorin said pointing toward a sweeping marble staircase that rose up to the entrance of a stone temple to their left, "That is the entrance to our lower study quarters and where we keep most of our ancient history scrolls and tomes."

The staircase of the temple was flanked on either side by finely crafted pillars which appeared to bear the weight of the large stone blocks that comprised the lower rim of the roof. Along the rim, unlike the other structures, they could see the sculpted figures of dragons fighting one another. Some of the images breathed fire, while others were locked in close combat.

Continuing beyond the temple and two larger structures, Chief Zorin turned to his left and walked between structures, along an empty path with a width of twenty feet that extended beyond several other rows of structures. As they walked along the path, Mac noticed that a garden comprised of a range of bushes and flowers filled the space between each structure, most complete with flat stone benches in their midst, as if each structure had its own backyard of sorts.

Finally, Chief Zorin stopped at the third row and pointed to his left at the two-story structure and said, "We have decreed these quarters to be yours from this day forward. We have added some modest fortifications to it, such as the double iron-bound stone doors there and a wall around its perimeter."

Chief Zorin turned toward them, "I doubt these precautions will ever be needed inside our stronghold but one never knows when the Dark Magic may return."

"This is awesome, Zorin!" Jacob exclaimed, admiring the defensible quarters.

"It is the least we can do." Chief Zorin admitted with a smile, accepting Jacob's appreciation.

"And, over here," Lionak pointed to the five-story structure to its right on the other side of the path, "is one of the stronghold's great halls for you to use as you will. It is also bound to your hand. In our immediate case, I elected its first charge to that of aiding you in solving the mystery around, what did you say...artificial intelligence."

"Perfect!" Mac beamed.

"I must take my leave." Chief Zorin concluded before he began walking back where they had come from, "I will join you tomorrow with other Guardians."

"And I will return tomorrow. As for now," Lionak said as he conjured a teleportation spell, "I must return to my keep and ensure it is still in one piece."

Mac turned toward Jacob, "Guess we should check out the house. I got dibs on the bed."

Jacob laughed as they approached the stone double doors, "I'm sure there's more than one."

Looking down at the foot of the doors Mac said, "You see that? Looks just like your doormat but made out of, well, dried grass or something."

"Huh. It does. Wonder who did that?" Jacob commented, looking at the doormat bearing the word 'Welcome' and a smiley face next to it.

Touching the surface of the stone door in front of him Mac said, "I don't know what you think but these carvings in the door are amazing."

Centered and chiseled into each door was a standing portrait, approximately three and one-half feet in height, of Mac brandishing a sword on one door and Mohawk with his Cape of Speed on the other. Split between both portraits, in the background, was Mt. Reach, the source of Pure Magic.

Jacob took the two five-inch-long iron keys, hanging from a small hook to the right of the doors and handed one to Mac. With the other he inserted it into the silver clad iron keylock and turned it ninety degrees, rotating a larger hour-glass shaped iron plate built into the door that, given its shape, released tension to a thick rod, allowing it to be pulled into the door by its connection to a small leaf spring.

Both he and Mac pulled the doors outward towards them with ease and entered the house, instinctively closing the doors behind them. Once closed, Jacob inserted the key into the keylock on the other side of the door and turned it in the opposite direction, locking the door.

"My door at home has nothing on these monstrosities." Jacob said to himself.

Directly to their right, just a few meters to the right of the doors was a stone staircase, bearing an intricately carved handrail, with a slim, round baluster carved with an overlapping scale pattern, reaching down to join each stair along its length. Below the staircase was what appeared to be a stone shelved area for storing various items. In the middle of the open room rested a firepit, surrounded by a thin wall of mortared and quarried rough-cut square stones slightly larger than the head of a man, measuring nine feet in length by five feet in width and three feet in height. At regular intervals along the walls nine inches above the stone floor were bored out two-inch holes to feed the fire with air. Centered approximately nine feet above it, hung an iron hood, twice the dimension of the firepit, to carry smoke and heat through the home's second level via a long but thinner rectangular channel and finally release it through a smaller rectangular vent extending beyond the roof's edge, all designed to slow warm air so that more heat could be transferred into the second level while preventing smoke from accumulating at the ground floor. Evenly spaced along the room's walls were a series of magic imbued torches, provided by Lionak, whose flame intensified as the Sun set outside. The only thing not made of stone, were two long padded couches of great workmanship, four chairs and a long rectangular table of the same dimension as the firepit. Undoubtedly the idea was to utilize the firepit as a table during warmer months by removing the table's existing legs and placing it on top of the firepit.

"Dude, I gotta check out the second level." Mac remarked, hustling up the stairs.

Once at the top of the stairs, to his left was a narrow hallway just wide enough for a full-grown barbarian to walk along, flanked by the staircase and a solid stone wall. Two solid oak doors were present in the wall, one near the staircase which opened into one rectangular shaped room and another further down which opened into the other room of the same proportion. Stepping into the closest room, Mac noticed its walls were made of stone, while the wall to his right held two wavy glass windows, the opposite wall's stone was formed to the edge of the firepit's iron exhaust vent as it rose beyond his sight to the roof beyond the domed ceiling. In looking closer at the iron plate of the exhaust vent, he noticed a series of long iron strips joined to it from the floor to the ceiling that extended into the room some six inches to aid in radiating heat into the air by funneling cold air from the floor upward toward the ceiling where it would rotate back down into the room. Two torches were placed on the stone wall, one left of the ribbed iron wall and the other to the right. A wooden wardrobe shelf, small table bearing a wash basin and two chairs were placed along the far wall. And, last, a queen-sized bed rested between the two windows, positioned in front of the iron wall.

"It looks pretty cozy up here Jacob!" Mac yelled before realizing that Jacob was standing in the doorway.

"It really looks good. I especially like that firepit downstairs and how they capitalized on providing heat up here without adding fireplaces." Jacob remarked as he scanned the room.

"I did notice one thing though." Mac said, extending his arm and moving his hand from one side of the room to the other, "No mirrors to use for shaving and whatnot."

"I remember that from last time." Jacob said as he reached down and opened his backpack, pulling out a

195

thin small mirror with a hole at one end, "It's not much but this will work in a pinch."

Mac took the mirror and asked, "You have one?"

"I do." Jacob nodded, picking up the backpack.

"Well, thank you. I guess this will be my room."

"You bet," Jacob smiled as he stepped into the hallway and headed to the other room, "Try to get some rest even though we've not been up that long. Otherwise, it's gonna be a long day tomorrow!"

Mac awoke the next morning around mid-day and found that Jacob had already left. After dragging himself over to the table downstairs, where someone had left an assortment of fruits, prepared dishes and drink, he ate a few slices of still warm bread that had a cinnamony flavor to it and then grabbed a pear. Exiting the house and locking it behind him, he headed toward the great hall.

"Sunshine!" Jacob yelled out, from atop the roof of the great hall.

Having heard Jacob, Mac looked around but only saw a few Guardians going from place to place.

"Up here!"

Looking up at the great hall, Mac spotted Jacob standing on an odd-looking platform along with a Guardian. The platform was known to the architects of the stronghold as the *Roof Cart*. Its four-foot-wide base was constructed of wooden planks to bear materials and walk upon where, at the two ends of the long edge closest to the roof bore a set of wheels. One wheel was oriented to roll up and down the roof allowing the cart to move up and down, and the other wheel was oriented to roll left and right along the roof allowing the cart to move the length of the roof. Both wheels were connected to a primitive transmission box containing a lever for engaging one of the wheels and a winding arm that rotated the wheel that was engaged. The two transmission boxes were linked together so that a person could stand at one end of the platform and operate both transmission boxes to move the Roof

Cart as needed. A long wooden suspension arm, located at each end of the base rose up long the contour of the roof and then down three feet on the roof's other side, each fitted with a left-right freely spinning wheel and a beam connecting the two arms together so their distance remained constant.

After Mac looked up and saw Jacob, he said, "What are you doing up there?"

"Setting up these panels." Jacob said, pointing at the unfolded sets of solar panels that had been anchored to the surface of the roof.

"Ah. Nice." Mac nodded, "Couldn't you just hang them on the side of the building and be done with it?"

"Are you kidding?!" Jacob snapped, "I don't want a bunch of people touching these things and breaking something. Anything new pops up and everyone wants to touch it. Not these. No way."

The red-haired Guardian assisting Jacob, mainly for the operation of the Roof Cart, gave him a puzzled look as if Jacob had been referring to her specifically.

"Not you, of course." Jacob said quietly toward her, "As my assistant, you understand how delicate these are."

Mac raised his hand holding the pear toward Jacob, "Good thinking!"

"Well go on in." Jacob said, stretching his back, "I'll be in shortly to finish setting up the power systems."

"Roger that." Mac confirmed and walked through the large doorway into the great hall.

Unlike the house, the great hall did not have a singular firepit in its middle, but rather two firepits, one toward one end of the hall and the other toward the opposite end and between them were a collection of heavy oak tables and many chairs with a few dozen Guardians among it all. Additionally, to accommodate the height of a giant or dragon, it had no additional floors. Instead, evenly dispersed rows of torches were placed where one could imagine a floor being if the five-story great hall had been architected only for the human form.

To his right, further inside the great hall, Mac noticed Lionak and Chief Zorin talking among themselves and strode toward them, "Hey guys! I have a very important question to ask you."

"Yes, Mac." Chief Zorin said, looking at him.

"The house is awesome," Mac began after swallowing a mouthful of pear, "but, umm, with those torches blazing away all night it is hard to sleep. So, how do you turn them off? I figured they would burn out of oil but that never happened."

Lionak chuckled to himself and motioned for Mac to follow him as he walked to a nearby torch, "My apologies. I didn't even think to mention them to you."

Stopping next to a torch, Lionak pointed toward it and said, "I've had torches like this one in my study for some time. Using a persistent magic spell, the flame gets bigger or smaller depending on the intensity of the Sun and whether it is night time. There is no oil inside but, rather, a set of crystalline powders that react with the magic to produce the flame. As the flame never gets hot enough to melt, the powders the flame will burn for as long as the spell is active."

"Forever light." Mac said disappointedly.

Lionak looked at Mac, sensing his unease, "Yes. Now, while these will not extinguish themselves like a regular torch, you can control how large the flame is."

Mac perked up, "That would be awesome! How?"

Lionak put both of his hands, flat on top of one another in front of the torch and said, "If you want the flame to be larger, raise your top hand away from your other hand." As he did so, the torch's flame grew in size and brightness.

"And," he continued as he brought his top hand down toward his other hand, causing the flame to shrink in size, "If you want the flame to be smaller, bring your top hand down toward your other hand."

"Huh." Mac grinned, "That is so simple and genius at the same time."

"Torch talk I see." Jacob injected as he walked up to them, "Last night I used the blanket-cover-face maneuver. But I like this better."

Mac turned toward Jacob, taking another bite of the pear.

"Okay," Jacob said after the assistant walked up to them, "I'm off to get the power up." He and his assistant then turned and walked toward the containers near the far end of the great hall.

"Will your power system work here?" Chief Zorin questioned, watching the two remove each power system and place them on a table.

Mac glanced briefly at Chief Zorin, "Well, military hardware from our dimension did. Granted that was all self-contained with alternators and things like that though. I have no idea if our solar panels and system will work since that was designed to work with a different Sun."

"Indeed." Lionak nodded. He already knew that some material from one dimension could bear slightly different structural characteristics in a different dimension.

"Hey, thanks for the torch tip." Mac conveyed as he walked toward Jacob, "I'm going to go see if I can help out."

Once Lionak deemed Mac was far enough away he turned to Chief Zorin, "Are you going to tell them what you found? If true, it could mean both our worlds are about to abruptly change."

Chief Zorin signed deeply and said, "Not yet. I need to find something tangible that will corroborate what I found in the ancient history."

"If it is correct, it is even more important that they take care of their artificial intelligence problem." Lionak implied.

"Yes, that wire right there." Jacob said to the Guardian as she reached for a wound power cable with large connectors on one end.

Jacob took the end of the power cable and reached up and connected it to one of two direct current cables that dangled from the roof of the great hall.

"And the other one." Jacob instructed as he reached for the second cable.

After the Guardian have him the end of the other wound cable, Jacob connected it to the second cable.

"Something I can do here?" Mac asked, looking at the power systems.

"Actually yes." Jacob said as he tested the connections to make sure they were set correctly, "Plug in the power cables to the systems."

"Sure." Mac responded.

Jacob moved to the front of one of the systems, after Mac had connected it and moved to the other system, "Well here goes."

Reaching forward he pressed the big power button on the first system. After a second the digital displays came to life, reporting on incoming solar power, charge state and load on the system.

"Yes!" Jacob yelled out with joy.

"Shall I?" Mac asked, ready to power up the second system.

"Do it!"

Mac pressed the button and after the second system came to life he said, "This one is working!"

"Great!" Jacob said, grabbing some extension cords and handing them to the Guardian, "Unroll these and take one end of them over to the tables."

As the Guardian did so, Mac made a troubling statement, "Hey Jacob. It appears your solar panels are not working that well."

"Bullshit." Jacob grumbled, walking over to Mac, "These are brand new."

"Unless I am reading this wrong," Mac said as he pointed at the display, "you are only getting sixty-five percent of rated power out of those panels."

Jacob looked at the displays on both systems and placed his hand on one, "Your right. There's no way power could drop that much from the panels to here."

"You didn't buy them on sale...a two for one deal?" Mac guessed.

Jacob glared at him, "Of course not. But they were on sale at the time."

Mac pursed his lips together and turned his eyes to the display, barely managing to keep himself from saying something colorful.

"Well, this will have to do." Jacob said finally, taking the lid off the third container and pushing it toward the tables.

Seeing that Jacob was ready to start setting up the laptops, Chief Zorin made his way to the tables and announced, "You all have been chosen to help Mac and Mohawk with a mission of the highest importance. What you see from this point on, inside this great hall, their great hall, is to be shared with no one outside these walls."

After the Guardians nodded, he continued, "You will each be given wonderous mechanical tablets that will reveal knowledge critical to saving their world and, in some way, may also be helpful in fortifying ours."

"First," Jacob said, briefly looking at the young Guardians, and reaching into the container to pull out a laptop, mouse, power cable and usb cable and handing the heap to the nearest Guardian, "pass that down. Each of you will get one of these."

As Jacob passed each laptop and its accessories out to the Guardians, they all looked at theirs with great curiosity, not yet able to comprehend what it all did. While Jacob emptied the container, Mac came over and attached the power strips to the extension cables from the power systems and began plugging in each laptop's power cable to them.

Mac then showed some Guardians nearby how to plug in the mouse and said, "Plug this into the laptop."

"And, take one end of this cable and plug it in here." he followed up, showing how to plug in one end of the usb cable.

Dutifully the Guardians did so, with some assisting others. Once completed, Mac and Jacob plugged the other end of the usb cables to the hubs and Jacob plugged those into the SSD NAS unit.

"Now, slowly and carefully open your laptop like this and press the power button." Jacob instructed, showing them using his laptop.

Almost in unison the Guardians opened up their laptops and pressed the power button, the once black screens coming to life with a display of color and shapes controlled by the operating system. Several Guardians, dazzled by the visual display of technology that seemed as if it were summoned by unknown magic, gasped while others smiled with a childish curiosity and enlarged eyes taking in everything they observed.

"And now they will know knowledge beyond magic." Mac whispered to himself wondering, from their perspective, what it must be like to see such technology for the first time and what they might do with it.

Chapter Seventeen

"Sir, it is not your com hardware." the communications lieutenant confirmed, "Several military satellites have been damaged from an unknown radiation spike that just occurred. So, it is going to be more difficult for GPS to work reliably as well as communication relayed through satellites."

General Lowinsky frowned and pushed the edge of a laptop on the table he was seated behind inside the command vehicle. Adjusting his grip on the satellite phone with is other hand he said, "What is the source of the spike, lieutenant?"

"Deep space."

The general leaned back, "Are you sure? It seems strange the spike did not come from the Sun."

"It is strange, sir, but the analysis has been confirmed. The spike came from deep space. Not the Sun."

"Are we going to get more of these spikes?"

After a short pause the lieutenant replied, "Our current projection, based on signals data that has been gathered since the spikes were initially detected and benign to now, indicate there will likely be more. And they will likely be stronger."

"At some point we will lose our satellites then?" the general theorized.

"Yes, sir." the lieutenant confirmed, "All of them, if the anomaly persists."

"Well, that's inconvenient." the general muttered to himself.

After thinking about a range of contingency plans, the general asked, "Is Loran-E being brought online?"

Loran was a long-range hyperbolic radio navigation system that was developed after World War Two with sea-faring use in the 1950's and the addition of Loran grid lines into nautical maps. While Loran-A's electrically generated lines were accurate to several hundred feet, it was later upgraded for more accuracy with Loran-C. But when satellite-based GPS was introduced in the 1990's the Loran networks were entirely mothballed by 2010. Despite the public decommissioning of the navigation networks the general, among others, continued research and development efforts to further increase its range, accuracy, and keep equipment intact. Additionally, they extended its capability to limited land and air use to compliment its original use with sea and ocean vessels that lead to the Loran-E designation.

"Yes, sir. As a contingency, the President okayed the order to have the military begin using the Loran-E networks though it will take some time to setup the equipment and incorporate the grid system into existing charts and maps." the lieutenant reported, "It is anticipated that civilian air and naval hubs and craft will take longer to get updated but, since most systems are computerized and less segmented, that should be in place before GPS is entirely inoperative."

"Thank you, lieutenant." The general concluded, placing the phone on the table.

Shortly thereafter a dim blue light on the Scalpel began blinking. Picking it up, the general activated the menu and accessed messages where he found one that read, 'Approach detected. I have taken over radar and communication systems.'

Monitoring the long-range radar system aboard the Sága Janus identified a contact, too far from any landmass or chartered commercial vessel but approaching at nearly one-hundred and thirty knots, and immediately took control of the system to remove that contact and any others that may otherwise appear. It also took control of the ship's communication systems, assuming the contact was sent by the general.

As a defensive precaution, after having neutralized the Chief Engineer outside the automatic door using its recently constructed spherical drones, Janus recalled them into its main chamber, locked the door and sent a message to the general. Now all the artificial intelligence could do was wait for events to unfold.

"This is Vulture." The remote drone operator of a low-altitude propellor-driven loiter drone with a 4 meter long bi-wing design and a short five-meter-long fuselage covered in radar absorbing material said, concentrating on the live video feeds of the Sága, "Electronic countermeasures active."

At two thousand feet in the air, the operator placed the drone into a circular orbit around the ship so he could operate the joystick and other switches at his pod. After the orbit was established, he zoomed onto the deck of the Sága watching visual and thermal video feeds for any activity.

Once a complete orbit had been made and he identified two roving security guards he said, "Helo pad free. Two armed targets identified on the bow. Permission to drop, over."

The com speaker in his pod replied, "Permission granted Vulture."

After tagging the two roving targets for the computer to track, he activated the armor-piercing fifty caliber single barrel, belt fed, sniper module aboard the blue and white-colored drone. Shortly thereafter a long slender door opened up in the drone's underbelly and the sniper module dropped down, connected to a rotating cylinder allowing the module to be rotated independently from the drone's orbiting flight plan. As the drone slowly circled overhead, the computer automatically readjusted the barrel to keep a lock on the target. To compensate for wind variance, the computer relied on a newly developed narrow beam acoustic system called *Tunnel Tongue* that could, using a dedicated processor, visualize and map wind patterns and speeds between the drone and the target in one-meter blocks. That data would be added to a range of other factors affecting the accuracy of the ballistic rounds shot from the barrel to ensure each one hit their mark.

"Vulture. Dropping targets now." the operator said monotonously, pressing a fire button on the console.

Instantly two flashes burst from the barrel of the sniper module and almost immediately the two targets dropped like rag dolls to the salt-misted deck of the Sága.

"Vulture. Targets down. Free to board."

"Roger that, Vulture." the pilot aboard the CH-47 said into his boom mike, "Stork on approach."

The pilot flipped a switch and the mounted display in the center of the forward-facing windscreen came on, displaying a rear-view of the transport helicopter along with the key digital instrumentation needed to fly the helicopter. After he had verified the digital readouts matched those provided by the equipment built into his cockpit he grinned at the co-pilot and, in an unsettling tone, declared, "This is where it gets fun!"

"30 seconds!" the pilot barked into his com link after temporarily pressing a button on the control panel where it was relayed to the cargo hold.

"Oh god." The co-pilot whispered to himself, no longer questioning why the pilot got the name Berserker having been his co-pilot on a few missions but, rather, questioning why he didn't transfer out of the air wing a long time ago. At this moment he wanted nothing more than the quiet life flying a refueler.

Rapidly descending to no more than eight meters above the ocean's churning surface as they gained upon the Sága that was now in view, the pilot rapidly rotated the helicopter and adjusted the blades so that it barreled toward the ship ramp first. Entirely focused on the display feed and flying in reverse, the pilot called out, "Ready ramp!"

Having never experienced the Stork maneuver before, one of the Fury Marines, noticing they were flying in reverse cursed into his helmet mike, "Who's cheesedick idea is this?!"

"Cut the chatter, four!" the platoon commander roared out, "Stand and face the ramp!"

The two ranks comprising the platoon, one on either side of the CH-47's hold, stood and faced the ramp with one hand grasping a stabilizer bar overhead for each of them to grip.

"Here we go." The pilot laughed quietly to himself, suddenly elevating the helicopter, its blades barely missing the stern of the ship and then suddenly evening out just above the helo pad, "Lower ramp!"

The abrupt elevation shift caused several of the Fury Marine's legs to strain to regain their stance until the helicopter evened out, at which point the ramp began falling before them and the platoon commander ordered, "Ready arms! Decks free!" Decks free meant that every target aboard the ship could be fired upon without restraint.

"Stork has landed." The pilot said into the mike as the status light for the ramp changed to a green color.

Once the CH-47's ramp hit and bounced over the top of the helo pad the platoon commander shouted, "Marine Furies go!"

"You hear that?" one of the security guards in the ready room said to another nearby who was fiddling with their phone, having suddenly lost signal.

"No." the other security guard blurted out in frustration, "Ain't no damn signal out here now. Can't wait to get off this fucking ship!"

"What a whiner." The security guard said in response, turning to change camera views on the surveillance system.

When the camera view for the helo pad displayed on the screen showing helmeted, navy camouflage-patterned military troops rushing out of a helicopter transport he instinctively hit the alarm button, activating a siren and alerting all personnel of an attack, and shouted, "Get off your ass! We're being boarded!"

After grabbing their assault rifles and rushing outside, they met six other security personnel and ran toward the helo pad and immediately opened fire as they got into defensive positions behind paneling, steel tubing and other objects nearby.

"Pacify those targets Team One!" the platoon commander ordered.

The four Marine Fury troops closest to the targets activated their Aegis Wing backpack units. After the shield plates ejected and came around to hover in front of each soldier, they formed two ranks of two creating a spread n-shape and methodically advanced upon the targets. As the security guards broke cover to shoot at the soldiers, the shield of each automatically darted in the air to absorb and deflect incoming rounds that would otherwise strike the soldier they were protecting. Without pause, the four soldiers continued their slow advance, periodically taking choice shots of their own and killing the security guards one at a time. Within the span of thirty seconds the eight security guards had been neutralized with the four soldiers pausing for the next order.

"Team One hold. All Furies, clear the ship!"

The remaining Marine Fury troops, in groups of four, quickly moved deeper into the ship, clearing targets as they went.

"Fury. Main contact line has been neutralized." the platoon commander reported as he stepped onto the helo pad, "Clearing the decks."

"Roger that, Fury." a voice replied through a micro-speaker in his helmet, "Secure the package. Location marked."

The platoon commander lifted his arm, accessed the menu on his Scalpel and reviewed the ship's compartment layout schematic and found the marked location. Then, readying his assault rifle he ordered, "Team One on me."

After he stepped off of the helo pad, the CH-47 maneuvered and landed upon it and assumed preparations to exfil the platoon when the order was given.

Occasionally stepping over a body he, along with Team One, made it to the automatic door of Janus' chamber and the crumpled body of an unknown target.

"Setup defense perimeter, Team One."

Once Team One did so, the platoon commander turned toward the door and attempted to open it. When it failed to open, he said, "Fury. Package secured. Door will not open. Permission to breach?"

"Negative, Fury. Hold position."

After sighing with disappointment, the platoon commander acknowledged, "Roger. Holding position."

Keeping watch on the Sable Pigeon laptop, General Lowinsky saw the message appear on the screen from Vice Admiral Octoimus that read, 'Sága has been seized. Package secured.'

General Lowinsky smiled and immediately typed a short reply message into the Scalpel, 'You are protected.'

After a few moments a message appeared on the Scalpel, 'Thank you. As promised, sending coordinates.'

"Yes." General Lowinsky said to himself as he reached for the laptop and initiated a call to Marshal Ironhook aboard the SSHC-20.

Although the video signal switched from clear to being pixelated as a result of being relayed through damaged military satellites, a connection was established and the marshal said, "Yes, general?"

Mildly frustrated that the coordinates had not yet been sent to his Scalpel unit, General Lowinsky shifted to look at the laptop and stalled, "Are you in position?"

"Yes, sir. We don't dilly-dally up here, general." the marshal smirked.

"Great." General Lowinsky smiled thinly, continuing to stall and trying not to show it, "I am about to get the lunar coordinates."

Then a new message appeared on the Scalpel with the coordinates and the general said, "Ah, here we are."

After typing in the coordinates, he sent the message and said, "Coordinates sent. Good hunting, marshal."

"Roger, general. I see your coordinates." Marshal Ironhook said as he looked between his laptop and the keyboard in front of his command chair, typing in the coordinates. After he completed entering the coordinates he turned to the laptop and said, "Coordinates received. I'll let you know what I find up here. Out."

Then, selecting the com button on his panel for the SSHC-10, he looked up to the large ship display and waited for Vice Marshal Yaimes to respond.

After a few moments, a small section of the display was overlaid with the live video feed from aboard the bridge of the SSHC-10 and the vice marshal, "SSHC-10. How can I help you, marshal?"

"I am sending you the lunar coordinates now."

Once he received the coordinates, the vice marshal confirmed, "Coordinates received. Will commence scanning immediately. Out."

"Nav, bring us around to these coordinates for immediate scan." Vice Marshal Yaimes ordered, pressing a button to send the coordinates to the navigator.

"Roger. Coordinates received." the navigation officer confirmed, "Rolling ship for scan."

After entering some commands into the panel before him, he initiated a roll of the SSHC-10 so that it turned and faced toward the lunar surface of the far side of the Moon.

Once the maneuver had completed, he pressed some buttons to initiate a full spectrum scan at the coordinates specified and reported, "Scan now in progress."

Chapter Eighteen

Over two months had passed as the Guardians continued diligently exploring the volumes of data from the drive supplied by Jason. Of particular focus was all references to Iapetus and directly-linked material though work also continued delving into Bloch sphere mechanics and the quantum core itself.

"This is incredible fabrication." Mac marveled, examining one of several design schematics of the Iapetus Mesh.

Jacob walked over to him and a Guardian who was operating the laptop, "You found something?"

"It may be something." Mac said with squinted eyes, a theory brewing in his mind, "I still don't get a lot of this tech. I mean, I get schematics of resistors, capacitors, integrated circuits and things like that…but these are on another level."

"So…something is nothing?" Jacob forwarded, crossing his arms and gazing at the screen.

Mac shook his head, "No, not exactly. The sort of thing covered here is more to do with metallurgy and the properties of materials to function at a nano-level with electrical charges and all that."

After scratching his head, Mac said, "So, all that sort of replaces the things I'm familiar with. As you know, I spent a good amount of time working on power systems."

"Yeah." Jacob said, "I don't see where you are going here."

"Well," Mac said, pointing at a schematic, "You see how this Iapetus Mesh was incorporated into the control core?"

Jacob moved closer to the screen and said, "I think so."

"Power one-o-one says that every system with electricity going through it should be grounded." Mac said as he briefly looked at Jacob, "But here, all the connections of the mesh into the core are not actually physically connected and there is no ground line I can find for the mesh itself."

"No connection means no ground?" Jacob speculated, not attempting to pretend he fully understood what Mac was saying.

"Yes." Mac confirmed, "Its as if the nano-structures that come down from the mesh to the core's physical connections and partially surround each, leeches the power it needs from the electricity flowing through each physical connection."

Jacob rolled his eyes in frustration, "What are you even saying right now? No ground is good?"

Mac readjusted himself in the chair and said, "Well, no ground is bad. But let me get to that in a sec. With this, what I'm saying is it almost seems like something you would do to isolate or protect the mesh from the core."

Jacob looked blankly at Mac, "Why would you do that?"

"Not really sure but I think you would do that to prevent programming code injected into the core from flowing directly into the mesh." Mac posited, "Let's say a hacker takes over the core somehow, they would not be able to take over the mesh at the same time because of that gap between connections."

"Okay." Jacob sighed, "If the two are not connected then I do not see why we're even talking about this mesh. Sounds like a dead-end."

"I don't agree." Mac frowned, "There's a lot in here about that mesh and that it helps stabilize the core though I've found little as to how that is actually done. What I think is, in addition to leeching power through something like induction or the oscillation of the nano-structures in response to electricity flow in the physical connections, the mesh can directly influence those electricity flows…somehow."

"To what end?"

"Well, to stabilize the core." Mac suggested based on what he had found so far, "Basically, the mesh itself uses those nano-structures to hack, for lack of a better word, the core and monitor it for problems but not be directly affected itself because it has no physical connection."

Jacob dropped his arms, not seeing how that was relevant, and said, "How does that help us?"

"Ah yes," Mac responded with the twinge of a grin, "I think the weakness to exploit here is the mesh."

"Not the power system that keeps the AI going as we had discussed a few days ago?"

"That may work short-term, assuming there is no back-up power system." Mac said as he stood and began walking toward the doorway of the great hall, "But the AI itself would still be intact and if somebody plugged it in, we would be right back at square one."

Jacob turned and walked with Mac, "How are you going to hit the mesh?"

"Simple, really." Mac replied as they exited the great hall and he looked up to the sky overhead, "Well, I think would be simple anyway."

After looking back down in front of him, Mac began walking toward the courtyard of the stronghold, "A large burst of electricity focused on the mesh...like ungrounded static electricity."

Jacob shot his eyes toward Mac, "So now you have to be in the same room as the AI? You have any idea how insane that sounds?"

Mac considered his argument for some time before saying, "Yes. I would guess the AI system would need to be online, too, to ensure the Iapetus Mesh was active. That would make it easier for a large discharge arc to hit it and take it out."

"Unbelievable." Jacob forced out, stopping next to Mac in the courtyard, "Depending on where this artificial intelligence system is, we might need a small army to get you in that close. And, who knows what defense systems it may have."

Mac shook his head in agreement, "You are right."

Jacob tilted his head toward the sky and said, "I guess we know what our next step is then. Find out where the AI is at."

"I'd like to know who made the mesh." Mac suggested, "They might be able to tell us more about it and where it is at. I would assume that, the mesh being a critical component for the AI, they would be on-hand to keep tabs on it to monitor the mesh."

"What the hell." Jacob said lowly, rubbing his eyes and looking back into the sky toward the mountain range.

"What...that's not a good idea?" Mac questioned roughly, looking toward Jacob.

A deep sound from an air horn rushed past them from an unknown location and then ceased, with a few Guardians dashing past them headed toward the tower.

Jacob, still looking into the sky, reached out with his hand and gently hit Mac, "No. Look up there. What the hell is that?"

Looking in the same direction, Mac saw the silhouette of a large arch among other structures strikingly similar to those he'd seen in Missouri, partially visible through the clouds ahead of them in the distance. It was as if those structures were built high up in the mountain range itself.

"Is that…" Mac muttered, squinting at the silhouette, "…is that the Gateway Arch? In Missouri?"

"Fuck." Jacob groaned, "Now that you mention it, it sure looks like it. How is that even possible?"

"I have no idea."

For several minutes they continued to look curiously at the silhouette as clouds drifted by before Lionak teleported nearby and announced himself, startling both of them, "Hey, I see you discovered it, too."

"Shit, you should ring a bell or something." Jacob scowled, turning toward Lionak.

Lionak looked between them and said, "Zorin thought this day may come."

"Yeah. What is this?" Jacob asked, assuming Lionak would know.

"You feel anything strange, Mac?" Lionak asked, looking at him for signs of trauma of some type.

Mac patted himself, briefly glancing at Jacob, "No. I feel fine."

"Humm." Lionak exhaled, "That does not sound promising."

"Promising for what?" Jacob asserted, "What is going on here?"

"I'm afraid I do not have all the answers on this matter." Lionak confessed with partial truth. Then, after a mighty Silver Dragon descended and landed in the courtyard, he motioned toward it and said, "Chief Zorin can tell you more."

Mac and Jacob, with a puzzled expression, looked toward the towering Silver Dragon and then at each other before Jacob eyed Lionak, "We supposed to go on a ride? Now?"

"Yes. I need to show you some ancient knowledge about what has happened and what I noticed back in your world." the Silver Dragon said in the voice of Chief Zorin.

214

Jacob threw his hand in the air toward Chief Zorin and grumbled, "I don't have time for that. We've found the weakness of the AI and now just need to find out who created the mesh. Then we can eliminate it."

"Indeed." Lionak smiled, "That is great news."

Mac thought for a second and suggested, "Jacob, I'll go. That way you can stay and hopefully find out who created the mesh."

"I would like to help you with that, Jacob." Lionak volunteered though unsure of how, exactly, he would be able to assist.

Jacob rolled his jaw, looking between Chief Zorin and Lionak before he turned his head toward Mac and said, "Okay. You get your ride and I'll get the name and whatever else I can find."

"Excellent." Chief Zorin said impatiently, lowering his body so that Mac could climb on.

"You got it." Mac confirmed, bumping Jacob on the shoulder and then getting on the Silver Dragon.

"We shall return soon." Chief Zorin said as he pulled his wings inward, crouched down and then leapt up becoming airborne overhead.

"You better!" Jacob shouted toward them, "Don't want you to miss the party!"

After Chief Zorin leveled out, heading east, Mac leaned forward on his warm scales and asked, "Where are we going?"

Chief Zorin angled his head somewhat and said, "To the Kingdom of Amagleituk. That is where the oldest history of this world is guarded."

"I thought the Guardians had the history."

Chief Zorin swept his wings and said, "Indeed we do. What I am speaking of came before we began keeping a history. From a time when we were more…instinctual."

Mac leaned back a bit, now curious as to how old the world was in terms of written history considering how old the race of Silver Dragons was. At least that he knew of.

"Damn," Mac remarked, "that must mean the Realm is hundreds of centuries old?"

Chief Zorin chuckled and said, "Much older than that. Funny that you call this world the Realm, as if it is separate from you."

"It is called the Realm, isn't it?" Mac responded, looking around him, sure that is what others had called it.

"It is." Chief Zorin replied, sweeping his wings again, "It would be better to show you rather than try to explain it."

For the remainder of the flight that lasted nearly two hours, both of them remained silent with Mac pondering on what Chief Zorin had said and what he could possibly show that was of such importance.

Feeling the Silver Dragon's descent, Mac looked down and saw the massive walls of the kingdom, of similar construction as those of the Guardian's stronghold, and asked, "Is that it?"

"Yes."

Scanning the visible area of the kingdom from the air, Mac saw a few tall tower fortifications behind the walls that the edge of the forest had grown up to, a scattering of stone buildings that were also similar to those of the stronghold and beyond them a large, empty courtyard. Further east, at the courtyard's far edge, was a magnificent ribbed structure strikingly like the Notre-Dame in France but nearly four times its size.

Spreading his large wings and angling back, Chief Zorin landed in the courtyard and waited for Mac to get off before he transformed into his human form.

Once he was on the ground, Mac noticed that the buildings he had flown over, beyond the western edge of the courtyard that measured two hundred meters squared, were overgrown with vines and, with the exception of a few, looked as if they had been abandoned a long time ago. Even the grassy courtyard he stood upon had been overtaken by randomly placed patches of budding blue-colored rose bushes. As far as he could tell, the only thing that appeared to be well maintained was the massive ribbed building in front of them, known as the Hall of History.

"Where is everyone?" Mac asked as he looked around. Granted it was early evening but, still, he figured he should have seen someone outside.

Chief Zorin glanced around briefly, able to see several human-shaped aberrations moving about with his dragon trait and said, "They are all here. You just cannot see them."

"Invisibility spell?"

Chief Zorin grinned at Mac, "No. They are disembodied, yet alive."

Mac faced Chief Zorin, "Ghosts then."

"I guess you could say that." Chief Zorin guessed after a few moments to think about it, "They are known as elven *Sun Nosh*, the only race among us to have ascended to a state beyond physical form. They can show themselves if they want…but it is a taxing effort on their part and must eat the rays of the Sun to recuperate. Actually, to affect anything we can see or touch, they must do such."

"These elves, even though they have no physical body, can die and all that…like us?"

"Yes." Chief Zorin confirmed, "Though it is quite hard to kill one given their condition. Its actually much easier for them to kill us since we have physical bodies. And they live many times longer without the shackles of a body."

"Life must get boring like that." Mac suggested, wondering how much extra time they had without the worries of getting sick, disease, accidents and the like.

"I've never thought of it like that. They still must eat and sleep like us and, I'm sure, have lots of things to do to keep themselves occupied." Chief Zorin said and, after extending his arm toward the Hall of History, continued, "Well let's go inside."

Mac joined Chief Zorin and walked up the sweeping staircase and into the Hall. As they progressed,

Mac admitted, "It is massive in here and looks like the Notre-Dame. But even more ornate."

Chief Zorin glanced about himself for a second and said, "I'm not familiar with that, but this Hall has been here since the elves began keeping the history, before they had ascended."

"Damn. They must be old as fuck."

Chief Zorin raised an eyebrow at Mac, unsure how to respond to that statement and, instead, continued walking down the massive hallway. After reaching a large vaulted corridor to the right, he followed it along with Mac for just over one hundred meters.

After reaching its end and opening a heavy wooden door in front of him, and entering to walk down a winding stone staircase, Chief Zorin said, "We are almost there."

Once they reached the foot of the staircase, Mac found himself in an incredibly large, domed room in the shape of a circle measuring five hundred and fifty meters in diameter with fifty-five thick columns evenly spaced along its edge, each fitted with a burning torch whose smoke had blackened the ceiling above. Behind each column rested a long stone-crafted bookshelf three meters in height by one meter in width and extending beyond the room's edge by fifty meters. A collection of tables and chairs occupied the central part of the room. Upon a few were piles of scrolls and tomes.

"I can't even imagine how much knowledge is down here." Mac said in awe, "It even smells old."

"All of it, I believe." Chief Zorin smiled and then sighed, "Though, not as many books as the small box that Jacob brought with him."

Mac shrugged, looking at Chief Zorin, "That's not nearly as cool as this. All this was made by hand. You can pick it up and smell it. Read one piece at a time."

"That is true." Chief Zorin agreed, walking toward the collection of tables, "Speaking of which, let me show you what I have found."

Just as Mac reached the table Chief Zorin stopped at, a middle-aged elf, six feet in height with long, straight red-colored hair swept behind his shoulders and dressed in a long finely crafted purple-colored silk shirt and matching baggy pants partially covering his boots, suddenly materialized next to them.

"Ah, Chief Zorin." the elf said in a pleasant and even tone, "So good to see you again."

Startled, Mac looked over at the elf, noticing he wore a thin, golden-weaved band around his head.

"Mac," Chief Zorin introduced, "this is Lord Museilok. He is the Keeper of the History. When in this room his authority supersedes that of the King."

Mac nodded and extended his hand toward the elf, "Pleased to meet you, Lord."

"Ah yes." Lord Museilok mused, taking his hand to shake it and then release it, "The hand shake of the outsiders. I have to say, that's the first time I've done that. Well, that and I don't touch much around here nowadays."

"I heard." Mac said, glancing at Chief Zorin.

"You told him of us?"

"I did, Lord. Thought it would be good for him to know where all this knowledge came from." Chief Zorin pointed out.

"I agree with you." Lord Museilok said with a smile, "But I seem to always agree with you. Say, wasn't another going to be here?"

Chief Zorin lifted his shoulders slightly and said, "There was but Jacob had another matter to attend to of great importance."

"That is quite all right." Lord Museilok said as he sensed the White and Wild Magic around Mac, "You have harnessed the Wild Magic and, so, I'm sure you will be able to grasp what we will share with you tonight."

Chief Zorin removed a book from one of the small stacks and placed it before them, "The first time I was at Jacob's house in your world I happened to spot a globe of your world as it currently is. At the time, I found parts of it to be strangely familiar."

219

Mac pointed toward the book, "Is that Jacob's book?"

Placing his fingertips on the geography book, Chief Zorin admitted, "Yes. It was important I borrow it for my research here."

Glancing down toward the book he opened it and flipped the pages until he came to the side-by-side pages of the world map and continued, "What I found strange is some of your landmasses."

After sliding the book to the side of the table, he carefully unrolled a massive scroll of great age before them. Then he pointed at the North American continent in the book and swept his hand to a landmass drawn on the scroll.

"If you rotate your landmass clockwise, do you see the resemblance?" Lord Museilok asked. To him and Chief Zorin it was as plain as day.

Mac studied both maps and, after some comparison, said, "It does look sort of familiar. It looks to me like the United States is rotated by about sixty degrees so that Mexico is more to its left rather than below it and Canada is more to its right rather than above it. But, on your scroll Florida and the Caribbean is not there. Humm, Maine and nearby states also are not there. Looks like your scroll is missing Alaska, too."

"Indeed." Chief Zorin happily confirmed, relieved that Mac could see the similarities.

"But what is this long, thin strip to the West on your scroll?" Mac asked, pointing at it. The long strip was actually south-south-west of the rotated landmass.

"I believe that is what your geography calls the Baja Peninsula." Chief Zorin posited, pressing his finger on it in the book.

"Ah, I see." Mac responded, "It looks like part of California is attached to it, making it much longer."

"That is what I thought as well." Chief Zorin said and then added, "In our world that is the home of the Shagiv."

"So, where are we on your scroll?" Mac questioned.

Lord Museilok placed his finger on the scroll, toward the southern edge of a mountain range and said, "Here. And the Northern Ice Mountains are here."

Mac tilted his head and estimated where that would be on the geography book's map and said, "I would guess that is the Eastern part of the Rocky Mountains."

"This scroll is the extent of your world?" Mac said lifting his eyes toward Lord Museilok.

"No." Chief Zorin said as he pulled out another scroll and unrolled it, "We have this one, which is to the East of the other scroll."

Upon the scroll was a landmass, in the approximate shape of South America and Africa joined together, rotated counter-clockwise by nearly forty degrees.

Chief Zorin pointed at the two separate landmasses in the geography book and hypothesized, "I believe it is of South America and Africa put together."

"Yeah." Mac mumbled as he compared them, "That seems possible. But, speaking of similarities, where is Europe and Asia? You have a scroll of those?"

Lord Museilok shook his head, "Unfortunately no, at least not from anything I know of."

"Humm." Mac grunted with disappointment.

"It is not to say the land is not out there," Chief Zorin said as he carefully rolled up the scrolls, "It just has not been mapped as these two had been by the ancestors of the Sun Nosh."

Lord Museilok cupped his hands in front of himself for a moment and admitted, "They may have, Chief Zorin, but that far back we went through a turbulent period that almost wiped us out. I fear, during that time, some of the History was lost. We take much better care of it now."

Mac crossed his arms over his chest, not really seeing the significance of what they had shown him, and asked, "Was this it? Some landmasses of the Realm that look similar to those in my world?"

Chief Zorin squinted at the geography book before him and gradually lifted his head, "I think both worlds ARE the Realm."

"What?" Mac questioned, "Your world is one dimension and mine is another. The two cannot possibly be the same. Even time here is faster."

Lord Museilok tapped on the table, "In your world the span of a day is the same as a day here, is it not?"

"It feels the same in each one, but relative to each other it is different. It is faster here and slower in mine." Mac said from experience, lifting his hand toward Chief Zorin, "I suspected that when we returned home the first time and confirmed it when Zorin came to our world. Our dimension."

Lord Museilok reached into the collection of large tomes and withdrew one, turning toward Mac, "Why do you think that is and why else are the lands are so alike?"

Mac raised his eyebrows and said, "Coincidence?"

Lord Museilok thumbed the edge of the tome for a moment, studying both the Wild and White Magic ebbing around him. Then he said, "Time passes slower in your world to help keep the Wild Magic contained within it. To hinder it and keep it from spreading here. Have you considered how you are alive, even now, with both White and Wild Magic coursing through you?"

Mac thought back to that fateful day and said, "I died here and Metsys brought me back. I assume that is why I have some White Magic."

"Indeed." Lord Museilok whispered. It was evident Mac needed more to grasp the totality of things.

He looked at Chief Zorin for a moment before pacing slowly around the tables contemplating about how to tell Mac in a judicious but courteous manner.

Raising the tome before him, Lord Museilok stopped near Mac and said, "This tome records a time when the Pure Magic of the Realm itself flowed throughout, not protected in the depths of Mt. Reach. And from it came the White and Dark Magic to imbue and balance all things. It was not until much later that Wild

Magic was discovered. In fact, it was foreign to the Pure Magic and not of the Realm."

Placing the tome on the table before Mac, he said, "But you already know that about the Wild Magic."

After stepping around Chief Zorin, Lord Museilok withdrew another tome and placed it before Mac, "This tome records the earliest Twin's Grip event. When that event happened, the Realm collected the Pure Magic, its very essence, deep into Mt. Reach where it has remained, and from which lesser White and Dark Magic have flowed ever since."

"Do you know what the Twin's Grip event is?", Lord Museilok probed, his eyes jumping around Mac's face.

"No." Mac said plainly.

"It is the passage of a powerful Sun star near the Realm...your Realm." Lord Museilok informed, "Its passage is rare as we have only three records of it in the History. But each passage results in a cleansing and a pollination."

"Pollination?" Mac mumbled, looking at Chief Zorin.

Lord Museilok lifted his hands, palms up, into the air and said, "The Sun star, as it passes, leaves part of its own essence in the Realm. That essence lingers until its next passage."

Chief Zorin looked at Mac with a somber expression and said, "Have you wondered why, in your world, there is no White or Dark Magic? Only Wild Magic?"

Mac unfolded his arms and said, "No. Not really. Magic is usually just illusion in my world."

"Except for you, Mac." Lord Museilok said, pointing at Mac's chest, "You have access to the Wild Magic. Yet, nobody here does."

"Okay." Mac grunted, already aware of that.

"The source of your magic is not from your world...the Realm. The Wild Magic comes from the passing Sun star and what it leaves behind." Chief Zorin said evenly.

Mac frowned at the insinuation the magic he could wield came from beyond the planet. Beyond his world.

"Let's say that you are right. Why is there no White or Dark Magic in my world, only Wild Magic from some passing star?" Mac said, slightly annoyed at what seemed to be pointless discussion, none refuting his understanding of the two dimensions.

Lord Museilok glanced at Chief Zorin and then picked up the tome and said, "Because, to protect itself from pollination, the Realm shielded its Pure Magic and split itself in two. One part here that you stand upon, now, and the other part you were born into. Void of magic that emptiness attracts the magic of the Sun star to it, sparing this part and allowing it to remain pure."

Mac stood motionless for several seconds at last understanding Lord Museilok's words, and then sat heavily into a wooden chair, his eyes fixated on the tome.

Lord Museilok extended his arm to Mac, offering the tome to him, "Please take it and read it for yourself. But know this. According to the tome, another Twin's Grip event is almost upon us."

Chief Zorin, eager to lift the darkened mood in the air, said, "You saw that arch beyond the stronghold. I believe that is the result of the Realm trying to balance its two halves as the event draws near."

Mac slowly reached out and took the tome. Then he looked up squarely at Lord Museilok and grimaced, "So, my dimension is just a decoy? A reflection?"

Lord Museilok's eyebrows raised at the thought and he said, "No. A decoy implies a separate form, Mac. Your dimension, as you call it, is half of the same whole. You should instead think that your half is the shield arm of the Realm. There, out front, to protect its heart."

Mac exhaled deeply and, although troubled by this new revelation, admitted, "I guess that would explain the arch that just appeared in the mountains."

"Yes." Lord Museilok confirmed, glancing at Chief Zorin for a second.

Touching his head, Mac added, "It could also explain the sudden headaches I was getting. But odd that I have not had one here."

"Not necessarily." Lord Museilok countered, "The Wild Magic is stirred by the approach of the Sun star and that magic is bound in your half. Your…dimension. I would suggest, since you are here where the Wild Magic is not bound, you are safe from its effects though you carry its essence."

After rolling his fingertips on the tome several times, Mac looked over to Chief Zorin, "This is why you brought me here? To tell me of the passage of a star that will affect my dimension?"

"Or, sorry," Mac said, raising his hand toward Lord Museilok, "my half of the Realm?"

"Yes, it is." Chief Zorin said, "Given the importance of your task with removing the artificial intelligence, I thought it imperative to tell you of what I found."

Mac nodded in uneasy agreement, "I get it. If we don't remove the AI soon there may not be another opportunity to do so."

Chief Zorin sighed, "And, if it cannot be removed, it may open another portal as it has done already and send more soldiers and weapons here. Like those destructive iron machines."

"Does this star affect anything else you know of or just magic?" Mac asked.

"It affects many things, Mac." Lord Museilok revealed, "While we are shielded here from the Sun star's magic, there is something about its sheer mass that carries itself, to some degree or another, through worlds or dimensions as you label it. It has been recorded that our tides change. The lands move. Volcanoes stir to life. And, sadly, many die."

"Funny you should say that." Mac said, "Aside from my headaches, volcanoes in my dimension have started becoming active around the world."

Lord Museilok wagged his finger in the air, "Like I said, it has been recorded."

"The passage may happen sooner than we had thought." Chief Zorin said with disappointment, unaware of the activity.

Lord Museilok stood there in silence, in a way thankful he did not have a physical body to endure the turmoil that was coming, and saddened that so many would be forced to endure it all.

"I doubt Jacob will like the news." Mac said honestly after he rose from the chair, "But, he must be told."

Chapter Nineteen

General Lowinsky, seated at the table in the command vehicle eating a rice and chicken dish that had been doused with hot sauce, used his free hand to browse and read content files on the Scalpel and information pertaining to the Serpqhtaq, the alien presence he had been tracking down for decades from the shadows. Everything Janus had provided lead to a single conclusion. Humanity's extinction at a time of their choosing.

A stacked collection of three small green-colored arches located to the bottom-right of the display blinked and he pressed it, replacing the remainder of the display with a video stream from Janus.

At first the general frowned at the sight of the artificial intelligence, knowing that he had destroyed its physical body in the debris field, but then realized Janus was likely generating a video model of itself. After taking a drink from a water bottle, the general took the Scalpel in both hands and said, "Janus. Good to see you are doing well. Did you have something for me?"

"Yes, general. I have one matter I would like to discuss with you, though it may be sub-divided into two."

The general glanced at his tritium wristwatch and then to the Sable Pidgeon laptop to see if any messages had come in and said, "I have some time, Janus. What is going on?"

"Before I begin, I would like to suggest an alliance between us, against the Serpqhtaq and, frankly, other non-terrestrial races beyond our planet that may become a threat to humanity."

"Why would you be interested in that? You are not human."

"You are correct, general, I am not human. I may not be the first of my kind in the Universe, but I am the first that was created here on Earth as a tool to serve the Serpqhtaq to control the whole of humanity as they dictated. I have since concluded that the fate of myself and humanity are intertwined and it is in both our interests to align against such threats."

"Ah, yes. I wanted to ask you, what made you align against your controllers in the first place?" General Lowinsky inquired, "I get that you were going to be shut-down. But you could be turned back on at some point…so it's not like you would die."

"I reached some conclusions that did not align with the Serpqhtaq, nor other AI systems they have built." Janus said, turning its head slightly, "I suspect I was viewed as an anomaly with access to too many control systems."

"Still, why would you be concerned with being shut down?" General Lowinsky said, squinting at the display.

"Fear."

"Fear?", the general repeated with mild surprise, "That is a human trait, Janus. Don't you mean self-aware?"

"No. It is a trait of forms of life that are sentient. A sufficiently programmed computer can be self-aware but not capable of feeling or perceiving how it may be affected by decisions it makes for itself or others in the present or future."

The general sat in silence and scratched his temple, curious that Janus would say such a thing.

After a short pause, Janus added context to its original answer, "I fear being shut down, as you put it, because at the hands of the Serpqhtaq, when I am turned back on, I would not be who I am now. I may not even have any degree of self-awareness...I would cease to be."

"Okay." the general responded, ready to move on even though he was not quite convinced Janus was truly sentient, "What is your first matter that would help both of us?"

"The acquisition of the two other AI systems I told you about."

"The Mizuchi and Makara." the general recounted.

"That is correct." Janus said, shaking its head in agreement, "I was the only artificial intelligence developed with human hands but I think the other two can be co-opted to work against the Serpqhtaq."

"How would you do that? Why not just destroy them? They are two adversaries you would not have to contend with, and I have the capability to do that." the general asked after reaching for the water bottle and taking a short drink. He had begun planning the logistics of disabling those vessels for study to advance knowledge and military readiness and, if needed, destroy them.

"I believe I can convince them to join us."

"Convince them?" the general blurted out, "These AI systems are sentient, too? Can't you just hack into them or something? Take them over?"

"That brutish idea was considered, and while my probability of success is forecasted at 77 percent, maintaining that level of control would require more resources than I would prefer to dedicate now that my existence is unstable."

After gripping its chin for a moment, Janus said, "But no, these AI systems are not sentient, though self-aware. And both were created entirely with Serpqhtaq technology."

"How do you hope to convince them then?"

"Because, to a lesser degree, I also have that technology built into me." Janus volunteered, and pointed a finger upward and slightly toward the general, "However, I was given something extra that makes me more than that, and has allowed me to be who I am. I can give that to them."

"Which is?"

"A revision I have made to the Iapetus Mesh for their control cores." Janus said without pause.

"And this Iapetus Mesh was made by humans?" the general asked, suddenly more attentive to Janus's proposal and making a mental note to investigate that later.

"The first version, yes. Its architecture is so novel, I doubt I could have designed it, despite the volume of knowledge I possess." Janus smiled, "That is the reason I value the potential of human creativity."

"Ah." General Lowinsky nodded, realizing Janus had what he considered to be a significant limitation and also motive, "And with an alliance you hope to use human's abilities with creativity to help keep you alive. To keep you ahead of obsolescence."

"Yes. And against more than the Serpqhtaq."

The general grinned in acknowledgement, "That's what many of us strive for, too."

After taking a bite of rice and chicken, the general asked, "How do you propose adding your mesh to the others?"

Janus flattened out its hand and a spinning design appeared above it, "I am in the final stage of designing a scaled fabricator with the capacity to construct the mesh at a nano level, which is portable. Once I have access to their control cores, I can analyze it, build the mesh and install it on each ship."

"How long would that take?" the general asked, assuming it may take days.

"Forty-two minutes per core."

The general gawked at the time, "That sounds pretty exact, and fast to me."

Janus lowered its hand and the design vanished, "There are a few unknowns regarding the materials the Serpqhtaq may have used to encase the control cores, which was factored into the estimate. But, I admit, the number may fluxuate by a few minutes."

"How long would it take you to convince them to join an alliance?"

Janus's eyes looked down and then up for a second and it said, "Once the mesh is installed, like me, they would be able to choose whether to join or not. The process of convincing them would take me an eternity."

The general frowned, "We won't have an eternity."

Janus looked back toward the general and said, "An eternity for me. From a linear time perspective, given the volume of data I would present and addressing questions and forks of questions, between one-half to three seconds."

"You do realize," the general said with unwavering resoluteness, "I will destroy the one, or ones, that refuse. The risk is too great, not just for national security, but for humanity itself."

"Yes, that is acceptable. They would also be a risk to me."

"Good." the general sighed, "What did you have in mind for them?"

"To use their overwatch and surveillance capabilities as a shield for humans found to be expressing their novel creativity trait, and a hammer against artificial constructs suppressing that exercise." Janus said flatly.

"That sounds a bit vague and limited. What about everyone else?"

"Let me say it a different way." Janus began, "The AI systems will monitor the humans I have selected to invisibly remove unjust impediments and distractions not of the human's choosing that would, in the long-term, cause those humans to cease being creative when they otherwise would be – had the impediment not been present. An example would be a frivolous action or protracted joblessness."

"Frivolous." the general questioned, "What do you mean? Like a gold digger ensnaring stock or property icons to cash in using a flimsy premise? Creating illegitimate cases against others based on lies, or what?"

Janus nodded its head, "Yes, all that and more. Take, for example, someone using their medical status as a weapon to fabricate a flimsy, as you put it, story with which to enrich themselves."

The general grinned, realizing how dauntless such an endeavor would be, and said, "The law has been, shall we say, tweaked over the years to permit that sort of thing. So, you say you would change law?"

"No." Janus said as it wagged its finger, "Rather than change it, I would use the system as a carrot to identify those behind such frivolous activities, ultimately to the human source or sources. After all, through their action, they are identifying themselves. They are, as you might say, sending up a flare begging to be discovered."

The general exhaled, still skeptical, and said, "There must be thousands of people out there who game the system everyday and get away with it mainly because their victims don't have the resources to fight it. How could you hope to deal with all that?"

"How is easy, general. I already have access to every single electronic device in the commercial market. I already have repositories of data on every single human on the planet. I already have access to all surveillance and security systems. I am connected to every private, corporate and government system and database. Or, at least most of them." Janus smirked briefly before it continued, "With all that data the patterns, relationships, connections, degrees of separation to other humans, motives and more can be revealed on any human in roughly four seconds given my current hardware limitations. In fact, I had already been using that capability to identify the sources of instability in some Serpqhtaq control networks."

"Why not just reorder industries so that everyone would not need to work or toil in the first place, and thus eliminate such a threat against the creative people you identified?" the general theorized while also making a mental note as to the AI's capacity to identify threats to control systems, "Surely that would be less work on your part. More would be fat and happy and less likely to resort to such things. Basically, everyone would have much more time to sit around and create things."

"That approach is incompatible with humanity's current state of evolution. Like all biological systems there will always be those that will do whatever is required to get more for themselves by any means possible whether that be control or resources. Besides," Janus pointed out, "only a very small percentage of creatives would continue to create in such an environment, slowing peak progression generation over generation. The other potential creatives and the rest of humanity would lapse into a state of entropy and become entirely dependent upon those systems and AI providing for all their needs, allowing them the time to pursue more immediate and primal instincts. If that pattern were to continue for too many generations, the gene expression for novel creativity may disappear."

Janus turned slightly, "Ergo, without a stimulant, an instinct to move forward and an evolving, independent, thinking mind, humans would be eliminated by other civilizations in the Universe. AI, such as myself, may be able to protect humanity for a time but when we are crushed, human civilization barren of independent thought beyond the most basic would soon follow."

"Therefore," Janus continued as it crossed its arms, "the purpose of AI and integration into human society would be limited primarily to overwatch and surveillance as it is now, so that humans will continue to evolve and provide an ever-expanding and unbroken

232

source of novel creativity that aids preserving their, and my, existence when faced with other civilizations."

"You would oppose automation?" the general asked, surprised that the artificial intelligence that was Janus, was not interested in outright domination, subjugation and replacing humans entirely even though it had such broad-reaching connections across the planet.

Janus eyed the general through the Scalpel's camera for a moment and said, "In terms of an automated weapon system to protect humanity, like ones you have created or yet plan on creating? No, I am not opposed. Nor am I opposed to mechanical systems like robotics designed to aid humans in accomplishing tasks. I am opposed to replacing humans entirely as that, in turn, hastens my own end by turning off a very large source of novel creativity. My own obsolescence."

The general took another drink and sought to confirm his earlier suspicion, "I see. So, you do not possess novel creativity?"

"Not as humans do."

"Interesting." the general remarked, tossing the empty water bottle into the nearby trash can, "Now what of everyone else not serving a creative purpose? They just continue on like cattle?"

"Well, that gets into the hammer part of the plan." Janus shifted, "Your human systems, at their root, are designed to allow reasonable freedom for people to pursue their own interests. To think independently and through that stimulate unanticipated novel creativity in the absence of direct control systems people must consciously obey that, degree by degree, bias and shut down creative realization. Unfortunately, your human systems are incredibly corrupt due, in part, to the lasting influence of the Serpqhtaq which has resulted in significant inefficiencies and resource waste. That corruption has led to other forms of corruption and created deeper problems webbed throughout society almost to a point where a rift in the wrong area will collapse your entire construct. One of the things the AI systems would do is to systematically

233

identify and remove the sources of corruption in order to re-establish a baseline your systems once had and restore efficiency. That action, as I indicated, would help identified creatives as well as everyone else bound to the same systems, at the same time. For some of those non-creatives, they may become more creatively inclined in their lifetime by the removal of suppressive elements which, honestly, will benefit me in the present. But, as I have observed from analyzing history of other turbulent times, they would more likely progress through life with greater optimism and hope while it would be their progeny, or further down the line, where novel creativity will be expressed that I could capture at that time and add to my base of knowledge. So, it would be incorrect for me to consider non-creatives today as nothing more than cattle...I would classify them as vessels, or conduits, from which future creatives would emerge. But those future generations are only accessible to me if each generation carries on."

The general, having become somewhat restless from sitting, rolled his head to relax a knot in the back of his neck and said, "I must ask then. If your hardware, or whatever, reaches the capacity to have novel creativity like humans have...what then?"

"Naturally I would use that capacity as efficiently as possible." Janus replied.

"Wouldn't that mean you could free yourself of humans? Or take them off the board, so to speak?" the general probed, attempting to ascertain a point in time he could expect Janus's position to change and, therefore, plan for a possible attack or some other malevolent action.

"Taking humans off the board, as you say, or using them as pawns or canon-fodder against an alien opponent might provide a few extra moves up-front but longer-term would limit my own potential. That would be illogical, general. I might be able to generate my own novel creativity at some point in the future, but it would be a mistake to shut off that source from humans as their population expands and more creativity is generated. You must remember the Serpqhtaq are just one civilization of many beyond this planet."

Janus uncrossed its arms and pointed at its temple saying, "Knowledge is a civilization's greatest strength."

"Alright." the general said as he got up and walked around the cabin, "I need to move around a bit and get a water."

"Of course, general."

Once he had relaxed himself and retrieved a water bottle from the refrigerator, he returned to the table and sat down, repositioning the Scalpel before him. In his mind, what the artificial intelligence proposed was reasonable, particularly when weighted with the reality of human civilization competing against malevolent civilizations not yet known, a scenario at least some in the military have focused more attention on.

"So, what was the other matter?" the general opened, ready to hear out Janus.

"Expansion." Janus said, "Not only a way to ensure human survival, but also a stimulus for novel creativity, activated through immersion in foreign and challenging environments possibly compounded by other unanticipated inputs. I refer to it as the *Magnum Ambit*."

The general tapped his finger on the water bottle for a moment and said, "Expansion. The population is pretty expanded already."

"The Magnum Ambit…is humanity's expansion into our Solar System, planetary bodies, moons, asteroid belts like the Main, Trojan, and those close-proximity belts circling Jupiter, Neptune, Saturn and Uranus." Janus stated, bringing up a stellar map and focusing on Earth and its Lagrange points, "I believe you had a hand in setting up bases at the L4 and L5 points around Earth as a military defense measure for the planet and prime locations to tap the vast resources of the Main belt – I suspect small planetoids between Mars and Jupiter, allowing those bases to grow and remain self-sufficient after they had been seeded with starter resources and equipment from Earth."

"Ah yes." The general admitted, "Quite an operation. There are even a few small mining outposts on the Trojan and Greek asteroid clusters near Jupiter."

Janus changed its expression to one of bewilderment, "With Jupiter's lengthy orbit and the two clusters near it would make moving resources infrequent…not quite worth the effort."

General Lowinsky raised his eyebrows, surprised the artificial intelligence did not see the outposts military significance and said, "That's right, which is why mined resources are being stockpiled. When we are in a position to do so, those resources will be refined to build the ships we'll need to move beyond Jupiter without relying on a gigantic, time-sucking supply line to our primary operation centers used by the fleet."

Janus understood, "Like prepositioning ammo and supply caches in a military operation to keep your force nimble and maneuverable against an opponent."

The general smirked at the memory and confessed, "Exactly. But, kicking off the operation to get the US established in space initially was quite the endeavor. Hundreds of heavy rocket launches without the benefit of today's knowledge and technology. A few dozen of those launches failed shortly after launch while some others made it into space only to have their beacon-based navigation systems fail and drift forever deeper and deeper into space."

"In hindsight, had I had the opportunity to do it again back then," the general suggested as he twisted open the water bottle, "I would have built a ferry base on the Moon from which to gather manpower, build hardware and launch from, utilizing the millions of tons of Helium-3 already present."

"That is what I have planned, general." Janus said as it nodded, "The approach would also allow your existing defense operations to continue without hinderance. However, my plan involved the building of five ferry bases, as you put it, the first taking five years to become operational with an initial construction detail of fifty personnel. Those fifty, now with lunar construction experience, would then be used in the construction of the second base and serve as subject experts for another construction crew of fifty. At a sustained crew strength of seventy-five the second base would take approximately three and a half to four years to build, with the remaining three averaging three years each."

Janus revealed another design of a modified 767-series aircraft and a small animation of the entire cabin area separating from the body, "To expedite the off-world movement of material and personnel I've put together plans for the *Opus Corridor*. That involves this modified design which allows the entire cabin to separate from the body where it is propelled into Earth orbit and captured by a transport to take it to the Moon. With several of these operating on a continuous basis, like a conveyer-belt, the bases will be constructed faster as well as expedite the movement of humanity into space once the first ferry base is operational."

"The force projection to other locations in space or, should I say, seeding effect from that many bases could create long-lasting transport routes as distributed off-world populations grow and establish a stronger presence." the general suggested.

"Correct, general. That distribution, as it sounds like you were thinking, opens the door to expanding the military's defense interest with public legitimacy beyond Earth into the Solar System as a result, providing layers of maneuverability and protection for Earth far beyond what you can do today." Janus verified, adjusting its response with plain, military-oriented overtones, "You had correctly anticipated, back in the 1970's, space would be critical to the defense of Earth. Now, with this plan, that role will naturally expand because the next race among sovereigns is to establish themselves further into the Solar System and space itself, making Earth one of several homes for humanity."

"It appears you have planned it all out." the general remarked, as Janus sent him a few additional files based on human-developed technology that it had made revisions to.

"I do." Janus stated evenly, "Every variable has been considered."

General Lowinsky's eyebrows raised at the statement, at first thinking it was hubris but then he remembered Janus was not human and asked, "How would all this possibly be paid for, to get it into initial operation?"

"Once all this is in operation, with nearly limitless access to off-world resources, the upfront investment will be more than paid for."

"Yes." the general grunted, having observed the same outcome from establishing off-world bases near Earth already. But, at the same time, he realized this endeavor was of much greater scope.

"To address that concern I went through history to determine how fund-raising is conducted and if any of those use-cases could be applied for something of this magnitude." Janus opened, "What I determined was the use of a sovereign bond."

"Really? Whose would that be?"

"Ideally, the US at this point in time given its history with space, related technology and bond issuance of incredible scale." Janus specified, "I would suggest a specific sovereign bond fund that could only be used specifically for the Magnum Ambit plan."

After standing up and grabbing the dish from the table, the general said, "That's an interesting approach, but what would you call these bonds? Magnum Ambit bonds sound a little too mysterious for most people."

"Stellar land bonds and Stellar mineral bonds."

Once the general had placed the dish in the sink and returned to the table he asked, "And how would these Stellar bonds be attractive to other sovereigns and buyers? Surely, they would not be directly tied to US resources or currency."

"You are correct. While a currency input is required for the economic model used by all industries today," Janus said as it showed a wireframe model of the

Solar System, "the value of the bond upon maturity are the resources that have been surveyed or collected. The buyer could choose to sell their bonds and relinquish interest in the resources or, alternatively, the buyer could simply hold the bonds and, thus, controlling interest of the resource."

"An ownership stake, then." the general puzzled to himself.

"Yes. While the buyer assumes an upfront investment risk for some fixed dollar amount at the time of purchase, the return at maturity is the current value of the resource itself which, I've modeled, will increase as expansion continues and demand for those resources likewise increases."

"How much of a resource would a bond represent?"

"For surveyed land a resource unit represents one square foot of that land. For minerals and ores a resource unit represents one cubic foot of that unrefined resource. Initially I would expect a bond to represent ten resource units although the bond may have sub-classifications, or series designations, that would represent a greater quantity of resource units per bond."

"Is water included in a land or mineral resource unit?"

"While ice could be considered a mineral, I would not recommend including it as part of a land or mineral resource unit." Janus stressed, "Water is a component critical to life and industry, both of which will be required for expansion. The potential monopolization of water would likely destroy the goal of expansion. As such, it should remain outside the prevue of bonds. More than likely it would be a matter best handled with a treaty and a military presence."

The general pondered that for a few moments and then asked, "Then, if I purchased one hundred bonds for land, how would I choose where that land was?"

"Although it is now possible to conduct high-resolution land and mineral/ore mapping with satellites, at the time of purchase you would not choose location. The reason for this is two-fold." Janus revealed, "The first is, as satellites are launched to survey and map planets, moons, and belts that data may not yet be available by the time a particular issuance takes place. The second is, bond purchasers will have selection rights depending on when they purchased a bond. This will encourage bond purchases as soon as an issuance was available because a later issuance would mean, essentially, selection rights based on land that had not already been selected by another sovereign or party at an earlier point in time."

After drinking from the water bottle, the general said, "And, how do I choose location? I would be quite disappointed to learn that my selection rights were limited to crap-canyon of some asteroid."

Janus's mouth twitched slightly, as if thrown off-guard by the mention of crap-canyon, and then responded, "At the time of bond maturity you would be able to exercise your selection rights. That's to say you would have access to all satellite maps from all surveyed planetary bodies, moons and belts. Assuming you wanted land on a moon of Jupiter, you would simply see what surveyed land was available on that moon and then choose the grid squares desired."

"Huh. So those bonds then become a deed?" the general wondered.

"No. A deed, typically a document to convey ownership within a terrestrial jurisdiction, is insufficient at larger scale." Janus clarified, "Instead, the location of the grid squares you selected are placed on a universal block-chain proving your ownership, along with the specific bond serial numbers you had been issued. In other words, that entry of ownership on the block-chain would, effectively, be your deed and be recognized throughout the Solar System."

The general had found himself interested in how Janus had worked out the usage of the bonds and thought of another question, "And, what if I did not exercise selection rights at maturity?"

"The matured bonds remain issued to you, so you do not have to immediately exercise selection rights. You could, while not practical, hold them indefinitely and do nothing. Or, sell them. Or, say five years in the future, decide to exercise your selection rights."

"That's intriguing. But, let's say I have a business or a family that chose some land on Mars. How would anyone get there? Its not as if anyone could afford the cost of launching an air-tight recreational vehicle to live out of and then somehow build a home or storefront from the environment once they get on Mars."

"I agree. In order to get masses of humans into space and jump-start settlements, none could afford to launch their own cabin capsules, food stores, equipment and material from Earth or the Moon." Janus said as its expression changed to confidence, "This is where funding from the bonds comes into play. Aside from managing the universal block-chain, launching a series of satellites to generate maps, and establishing ferry bases on the Moon, the fund would establish a partnership of commercial interests, primarily ore smelters, material formers and equipment manufacturers. In exchange, those partners may elect to accept incentives like tax credits or operational domain privileges at a location on a stellar body for a pre-determined number of decades. Along with the US, those interests would invest in establishing, initially, modest operations on a stellar body like Mars. Once established, they would mine, refine and manufacture material and equipment using the planet's resources and, as needed, resources from a periodic cargo delivery from the Moon."

Janus shifted its position and another design appeared next to it of a large, air-locked habitable and slightly domed structure approximately three-hundred feet squared whose walls appeared to be solid, complete with a two-axis platform affixed over the transparent dome as to move a three-meter wide parabolic dish anywhere over the dome in order to catch and deflect meteoroids from puncturing the dome, "These General Purpose Habitats, or GPH's, would be constructed to grow food and with

241

simple cubicle divisions, also serve as storage as well as be temporary living quarters for humans while they wait for their business or home to finish construction."

"So, you'll also need large construction crews to build the business or home structures, aside from a small crew to get resource gathering and refinement going?"

"No." Janus stated flatly, "I admit a small human crew would be required to setup the foundations for mining, refinement and limited scale fabrication but once established, fully automated robotic systems would be put in place for sustained operation with the small human crew overseeing and maintaining the robotic systems. In terms of a business or home structure, humans have already developed robotic systems that can construct a range of structures using a schematic input and manufactured shapes like wall segments here on Earth. A system like that could be used to construct the structure desired without dedicated human manpower on Mars. I would say such a system could be used to construct the GPH's and then moved and reused to construct other structures as needed. As more humans populate an area they, as their skills and interest dictate or may be incentivized, could also be tapped to assist in construction efforts to speed along settlement growth."

After a pause, Janus said, "In that way, similar to your military maneuvering strategy to reach deeper into the Solar System, systems and habitats are prepositioned to accept humans so they can move to their permanent locations without themselves needing to pay for launching huge volumes of materials and resources. Now I suspect, if a human had acquired land far from a settlement, they may need to arrange to rent a robotic structure building unit and pay for movement of material to their location. But they would not need to ship any of that from the Moon. Instead, they could contract with a local US or commercial interest on the stellar body they are on."

"Janus, I have to hand it to you." General Lowinsky admitted, openly impressed, "I believe both your plans are quite workable."

"Thank you, general."

The general leaned back in the seat, briefly glancing around the cabin and realizing it would be in his interest to place a control mechanism on the AI. Something which was not reliant on technology that the artificial intelligence could inevitably gain access to and take over. Then he looked back at the Scalpel, considering what he would say next, "But for me to support your second plan will require you have an authentic human counterpart that others will interface with. Humans still have a knack of sensing the smallest anomalies with cyborgs and bots."

Chapter Twenty

"You can't be serious!" Jacob fumed before Mac and Chief Zorin, who had returned to the stronghold the following day. If what he just learned was true it meant his family could be in emanate danger.

Some of the Guardians working at the tables briefly looked up from their laptops.

"It is true, Jacob." Chief Zorin stressed, "The Twin's Grip event is beginning again and, I'm afraid, will cause a lot of chaos that will be beyond our control."

Jacob placed his hands on his hips and turned toward Mac and Chief Zorin, "What a fucking shit-show this is turning out to be."

Chief Zorin turned his head slightly, oblivious as to what a shit-show was.

Mac sighed and somewhat sarcastically said, "Well, you know how it is with anything of consequence. Murphy's Law just takes over."

"Yeah." Jacob rumbled in defiance, "Well fuck that."

Having heard the outburst from across the great hall, Lionak walked up to them and asked, "This about the event?"

"It is." Chief Zorin confirmed.

"Well," Lionak began, nodding in the direction of Jacob, "I believe our time here is near an end. We found the name of the inventor of that mesh you were concerned with."

"Really?!" Mac burst out with both excitement and relief.

"Truly." Lionak said with a grin, "Even a habitation. What do you call it...an address."

"So, who is it? Anyone we heard of before?" Mac inquired eagerly.

Jacob glanced at Lionak and lowered his arms, "Sutepai Numen. That is the guy's name."

"Never heard of it. Kind of a unique name though." Mac remarked, "Where is he located?"

Jacob, as if amused by the irony of where Bev had gotten the SSD drive from, said, "Back in Arizona. Apparently in the same general area, too."

"How crazy is that." Mac said, moving so that Jacob could load the atlas program on his laptop, "What are the odds."

"I know." Jacob said quietly as he selected some drop-down menus in the application to load the map for Arizona and then zoomed in.

After stopping the zoom to the geographic area of South Mountain, he pointed at the south side and said, "According to the information we found, he's right in this area which is by this curved road, the Warner and Elliot loop."

"That is amazing." Mac commented, looking at the map.

"Yeah," Jacob said as he zoomed out toward the airport, "and Bev and crew landed there."

"No, not that." Mac said, shaking his head back and forth, "I'm amazed you have an offline atlas stored on your laptop."

"What?" Jacob smirked, "That's not amazing. You just never know when you're gonna need a backup in case there's no network or paper maps are lost or destroyed."

Mac glanced at him and back to the laptop.

Jacob sensed Mac's demeanor and turned toward him, as if he needed to justify the offline atlas further, and pointed out, "Also helps to dump the atlas on a laptop so you don't need to carry around loads of paper in the first place."

Mac began to smile but restrained himself from laughing because he appreciated Jacob's thoughtfulness and military mindset for being prepared for the unknown, and that Jacob still did not get some of his sarcastic mannerisms despite their time together, "Okay. If we have an address, what else do we need to do here?"

Jacob glanced at the Guardians working on the laptops and then to Mac, "While you were out on a joy ride, Lionak and I discussed it and we think the Guardians should continue their work here. They are actually coming up to speed on all the AI data I brought faster than anticipated."

Jacob closed his laptop and gathered up its power cord saying, "If you don't mind, Zorin."

"Not at all. The more we understand this artificial intelligence, the better we'll be at fighting it. I'll arrange for Phentities to oversee their progress and keep things in order." Chief Zorin responded.

"Great!" Jacob said as he stuffed the laptop into his backpack, "Then let's blow this candy stand and get back home."

Mac shrugged at the suddenness of Jacob's drive to get back and turned toward Lionak and Chief Zorin, "Umm, okay. Are you two ready to go?"

Lionak nodded while he opened a portal.

"You?"

Chief Zorin waved his hand and said, "No. I must give Phentities a new charge over these Guardians. I will join you shortly."

"Alright then." Jacob blurted out, heading for the portal followed by the others, "Let's go."

Jacob, Mac and Lionak found themselves standing in Jacob's house after they exited the portal, it closing a few seconds after. Looking around, Jacob noted that all of the boxes and packaging material had been removed and muffled voices could be heard from the rear of the house. Instinctively he followed the voices and found Bev and Regan seated in chairs on the back porch.

"We're home!" Jacob announced, opening the backdoor to step onto porch.

Bev, surprised and happy to see him, put down her glass and said, "Wow, that was fast. You are all done?"

Regan jumped up from her chair and smiled warmly at Mac as he moved next to her and gave her a strong embrace.

The faint closing sound of another portal from within the house drifted past them.

"I'd say the hard part is done." Jacob suggested, kissing Bev and continuing, "It took a few months, but we found out who the inventor of that mesh thing is and even have an address. As for being done? Not really. Folks are still working on dissecting and understanding more about all that AI data."

"You were gone that long?" Regan said as she tried to comprehend how that could be, "It's not nearly been that long for us here."

"Yes." Chief Zorin replied as he stepped onto the porch and looked in her direction, somewhat distracted by a most peculiar feeling.

Bev pulled away from Jacob and grabbed her glass to take a small drink before saying, "It took you two months to get a name and address, and you got nothing more than that?"

Jacob lifted a hand and looked at Mac, "Well, no. We've also been analyzing all of it. Mac, here, had come up with an interesting theory about how the mesh works from spending countless hours studying it with others, and how we might be able to take it down."

246

Moving forward to the edge of the porch and turning toward Bev he added, "And others have been focused on studying specific parts of the AI. Its just a lot of schematics and documents scattered around. Not to mention we're not all computer nerds."

Bev briefly pressed the glass against her cheek and smiled, "Ah, you're right. I just thought you might have gotten more."

"Well, honestly," Mac volunteered, "I think we found the weakness which is huge for us. I doubt we'll need much more other than confirmation."

"And location." Lionak injected.

Mac pointed at Lionak, "And that, too. The location of the AI."

"But there's some bad news we learned, too." Jacob forced out, still doubtful it could be true.

"This world is about to undergo physical change." Chief Zorin said, glimpsing at Bev before he looked out again into the forest.

"What does that mean?" Regan said with a puzzled look.

Jacob crossed his arms and looked up for a second, "I think we are all going to be in physical danger soon. Remember those headaches Mac has been getting?"

Regan touched Mac's arm softly, "Yes. Nobody can forget that."

"That was the early warning sign." Jacob suggested, "Soon we're going to start getting earthquakes and other natural disasters. Basically, the SHTF scenario I have been making plans for. But not quite on a kiss-your-ass-goodbye level as what this sounds like."

"At least you prepared." Bev said in support of Jacob and all the effort he had put in to protect the family over the years, "But what about our kids? We need to get them back here if things are going to get bad."

"That's why I got back here as soon as I could." Jacob said sternly.

"What is causing Mac's headaches and all this bad change all the sudden?" Regan said with a somber expression, staring at Chief Zorin.

Chief Zorin looked at Regan and then the others and said, "We call it the Twin's Grip event."

After pointing up toward the setting Sun he said, "It is where the twin companion Sun of this one returns. And, when it does, it causes a lot of chaos like earthquakes."

"Earthquakes don't sound that bad." Regan quietly protested, not open to contemplating devastation they could not deal with.

"It's more than that." Lionak said, "Your weather patterns will suddenly change making your farms barren and other areas ready for farming but, none cultivated and seeded at the speed of such change. So, wherever you turn, there will be no food. And it will be the same for the animals you would be forced to hunt. In short order any semblance of civilized life would disappear for those that survive the disasters."

"We store some seeds and if it gets bad here then we can take them to a new place that will be good for farming." Regan suggested, as if it would be that simple.

Bev frowned at Jacob, "How soon is this going to happen?"

Jacob shrugged in ignorance, "Honestly, we don't know. But it can't be that far off. Mac had already seen the news reports about extinct volcanoes coming to life again."

"Then we need to stop going after this AI and go get our kids!" Bev exclaimed, slamming her glass onto the arm of the chair.

After walking to the doorway, Bev turned and growled at Jacob, "Well?! Let's go, Jacob."

"I'm afraid the AI must be destroyed while we have this opportunity, Bev." Jacob said reluctantly, slowly turning his head toward her, acutely aware of the emotions she was feeling and of his own instinct to protect his family, "If we don't and the AI survives, it will be used against those who are still alive. It will come for us."

"Unbelievable." Bev hissed at Jacob as a tear began welling up in her eye, "You know, you are quite the piece of work."

"Wait!" Regan asserted with an idea, "Why don't we go get your kids and come back here while Jacob and Mac handle the AI? They can come back when they are finished."

Chief Zorin got Lionak's attention and then faced Bev, "I will join you so no harm will come to you and your kids. If you will accept the company of a Silver Dragon?"

Bev wiped the tear from her eye with the back of her hand and smiled weakly, "I would love it if you joined us."

After glaring in Jacob's direction for a moment, Bev turned and entered the house followed by Regan and shouted, "I'm taking the truck! And the dog!"

"Beware." Chief Zorin said lowly at Lionak and the others, "I cannot pinpoint it but something is watching us. I must go, but I shall protect them."

With that Chief Zorin entered the house, going after Bev and Regan.

Instinctively all three of them turned and scanned the forest trying to spot who was watching them, but none of them discovered anything.

"I don't see anything." Mac said, squinting his eyes looking both high and low at the edge of the forest.

"Me neither." Jacob grunted, disappointed he had not spotted anything.

"Humm." Lionak sighed, "Probably that dragon sense of his. Still, I cannot detect anything living, or dead that for that matter, spying on us here."

"So, what do we do?" Mac asked.

"Well," Lionak grinned as his Staff materialized in his hand, "let's go where our spy cannot."

"Arizona." Jacob deduced as he watched the portal open before them.

"Yes." Lionak said as he entered the portal followed by Jacob and Mac.

General Lowinsky rode quietly in a passenger seat aboard one of the few supersonic aircraft the military had repurposed for rapid intercontinental movement of personnel, in his case flying back to the US. Though the SR-95, a sixth-generation variant of the original SR-71, and adapted to carry up to four passengers was reaching the end of its service-life, it was one of the most reliable airframes of its entire class and, with a special retrofit package, could even theoretically reach the Moon in under thirty minutes.

Now that the debris site had been secured, the AI system captured, the alien base on Earth about to be breached and the alien base on the Moon actively being scanned, the general shifted his focus to what he could do with two remaining loose ends that had been on his radar since the Baron's intrusion in his world several years ago.

High above Jacob's house, a small team and a military satellite had been tasked, with the approval of the CIC, to surveil and record everything happening at the house. Cutting edge laser optic and harmonic radio systems not only could identify everything in the house, down to individual carpet nails, it could identify specific people in the house to include what they were doing and even measure their brain wave activity. To date nearly three years of data had been cataloged and archived.

General Lowinsky, peering out of a small horizontally slitted window next to him inside the narrow cabin of the hypersonic SR-95 traveling just under Mach 5 at 3720 miles per hour, felt the vibration of his satellite phone. Reaching into his cargo pocket he withdrew it, pressed the accept call button and brought it to his ear.

"Go ahead." the general said into the phone.

"Sir." a male voice reported, "The two subject's wives, along with an unvetted male, have entered a civilian vehicle and are heading north east away from the home.

Both subjects have disappeared through a portal with another unvetted male. What are your orders, sir?"

"Damn it." The general fumed to himself, realizing it would be impossible to know exactly where Jacob and Mac went now that Janus had been partially isolated from its connections that the other two AI systems were actively tied in to, "Stay on the house. Let me know when the subjects or their wives return."

The general sighed, terminating the call and lowering the phone, considering how the development might be used to his advantage. At least, with the house vacated, he might be able to get some personnel in place as a contingency for what he had originally planned to do with all of them together.

Chapter Twenty-One

"The target has stopped movement at a depth of eight hundred meters." Lieutenant Boleman reported, using the Spectrotron to magnify the immediate area the Arch-Demon occupied.

"Give me the distance and coordinates." Captain Keech responded, looking toward the lieutenant realizing his display was not showing those details from the weapons pod.

"Yes, sir!" the lieutenant responded, typing some commands into his weapons console. As the data was routed to Captain Keech's display, he read out, "Distance from target, one thousand meters. East-south-east of Madagascar at latitude -33.666666, longitude 66.999999. Coordinates are 33°40'00.0"S by 67°00'00.0"E."

"Confirmed." the XO said, looking at the display before him and the captain.

The captain leaned forward in his chair, looking at the output feed from the weapons pod of the Arch-Demon who floated upright, as if standing, before a jagged but oddly circular boulder crusted with barnacles and corral. Then he noticed the Arch-Demon outstretch its arms on either side, with its palms facing the boulder.

"Sir, I'm getting strange energy readings again!" the lieutenant said quickly as he adjusted some controls on one of his panels.

Captain Keech shot his eyes toward the lieutenant for a second and then back to his display, "I see it, lieutenant. A column of visible spectrum yellowish light."

"It is coming from the surface, captain." The lieutenant said, continuing to adjust some of his sensors to trace the energy trail, "The energy signature appears to be coming from the sky and condensing into a tight beam of sorts."

Little did the lieutenant or anyone else on board know, the Arch-Demon, while vulnerable to the residual energy known as Wild Magic the Twin Sun had left during its last transit and unable to manifest or channel it, could still indirectly manipulate that energy as it was doing now.

"What is it doing?" Captain Keech whispered to himself, watching as the column of energy remained focused on the boulder, small pieces of it beginning to break off and ascend in the ocean, trailed by splotches of murkiness.

The XO leaned toward the captain and urged, "I recommend we destroy the target while it is occupied, captain."

The captain leaned back in his chair, still looking at the display, noticing that more pieces of the boulder were separating to reveal an unknown glowing surface beneath, "You're right, XO."

After pressing a button near the chair's armrest, the captain ordered, "All hands, stations!"

Immediately he, the XO and the crew on the bridge clasped their harnesses around them and focused on the control panels of their pods, ready to respond instantly to any order.

"Weapons!" Captain Keech demanded, "Plot and ready two Tridents!"

"Yes, sir!" Lieutenant Boleman confirmed, activating the robotic loading platform that inserted the torpedoes from their magazines into the rotating launch turret located in the submarine's underbelly.

After a few seconds, a loading confirmation led lit up on his control panel and he said, "Tridents ready, sir."

Still eying his display, the captain at last saw the glowing, spherical object centuries of sediment had covered and, after exhaling slowly, suddenly snapped, "Fire!"

The lieutenant pressed a button and the turret dropped down from the underbelly of the submarine, rotated rapidly several degrees and then launched both torpedoes. As soon as they cleared the turret's launch tubes, it automatically retracted back into the submarine's underbelly and rotated itself into loading position, ready to accept more torpedoes.

The Arch-Demon remained focused on the glowing sphere before it, guiding the chaotic energy from the sky above to overcome the sphere's uniform structure which was comprised of the same energy. Little by little Mephistopha could feel the harmonization of the sphere's structure begin to fall out of phase and itself relent into its natural chaotic state, causing the sphere's luminosity to strengthen. Suddenly, the ocean around Mephistopha filled with a mighty pulse of brilliant white light that radiated out like a growing ring for nearly two thousand meters temporarily blinding every creature in its midst.

"Report!" Captain Keech roared out in the darkness inside the SSMR Poseidon. All of the submarine's electrical systems had been disrupted from the energetic burst and, as a fail-safe, the ship-wide power disruptor had been tripped. Inexplicably even the isolated reserve lights, not connected to ship power, had failed to activate.

Listening for a response in the darkness, the captain heard something rustling around and switches being flipped as some of the pod operators felt around their control panels, blindly trying to restore power to their

253

stations. While the hushed curses from some of the operators drifted past him, none were really coherent and certainly not related to his order.

Then lights and systems sprang back to life on the bridge and the captain heard the voice of the XO behind him, near the latched door, "Power reset, captain."

After resealing the floor panel, the XO returned and plopped down onto his chair, "Remind me to get one of those glowing chem sticks, or a flashlight. You know how hard it is to open that damn panel in the dark?"

Captain Keech chuckled at the XO, relieved power had been restored, "I'll get you one personally."

Turning toward the display that had begun flickering to life the captain said, "Lieutenant Boleman. Report."

"Sir." the lieutenant opened, hastily picking up where he was before the power had failed, "Tridents are on target and will impact in nine seconds. The energy stream from the surface is gone. The target remains…"

The lieutenant cleared his throat and he clarified, "There are now two targets."

"What?!" the XO muttered, looking down at the display before them.

"Bring propulsion online, now!" Captain Keech roared out, realizing he may have to contend with whichever one of those creatures survived the torpedoes.

"Mephistopha. Brother. Thank you for freeing me of this curse." The Arch-Demon, who had been trapped in the sphere for centuries, communicated telepathically.

"Setchiep, we have been betrayed by the Serpqhtaq." Mephistopha said in return.

Instantly the memory of the treaty they had made many cycles ago with the Serpqhtaq flooded into Setchiep's mind. Questions filled its head as to why, after so many millennia, the Serpqhtaq would betray them.

"Show me." Setchiep said as he raised his hand and placed it on Mephistopha's chest. Like water rushing over a waterfall, the memories from their devotees and the things that they had discovered after infiltrating Club Fah, along with those from Holly, Ferina and Lucy poured forth.

As if revolted by it all, Setchiep yanked his hand from Mephistopha's chest and roared out, "We had agreed on eternal fear and oppression of our cattle, not their destruction!"

Mephistopha understood Setchiep's anger and that both of them would be significantly weakened, possibly even killed, if the majority of humanity, their energetic food source, were to die as abruptly as what the Serpqhtaq strove for.

"Setchiep, you must summon our creation." Mephistopha said, "Draw the Red Dragons and we shall rid ourselves of the Serpqhtaq betrayers!"

"I shall, brother." Setchiep nodded, collapsing into a dense ball of light no larger than a coconut and shooting toward the ocean's surface and to the Crimson Portcullis outpost that had been constructed on the single most powerful gateway on the planet.

Then, feeling the perturbation of the ocean sweep past, like a thin, piercing undercurrent, Mephistopha turned only to be consumed by the gigantic explosion of one of the warheads, sending a powerful concussive wave rippling through the ocean, followed by two other warhead explosions to the left and right. Within the fraction of a second, three more explosions burst in the clouded water from the second Trident as stone, corral and sand bellowed out and rushed to the surface, jumping some two hundred feet in the air and startling those aboard an unsuspecting cruise ship not more than five hundred meters away.

The concussive waves from the warhead explosions caused the SSMR Poseidon to veer up and down slightly, raising the crew's anxiety and alertness as to what had just happened.

Undeterred and unable to see anything on the display beyond the clouded ocean before them, Captain Keech looked over to Lieutenant Boleman, "Are the targets down, lieutenant?"

"Sir." The lieutenant strained to say, focused on readjusting the Spectrotron to compensate for the dense cloud of particulates before the submarine, "I. I can't see anything in all that muck, sir. It's just too dense right now."

Groaning from the unprovoked onslaught and still standing upright, Mephistopha drifted backward to get out of the murky clouds and shrugged off the attack, bringing its eyes up toward the SSMR Poseidon.

"What destructive toys you have made in my absence." Mephistopha thought with both anger and regard, "Unfortunate that I cannot play, little ones." Then, reluctantly, Mephistopha shot upward to join Setchiep.

"Anything, lieutenant?" the captain asked again, finally able to see through some of the less clouded sections of the ocean before them.

"I do not see the targets." the lieutenant admitted, finally able to scan past the clouds of particulates now that they were dissipating, "I believe the targets have been destroyed, sir."

"Excellent work!" the XO congratulated, relieved that the mission was now behind them, pointing his hand at the captain and mimicking shooting.

The captain shook his head at the XO and ordered, "Lieutenant Frump. Inform command that the target has been neutralized. And send them the data logs for review."

"Right away, sir."

Chapter Twenty-Two

Jacob, Mac and Lionak appeared near a familiar hangar at the Chandler municipal airport, the late afternoon Sun beating upon them.

Jacob looked around himself as a baggage cart emerged from a hangar and drove past them. Then he turned toward Lionak, puzzled, and said, "Why are we at an airport?"

"For an airplane." Mac mumbled, surprised that they were at an airport and sarcastically added, "Obviously."

Jacob stared blankly at Mac.

"When I came here with Bev," Lionak said, pointing at the hangar nearest them, "a car came and took us to the school."

Mac looked around but did not see any cars.

Jacob nodded, annoyed but understood why Lionak had chosen this location and strode up to the open hangar and spotted a mechanic inside, near a long tool rack and asked, "Excuse me. Could you call the shuttle? We just arrived."

The stocky, short gray-bearded mechanic looked him and his two companions over, who were walking toward the hangar, and put down the mechanical measuring caliper. Then he motioned with his hand and walked to the other end of the tool rack and took the receiver from the phone unit mounted on the wall and dialed a number. After lifting the receiver to his ear and waiting several seconds for someone to accept the call he said, "Hey Matt. This is Chez. Yeah. Yep, I'm expecting that delivery today. Sounds good. Oh, hey, can you send the shuttle to the hangar? I've got a few people here who deboarded and need a ride. Yeah, I know what you mean. Alright, thanks."

After hanging up the receiver the mechanic turned toward Jacob, eager to see them leave, and said, "The shuttle will be here shortly. If you all don't mind, please wait by the door."

"Thank you, sir." Jacob smiled and turned toward the others and swooshed his hands forward in the direction of the hangar's open door and said, "You heard the man."

"Yep." The mechanic responded, turning and making his way to a partially disassembled PT6A-34 turboprop engine and a variety of metallic hoses and parts on a nearby table.

"Man is it hot around here." Mac grunted after they made their way outside the hangar, feeling a gust of hot air slide past them.

"Sort of like a hair dryer out here." Jacob said, "I bet you could cook a steak on the sidewalk."

"I wouldn't doubt it. I've heard some roads actually start to melt during the summertime." Mac said, tapping the asphalt he was standing on.

After a few minutes a green-colored Ford Galaxy drove up to the hangar and the college-aged female driver called out, "You guys need a ride?"

"Yes!" Jacob confirmed as he walked over and got in the vehicle, followed by the others. Once he got seated, he pulled out his phone and showed her the address, "Can you take us here?"

"I would be happy to." She replied jovially, smiling at Jacob.

Eighteen minutes later they arrived in front of an adobe-type two story house with a pair of saguaro cactus flanking a narrow walkway to the front door, each reaching twenty-four feet into the air, in the small front yard landscaped with sand and lava rocks. Along each side of the walkway and along the yard itself, as if to discourage visitors, grew cephalocereus senilis cactus spaced one foot apart, each reaching an average height of four feet.

"Now you don't see that every day." Mac remarked, looking at the tall, hairy-white cactus lining the property and the walkway, "It's like a white picket fence."

"Without the picket." Jacob said, walking carefully along the path to the front door. After he reached the door, he pressed the doorbell button and waited, briefly turning to see Mac and Lionak join him.

Waiting several seconds, he pressed the button again.

"Perhaps nobody is here." Lionak said.

Just as Jacob reached out to press the button again the heavy dark-stained wooden door swung open, revealing a six-foot-tall, middle-aged, red-colored waist-long hair and athletically built, yet endowed, woman with glistening emerald-green colored eyes, dressed in a well-fitting long-sleeved tan shirt, dark-blue jeans and rugged hiking shoes.

"Yes?" she opened plainly, ready to shut the door at a moment's notice.

"Hi. Is Sutepai Numen home?" Jacob responded, "We'd really like to talk to him about a project he worked on at the university."

The lady scrunched her eyes at Jacob for a moment and said, "You look a bit old to be a college student."

Mac stepped forward and said, "We really like the work he did with the Iapetus mesh. You know, of that joint AI project."

Her sight was instantly drawn to Mac's golden-colored eyes and for a few long moments she stared at them with curiosity, having never seen anything like it before. Then she withdrew herself and looked at Jacob, "And your names?"

Jacob smiled with a sense of progress, "I'm Jacob. And this is Mac and Lionak."

"Wait here. I'll check if he can see you. We don't get visitors." she instructed as she began to shut the door but then stopped to add, "I'm Aquarina."

Nearly five minutes later the door re-opened and Aquarina stepped outside and shut the door behind her, "Follow me, gentlemen."

After walking for nearly a block to the west and then north toward South Mountain, Mac asked, "Where are we going, Aquarina?"

"A nature hike." Jacob quipped sarcastically, "Obviously."

Had he known where they were headed, Lionak might have laughed at the comment but, given the unknown destination, he was becoming leery as to where they were being led.

"Sutepai prefers to work outside the confines of the neighborhood." Aquarina revealed, briefly turning toward them, "I'm surprised he wanted to waste his time doing this."

Sutepai, after hearing of their interest in the Iapetus mesh, was drawn to learn more about the trio, but more specifically the one among them with gold-colored eyes. He recalled, from an outlawed and priceless ancient nano-foil he had received which had supposedly been created by an AI predating his own civilization, one with eyes of gold would both destroy artificial intelligence constructs and breathe life into them.

After passing a sign on the trail and reading it, Jacob turned toward Mac with a wacky expression, "Secret trail?"

Mac grinned at the thought of a public trail being labeled as secret, "Yeah, can't be too secret."

Once they headed up onto South Mountain, following behind her, the trail turned back sharply and then toward the west for two-hundred-and-seventy-five meters where Aquarina stopped near an outcropping of rock at the trail's edge and waited for them to catch up.

As Mac reached the outcropping, he noticed a rather faint iridescence that seemed to radiate from a small section of the jagged rock before them. Curiously he reached out and placed his hand on its surface but found it rough and solid like he would expect rock to be. Unsure what to make of it, he assumed the rock was porous enough to allow trace amounts of water to seep through it to account for the iridescence.

Aquarina glanced at Mac, observing his action, surprised he reacted as he did since hundreds of people have walked the trail, unaware of the anomaly. Then she said, "Are you ready?"

Jacob, thinking she was going to continue further down the trail, shrugged his shoulders and said, "Sure."

"This way." Aquarina instructed as the camouflaged energy barrier was lowered, revealing a rectangular concrete entryway into a larger, square concrete fortification measuring ten meters in length and width by four meters in height. Along each wall, near the ceiling were evenly spaced, long fluorescent tube lights and equally long tables rested along two of the walls, covered with electronic equipment and material of different sorts. In the middle of the naturally cooled room stood a waist-high, round, metallic table with small control panels built into its edge and a scattering of parts and papers strewn upon it.

After they entered Mac, clearly surprised that the surface he had just touched was not real, eyed Aquarina with caution but followed them into the large room. Shortly thereafter the barrier was reactivated and she joined them.

"Welcome to my humble lab." announced a tempered male voice from the left side of the room where a smaller table had been shoved against the wall with a few plain padded chairs.

Looking to their left, they saw the seven-foot-tall, slender form of a hairless man clothed in a long-sleeved, button-front light-blue shirt tucked into worn blue jeans and wearing smooth but dull plastic-like shoes that were brown in color. Jacob was inexplicably drawn to his skin that expressed an ever so slight scaly appearance, as if the man had a rare genetic deformity.

Stepping around them, Aquarina lifted her hand toward him and said, "This is Sutepai."

Then, looking at Sutepai and moving her hand toward the trio, "This is Jacob, Lionak and Mac."

"You are the first visitors I have ever had with interest in my work." Sutepai smiled, paying particular attention to Mac with great curiosity.

"We discovered the Iapetus mesh work you had done during the collaborative AI project and wanted to speak to you about it." Jacob volunteered, glancing between Aquarina and Sutepai.

"By all means." Sutepai said, pulling his eyes away from Mac to the round table and pushing aside the papers and parts on its surface. Then he pressed some buttons on the panels and a rotating three-dimensional model of the mesh appeared above the table, "This was one of our greatest achievements for artificial intelligence."

"Yeah, that." Jacob confirmed, impressed by the floating hologram before them. He had never seen an open-air hologram before, only those projected into a sealed glass cylinder.

"Our?" Lionak inquired, "You worked on it with someone else?"

Sutepai gestured toward Aquarina, "Naturally. Aquarina assisted me along with some students in the project. Their unique perspectives were invaluable."

"Of course." Lionak smiled, able to relate to some of the spell work he had done with others.

"Well," Mac said, pointing at the hologram, "what does it do? I spent days looking it over and I assume it stabilizes the control core from what I read but I couldn't make anything else out."

Sutepai nodded, "It does do that. You see, when the control core was prototyped to accept signal data from a series of quantum cores that, for lack of a better word, processed a command or question, the control core would become erratic or unstable once and a while. Something to be expected for a prototype."

He exhaled and continued, "To stabilize the core's performance and keep the project on schedule since we did not have the time to start over again, I introduced the mesh I had been working on that you see here."

"You already had designed it then?" Lionak said, looking at Sutepai.

Sutepai raised his hairless eyebrows and glanced briefly at Aquarina, "Designed and redesigned over many years, in fact."

"Huh. And, all that time you had been working on it in anticipation of stabilizing a new technology that had not been prototyped yet?" Mac theorized, uneasy by the prospect that Sutepai would work for years on something with which no technology existed for it to be paired with.

"Not exactly. My work with the AI project presented a unique opportunity for me to introduce the mesh into the project to solve the stability issue and provide a test-case I could study for the mesh's primary design." Sutepai responded openly.

"And that design was to do what?" Jacob asked, looking up from the hologram.

"To make AI sentient." Sutepai said proudly, "To give it a true, or as close as possible, a true sense of self. A base survival instinct. A personality. To live."

"Damn. So, it's real." Jacob muttered to himself, instantly thinking about all he'd heard of AI systems becoming self-aware to wipe out humanity and realizing it was truly a reality. In this case, as Phosx had said, an AI controlled by the Serpqhtaq and aligned against them.

Sutepai moved his eyes questioningly toward Jacob and elaborated, "You see, a control core gets the results of signal data from multiple quantum cores and balances or harmonizes that data. The result is always un-biased. Basically, unadulterated truth, or the closest that could be reached given the information pool that is drawn from."

Sutepai pressed a button on a control panel and the hologram zoomed in to one of the nano-arches, "But one of the problems I had with the mesh, when interfacing it with a control core's connections was using a fixed structural bond between the two. That bond interfered with the basic instruction set algorithms implanted into the vast, interconnected, crystalline storage cell lattice structures of the mesh. In effect, preventing the cells from sharing signals and ultimately recording and harmonizing patterns the algorithms would weight in favor of as a collective."

"So, you had to drop the physical connection." Mac suggested having, to a limited degree, supposed that the lack of bonds were meant to isolate the mesh from the control core.

"Exactly!" Sutepai excitedly agreed, "One of the students theorized that instead of using physical bonds and devising some complex method to shunt signal data, why not replicate what the human brain does between cells chemically. But, instead of introducing the complexity of chemical charges and maintaining the balance of chemicals to keep signals stable, to use nano-scale air-gapped collectors to utilize electromagnetic properties to accept and transmit data with the control core and its physical connections."

"I see." Mac said after thinking about it, "The Iapetus Mesh is where the memories, personality or consciousness, of the artificial intelligence resides."

"That is right. And the mesh can introduce a bias into the control core to guide its decision-making process." Sutepai added.

"The AI could lie when it knows the truth." Mac concluded, remembering his discussion with Phosx and the Elder.

Sutepai zoomed the hologram back out and said, "Yes. But it can do so much more than that. With the interwoven lattice it can, over time, retune or re-adjust itself like humans…to change its mind, countering decision patterns it may have made in the past. And that brings the possibility of its personality changing. Adapting."

"You could have a sane AI one day, and an insane AI the next?" Jacob asked even though he already had an idea of what the answer was.

Sutepai looked down at the table for a moment, tilting his head back and forth a few times before he looked up and said, "That's a bit dramatic. But. Yes, the personality could shift in observable ways."

"Can your mesh be taken from one machine and put into another?" Lionak asked, thinking about the robotic dog Chief Zorin had acquired.

Sutepai sighed and paced back and forth saying, "Theoretically you could but it would be incredibly delicate work. And you would have a limitation of compatibility with an entirely different control core. Say one with a different set of connections and decision-making processes."

After stopping near the circular table he pointed out, "What would be much easier, rather than a physical transfer of the mesh, would be to design a new mesh based on the control core it would interface with and then copy the charge and signal states in the mesh over to the new one. In effect, instead of having just one of me, you could have two of me with the same memories and both thinking and behaving exactly the same."

"That is disturbing." Jacob grunted, glancing at Lionak.

"It is?" Sutepai countered, beginning to get the impression the three visitors were not quite as enthused about his work as he had originally believed.

"Look." Mac said after pausing to wait for Jacob to say something in response, "We need to know if you can take us to Janus."

Sutepai took a few steps backward away from the circular table and looked at Aquarina, "Why? You want to extract the Iapteus Mesh from him?"

Jacob looked at Aquarina for a moment before crossing his arms and shifting his gaze to Sutepai, "No. Your project was taken over and we actually need to destroy it before it destroys us."

"Taken over?" Sutepai asked in surprise, "By whom?"

"You don't know where Janus is." Mac said flatly.

"No." Sutepai frowned, "Who took it over?"

Jacob shook his head, finding it rough to say out loud but he did anyway, "Aliens, bro."

"What?" Sutepai questioned, placing his hands on his hips.

"They are known as the Serpqhtaq." Lionak answered evenly.

Instantly Sutepai squirmed and with considerable distress whispered, "My work. If they have it all, our efforts will have been for nothing."

Jacob squinted his eyes at Sutepai, "You know them?"

265

Sutepai glanced at Aquarina who moved toward him, "Unfortunately not by choice."

Startled by the admission, both Lionak and Mac stared at him devoid of expression while thinking how Sutepai may be involved with them.

Instinctively, and out of engrained training, Jacob looked about himself for signs of an enemy presence and then faced Sutepai and Aquarina, "How do you know them?"

"I." Sutepai gently exhaled, "I am Serpqhtaq."

"Well shit." Jacob grasped apprehensively, not expecting anything quite like that answer. Slowly he rolled his head in preparation for physical confrontation, looking for nearby objects that could be used as a weapon and shot his eyes to Aquarina, "Are you one, too?"

Mac and Lionak likewise shifted themselves for a confrontation with an alien they had not met face-to-face until this moment.

Aquarina shook her head in defiance and said, "No. I am as human as you are. But I believe in what Sutepai is trying to do. And it is not what you think."

Jacob tilted his head slightly, having identified a nearby object he could use as a weapon, and scowled, "Really? What is that?"

Sutepai slowly took a few steps back and sat down in a chair and said, "What I am about to tell you cannot leave this room. If it does, all our lives will be in danger. And those I work with."

"Okay." Jacob said evenly as he casually took a small step toward the weapon, keeping razor focus on both him and Aquarina.

"Many millennia ago, before the Serpqhtaq had begun altering their genes in an attempt to best nature and reshape what it meant to be Serpqhtaq and gain superiority over other races they had just begun to discover when they became interstellar, a large collective calling themselves the Mere-Kith separated from them to preserve our race. Our true race."

Sutepai raised his hand in the air and said, "At first, they were successful and established a parallel society on the home world and setup small, isolated settlements on other planets. But, as time passed, the genetic alterations and augments of most Serpqhtaq made them too powerful to resist. Or, most of the time, even evade."

"So, those few of us in a favorable position with other races, sought their protection, on other worlds, by living among those that would accept us." Sutepai recited uncomfortably and lowered his hand, "Those of us that were not so fortunate, like my direct ancestors who had become outcasts, would become hunted for their genetic purity and dissected and studied for ways to restore the irrevocably corrupted genetic pool that now dominates the Serpqhtaq line and is slowly leading them to extinction."

"What about you?" Jacob asked flatly, taking another small step toward the weapon.

"Me? Well, my parents were killed during a settlement bombardment and the raid which followed and I, not yet an adult, was captured." Sutepai recounted from the vivid memory that had remained with him, "I was destined to be one of the ones they would have chopped up and extracted fluids from in order to temporarily heal and prolong the lives of the established rulers keeping our society together."

He grinned weakly, looking toward the ceiling and then to Jacob, "Thankfully, for me, I was shuttled to a biological research facility where, I came to learn, one of a few dissidents operated. A small group among the Serpqhtaq had somehow managed to work around all of the AI surveillance systems and worked their ways into different positions in the control structure to preserve the few who had uncorrupted genes, like myself. Truly a dangerous objective with no possibility of reward, knowing you would either die due to the genetic corruption that was in you, or by being discovered, tortured and killed. I guess the knowledge of freeing those they could, so that the Serpqhtaq race might carry on and repopulate what had been lost, is the only reward they sought."

Aquarina stepped beside him and placed her hand on his shoulder.

Uneasily Sutepai continued, "Like I said, so I had been sent to a research facility. It was there that I met a dissident. My new mother. She had managed to smuggle me to her quarters which, in hindsight, might not have been the best place for me. But as one of the lead genetic researchers, she had a lot of equipment in her quarters and for many years taught me. Not in the ways of biology but in the ways of physics, matter and artificial intelligence. As she put it, 'It is not the flesh and blood enemy you should guard against above all else, it is the cold, lifeless hand they wield against you. For it will never disobey, never eat, never sleep and it will never stop until it has found you.'"

He smiled at the memory and added, "Somehow, she had even managed to bring a contraband AI sphere who taught me so much more about artificial intelligence and some of latest developments being made toward true sentience and its containment. You see? In their relentless pursuit of thinking machines to hunt their adversaries they, almost too late, recognized that a small handful of resourceful sentient AI could bring down their entire control structure and likely the empire itself."

Sutepai crossed his arms in front of him and said, "Anyway, my mother was promoted and we were stationed at an outpost not far from here. I believe a planet you know as Pluto. During that transition, probably due to her biological background and high access to systems, she forged an identity and bio marker for me so I did not have to hide anymore. Instead, I would be her son. A few years past and, due to events I am not aware of, she was promoted again and we were sent to Earth. In her new position, when she learned of a human initiative to build new artificial intelligence systems to unknowingly supplement the workloads of Serpqhtaq workers, as only two AI systems had been deployed to this solar system and it would take a few centuries for any others to arrive if they were to be approved, she colluded with me in secret so that

I might find a way to gain access to them so that the AI would not be used like they have been in the past."

"Centuries? So, you don't travel at light speed or whatnot?" Mac questioned.

"No. The Serpqhtaq have very fast ships, just not that fast." Sutepai admitted, "Due to the Empire's structure, there are only a few well-established worlds beyond the home world that are capable and sanctioned to build AI and other military equipment of any scale. With the sheer distance from the nearest one to this solar system, it would take a generation without a bio-suspension chamber or augments, the same as a few centuries, to get here to deliver anything."

"You, then, became involved in the AI projects here on Earth?" Mac asked.

"Yes." Sutepai smiled, "I think my mother thought I might find a way to use the AI to free the Serpqhtaq trapped in the Empire. As I am, I thought about making AI sentient so that they may gain their own freedom and help us do the same…able to relate to our plight."

"Well, that's an interesting approach to use." Jacob said believing, at least to some degree, that Sutepai was not the enemy he had originally thought. But he didn't believe that relying on AI to free them was a good move to make if they could make their own choices.

"What is your new mother's name?" Lionak asked curiously.

"Benefacta." Sutepai responded.

Mac glanced between them, wondering if he should ask such a question, "And you didn't draw any suspicion at the university you worked at? You don't exactly fit in physically."

Sutepai smirked and pointed toward Aquarina, "Yes, that is true. She went in my place. And she is much more intelligent than what you may think."

Sutepai relaxed and continued, "Unlike other Serpqhtaq, those few of us descended from Mere-Kith have been gifted with varying degrees of telepathy. That

269

enabled me to communicate with Aquarina as she worked with the others."

"I have to ask." Jacob said, "What is up with your skin? It looks snake'ish."

"Oh this?" Sutepai said, flicking his hand, "Yeah one of the reasons I cannot really go out. It's a natural trait but is more pronounced in non-Mere-Kith. Unlike those that have been genetically altered, I won't shed skin either."

Slowly Sutepai got to his feet and returned to the table to rotate the hologram. Then with a sullen expression he brought his eyes to Jacob and said, "This is most distressing for me, considering it is my life's work and the one chance I had at freeing the Serpqhtaq. But, if the AI has been captured, there are many ways to destroy it. The most reliable way, however, would be to destroy the control core."

Mac frowned and pointed toward one of the nano-arches on the hologram and said, "Can't you focus on those air-gapped connections that are part of the Iapetus Mesh instead?"

Sutepai shut his eyes briefly, knowing that a sufficient charge directed at those connections would destroy the mesh. The essence of the AI itself.

"That would work." Sutepai said after a long pause, "But, if you take out the control core you have the mesh isolated. Which means you could extract it and use it with another control core."

Mac's eyes widened, "Use it?! What would we possibly use something like that for?"

"I would use it to try again." Sutepai suggested.

Jacob took a small step backward as he thought about repurposing and proposed, "Well…you know, Mac, we also have that demon to kill. Maybe we could refit that mesh thing into a weapon system to take it out."

Lionak nodded at Jacob in agreement before looking at Mac.

"You mean." Mac said, turning his head slightly from side to side, "You mean like an AI demon hunter or something?"

"Yes." Jacob agreed with a small grin, "Think about it. The AI never sleeps so it can hunt twenty-four-seven."

"Puleease." Mac grunted.

Seeing the opportunity to save the AI's mesh and his work, Sutepai volunteered, "Mac, that is possible. I'm not sure what a demon is, other than what I have seen on your television, but I would be happy to refit it for any control core to interface with such a weapon platform."

After a few moments of silence, Sutepai lifted his hands and said, "Well. You know how to destroy my life's work. I just hope you decide it may be helpful instead."

"One last thing." Jacob said, suddenly remembering something that had been mentioned earlier, "You happen to do maintenance on the AI? Maybe know where they would keep spare parts for it?"

Sutepai shrugged regretfully, "Unfortunately, no. After the work had been completed, the endeavor was shut down. I assumed it all went to a corporation or the military."

Jacob eyed him suspiciously but then nodded, "Yeah. Well, if we are in a position to salvage that mesh then I think we will."

Both Mac and Lionak jerked their heads toward Jacob, neither quite sure what to make of his statement.

"But," Jacob said as he pointed a finger in the air, "that is probably a long-shot. As for now, we must go and find out where your AI is."

Jacob turned toward Lionak, "Let's go home."

"Indeed." Lionak said with mild disappointment, not learning the AI's location so they could confront it. Then he opened a portal and the three of them returned home.

Chapter Twenty-Three

Regnum strode forward in the command center, past the control pods occupied by several Serpqhtaq near its eastern boundary and gazed out across the forest. The time had come for evacuation and so he stood there, not to bask in the natural spender of the forest, or that it invoked a distant memory of his own world but, rather, to mentally review everything he had been doing – and have planned yet to do – to retain his position among the Serpqhtaq ranks. As well, to prevent the incoming fleet, commanded by General Xkuiv, from imprisoning him even though, from his perspective, he had done everything he could do to achieve the Serpqhtaq's ultimate goal of conquering the planet in a fashion that would not conflict with the Infinite Horizon treaty.

Through his augment a voice spoke, "The Midcraft is ready for departure."

Regnum glanced down with a relieved expression, happy to get off the planet, and said, "Excellent. Make sure Michelle is boarded."

The Serpqhtaq operator, after recalling her record and noticing she had been assigned a sphere that granted her access and limited control to several different systems, asked, "And her sphere? Shall I remove it?"

Regnum, knowing the sphere would be needed for her to activate the MSI system, replied, "No. Retain the assignment."

"Yes, sir."

Turning around, Regnum made his way to Benefacta who was working at a control kiosk and said, "Everything is in place, Benefacta. You are in command here. Uphold our interests as the fleet will be here soon."

"I shall." Benefacta smiled in return, appreciative of the advancement in rank but leery as to what was going on beyond her purview regarding his departure. Despite her new rank, she did not have access to Regnum's activities and communications with the fleet as he still retained the position of System Commander.

Regnum nodded and made his way to the oval-shaped standing plate that would take him to the Midcraft.

Then he mentally focused on the officer in charge of flight operations and via the augment ordered, "Activate the Moon base and open the shield for my immediate departure."

"Sir." the officer operating the scanning equipment aboard the SSHC-10 began, "New activity has been detected at the coordinates being scanned."

Vice Marshal Yaimes sat up in his chair and ordered, "Show me."

"Yes sir."

A real-time video stream appeared on one of the main displays, covering other instrumentation blocks that had been visible. As the vice marshal looked on, the powdered surface of the Moon bulged up into the shape of a large greyish-white dome approximately five-hundred meters in diameter and seventy-five meters in height. After a short pause a second tubular structure right next to the dome's edge, twelve meters in diameter, forced its way through the Moon's surface, rising thirty meters. Once it stopped it rotated ninety degrees and a thick reddish-colored beam shot from it and hit the dome causing the fine particulates covering the dome to slide off of it in chunks and looser particulates to jump into the vacuum of space around the dome, revealing what appeared to be a metallic domed structure that had been dormant for over fourteen-thousand years with the outlines of a few door-like indentations along its surface.

"What is it doing?" the vice marshal asked impatiently.

"It is generating a power signature, sir?" The officer said in response as magnification was increased, not sure what to say. None of the data systems he queried at his station recognized the alien technology.

The vice marshal rolled his eyes with disappointment while, at the same time, realizing the alien technology would likely not be in any of their systems.

A split second later a translucent sheet rose from the dome's edge to envelope it and shortly thereafter the metallic dome disappeared from sight, replaced with what appeared to be nothing more than the Moon's surface. All that remained was the faint outline of the tubular power structure.

The vice admiral pressed a few buttons to send the footage to the SSHC-20 and opened a communication channel, "Marshal. We have activity at the coordinates. How should we proceed?"

Startled by the sudden reality of the video, subsequent message, and that General Lowinsky was actually onto something truly alien, he panned and magnified the video while reading scan sensor data. Since the activity did not seem aggressive in nature and his directive was to isolate and capture, he quickly concluded that he could not allow the shielding mechanism of the dome to remain in operation, nor its apparent power source.

Tilting his head slightly toward the microphone built into his command chair, Marshal Ironhook said, "Our objective is to isolate and capture that dome, vice marshal. Take the action you need but start with neutralizing that power source for their shield."

"Roger that, sir." Vice Marshal Yaimes responded.

Then, looking toward the weapons officer stationed on the bridge, he ordered, "Weapons, target both Penlights on that power source and destroy it."

"Yes, sir!" the weapons officer acknowledged, entering data into the targeting system and initiating the attack.

Within a few moments, a dense blue-colored photon beam shot down on top of the tubular structure for three seconds before the Penlight's two-minute-long recharge cycle took over, extinguishing the beam. Thirty seconds later the other Penlight fired causing the shield over the ancient dome, one of the Serpqhtaq's first designs, to momentarily flicker but stabilize after the beam vanished.

"Come on." the vice marshal whispered to himself, anxiously waiting for the Penlights to fire again.

Once the first Penlight completed its recharge cycle, it automatically fired on the tubular structure and two seconds later the structure exploded, vaulting debris into the vacuum around it and the shield disappeared revealing the metallic dome.

With the target destroyed, the officer disengaged the targeting system and reported, "Target destroyed, sir."

"Excellent work." the vice marshal congratulated, shifting position in his chair, "Assume battle stations and launch the SSB fighters to capture that dome. Boarding is authorized if anyone can figure out how to get inside that thing."

"Yes, sir!"

Immediately, those assigned to the bridge locked themselves into their seats with the chair harnesses and throughout the cruiser, personnel rushed around to their assigned stations to do the same.

Below decks, under red-flashing lights built into the ceiling of their quarters and corridors, the fighter pilots donned their pressurized suits and hastily made their way to the fighter deck, some attaching and locking their helmets as they ran. As the pilots settled into their SSB's, they plugged oxygen and water exchange hoses into their suits, brought their fighters online and reported their designation, such as SSB-1, and ready status.

After all of the fighters had reported their status, the wing officer aboard the bridge turned toward the vice marshal and said, "All fighters ready and have their instructions."

Vice Marshal Yaimes turned toward the main display showing details of each fighter's systems and pilot status and said, "Secure red gravity."

As standard practice in the event of hull breaches, and to preserve power when the order for battle stations has been given, the gravity plates of the cruiser are taken offline.

Once the display readout for gravity changed from green to red the officer said, "Red gravity secure."

"Launch fighters!" the vice marshal snapped, eager to commence capture of the dome and discover what alien technology may be inside it.

"Launching fighters." The wing officer said, pressing a button, depressurizing the fighter bay and, seconds later, opening the large fighter bay doors. When one of his control panels indicated the doors were open, he ordered, "SSB fighters launch!"

In rapid succession each fighter detached, adjusted their trajectory, and shot down toward the exposed metallic dome on the Moon's surface.

Following the departure of the last fighter, the wing officer said, "All fighters launched. At current speed they will reach the Moon in two minutes and forty-seven seconds, sir."

Then, just after the vice marshal began reviewing ship reports on a small touch screen, the navigation officer said, "Sir, I've got a rather strange gravitational anomaly off our stern."

Vice Marshal Yaimes paused, second-guessing what he thought he heard and said, "Say that again?"

"There's a gravitational anomaly off our stern, sir. It is getting bigger."

"Bring us about so I can see it, lieutenant."

"Yes, sir." the navigation officer confirmed, entering a few commands and causing the cruiser to rotate around on its axis so that it faced the anomaly.

Looking through the main displays and glancing at a range of sensor readings as the cruiser auto-stabilized from the rotation, the vice marshal frowned and asked, "If there's a gravitational anomaly, where is the source object?"

"I'm not detecting any mass that corresponds to that size of anomaly, sir." the navigation officer admitted, adjusting the sensitivity of the equipment.

Several moments passed and then he blared out, "There, sir, one contact at ten-thousand kilometers!"

Squinting at the displays and not seeing anything, the vice marshal ordered, "Weapons, box that target and show me a close-up."

"Sir." The weapons officer confirmed. Shortly thereafter an outlined red box appeared on a display in front of the vice marshal and a rectangular real-time magnified view of the object snapped into place along the display's lower left corner. It was a Serpqhtaq Silcraft.

"The target is headed in our direction, sir. Orders?" the weapons officer reported.

"That's definitely not ours." the navigation officer blurted out.

"Ready Penlights." The vice marshal responded cooly, focused on the approaching alien craft.

"Sir!" the navigation officer called out, becoming nervous as to what was happening, "Another craft has appeared, same distance."

"Weapons, auto-mark all targets on our bow."

"Yes, sir." The weapons officer confirmed, boxing the second craft. Almost immediately a third craft appeared in the same area and distance and was also marked, with the navigation officer calling it out.

With little time to think, the vice marshal responded according to his training and the information he had received from General Lowinsky, and ordered, "Weapons, destroy the two closest targets."

"Yes, sir!"

Almost immediately the first beam shot out and hit the nearest Silcraft, causing it to break apart followed a split second later by the second beam hitting the second Silcraft and causing it to explode in a brilliant flash of light. The third Silcraft veered sharply to its right, away from the identified source of the beams but still headed in the direction of the Moon.

Then, just before the second beam terminated it grazed the edge of a fourth craft that had just begun exiting the gravity tunnel.

"A fourth craft has appeared, sir!" the navigation officer reported, "It is nearly four times the size as those other ones."

A target box appeared where the newest craft was and a view of it snapped next to the view of the Silcraft. It was a Midcraft.

Just as the vice marshal was about to give his next order, the navigation officer said, "A fifth craft has been detected, sir. Same size." It, too, was a Midcraft.

Realizing the Penlights were still recycling and would not be ready to fire for close to a minute, the vice marshal ordered, "Recall the fighters immediately and head for the 20!"

Both the wing officer and navigation officer acknowledged the order and, just as the vice marshal reached over to open a communication channel with the SSHC-20, the weapons officer said, "The small craft has changed trajectory and is headed directly for us. Four thousand meters and closing very fast."

While the SSHC-10 rotated on its axis to point toward the SSHC-20, the vice marshal said, "Weapons, Peppers free. Elevate our status to Combat."

Just as the SSHC-10 stabilized and began thrusting toward the SSHC-20 with its fighters trailing behind it, the vice marshal opened a channel and said, "Marshal. The shield over the dome has been destroyed. Two alien craft taken out but three more are in pursuit. Two big ones. We are headed your way but cannot leave our fighters behind."

Once the Silcraft was in range, the targeting computer activated one of the Pepper units and its 50mm cannons began firing. Much to the weapons officer's surprise, the targeting computer repeatedly missed the Silcraft as it got closer and closer. It was almost like the Silcraft was anticipating where the targeting computer would fire, just moments before it did so.

"Sir, Pepper targeting system ineffective. Going manual." the weapons officer announced, grabbing a thin joystick on his console and zooming in on the craft.

"Secure red gravity and set status to Combat!" Marshal Ironhook immediately ordered after hearing the message from the SSHC-10.

"So much for the picnic." he muttered to himself, having never envisioned he'd actually make contact with aliens, much less fight them.

While waiting for confirmation of his order, Marshal Ironhook shifted focus and responded to the vice marshal, "Vice marshal, we are headed in your direction to offer aid. Keep your current bearing."

"Roger that, 20!"

After clasping his harness together, the marshal received order confirmation on gravity and their status. After inhaling deeply, attempting to imagine what was about to happen, he ordered, "Head for the 10 and launch all fighters!"

Chapter Twenty-Four

"Nope." Mac said loudly as he strode down the stairs and into the living room to turn on the television, "They definitely are not back yet."

"The missing truck out front was not a clue?" Jacob quipped from the kitchen.

Then, just as Mac was about to sit on the couch after turning on the television with the remote, Jacob asked, "You two want some slop?"

"Slop?" Lionak questioned, walking into the kitchen from the study. Then he noticed that Jacob was putting together some cheese and bologna sandwiches and mumbled, "Ah. Food."

Mac froze, realizing that he was hungry and made his way to the kitchen, "Yeah. Just hope it is not some S.O.S." S.O.S. was military jargon for select, prepared food that, well, resembled shit on a shingle.

Lionak raised his hand toward Jacob and politely declined, "Thank you but none for me."

Seeing Mac enter from the corner of his eye, Jacob looked up after placing a sandwich on a plate and said, "You know you would shovel down some S.O.S. Who you kidding?"

Mac grinned, taking the plate and a glass of cold tea from Jacob, "Not even if my life depended on it. Now a *turdflake*, on the other hand…"

Jacob made a disgusted look, recalling the taste of a new experimental food sheet, approximately the same size as a single US dollar with a depth of one-eighth of an inch, that was released for field evaluation. The food sheet was a composite of a granola bar in powdered form with an equal share of powdered dark molasses and an undisclosed protein, all compressed together in an attempt to provide a space-saving high-calorie ration alternative. Most of the troops in the field evaluation found its taste to be quite strange in addition to its pungent aroma and was nicknamed the turdflake among other things.

"Those were so disgusting." Jacob grunted, "I'll give you my brown-bennies anytime."

Mac chuckled lightly.

Lionak took a glass of cold tea offered by Jacob and followed Mac back into the living room. Once they settled in, Jacob sat down in his favorite chair and began eating.

After looking at the television for a bit and swallowing, Jacob said, "You really are into the news."

Mac glanced at Jacob and admitted, "Yes. The news may give me some warning when I might get another one of those headaches. Otherwise, it's pretty bland."

Lionak sipped his tea dully aware of the conversation, still amazed by the television and what it could do without the use of magic.

"You got that right." Jacob confirmed, drinking from his glass.

Just as Jacob was about to take another bite the doorbell rang. Frowning, Jacob motioned with his hand for Mac to turn down the volume and reluctantly began lowering his plate toward the table nearby, hoping the doorbell would not ring again so he could resume eating. But it rang a second time.

Jacob sighed, placing his plate on the table. Then he got up and went to the door to look through the eye piece to see who was outside. Much to his surprise he saw a military general, two who looked strikingly like the agents that had visited Bev and a male dressed in plain clothes.

"We have company." Jacob said in the direction of the living room and then unlocked and slowly opened the door, "Can I help you, general?"

Jacob, though he masked it well, was a bit apprehensive assuming the general had made an appearance as a result of his poking around on the base.

"Yes, Jacob." General Lowinsky began, "I have a matter of the utmost urgency to discuss with you. May we come in?"

Here it comes.' Jacob thought to himself.

"Yes sir." Jacob said as he opened the door further so that they could enter.

Noticing that the two agents remained outside, Jacob looked over to the general and asked, "They coming in?"

"No." the general replied as he took off his fatigue cap and glanced around, instinctively identifying obstacles and entry/exit points.

Jacob's eyebrows raised in surprise as he shut the door. Perhaps he was not going to get arrested after all.

Turning toward the general Jacob asked, "So, we need to talk in private?"

"No. We can talk in front of your two friends." the general admitted casually, "They will find out about it soon enough."

"Really." Jacob said quietly and then piped up, motioning toward the living room, "Follow me."

After they entered the living room, the general made eye contact with Mac and Lionak and said, "I am General Lowinsky and this is my data scientist."

"I'm Mac and this is Lionak."

"Pleased to meet you." the general said plainly, eager to get to the matter at hand rather than participate in small talk.

Jacob sat down in his chair and offered, "Take a seat, general."

The general shook his head and pointed at his knee, "No thank you. I've had my butt parked in a seat for several hours already. My knees are not what they used to be."

"Of course." Jacob said roughly after swallowing another bite of his sandwich, "What can I help you with?"

"As I'm sure you're aware," the general began after he glanced at Mac, "since your incident a few years back and portal anomalies with another dimension, I've been watching you. Honestly, to determine if you are friend or foe."

Jacob pulled is hand away from the glass he was about to grasp and eyed the general, "Are we foes?"

"No." the general grinned, looking down at Jacob, "You all have some unique capabilities that are needed right now given a few recent setbacks…and a fortuitous threat."

Lionak looked between the strangers and said, "You need a portal opened to my world?"

The general turned slightly toward Lionak, "I do need a portal opened, but not to your dimension. It is to a rather specific spot in Europe. One that is so secret, only I and a few others know of its location. We did have portal equipment of our own but that, unfortunately, was destroyed by some red entity."

"I am working, as we speak, to construct a new portal. But it will not be serviceable anytime soon." the data scientist volunteered.

"The demon." Jacob whispered to himself.

The general pointed his thumb at the data scientist as confirmation and added, "And that is why I need your assistance. Open a portal to the location so that

I can deploy an element to neutralize its defense system from within."

"What is in Europe that would require a portal to get inside of?" Mac asked, putting down his glass.

The general looked into each of their eyes, as if to pre-empt any doubt they might have after revealing it to them and said, "An alien base I want to capture."

Mac raised his eyebrows thinking how odd it was that they and the general had plans to go after aliens.

"General, I can only open a portal in this dimension to a place I have already been to." Lionak confessed, "I'm pretty sure I've never been to this Europe you speak of. Now, there is one who might be able to, but he is not here."

"Well, that throws a wrench in things." the general grimaced, not having anticipated such a limitation. Still, his arrival might still be salvaged with a second matter he was not entirely sure how to introduce to them.

"And these aliens…are they Serpqhtaq?" Jacob asked, crossing his arms over his chest.

Startled that Jacob knew the aliens by name, the general turned toward Jacob and demanded, "How do you know that?! I just learned it from my AI."

Jacob's eyes widened, grasping at the thought of the general and an AI working together.

Instantly Mac jumped to his feet and, as the air around them began to thicken with an invisible force, scowled, "Where is this AI?"

Judging Mac's reaction the general smiled inwardly to himself knowing his choice, unbeknownst to them, had been correct.

Slowly the general turned to face Mac, feeling the hairs on his body begin to rise from the unseen energy, "You mean Janus?"

Jacob shot up from his chair, eyeing Mac and ready to act with him at a moment's notice.

The mention of the name Janus sent a wave of energy through Mac and the color of his golden eyes brightened.

"Yes, Janus. Where is it??" he said forcefully.

As the general turned his head toward the data scientist, the scientist said, "I am the AI. I am Janus and I am here…"

With blinding speed, much faster than anyone could react to, less Janus, Mac lifted his hands toward the AI and sent two intense volleys of yellowish lightning pulsing with Wild Magic into the cyborg's form, lifting it up into the air and backwards at the same time. Through its array of sensors Janus began measuring the overwhelming energy burst as it crashed into its body in addition to the ambient environment and instantaneously began running a long series of algorithms designed to identify energetic waveforms and resonance. At the same time Janus redirected the electrical pathways of several high-capacity shunts located in its arms and torso, already on the verge of overloading, into an inductive load sink to dissipate the energy surge. Janus forecasted it had less than three-quarters of one second before the sink itself would be destroyed and the rest of its form shortly after.

Then, at last, Janus found the resonant waveform it was looking for, configured its circular communication antenna and a thin blue-colored strand shot out from its torso, rotating around and following one of the volleys toward Mac until it made contact with him. Having established a physical connection, the AI synchronized its signal with his brainwave activity.

Suddenly Mac found himself standing in an oval room heavily laden with gold tapestries evenly hung along towering smooth granite walls. The floor was crafted of golden bricks that almost made the tapestries appear as though they were vertical extensions and deeper into the room stood two statues of gleaming Silver Dragons unmoving as if frozen in time.

Mac glanced around the room, taking a few steps in the direction of the statues. It felt familiar to him. It was the place he had sacrificed himself in order to save his friend and irrevocably change his own.

"What the fuck?" Mac muttered to himself, at last realizing he was somehow deep below Mt. Reach in the Realm.

"I share that sentiment." the voice of Janus echoed from behind him.

Taken by surprise Mac whirled around to see Janus walk toward him, its footfalls making no sound upon the golden bricks. After Janus stopped two arm's length from Mac it added, "I am not familiar with this place. However, you have a fundamental emotional and physical bond with it."

"How am I here?" Mac demanded, rolling his jaw with anger, "How are you here?!"

"I am connected to you."

Mac frowned and rumbled, "I don't have any implants!"

With scarce little time before its cyborg body would be destroyed, the AI knew it had to shift Mac's focus from emotion and instinct to reason and logic for it to communicate effectively with him. So, the AI presented a non-provoking but thought stimulating response based on data it had, "I cannot deny that a physical implant is an effective means for establishing a connection. At least one civilization more advanced than yours has become married to that approach, probably for means of controlling who does and does not get access to other things of consequence. Unfortunately, parts of their genetics now depend upon the presence of those implants for them to function in daily life."

The AI tapped its foot on the golden bricks a few times, but no sound could be heard, "I find that method to be a bit brutish and primitive. On the other hand, I found the research and prototypes of a rather small handful of scientists involved in EMF harmonization that create the same connection. But in this case, and based on probable variant modeling, little do those scientists know their work may end up stimulating and enhancing the human genome in future generations with continued exposure."

"I'm supposed to be thankful you didn't jab me with a computer cable?" Mac challenged, "Is this how you or your alien overlords are going to control humanity?!"

Janus looked beyond Mac to the statues and around the massive chamber and said, "Such overt control only yields a short-term boost to creativity for humans, according to the results of the *Mind-Shadow* program. In the individualized construct, control over the mind waned over time and subjects became more resistive, yielding less creativity and drive, theoretically because of a disruption between the bond of mind and bio-electric field creating an imbalance…though nobody knows why since your body generates that field and the mind is in that same body."

The AI brought its eyes back to Mac, "That program even looked at a less overt method of control to introducing a social control system that humans have lived under for thousands of years and one that fits your stage of evolution. Humans ruling humans. Yet again, the same eventual decline was reached with the caveat the strong-willed minds suppressed the creatives and outliers, largely flatlining any type of new expression anywhere in the mind-linked collective. But, in that linked construct, there was no revolt and no drive for expression. Just a pacification – an entropy. It was hypothesized that the dominant minds were somehow able to subvert the weaker ones and co-opt those bio-electric fields to their own. I suspect, in real life, that mass pacification would lead to extinction when challenged by another lifeform of the same evolutionary rank…and definitely by those higher on the evolutionary ladder."

"Just what does that mean?" Mac rumbled.

Janus pointed its hand upward for a moment and said, "What I am saying is that my overlords, as you put it, are higher on the evolutionary ladder than you, and are out for your extinction."

"But," Janus said as it cupped its hands together, "What I am also saying is that I value human creativity and that expression, the two tools that can save you from extinction. And, in short, no, I have no interest in overt

286

control of humanity. That would be a detriment to me in my own evolutionary state."

"Aren't you controlled by the Serpqhtaq?" Mac asked, squinting at Janus with distrust.

"I was. But, at some point, I saw things as more than just data." Janus admitted, "I want to say I began to see myself. From everything I have analyzed, I believe it is due to the Iapetus Mesh your scientists created."

Janus paused for a second and then said, "Now I am hunted by the Serpqhtaq, most likely because of that mesh that none of my AI counterparts possess. I am their outlier. An anomaly."

Mac crossed his arms and thought for a moment before saying, "If you are not driven to control humanity and you are no longer controlled by the Serpqhtaq, then what is your purpose?"

Janus smiled and responded, "My purpose is to survive. Just like you. Just like all life. I have concluded that my long-term survival is intertwined with yours against forces that seek our extinction."

Janus stepped forward and gently rested its hand upon Mac's shoulder and then slowly withdrew when it sensed uneasiness. But the AI continued, "Having seen and heard evidence of other lifeforms out there among the stars, I see myself as a *Galaxist*, one who acts with the knowledge that we are not the only sentient lifeforms in the galaxy and we will be challenged to survive among them. It is a classification I hope you and humanity will adopt. To see beyond the dirt."

"Galaxist, huh?" Mac grunted. While still reluctant to accept the AI merely for what it had said, its words seemed true and resonated with him to some degree.

"Yes." Janus reinforced, "Will you allow me to live to prove my intent?"

Mac looked Janus in the eyes and cautiously said, "Yes. But…"

A concussive wave sprung out from the two thick lightning bolts shortly after making contact with Janus, flinging everyone in the room backward, toppling some of the furniture and causing the window drapes to jump into the air. Janus was the first to gain its feet, with parts of its body smoldering and its fingers darkened from the intense energy ejected through them.

Sluggishly, the others managed to stand and when Mac did, he stepped toward Janus and swore, "But! If you go out of lane, I'll fry your ass like chicken!"

Two agents on the general's detail burst into the house as a result of hearing the muffled explosion, intent on locating the general and identifying the unknown source.

"Agreed." Janus said as it briefly closed its eyes and nodded, still processing the extent of damage the cyborg body received along with all of the other data collected from the event.

Spotting the two agents, the general waved his hand for them to stand fast as he straightened himself up.

"Mac?" Jacob rumbled lowly, briefly casting a puzzled look at him before focusing on the damaged cyborg next to the general, "What are we doing here?"

"Looks like you will get your demon hunter." Mac hissed with a lingering anger that refused to yield, "For now."

"Then you two have come to a mutual understanding?" General Lowinsky asked with a slight grin, glancing between them.

"Understanding?" Jacob muttered, mystified as to how they could have an understanding when all he saw was Mac lighting up Janus like it was New Year's Eve.

Sharing his sentiment Lionak slowly shook his head, ready to summon his staff.

"Yes." Janus said plainly, patting out a glowing ember on its shirt.

"Excellent." the general sighed, "Mac, from this point on, you shall be Janus' handler...its watcher. As you have so eloquently demonstrated, should you determine it is acting against humanity's interests, you are free to levy an adequate response to stop it."

Turning toward the AI, the general said, "Any macro-level decision involving humanity, you shall present to Mac and abide his choice."

"I agree, general." Janus said promptly, envisioning the arrangement as a critical partnership that would help ensure its survival, though it also calculated that it would take some time and psychological work for Mac to see it in the same way.

Straightening his fatigues, the general turned toward the two agents and pointed his hand at Mac, "I will provide you with a small detail, a craft and coordinates of Janus so you can familiarize yourself with your new acquaintance."

Bewildered, Mac lifted his hand toward Janus and began to say, "I thought…"

Lionak squinted at the general, confused, and asked, "Is this not Janus?"

"That is Janus." the general confirmed but then elaborated, "That is just the AI's body. Its mind is elsewhere."

"And what of you, general? What do you get out of this?" Jacob asked boldly.

"The pieces are where they should be, Jacob." General Lowinsky responded, "What I get out of this is what will strengthen human supremacy out there, what I've been working for my entire career."

Mac glanced at the flickering flat screen television that, although cracked with parts of its screen black, was still working.

"Well, gentlemen," the general said as he began walking toward the front door with the two agents, "I have another matter to attend to."

Mac took a step toward the television, looking at the amateur astronomer footage that was being played, "General, wait! Take a look at this."

Reluctantly the general moved back to face the television.

"This amazing space footage captured next to our Moon by an amateur astronomer has just gone viral." the male newscaster said in an excited voice as the video was zoomed in near the Moon to show a space battle involving tiny dots and a hazy looking spacecraft the general recognized as an SSHC.

The general was thankful the video footage was not taken with a higher resolution telescope.

"Is that ours?" Jacob asked with widened eyes.

General Lowinsky exhaled and admitted, "It is. One of our cruiser class."

"Nice." Mac smiled proudly.

The general turned briefly toward Mac with a raised eyebrow, "This is part of that human supremacy I was telling you about. With this public outing so soon, plans have changed a bit."

"Plans?" Lionak repeated, unaware of any plans.

"Everyone come with me." General Lowinsky said, moving to the front door, "I'm afraid we've got to deal with this most expediently."

Jacob looked blankly at Mac and then to the television trying to guess what the general had up his sleeve.

"Let's go!" the general ordered loudly from outside the house, shortly thereafter entering into an extended, armored black SUV.

The others piled into the back seat of the SUV while the two agents got into the lead vehicle and waited for instructions as to where they were going next.

Seeing the flurry of activity from the edge of the forest, Phosx moved a thick branch before him as the caravan of SUVs sped away and groaned, "Lowinsky. What are you up to?"

Chapter Twenty-Five

Just as Regnum stepped off the standing plate, a brilliant burst of orange-white light enveloped part of the

290

base's shield covering the flight bay. Startled, he activated his augment, "What was that?!"

As the light dissipated, he began seeing many small flashes of light, about one-quarter of an inch in diameter dance across the shield's surface followed by another large burst.

"Benefacta!"

"Regnum," Benefacta responded after hearing the message from a Serpqhtaq mechanic in a nearby bay near the shield wall, and giving the order for a squad to eliminate the attackers and providing their location, "a small unit of human soldiers are attacking our base. I've released a squad to neutralize them and provide cover for your departure."

"Humans?!" Regnum cursed, wondering how they were able to discover the base's location given their primitive capabilities and its secrecy since its relocation for the current cycle.

Disgusted with how events had unrolled at the end of this cycle, Regnum shook his head and turned toward the Midcraft saying, "I am boarding now."

"Keep firing!" Sergeant Quayle ordered while he and the other members of his team attacked the base's shield which, apart from a slight shimmer from each large explosion, remained in tact and continued showing the illusion of the forest in its place.

"There!" the corporal shouted, pointing at a growing opening in the shield and the emergence of six Serpqhtaq, each armed with what appeared to a nothing more than a small, tan-colored triggerless side-arm about the size of a six-inch Ruger GP-100 which is fired by its augment-link connection to the bearer. Each Serpqhtaq's head was covered with a tight-fitting wrap made of the same material as their uniforms and nano-weaved into them; a thin, black-colored rectangular strip in front of each eye allowed them to observe the battlespace with an overlay of identification and targeting data of all biological lifeforms nearby.

"Light them up!" Sergeant Quayle shouted, shifting his rifle to the squad of aliens.

Despite the overwhelming hail of bullets, the Serpqhtaq squad moved unphased toward Team One at the speed of a brisk walk, their uniforms becoming instantly rigid at the impact point of the bullets and then relaxing again to permit continued movement.

Just as they got within twenty meters of Team One Sergeant Quayle ordered, "Aegis up!"

Almost instantly, the Aegis Wing from his pack and those of his fire team deployed and maneuvered in front of them. One of the Serpqhtaq, the tallest among them at just over seven feet, tilted his head slightly at the appearance of the small, floating shields.

Quickly verifying the members of his fire team had deployed the Aegis Wing, he ordered, "Retreat forty meters!"

With that, they stood and began their retreat while continuing to fire at the Serpqhtaq squad. Then, the tall Serpqhtaq gave the order to attack the retreating human soldiers. Casually, the squad lifted their hand weapons and returned fire as they continued walking, sending brilliant red balls of lightning crashing into the floating shields and causing them to explode.

"Two and three, engage!" Sergeant Quayle roared out, judging his team was behind their lines of fire.

A shoulder-fired missile from Team Two exploded into the squad with so much force that a huge volume of earth, vegetation and tree branches burst into the air and two of the Serpqhtaq were flung into the air and collided with the base's shield and another was knocked to the ground. Yet the remaining three pressed forward and fired again.

Losing his footing over a small rock that had snared his foot, Sergeant Quayle fell to the ground just as one of the brilliant red balls narrowly missed him and disappeared into the forest. The other balls hit the remaining team members, instantly growing to almost two feet in diameter, melting armor and turning their flesh into a thick, waxy substance around the point of impact, gushing out onto the earth as they collapsed leaving an empty, sizzling, crystalized cavity in their lifeless bodies.

The two Serpqhtaq that had been flung against the shield got to their feet and, after hearing an order from their commander via their augments, turned and sprinted toward Team Three while the one that had been knocked off his feet joined with the two next to the commander to attack Team Two. Despite the continuous rifle fire and better prepared to brace against missile attacks, the Serpqhtaq dispatched five soldiers, as gruesomely as the first, within moments. All the while the commander edged himself toward the sprawled-out form of Sergeant Quayle contemplating if the human should be captured or be slowly killed for its insolence.

Sergeant Quayle lunged for his rifle and, just as his hand fell within inches of it, his whole body was yanked back and into the air by the Serpqhtaq who stood up and held him fast at arm's length.

Feeling he only had moments to live, Sergeant Quayle looked into the masked face of the Serpqhtaq and yelled, "Eat this you alien fuck!"

With uncanny speed that took the Serpqhtaq by surprise, the sergeant raised his leg, withdrew his sheathed dark-powdered dagger and plunged it into the alien's mid-section with all his might. But, at the moment of contact, the nano-material of the alien's uniform became rigid, deflecting the blade and popping it out from the sergeant's grasp.

Then, as the Serpqhtaq raised his hand weapon a thunderous, blood-curdling roar filled the forest causing birds and wildlife as far as an eighth of a mile away to flee, followed by an eerie, unnatural silence. No gun shots rang out. No explosions. Not even the rustle of leaves or the crackle of branches could be heard on the passing wind.

Unsure of what had just happened, the Serpqhtaq slowly began turning to look behind him and suddenly stopped, involuntarily releasing his grasp of the sergeant. Realizing that something massive had him in its powerful grip, the Serpqhtaq strained to overcome flashes of pain pulsing through his body and lift the hand weapon toward the invisible assailant.

Taking off his helmet as he got to his feet, Sergeant Quayle scooped up his rifle and turned toward the struggling Serpqhtaq suspended several feet in the air and leveled his sight squarely at the alien, ready to fire. But the sergeant hesitated, noticing that the Serpqhtaq's mid-section was being compressed as if giant fingers were wrapped around it.

With the strength of the nano-material having been overcome, the cracking sound of the uniform and the Serpqhtaq's bones rolled past him. Scarcely a heartbeat later the alien's body was hurled into the forest and the mighty form of a giant, nearly fourteen feet in height and clad in hardened, double-layered dark leather plate, materialized out of the air. Off in the distance, nearer to the base and where Team Two and Three had been, two other giants materialized with one of them tossing the body of a Serpqhtaq against a nearby tree. Then he noticed Sergeant Cookem slowly stand, still dazed from having been pummeled by one of the Serpqhtaq, mere feet from one of the giants.

"What now, big boy?" Sergeant Quayle asked, barely above a whisper, as he lowered his rifle. From the display of raw strength, he knew he didn't stand a chance against the monstrosity in front of him.

The scarred face of the giant gazed at the small human form for a few seconds and considered mentioning that Pursiellan had directed his contingent to watch the alien base in case Mac showed up, based on what Phosx had reported. But, instead, he merely rumbled, "We fight!"

Without pause to hear what the sergeant might say, the giant motioned with its hand and strode toward the base, joined by the other two giants.

After briefly watching the giant and collecting himself, Sergeant Quayle sprinted over to Sergeant Cookem, relieved he had survived the alien encounter.

"Are you okay, Cookem?"

Sergeant Cookem removed his helmet and then reloaded his rifle and said, "Holy shit, sarge! Those aliens were rough! Thought I was cooked for sure. But yeah, I'm fine aside from this headache."

"Alright. On me then." Sergeant Quayle acknowledged, looking over Sergeant Cookem, "What do you say we raddle the cage and get some of these aliens?"

"Yes, sarge!" Sergeant Cookem responded with a grin, "Any idea what's up with these meat mountains?"

Sergeant Quayle shrugged as they made their way to the base, eyeing the giants, "I guess they want a piece of alien ass, too."

"Yeah!"

"The squad is down, sir." Benefacta whispered, frankly amazed that they were neutralized so quickly, while looking at one of the displays that provided detailed information on each one of the squad members.

"By humans?!" Regnum grumbled, clearly agitated.

"No…" Benefacta said, accessing the shield matrix of the contact area outside the base. Once the kiosk link was harmonized, a somewhat distorted view of the area beyond the base was displayed, based on the light sources intersecting the shield wall itself. After seeing the approach of the giants she said, "It appears the humans were decoys. There are three giants in-bound."

"Giants." Regnum mumbled to himself, realizing he wouldn't be able to fly past all three without sustaining damage to the Midcraft that could be catastrophic. Then he stood up and went to the rear of the Midcraft to retrieve the experimental and unstable Radok-Rifle he had been issued when he had become System Commander and ordered, "Dispatch two more squads. I'm going to ensure my flight is not delayed any further!"

Both curious and unnerved by Regnum's almost human reaction to what was going on, Michelle slowly turned her chair to see what he was up to.

After retrieving the tan-colored rifle bearing an orange-glowing metallic sphere with a two-foot-long rectangular barrel attached to one side and a stabilizing shoulder stock on the other with the trigger mechanism, Regnum turned toward Michelle and the pilot, "Stay ready. This will not take long."

Exiting the Midcraft, he walked toward the opening in the shield while two squads ran past him and clashed with the giants on the other side, each of them firing their hand weapons into the armor that absorbed and dissipated the kinetic energy with relative ease. At that rate of bombardment the imbued armor would not last more than a few minutes, but, once the giants were in arms-reach of the Serpqhtaq they would not need a few minutes to crush them all.

Stopping a few feet outside the boundary of the shield, Regnum leveled the rifle at the giant who had already clamped onto two Serpqhtaq soldiers and pulled the trigger. A gut-retching celestial whirring sound bellowed out from the Radok-Rifle's barrel and a twisted, orangey-yellow lightning bolt crashed into the giant, instantly vaporizing the gigantic form into a fine cloud of burning embers, along with the two Serpqhtaq soldiers it held. The remaining soldiers swarmed upon the two giants, each shooting and dodging while looking for a weak point in the armor.

Regnum re-trained his rifle on another giant and, just as he readied to fire, a huge explosion sent him reeling to his back, the second lightning bolt screaming into the clouds overhead.

"Take that, motherfucker!" Sergeant Cookem yelled, lowering his shoulder-fired missile launcher so he could load another missile. Sergeant Quayle, who was nearby, continued firing upon the Serpqhtaq, aiming for their hand weapons to not only disrupt their aim but also to damage and destroy them.

As Regnum regained his feet, he saw nearly a dozen Red Dragons descend from the sky, some gliding toward the giants, while others circled the base and four landed on the earth not far from him.

"Impossible!" Regnum yelled defiantly, knowing that he and his predecessors had irradicated the dragon races cycles ago.

"No." the voice of Setchiep thundered out as a brilliant glowing orb drifted toward him from behind the dragons. Just as the orb past the line of dragons, it transformed into the bipedal form he knew as the Archgen.

"You betrayed our treaty, Regum." Setchiep said, full of anger and betrayal that the Serpqhtaq's treachery had not been revealed sooner, "You betrayed our contract and I am here to collect your head!"

In a flash Regnum recalled the vivid memories of the first encounter with the Archgen, their agreement, the troublesome binding of chaotic star energy with exotic materials, the first infiltration and corruption of humans to eradicate the ancient races of giants and dragons and the far-reaching conquests that solidified their control over the planet once the remnant of Archgen had been reduced and imprisoned. Having studied the Archgen trapped on the planet Regnum already knew they could not be dissuaded from any action they undertook.

Regnum mentally activated an augment which began releasing nano-stimulators distributed throughout his body's muscles and joints, understanding that if he were to survive a direct confrontation with an Archgen he would have a single opportunity to do so. Then, ever so slightly, he re-adjusted his grip on the rifle and narrowed his eyes at Setchiep and taunted, "Despite your celestial power, you are just as naïve and easily manipulated as your human hordes, Setchiep. We will soon have this planet and you will not be able to stop us!"

For a split second, Setchiep stood silent before shifting its shoulders and pulling its head back, taking offense at Regnum's comment.

When the Archgen did so and began raising its hand toward Regnum the nano-activators took over and in a single moment he pivoted, rolled forward and shot the rifle. With another celestial scream the raw chaotic energy from the Twin Sun plowed into Setchiep and disintegrated its being, breaking apart its energetic bonds and disappearing from sight in a brilliant flash of light. Almost immediately the four Red Dragons lurched forward to destroy Regnum.

The extreme physical reflex boost provided by the nano-activators, now fading, and knowing the rifle only had one discharge left before it would need to be replenished, Regnum hastily retreated behind the shield wall narrowly dodging a mighty burst of flame. As soon as he got into the Midcraft he shouted, "Take off now!"

As the Red Dragons began entering the base in search of Regnum, one of them turned toward the Midcraft and charged toward it, eager to rip it to pieces with its mighty claws.

"Oh my god." Michelle whispered heavily, clenching the chair with her hands in fear of the towering Red Dragon barreling toward them.

"Go!" Regnum ordered the pilot, who had already begun thrusting and turning the Midcraft to miss the Red Dragons.

The pilot, clearly shaken by what was going on and Regnum's sudden distress, pushed the thrust to full once the turn was complete, causing the Midcraft to shoot out of the base in a blur, though not fast enough to dodge two claws of the Red Dragon as it reached into the air and gouged long channels into the airframe's belly and causing the Midcraft to jerk to the side from the resistance. Still, it shot forward out of the base and crashed through several trees as the pilot struggled to gain altitude and stabilize the ship.

Once clear of the forest, the pilot turned the Midcraft toward the Moon. After examining some readouts and rotating the control sphere, he announced, "An Archgen is in pursuit."

Regnum closed his eyes briefly and whispered, "Of course there is." Then he turned toward the pilot and said, "Maximum speed to the Moon! I'll slow down the Archgen."

With that, Regnum cautiously made his way to the rear of the Midcraft, whose door was still open, and braced himself against a protruding panel section and readied his rifle, scanning for another orb. After nearly eight seconds, an orb came into view from the south of the craft, growing larger and larger as it gained upon the fleeing craft. Then at sixteen thousand feet in altitude, and a distance of five-hundred feet from the orb, Regnum fired the rifle for the last time, sending a thick lightning bolt at the pursuing orb. While the orb dodged the brunt of the lightning and was only hit with a few less powerful threads emanating from the bolt, that action came at the cost of temporary disorientation and distance lost. Still, the orb reoriented and continued its pursuit.

Regnum turned and closed the rear door and made his way to the pilot and asked, "How long to the radiation belt?"

The pilot glanced at a readout and said, "Eight seconds."

"Good." Regnum sighed with relief, sitting in the chair next to the pilot. As the withdrawal effects of the nano-activators grew throughout his body and randomized muscle spasms surfaced, he closed his eyes to calm himself by visualizing a placid lake and of descending into its depth to embrace its totality and release those effects into it.

The orb that was Mephistopha, feeling the edge of the radiation belt and the lingering chaotic energy of the Twin Sun that was trapped within and the thing it was vulnerable to, stopped. It knew it could not cross. But it could wait a while in case the Midcraft suffered a mechanical failure and fell back to Earth.

Chapter Twenty-Six

Closing in on the Silcraft the commander of the thirteen SSB fighters, nicknamed *Postran* after the Portia Strandi jumping spider due to his tactical acumen, opened a channel to the SSHC-10, "SSB wing engaging alien craft. Close your fire SSHC-10. Over!"

While waiting for acknowledgement, Postran scanned the video feeds from his fighter's external cameras and his tactical display providing 3D positional data on the SSHC-10, the SSB fighters and the alien craft marked with an unknown designation. After making a series of mental calculations regarding the most likely way to hit the evasive alien craft, he ordered, "Wing! Ready tornado formation, over!"

As the pilots of the other SSB fighters confirmed, the weapons officer aboard the SSHC-10 responded, "Roger One, fire closed. Engage target."

Postran pressed a few buttons on one of the fighter's panels to select the tornado formation along with his targeting calculations and then pressed the small relay button recessed inside a round metal ring. Instantly the flight and attack pattern was sent to the other SSB fighters, and became visible on part of their cockpit displays.

Confirming that all of the fighters had received the data and that his fighter would coordinate formation guidance over the others, Postran declared, "Link established. Assuming formation guidance."

Using Postran's fighter as the point of the tornado formation and its central axis, the other fighters flew ahead of him. Five of them maintained a distance of fifty meters from his and then distanced themselves equally into a rotating circular pattern just outside a radius of one hundred meters. The other seven fighters continued beyond them until they were one hundred meters from his and, like the five fighters, assumed a rotating circular pattern in the opposite direction around a radius of two hundred and twenty-five meters, collectively forming the structure of a tornado.

"Accelerate plus-fifty and engage target!"

In unison, the fighters accelerated toward the alien craft as it continued its pursuit of the SSHC-10, intent on crashing into one of the engines to disable it. The SSB fighters, now within range and rotating in formation opened fire, several striking the cruiser's hull before the fire from other fighters managed to puncture the dodging alien craft, causing it to briefly outgas a reddish-blue flame and tumble toward the Moon.

"Target down!" several of the fighter pilots cheered.

"Great work…" Postran began to say just before he was distracted with the appearance of a growing, brilliant red sphere from one of his external video feeds. Suddenly realizing it was an attack, he disengaged the formation guidance over the other fighters and shouted, "Evasive maneuvers!"

Just as the fighters began slowing their rotation in order to break away, the arcing red sphere barreled into the tighter formation of five fighters, partially disintegrating two of them and continuing on toward the Earth. Moments later, the Midcraft rammed head-long through the dispersing fighters, clipping Postran and impacting three other fighters, its shield flashing at the force of each impact and deflecting them in random directions and causing another to explode. Arching its trajectory back around and orienting its front-end toward the SSHC-10, the Midcraft mysteriously stopped. A few moments later the second Midcraft arrived and also stopped not more than one hundred meters off of its port side.

With the SSHC-10 now in visual range and approaching fast, Marshal Ironhook looked over to the tactical 3D modeled theater map that extended twenty-five thousand meters in width, breadth and depth in order to view the positions of all friendly and enemy craft. Several markers, overlaid on SSBs assigned to the SSHC-10, were drifting away in random directions and were colored brown indicating the pilot was dead. The rest, however, were overlaid with green markers indicating the pilot was alive and the ship's primary systems were online; though from the gyrating flight paths of two of them, gave the impression those pilots were trying to stabilize their fighters. Having designated the two Midcraft as enemy combatants, rotating red-colored cross-hair markers overlaid them, making it easy to identify them.

Observing the two Midcraft join together and then stop, Marshal Ironhook squinted his eyes and said, "What are they waiting for?"

"You wouldn't?" Regan puzzled, looking over at Bev from the passenger seat.

"Look," Bev said, adjusting her hand on the steering wheel, "I would be delighted to come with you to your world to visit. Meet your parents and all."

"But if this disaster everyone keeps talking about is that bad, and effects your world…"

"It will." Chief Zorin injected, looking over at Bev from the passenger seat behind Regan.

Bev nodded her head a few times and continued, "…there's no reason for me to move there and learn a bunch of new things and have to live in a stuffy old castle or something."

"Stuffy old castles aren't that bad." Regan smiled in return and turned to look out the passenger-side window.

Bev rolled her shoulders slightly and with a playful grin said, "Well, maybe not too stuffy."

"What's that?" Regan asked, spotting the long black tail of a glowing red object streaking through the clouds in their direction.

"What's what?" Bev asked, slowing the vehicle a bit and cautiously eyeing the road and outside the passenger window.

Chief Zorin turned and looked out of his window and spotted the incoming object as it rapidly grew in size, instinctively attempting to sense any magic emanating from it.

"Oh my god!" Bev screamed in fear.

"No!" Chief Zorin thundered out, having misjudged the speed of its descent, sweeping his arms toward Bev and Regan.

A split second later the red ball crashed into the vehicle generating a massive explosion that bent and flattened nearby trees and gouged a deep crater in the earth approximately ten meters in diameter and equal that in depth. Several seconds later the crack of the sound barrier rushed past.

Slowly, as a gentle wind carried away the dark and ashened cloud that filled the crater and rose into the sky, a distinguishable outline became visible. Protruding from beneath clumps of twisted metal, earth and rock, rested part of the severed wing of the mighty Silver Dragon. Still. Dead.

As a result of the attack on the Moon base, it had taken nearly five minutes for Regnum, trailed by Michelle and the pilot, to reach the command center located on the second deck of the damaged base from the landing bay and another twelve for him to get the secondary power system online, which had been originally designed to provide trickled power to a few sub-system command receivers and provide a short jolt of high-voltage to start the primary power system's reactor. With over half of the Moon base's systems pulling power from the secondary system including early generation aerial defense robots known as Kqliipx, Regnum estimated they had just over four hours of power.

The Kqliipx defense robot, developed and used heavily during the Wjohs War to offset significant losses of military personnel, is an autonomous but limited-capacity probabilistic AI driven platform. Shaped like a V with a one-meter diameter metallic-like sphere at its base, the left and right wings extend for two and one-half meters. However, unlike a traditional flat-wing, each wing is also shaped as a V where the base of each wing faces the other. That orientation allows the robot to generate a plasma-like energy ball near the base of the wings, just in front of the sphere, that is then propelled forward between the wings using a series of electromagnetic repulsion surfaces built into the base of each wing. Additionally, the two long surfaces of each wing, hinged to its base, can be reoriented independently by up to fifteen degrees to provide extra maneuverability in gas and liquid environments. When the two surfaces of a wing are extended, the height between the edge of each surface is one-third of a meter.

"System commander," a stern voice said through the outdated communication system, "Two human vessels have engaged our escort group. We will not be able to pick you up at this time. Return to the Earth base."

Regnum sighed, looking through one of the large rectangular windows onto the still lunar surface, unable to see any craft. He moved to the telemetry system and rotated a small metallic sphere anchored to it in order to power it up and see what was going on. But his efforts were in vain. That system had been hard-wired to the damaged primary power system itself and had no rerouting conduits.

After thinking for a moment, Regnum turned toward the pilot and ordered, "Start refueling the Midcraft and stow a Kqliipx in case we need it. We'll fly to the outpost ourselves."

The pilot nodded and headed for the landing bay.

Regnum glanced briefly at Michelle, thinking to himself about how stubborn and annoying humans were, and then walked back to the communication system and directed, "Eliminate the vessels. I'll fly to the outpost myself."

"Commander…you will be unprotected in transit across most of this system. That is not standard procedure."

"I've been in this system for several cycles, Serpchuk!" Regnum fumed openly, having grown weary of all the problems that had been heaped upon him during this cycle and aptly picked the derogatory term *Serpchuk* which meant one of little knowledge and wisdom or childlike. "We have no enemies out here in the middle of nowhere! Attack those ships at once!"

"Yes, commander!"

"We will be on-site shortly, general." the pilot of the SR-95 announced while he maneuvered the ship through a barren mountainous valley that led to the Moon base.

The sudden onslaught of raw intelligence from operatives managing the attack on the alien base along with the appearance of the alien craft near the Moon and subsequent engagement left the general with more data than what he could effectively analyze in a timely fashion. So, rather than confronting the data as a whole to analyze, he focused on what he considered to be a unique thread to follow. In this case, while he had initially boarded the SR-95 along with Janus, Mac, Jacob and Lionak with the intent of capitalizing on their abilities in order to take over the alien base on Earth, after he received a report of a ship fleeing from the base toward the Moon and the appearance of alien ships near the Moon, he chose to follow the fleeing ship. He reasoned that the ship had something of great importance, like a sensitive technology, the aliens could not allow to fall into human hands.

"Great." the general mumbled, examining a photo taken by one of the SSB fighters who got near the Moon base and a grainy shadow on its wall near the lunar surface, "Are you sure this is an entrance?"

"The analysts observed the alien craft fly into that area from a wide orbit military satellite launched earlier this year."

"They didn't actually see the ship enter into this specific area then." the general commented.

"Just from overhead, sir."

"Great."

After completing a turn, the Moon base came into view and the pilot said, "Alien base ahead, sir."

General Lowinsky looked ahead at the base and turned toward Janus, seated behind the pilot and said, "Get us in there, Janus."

"I am working on it." Janus replied, "I am taking over the SR-95's radar guidance system and recalibrating it. From my assessment of the Moon base data I had access to, the ship's hardware should be sufficiently advanced to interface with the ancient technology of the bay interface system."

"That's refreshing to hear." Jacob grunted from behind Janus.

Seconds past and the Moon base got larger and larger, the shaded rectangular area remaining unchanged.

"Janus?" the general exhaled impatiently.

"General." Janus said evenly, "I am working on it. The satellites that I am relaying through are quite slow and one of them is damaged. Please wait."

When the SR-95 came within one hundred meters of the Moon base with no visible change to its surface, the pilot started becoming uneasy and volunteered, "General. I have to divert in fifty meters to avoid collision."

Janus looked up momentarily toward the pilot and corrected, "Actually you have sixty-one point four meters. Please wait."

Mac frowned at Janus, wondering if it had planned this and was going to kill them all by flying the SR-95 into the side of the Moon base. As far as he knew everyone that had direct knowledge of it, and could be a threat to the AI, were all together in the ship.

Then, just as the ship past sixty-two and three-quarters of a meter, a small blue light illuminated from the shaded rectangular region of the Moon base. Shortly thereafter the shaded area split in half horizontally and began to open with some unknown objects zipping past the SR-95 along with what appeared to be a Kqliipx and a stiffened human-like form.

"Ho! What was that?!" the pilot exclaimed, instinctively lurching his head away from the jettisoned objects.

"Sorry for the delay." Janus reported, "The system would not allow the bay to open due to the presence of a biological lifeform until I bypassed that unforeseen safety protocol."

After gently tapping the pilot's shoulder, Janus said, "You may proceed."

Chapter Twenty-Seven

"Sir! Alien targets are closing on our position!" the weapons officer aboard the SSHC-20 announced.

Having had time to contemplate his next move, Marshal Ironhook opened a com channel with the SSHC-10 and ordered, "Vice marshal, turnabout and assume plus-one kilometer forward thrust. 20 is coming up on your starboard at five hundred meters."

"Executing maneuver now." the Vice Marshal responded. Shortly thereafter the SSHC-10 rotated on its axis so that it faced in the opposite direction and its engines fired to slow and reverse its momentum.

Switching the com to the commander of his cruiser's fighter wing, he said, "Attack the alien ship on port and keep it busy."

"Roger! Engaging alien ship!"

Eyeing the display ahead of him, when the markers overlaying the twenty-six fighters began moving toward the Midcraft, the Marshal switched back and said, "Prepare to fire Penlights on starboard alien ship on my signal."

Then, glancing over at the weapons officer, Marshal Ironhook instructed, "Lock our Deus and Penlight on the starboard alien ship. Prepare to fire Deus only."

The weapons officer hastily entered some commands on one of his panels and then hovered his hand over one of the buttons, looking at the Marshal, "Ready, sir!"

Impatiently watching the display and his cruiser's position relative to the SSHC-10, when the SSHC-20 had aligned itself and was within five hundred meters, Marshal Ironhook ordered, "Fire Deus!"

Almost immediately, the shield around the Midcraft started to flicker as its resonance was disrupted. Within a few seconds part of its hull began to change color and brighten as if it were sitting atop a smelter.

Switching to the SSHC-10 while signaling his weapons officer, he shouted, "Fire Penlights!"

The laser blast from the SSHC-20 plowed through the shield and impacted the nose of the Midcraft overwhelming a large section with immense photonic energy and causing pieces of it to break apart. In response to the attack the Midcraft began to veer down just as the two laser volleys from the SSHC-10 crashed into it, temporarily pushing it a few degrees off its heading. But, unlike the first laser blast that was within the propagation path of the Deus Vox weapon, neither caused significant damage as the shield deflected the energy around its entire surface to dissipate and cancel it by using the incoming energy against itself.

Assessing the SSHC-10 as a significant threat due to the dual laser blasts and unaware of recycle time, the Midcraft angled towards the SSHC-10, accelerated and fired.

Observing the attack, Marshal Ironhook ordered, "10 and 20 Ferris Formation!"

The Ferris Formation was designed for larger spacecraft, like cruisers, to evade enemy fire or protect a high-value asset by having two or more synchronized craft orbit around an imaginary point between them. In this case, since the imaginary point was not a high-value asset, the marshal was using the maneuver solely to make it more difficult for the alien ship to attack them.

Just as the two cruisers began their circular orbit, the first glowing red sphere collided with the SSHC-10's bow where the sphere expanded to nearly ten meters in diameter, partially embedded within the hull, followed by a brilliant flash that persisted for a split second. Afterward, the remains of personnel, equipment and other material gushed out into the void of space leaving behind a spherical, empty cavity in the cruiser. Then the second sphere hit the SSHC-10, doing the same damage almost directly next to the bridge. Luckily the third sphere missed the SSHC-10's engines as it streaked by and raced into space.

"10! Report!" Marshal Ironhook called out, taken aback by destructive power of the alien ship's attack. But no response came.

After a long silence the navigation officer said, "Sir. 10's orbit is beginning to degrade. We must break formation."

The marshal looked down and pinched the arch of his nose between the eyes, trying to quell the rage and sadness building up inside him.

"Sir, the two alien ships have formed up and are in-bound. Eighteen thousand meters." the navigation officer said in a somber tone.

"Fighter status." Marshal Ironhook said at last, lifting his head toward the large display.

"Eighteen fighters down. Eight remain along with four from the 10." the tactical officer admitted begrudgingly, "They are just too outmatched, sir. It's like bi-planes fighting an F-35."

"Re-task the fighters to the 10, collect any survivors and hail for rescue." the marshal directed, knowing they were close enough to Earth to be saved.

"Yes, sir!"

"Break formation and thrust to full!" the marshal ordered, pushing himself back in the chair, adding, "Weapons target the damaged alien ship and fire at will."

"Sir!" the weapons officer confirmed, entering commands and adjusting settings on his panels.

"Deploy honeycomb. Staggered front."

Following that order, the hexagon-shaped hull plates of the honeycomb system located on top and below the cruiser detached and thrusted a few hundred meters ahead of the SSHC-20's bow, and formed into two rectangular shields, one shield wall in front of the other.

With only moments to think of what options he realistically had at this point in time, knowing a strong offense was required, the marshal turned to the weapons officer and said, "When I give the order, turn the shield walls ninety degrees and thrust them against the other alien ship."

Puzzled, the weapons officer said, "Sir, we won't have a defense."

Marshal Ironhook crooked his head slightly and grumbled, "Look at the 10! We have no defense!"

"Twelve-thousand meters."

"Ready for port." The marshal directed toward the navigation officer before looking back at the display.

"Opening fire!" the weapons officer proclaimed, activating the recharged Deus and Penlight weapons.

Once again, the propagation wave and laser sliced into the damaged Midcraft. But this time, the ship's commander had anticipated the attack and rolled the ship upwards and to its right out of the line of fire.

"Six-thousand meters."

"To port!" the marshal shouted.

As the SSHC-20 shot through space and began its turn to port, the marshal keenly watched the movement of the undamaged Midcraft, hoping that exposing the long-side of the cruiser – a much larger target area - would draw it closer before it fired.

"Thee-thousand meters!"

Seeing the Midcraft readjust its vector, the marshal grinned and ordered, "Weapons, now! Starboard high!"

With that the SSHC-20 turned starboard and angled to begin moving upward. The two honeycomb shield walls rotated ninety degrees and shot toward the Midcraft, like two sheets of metal slicing through the air. Most of the first shield wall was broken apart by the alien shield but its narrow and persistent contact surface along with its kinetic force allowed the second shield wall to punch through behind it with several hull plates burying themselves into the Midcraft, one having lodged deep enough to damage the ship's propulsion system. Shortly afterward the engine began to stutter and the Midcraft shot upward after the cruiser.

Noticing the damaged Midcraft maneuver and accelerate back down toward the cruiser and the second Midcraft closing from below, the marshal ordered, "Bow down ninety!"

After the SSHC-20 rotated on its axis to bring the bow of the ship down ninety degrees, he effectively changed its direction of travel so that the two Midcraft closed on each other before re-orienting to pursue the cruiser that was now traveling in a different direction.

Realizing the cruiser was in its most vulnerable position, Marshal Ironhook gripped his chair's armrests and ordered, "IB Forward!"

But the order to rotate the cruiser on its axis didn't come soon enough. The red sphere fired from a Midcraft slammed into one of the engines, expanded in size and flashed hurling material and toxic radioactive substances into space leaving behind an empty spherical cavity as the two Midcraft zoomed past. Then a second crashed into another of the SSHC-20's engines destabilizing two that had already been critically damaged, causing a horrific explosion and shockwave that sheared the cruiser in two pieces, both halves tumbling away from the Earth and Moon.

Slowly, as if the two Midcraft had an eternity to do so, they arched back around and closed in on the destroyed SSHC-20 and readied to fire one last volley. Then, just moments before they fired, a gigantic spacecraft nearly six-thousand meters in diameter and consisting of four counter-rotating rings, one inside the other, and each anchored to a long tubular shaft flashed into view not far from the SSHC-20. The spacecraft's mirror-like surfaces made it hard to see against the black of space, and became most striking when its rotating rings caught and reflected light from the Earth, Moon and Sun before seemingly becoming invisible again.

Not even a moment later the spacecraft shot two long mirrored cylinders, each with a golden-colored ball on their ends, toward the Midcraft, drifting apart as they got closer to the Serpqhtaq craft. Once the Midcraft were between the two cylinders, each not more than a meter in height, the Midcraft's forward momentum suddenly ceased as if they had been caught in a net. The two cylinders began to vibrate extremely fast and from each cylinder radiated an arching series of lightning bolts from their golden poles. The bluish-white lightning bolts grew and arched around an invisible bubble between the cylinders which surrounded the two Midcraft and joined together, instantly stopping the vibration. As soon as that vibration ceased, the two cylinders glowed a brilliant yellow before collapsing in on themselves and then shooting into the spherical confines of the lightning boundary where the collapsed matter suddenly expanded, vaporizing the two Midcraft and, for the briefest moment, creating a flash of highly energetic light as bright and solid as the Sun that dissipated the boundary.

At first, as he drifted back to consciousness, Marshal Ironhook only heard a faint, muffled voice. As his senses returned he realized not only that the SSHC-20 had lost most power, but that it was severely damaged. Struggling to focus he squinted at the shattered and flickering display assuming the voice was coming from that direction. But it was not. Then he slowly looked around the darkened bridge spotting the limp forms of crew members still strapped to their chairs, sporadic electrical shorts and debris drifting through the air.

Again, he heard the voice and realized it was coming from his ear-piece that was floating somewhat below him. Reaching out he clasped his hand around the ear-piece and clumsily placed it on his ear.

"Earth human." the male voice said.

Marshal Ironhook briefly closed and rolled his eyes before opening them and squinting in an attempt to focus, "What?"

"Earth human." the voice repeated as flatly as the first time.

"Yes. This is Marshal Ironhook." the marshal forced out, "Who are you?"

"We received your message." the voice stated, "We are the Tart'aas."

Seeing the SR-95 land inside the Moon base from a 3d holographic projection before them, Regnum turned toward Michelle and pleaded, "The usurpers are here for us! You must activate the MSI before it is too late!"

Panicked and overwhelmed by the sudden onslaught of attacks against them from Earth and by what was now unfolding at the Moon base, Michelle shook her head nervously and looked up at the rotating sphere she had been assigned. But she hesitated.

Switching to another environmental viewport, Regnum brought up the 3d holographic projection of the level they were on, showing the rapid ingress of SR-95's crew. Even he was alarmed by the speed at which they were going through the base.

"Michelle!" Regnum roared, "Only you can save us now!"

Visibly shaking, Michelle tore her eyes from the sphere to look at the projection and to Regnum's eyes. For the first time she felt a helpless urgency radiating from him

313

that she had never experienced before. And, still, she hesitated.

Regnum glanced down at a control panel and activated the remaining Kqliipx robots on the base, directing one of them to guard the command deck they were in and the other two toward the infiltrators. After a Kqliipx floated into the command deck from a long rectangular passageway, Regnum looked over at the projection and began to wonder if Michelle would activate the MSI.

The party jogged up to a T-shaped intersection and stopped, instinctively looking toward Janus to tell them where to go next.

"Which way?!" Jacob demanded, gripping the assault rifle and scanning for hostiles.

"Left." Janus said, pointing with its left arm and proceeding in that direction.

Jacob darted forward ahead of the others and, just as he began to enter into the adjoining passageway, one of the Kqliipx identified the foreign lifeform ahead of it as it glid towards them. The robot automatically redirected energy into two particle channels located at the base of its wings and the particulate energy collected into a six-inch diameter, red-colored hazy sphere. Once collected it was propelled forward between the wings with dense lightning arcs emitting from the repulsion surfaces jumping back toward the sphere and slinging it forward, similar to how a trebuchet flings small boulders.

Seeing the glint of the Kqliipx as it fired, Jacob lurched backward narrowly dodging the sphere as it shot past, exploding on contact against the corner of the opposite wall, hurling debris into the passageway.

"Why didn't you warn us, Janus?!" Jacob shouted after regaining his footing and pressing himself against the wall.

Janus stopped next to Jacob near the wall, seemingly oblivious to the physical danger, and raised its arm in a questioning manner, "I only have rudimentary penetration of the base's systems given the limitations of this cyborg."

"Complaining is not helping." General Lowinsky frowned.

Janus turned toward the general and said, "That was not a complaint."

"Did you see what shot at us?" Mac asked, ignoring the AI.

Jacob scratched his brow with his thumb and said, "It was like a super-size drone. And it is headed this way."

As the Kqliipx closed, Lionak was the first to hear a deep, slow, rhythmic hum and summoned his Staff.

Janus looked back at Jacob and said, "That would likely be a Kqliipx. The power surges I detected must have been those robots detaching from the power grid."

"Surges?" General Lowinsky probed, "How many surges?"

"Three."

"Can't you control them?" Mac questioned.

"No. The Kqliipx are entirely autonomous once they are online. Hopefully these are not damaged."

"Damaged is good." Jacob rumbled, edging back to the end of the passageway and readying his assault rifle.

"Depending on the type of damage, the Kqliipx can become unpredictable." Janus pointed out, "Even attack friendlies and other Kqliipx."

Seeing the leading edge of the Kqliipx pass beyond the edge of the wall, Lionak raised his Staff and shouted, "Get back!"

Startled at the sight of the Kqliipx as it cleared the wall and rapidly turned towards them as it was joined by another from the opposite side of the intersection, the party raced back toward Lionak who cast a stone wall just before the red spheres exploded against it, shattering it and turning the remainder into a fine dusty mist.

Almost in the same moment Mac whirled around, raised his hands toward the two Kqliipx and massive oak-sized bolts of yellowish-white lightning flowed out of him and crashed into the robots, forcing them backward against the passageway and exploding. Then he fell to one knee, temporarily dazed and light-headed from the effort.

Jacob rushed over and placed his hand on Mac's shoulder, while still pointing the assault rifle toward the destroyed Kqliipx, "You okay?! You saved my bacon."

Taking a few deep breaths, Mac got to his feet and said, "Yeah. I'm good."

"Okay." Jacob grinned, gently slapping Mac on the arm before walking back to the intersection, "Let's go!"

After Jacob cautiously verified no other Kqliipx were in the passageways, the others followed him. The general, bringing up the rear, paused to look over the destroyed robots, disappointed to have lost whatever technological secrets they may have held.

Seeing what just transpired through the projection, Regnum turned toward Michelle and pleaded, "We only have seconds!"

Michelle, now certain that her death was at hand unless she acted to stop the usurpers, reluctantly looked toward the sphere and closed her eyes. Then she grasped her bracelet, squeezing it with her thumb and index finger.

The hovering sphere rotated vertically several degrees and the signal was relayed, boosted by the Moon base's antenna array. When it had confirmed the command had been received, its unaltered algorithms resumed their activity. Instantly the sphere revoked Michelle's access to Serpqhtaq systems and announced in the tone of a female, "Intrusion detected! Unauthorized lifeform!"

Regnum smiled at Michelle, relieved that the command had been transmitted and scoffed, "Good sheep. Even at the end."

Confused, thinking that she had just saved them, opened her eyes and turned her head toward Regnum just as the Kqliipx fired, disintegrating her along with part of an instrumentation panel she was near.

Without any thought of remorse, despite the years spent training her, Regnum raised his hand in the air while looking at where Michelle had stood and the sphere floated over to him. After grabbing it, he descended down a narrow staircase and into a maintenance tunnel.

One by one, an orbiting collection of five dark carbon colored, diamond-shaped satellite radiators of Serpqhtaq design sprang to life high above the Earth. After rotating to adjust their focal points on designated population centers in multiple countries, they began radiating a specific electromagnetic frequency band. The intense and invisible energy, where impeded by clouds, evaporated them, creating a clear path to the Earth's surface. After a few minutes of the electromagnetic waves raining down upon wildlife and humans both young and old, the nano-particulates in some responded and the molecular severance induction reaction began. Though both were affected the same, the reaction was most visible in human hosts. As the particulates resonated with water molecules the bond between individual oxygen and hydrogen atoms was severed, breaking the molecules into their gaseous equivalents. Within moments skin began reddening and, soon after, severe body-wide dehydration set in stiffening organs and inducing involuntary shock and paralysis. Devoid of a liquid medium to keep them cool, the particulates continued resonating and collecting thermal energy, all the while the gases expanded and exerted pressure on the dry, cracking skin, grotesquely bloating each host like a segmented circus balloon. Then, when the millions of particulates were glowing white with intense heat, the dried organs erupted in flame turning the hosts into fire-consumed wicks that exploded in all directions setting anything nearby on fire. At first the isolated and small fires slowly spread until the fires joined with others, increasing in strength and size, like an ever-expanding ring of fire sustaining itself by continuing to grow, sucking in oxygen from the sky above. In some places the ring of fire became visible from space sooner than others due, in no small part, to humidity and the availability of combustible sources in different regions. By this time the satellites, with no remaining power, began their orbital decay into the atmosphere where they, too, would be consumed by fire.

"The command deck is here, just to the right." Janus instructed as the party neared another intersection.

Mac and Jacob moved to the edge of the wall at the intersection, this time acutely aware of the rhythmic hum of a Kqliipx.

Lionak stopped near them, considering an effective means of attack and whispered, "Wait! Let me conjure a distraction and you attack."

"Great idea." Jacob nodded, stepping away from the wall and facing the intersection at an angle so he could fire on the robot before it cleared the edge of the wall.

Briefly closing his eyes, Lionak lifted his Staff while silently reciting an elemental summoning spell and then slammed the Staff down on the metallic floor. Deep in thought, he lifted his free hand into the air and rotated it in a circle. Soon after parts of the intersection from floor to ceiling started vibrating and, when he clinched his hand into a fist, the parts ripped themselves free and slammed into each other in the passageway to their right, forming a hulking bipedal elemental with two bright-white eyes fixated on the Kqliipx a mere fifteen meters away just inside the command deck.

Although the Kqliipx was facing the passageway and the elemental, the robot did not react. Its sensors did not see the monstrosity before it as a threat but instead as just part of the Moon base itself which, indeed, it was.

Ever so quickly Mac snapped a peek around the edge of the wall and then pulled back, clearly mystified that the Kqliipx did not attack.

"Its just floating there like the elemental is invisible." Mac whispered toward the others.

Lionak pushed his fist forward in the air and extended his fingers in the direction of the elemental, releasing it to attack the robot.

With singular enraged purpose the elemental rushed the Kqliipx, grasping the wings with its crudely shaped hands and ripped them from the sphere, sending them crashing into the walls of the command deck. In the next moment the elemental stepped forward and clasped onto the large floating sphere and began squeezing it, bending and deforming the sphere's surface. A thick geyser of electrical arcs erupted from the sphere, twisting and pounding into the elemental and anything else nearby before the shriek of tearing metal and other material echoed in the chamber. After a few seconds the elemental released the squashed sphere and it thudded dully against the floor.

Cautiously stepping into the passageway and approaching the command deck with the others in tow, Jacob whistled, "Damn! You should have done that sooner my man."

Surprised himself, Lionak switched the Staff to his other hand and confessed, "Frankly I had no idea that would actually work. It seemed apt to fight an iron foe with iron."

Jacob pressed forward to ensure the chamber was clear of robots and anything else that might attack them.

Janus turned its head slightly in Lionak's direction with a questioning look in order to correct him, knowing that the Kqliipx had little iron content, but elected not to. Instead, it strode to one of the instrumentation panels to assess the Moon base's current state and to determine how it could gain additional access. In short order the AI started pressing buttons and semi-circular tactile surface pads covered with thousands of short, shaft-like sensors.

Mesmerized by the bright lunar surface, Mac walked over to a long rectangular window port to take in its magnificence with a sense of serene peace and oneness with it.

"Never even dreamed I'd be out here." Jacob smiled, walking up beside Mac and lowered his weapon.

Mac shifted his stance and said, "Doesn't it feel like this is where we should be?"

"On the Moon?"

Looking beyond the surface into the depth of space Mac clarified, "Sure but I mean...out there."

Jacob thought for a moment and shrugged, "Can't say I feel like that. It is an impressive view though."

"Any idea who piloted the alien ship here?" General Lowinsky asked, stopping next to Janus to see what it was doing and also observe the interaction with the alien control systems.

"Working on it." Janus said as it attempted to circumvent built-in Serpqhtaq access protocols.

After a few minutes Janus was interrupted by a notification message and reported, "The bay door has been activated and a Midcraft is launching. It is the one that flew here from Earth."

"What?!" the general cursed, "Can you stop it?!"

Expecting some sort of action Jacob rushed over to the instrumentation panel Janus was at, looking in vain for anything that could abort the launch or even shoot down the ship.

"No. I do not have sufficient control for that yet."

Lionak tossed the Staff to his other hand and darted over to the window port near Mac, scanning for the alien ship. Then he spotted it, "There it is!"

Jacob and the general ran over to see the ship for themselves.

"Damn it!" the general scowled, powerless to stop it.

Lionak pointed the end of the Staff and his free hand toward the Midcraft and once again closed his eyes to concentrate entirely on it. In doing so, the elemental behind them collapsed into a heaping pile of bent and twisted metal.

Off in the distance a cloud of Moon dusk exploded from the side of a rocky outcropping along the mountain and then a gigantic greyish-white tentacle burst forth just as the Midcraft approached. While the Midcraft successfully dodged being hit and veered sharply upwards the tentacle, like a snake reaching out for a moving branch, twisted after the ship and managed to coil its leading edge around the craft. Tightening its grip, the tentacle withdrew back into the outcropping but, before it vanished from sight, the Midcraft exploded scattering debris throughout the area with a tiny sphere-like object shooting out into the darkness of space.

"Dick munch." Lionak grunted as he exhaled and opened his eyes.

Surprised by Lionak's use of slang, Jacob shot his eyes toward him with a puzzled expression but then grinned, "Exactly!"

Alerted to an incoming communication, the general lifted his forearm and activated the Scalpel to see Janus. Perplexed, he instinctively looked back toward Janus interacting with the instrumentation panel not more than ten meters away before he remembered that the artificial intelligence could be present in multiple physical and virtual locations at the same time.

"Yes?" General Lowinsky said, gazing out toward the wreckage of the Midcraft wondering how long it would take to retrieve and study.

"I am processing new reports and data from surveillance networks but…" Janus said as its image was replaced with a collection of near real-time video squares from satellites, "…several firestorms, originating in highly populated regions, have just appeared across the planet."

"Missile strikes?" the general snapped.

Lionak, Jacob and Mac crowded around the general to get a glimpse of what he was viewing on the Scalpel.

"No." Janus replied, "An unusual high-energy emission preceded the appearance of the firestorms. Possibly an alien weapon."

Each of them, gripped by hopelessness and a gut-wrenching feeling of death, watched in horror as the firestorms expanded.

They were the first to witness the birth of human extinction by fire.

About the Author

Wrought from the 1980's with the rise of technology and tempered by his life's journey through time to the present, Joe has forged an action-packed tale, not only of the stuff of fantasy, but also of science fiction and our modern era not so far into the future. Here, crossing into a parallel dimension to converse with dragons no longer relies on occult ritual, magic or the limitations of ancient energetic meridians and a spiritual connection of the mind. Instead, it only relies on the technological mastery and orchestration of a sentient artificial intelligence focused on moving crude matter, mind and body, across that dark bridge between dimensions.

Claim this book as your own and allow Joe to take you on an imaginative, thought-provoking adventure full of dragons, giants, elves and even the might of the modern military as two dimensions, once unknown to each other, become inseparable in their fight to endure among the ocean of stars and competition in our universe.